THE TEMPUS PROJECT

PROJECT

A Brigitte Sharp thriller

Antony Johnston

Published in 2020
by Lightning Books Ltd
Imprint of EyeStorm Media
312 Uxbridge Road
Rickmansworth
Hertfordshire
WD3 8YL

www.lightning-books.com

British Library Cataloguing in Publication Data
A catalogue record for this book is available from the British Library.

Printed by CPI Group (UK) Ltd, Croydon CR0 4YY

ISBN: 9781785631795

In memory of Tails, Lu Wayland,
and all the others who urged us to live

'You naughty boy,' I whisper. I'm almost impressed by his balls.

He's been discreet so far. Maxim has had meatspace agents on his tail for weeks, waiting for him to slip up, but so far they've got nothing. There have even been times I've wondered if Maxim's intel was correct — but not out loud, not even in private to others here in the workshop. Hackers gossip like anyone else. I learned that last year, laughing it off like a silly joke. I'm pretty sure I got away with it, but since then I've kept my mouth shut around these loose-lipped motherfuckers.

I also scrubbed my browser history and bookmarks five times over. Just in case.

But it turns out Maxim's source was right. As well as following the target, the agents have been doing garbage dives. They take at-site photos of everything, steal anything useful, and bring it all to me.

The target and his wife have a four-month-old child. After one recent dive I saw a discarded baby monitor box in a photo. A modern type with camera as well as sound, and more importantly networked so the parents can go out for dinner or whatever and still watch over their little angels.

(Strike one: that box should have been in the recycling, where the agents might not have found it.)

I looked up the manufacturer, a Shenzhen outfit that makes

branded goods for big tech companies then uses the same machines and templates to pump out white-label versions to rebadge and sell as own-brand devices around the world. The Chinese government owns ten per cent of the company, but that doesn't make much difference either way. Design theft like this is standard practice at Asian tech facilities.

(Strike two: never trust a connection inside your house to a generic Chinese manufacturer.)

I asked around the workshop, and the black hat community, but there were no existing hacks or code injection methods for this particular device. So it was down to good old brute force.

I went to a retailer — an actual store, where I had to talk to actual people, hating every actual minute of it — and bought the same model of baby monitor. I took it home, set it facing out the window of my apartment to trigger the motion activation, and hooked it up to my guest network (firewalled off from the real thing) with default settings. Then I returned to the workshop and started poking it over the internet.

By the end of that day I had a crude but effective man-in-the-middle attack that captured every fifth frame of video from the camera, watching people walk by the street below my apartment. No sound, but the video was what mattered. Every fifth frame may not sound like much, but these cameras run at 30fps so it was plenty.

I'd hacked my own monitor. Now it was time to hack the target's.

I went old-school, locating it by 'war-dialling'. Back when dinosaurs roamed the internet, war-dialling meant using a program to call every possible phone number in an area by simple number incrementation — 0000000001, 0000000002, 0000000003, and so on — and see if any of them answered with a modulated audio signal instead of a human voice. If they did, the program knew it had found something electronic. Something that could be hacked.

I war-dialled local IP addresses for the baby monitors' manufacturer code. I found a few hundred in the city, so narrowed it down to the target's residential area. That left me with a dozen possibles. Half the owners hadn't changed the default login settings, and the ones who did had used crappy, obvious passwords.

I hacked them all.

That afternoon I piped the output from each camera into separate image directories, then wrote a quick script to automatically stitch the frames into Matroska video files and apply a motion-smoothing algorithm. It's like watching a 1970s soap opera starring robots, but it's fine.

At the end of each day for the past week, I've played all the day's files simultaneously, spread over my tri-monitor setup. Because each camera is focused on a crib, it's mostly sleeping babies. The camera only operates when they move, so they look like the most restless kids in the world. It's boring as fuck.

But patience is a virtue. Every so often, a parent leans far enough over their baby to be seen. Or they pick up the monitor and move it, to adjust the angle, clean the crib, or place it in a different room where the baby's fallen asleep. One by one I've seen each baby's parent and been able to eliminate their video feed.

Until yesterday, when I recognised the target's wife.

I spent the evening disconnecting from all the other monitors, securely deleting their feeds, and covering my tracks. Nobody would know I'd ever been watching. Meanwhile, the stream from the target's camera has continued recording in the background, waiting for something to confirm the intel from Maxim's source.

I didn't have to wait long.

(Strike three: never take your mistress back to your own house.)

'You naughty boy,' I whisper, and smile. Today's video feed shows him leading a young woman by the hand, down the hallway. It's only visible in the corner of the monitor's camera, and the image quality isn't enough to positively identify the woman, but anyone can see it's not his wife.

I don't know what Maxim has planned for this unfortunate sucker; what horrible treachery he'll have to perform to stop this video falling into the wrong hands. But I do know that young woman won't stay unidentified for long. Maxim will be happy. When Maxim is happy, we're all happy.

I light a cigarette and take out my phone. At the desk behind me Saskia mutters, 'For fuck's sake,' and I don't need to turn around to know she's waving her hands in the air, wrinkling her nose at the smoke.

I laugh, blow a thick cloud at the ceiling, and call Maxim's number.

2

SCAR. Committee unanimous. — G

Brigitte Sharp read the text message and shook her head in disbelief. 'Fucking boys playing,' she muttered.

'What was that?' said the voice in her earpiece. *'Trouble?'*

'No, nothing,' she replied, blowing smoke. 'Just the usual politics.' Bridge switched to the flight tracker app on her iPhone and noted the plane's position. 'Wheels down, two minutes. Stand by.' She stubbed out her cigarette and returned inside the building.

Andrea Thomson and her MI5 team would be at London City airport by now, waiting for the morning's inbound flight from Estonia. Registered on board that flight was Artjom Kallass, a Tallinn-based journalist carrying information about alleged Russian-backed 'hacking workshops' operating in cities throughout the Baltic countries, including Tallinn itself, to penetrate and undermine other countries' security systems.

Kallass had conducted investigations into the workshops for some time, but when he'd tried to publish his revelations of Russian meddling and proxy cyberwar operations in Estonia's national newspapers, he found himself running straight into a brick wall. Estonia, Latvia, and Lithuania hadn't been Soviet Bloc countries for decades. Even the Bloc itself was a distant memory, the province of cold war history nerds obsessed with Stalin, Khrushchev, and the Iron Curtain. But the depth of feeling and sympathy for Russia in the so-called 'Baltic triangle' remained strong, and every newspaper in the region was run by someone with strong political connections. None of them would risk angering Moscow.

So Kallass turned to the UK. He contacted Gregory Hughes, the cultural attaché at the British embassy in Tallinn. It was an open secret that wherever you went in the world, 'British cultural attaché' was often a synonym for 'SIS officer', and Hughes was no exception. He was the station chief for all three countries in the Baltic triangle — and the sole officer, thanks to a combination of budget cuts, the territories' small size, and a distinct lack of anything interesting happening in them.

Until Kallass. He was interesting.

If what the journalist said was true, Russia's extra-military 'hybrid warfare' units — in other words, government-sponsored teams of hackers — weren't restricted to Moscow-based groups like APT29, the Advanced Persistent Threat team responsible for many recent high-profile incidents such as hacking the emails of American politicians. Kallass' investigations alleged that the Kremlin also created, financed, and managed similar groups outside Russia itself, in friendly extra-national territories such as Estonia, to conduct cyberattacks against its targets. Targets like the UK.

This wasn't news; almost everyone working in international cybersecurity accepted it to be the case. But Artjom Kallass claimed he had proof.

The UK was eager to see it, but the journalist feared reprisals and refused to release it until he was safely out of Estonia. If Russia was already backing a hacking workshop there, it was natural to assume they also had officers of their own Foreign Intelligence Service, the SVR, operating in the country.

Gregory Hughes took Kallass seriously and contacted SIS headquarters at Vauxhall, in its squat, aggressively postmodern edifice of glass and steel overlooking the Thames. The Head of Station for north-east Europe had in turn passed the intel to Giles Finlay, the man in charge of SIS' Cyber Threat Analytics unit and one of the few senior officers inside the Service with experience and understanding of hacking.

It was Giles' CTA team, including Brigitte Sharp, who had prevented a recent terror attack in London; a 'dirty bomb' of radioactive waste carried by drones, following the theft of computer code from an Anglo-French military project known as *Exphoria*. Brigitte, herself half-French, had reluctantly gone undercover to root out the mole inside the project, before returning to London to foil the attack.

Following the mission's success, Whitehall realised the threat could have been dealt with more quickly if SIS, MI5, GCHQ, and the Ministry of Defence had communicated better. Giles was ordered to assemble a cross-departmental task force that could facilitate such information-sharing, and also take necessary action. He'd asked Brigitte, whose skill, insight, and intuition had saved potentially thousands of lives and brought a deranged terrorist to justice, to lead it.

Bridge wasn't the least bit confident about becoming a leader. She was perfectly comfortable working either as part of a team or flying solo, but being responsible for other people and giving orders was an entirely new experience, and not something she'd wished for. Still, the success of Exphoria gave her a renewed confidence in her own judgement.

Confidence that had now been undermined by a single text

message.

It was a tiny thing, not worth getting worked up about. She wasn't even sure why she'd given it so much thought in the first place. But she had, and now Bridge's suggestions for the new team's name had evidently fallen on deaf ears. Her ideas were logical and sensible — *Multi-agency Cyber-Espionage Unit* (MCEU), *Combined Cyber Task Force* (CCTF), *Anti-Terror Shared Intelligence* (ATSI), *Direct Cyber Operations* (DCO). She liked that last one; it was simple, to the point, and as much as she regretted how the word 'cyber' had become a synonym for all things internet, she was willing to make a concession to ensure everybody from Whitehall to MI5 understood the unit's purpose. Besides, 'The DCO' just sounded like an official department.

Giles, ever the Boys' Own public schoolboy, wanted to call it *Shared Cyber Anti-terrorist Response*. SCAR.

'You can't be serious,' Bridge had said with a grimace when he first suggested it. 'It doesn't even make sense.'

'And nobody cares,' said Giles. 'You've got to give them something sexy, something they can say out loud with gusto. You don't think "COBRA" was a happy accident, do you? It's not like the Cabinet Office also has a Briefing Room "B".'

Now Giles' text message confirmed he'd been right. Of course he had, and Bridge was angry at herself for daring to think the committee might listen to her suggestions over his. For even letting herself care whether they did or not.

So now here she was at Orly Airport, thirteen kilometres outside Paris, undertaking SCAR's first provisional operation — a simple C&C job to 'collect and convey' Artjom Kallass to safety. It was a suitable demonstration of the cross-agency premise at work, as it involved co-ordination with MI5. Andrea

Thomson, Giles' counterpart across the river, had agreed to take a team to London City Airport and wait for the morning flight from Tallinn.

Kallass, though, would never step off that plane. He was registered to travel, and the flight manifest would confirm he was on board, but it was a ruse; sleight of hand to throw off anyone monitoring those records or watching Kallass' travel activity. The journalist's meetings with Hughes in Tallinn, and the subsequent movement of information up the chain through SIS and finally to SCAR (*ugh*) were conducted with the utmost secrecy and care. But it was impossible, not to mention foolish, to assume that would prevent the Russians, or even Estonia's own intelligence community, from knowing Kallass intended to throw himself on the UK's mercy.

So Bridge had called on Andrea at MI5, and GCHQ analyst Steve Wicker, to help her arrange for Kallass to fly in to London this morning. Anyone following official activity, or the journalist's online movements, would have 'seen' him catch that flight. They'd expect him to land imminently at City Airport, where he'd be met and escorted to safety by the UK's very own domestic security service.

They'd be disappointed, because Kallass wasn't on the flight to London. He wasn't even flying to England.

'It'll take him ten minutes tops to get through passport control,' said Bridge. 'I'm en route.'

'*Roger*,' replied Henri Mourad, SIS' Paris station chief, in her earpiece.

Bridge set off through Orly concourse, heading for the arrivals area. As she went she tied back her hair in a neat pony tail, donned a pair of white gloves, and removed a name card from inside her blazer. She reached the open area in front of the arrivals door looking like all the other chauffeurs, taxi drivers, and personal assistants waiting for clients and bosses to clear customs. Next to the professional drivers waited groups of family members, eager to greet their loved ones, and a few unbooked taxi drivers looking for an easy fare. The same crowd as any other airport, in any other country.

None of the drivers or family members looked overtly suspicious. A good spy never would, of course. But certain stances, a particular sense of tension in the body, gave most operatives away. Chauffeurs were the trickiest to figure out, because so many were ex-soldiers — not only in England or France, but all over the world — and a military bearing was something one never completely lost, even after decades working civvy street.

Bridge had never served in the forces herself, but in addition to practising karate since she was a teenager, she'd undergone military-style instruction at 'The Loch', a secret training facility for UK intelligence officers in the Scottish Highlands. Just as she was confident she could tell which of these drivers were former squaddies, she was equally sure any intelligence officer worth their salt would clock her right away, behind her façade of 'bored limo driver waiting for a client'. Bridge's last line of deniability was the name card she held in her hand, which didn't say 'Artjom Kallass'. Instead it read 'Helmut Wasserman', a pre-agreed alias under which the journalist was travelling, complete with fake passport supplied by SIS and passed to Kallass by Gregory Hughes before he left Estonia.

She'd seen and studied photos of Kallass, and read his bio multiple times, but was nevertheless surprised when he emerged. In the past couple of weeks he'd grown a goatee, and today he'd also removed the spectacles he wore in every photo of him she'd seen. It wasn't the most ingenious disguise in the world, but it was effective. Even Bridge had to look twice. She caught his eye as he looked over the drivers, pointed to the name card, and held out a white-gloved hand.

He approached and shook it, looking up with a nervous smile. Bridge had a good six inches of height on him, but while she was used to often being taller than male acquaintances, it seemed Kallass wasn't, and he looked in danger of losing his composure. She couldn't afford him blurting out something inappropriate while surrounded by people, so Bridge quickly returned the smile and said, *'Bonjour, Herr Wasserman, et bienvenue à Paris. Suivez-moi, s'il-vous plaît.'* Kallass spoke French; it was why they'd arranged to meet him here in Paris, with the bilingual Bridge making initial contact. She hoped calling him by his alias would be enough to remind him where he was, and what they were doing here.

He nodded in reply. *'Merci. Pouvons-nous aller voir un buraliste en route?'*

'Oui, pas de problème,' said Bridge, relieved.

They wouldn't call at a store, of course. It was a code phrase, a simple way for Kallass himself to verify that this woman waiting for him at the airport wasn't an imposter. She turned on her heel and led him out of the building, across the walkway to the car park.

Airports, train stations, and bus stations were equal parts blessing and curse for C&C jobs. On the one hand, the sheer number of people present made it easy to blend into the crowd, to move unnoticed and rendezvous under seemingly normal circumstances. On the other hand, your adversary had those same tools at their disposal; they might have difficulty spotting you, but you'd have as much difficulty spotting them. Even the most broad-shouldered operator could look innocuous by the simple addition of a shoulder bag and smartphone. If they were willing to wear a T-shirt and sandals, even better.

It was also possible there might be rival operatives working jobs that had absolutely nothing to do with your own mission. Especially here at Orly, with nearly a hundred thousand people passing through every day.

So, aside from taking the usual precautions, Bridge was fairly relaxed as she led Kallass out of the main building to the car park. The journalist, on the other hand, couldn't keep his head still for more than two seconds, despite Bridge's whispered insistence to fix his eyes on the back of her head.

'*He's spinning like a bloody top,*' said Henri Mourad in her ear as they descended from the footbridge to the car park. He was parked on the other side of the same circular lot, watching them walk. '*If he carries on like this you'll have to strap him down inside the car.*'

Bridge didn't look at Henri, or respond. Instead she focused on Kallass as they approached the primary vehicle, a BMW she'd rented under a false name, and opened the rear door. The journalist took one last nervous look around, to her further annoyance, then climbed in. She quickly dropped into the driver's seat, engaged the central locks, reversed out of the space, and drove away.

'All good,' she said. 'Fifteen seconds.'

'*Wilco,*' replied Henri, and waited fifteen seconds before following her in a small Peugeot, rented from a different vendor in a different part of town, also under a false name.

Outbound traffic from Orly was heavy at this time of morning, with lots of businessmen arriving for the day, like 'Herr Wasserman'. So when they reached the main spur road leading to the A6 artery, several cars separated Bridge and Henri. They'd expected that, and used it to their advantage: before leaving the spur road, Bridge pulled off towards a small all-day restaurant, parked and waited. A minute later, Henri's rented Peugeot pulled in beside her.

Henri had selected this restaurant because it had no security cameras facing its car park. So long as they remained here they couldn't be seen from the road, or by recorded surveillance. Bridge exited the BMW and opened the back door.

'*Sortez*,' she said, gesturing at Kallass to get out. He was understandably confused, but did as he was told. Bridge turned to Henri, who was pulling clothes out of the BMW's boot. He donned a chauffeur's hat, pulled on a pair of white gloves, and buttoned up a smart jacket — while Bridge removed the counterpart items she'd been wearing, tossed them in the boot, then let her hair down from its ponytail. Finally, she and Henri swapped keys.

'*Bon courage*,' he smiled, and slid into the driver's seat of the BMW. The whole diversion took less than two minutes, and now the BMW was heading back to the spur road, following the highway entrance onto the southbound route of the A6. If anyone followed the car, Henri would lead them on a leisurely and fruitless drive to Étampes, more than sixty kilometres from Bridge's true destination to the north; the British Embassy in Paris.

Bridge opened the Peugeot door for Kallass, but this time invited him into the front passenger seat rather than the rear. It was one more thing to change, one more alteration to confuse anyone trying to follow them. He climbed in, leaning back to deposit his bag on the rear seat. Bridge adjusted the driver's seat to her height, then reversed out of the parking space and rejoined the spur road, driving north to Paris. From here it was a simple half-hour journey, straight up the A6 and through the city to the embassy. During the mission brief Bridge had assumed reaching it would ensure their safety. 'That's British soil, isn't it?' she'd said. 'Get him there, job done.'

Giles had at least had the decency not to laugh, but his tone said all it needed to. 'You've been watching too much TV, I'm afraid. The idea that an embassy's land somehow magically becomes sovereign soil is a myth.'

'But then why couldn't someone simply walk in and arrest Kallass after we get him there? Or what about Assange, in the Ecuadorian embassy?'

Giles pinched the bridge of his nose. 'Protections and immunities granted under the Vienna Convention of 1961. The land upon which an embassy sits remains the host country's soil, but that state's laws are suspended within the property's bounds.'

Bridge could hardly believe her ears. 'Are you telling me it's nothing more than a — a gentleman's agreement?'

Giles gave her a lopsided smile. 'All diplomacy is a series of gentleman's agreements. But some are more vigorously enforced than others. Let's say Estonia decided to ignore this one, and chased us into our Paris embassy. Suddenly, all bets are off. We could march into their London embassy with ample justification, and maybe also the French embassy, seeing as they failed to afford us protection from the Estonians.'

Bridge had seen the sense in it, of course. Without honouring those gentleman's agreements, diplomacy would be an impossible task, devolving into tit-for-tat chaos at the first sign of trouble. For the sake of avoiding international incidents, the sovereignty of embassies was a convenient legal fiction. And given the potential scale of this incident, Kallass wouldn't be truly safe until he'd been transported to genuine British soil. But delivering him to the embassy first would make that transport an order of magnitude simpler to arrange. A secure detail was already standing by in Paris to whisk Kallass away in the 'diplomatic bag' when the coast was clear.

At least, that was the theory.

They'd been driving for about ten minutes when Bridge's suspicions were first aroused. She was keeping a regular, easy pace, about ten kilometres per hour below the speed limit so as not to draw attention. She had no desire to be stopped by the police for speeding or reckless driving. As a result, a steady stream of cars passed them by, and the only cars behind Bridge were smaller and older models, like the Peugeot itself.

Except for two black Audis, a few cars back. They could have breezed past every car in front with the lightest touch of acceleration. But they didn't. Instead they remained behind, matching speed with the slower cars.

She tested the theory by speeding up a little, enough to overtake a couple of small cars in front. Sure enough, the lead Audi driver finally put his foot down to match pace with Bridge. Then she eased off again, pulling back into the slower lane, and the Audi did likewise. The second Audi, meanwhile, leapfrogged a couple of cars further back.

The *why* of it was simple enough. It proved Kallass was right, and that his evidence was solid — or enough people at least believed it was to have him shadowed, which was more or less the same thing. Either way it suggested he was onto something, and that in turn suggested the *who* of it; Moscow. Bridge had already inclined in that direction, partly because of the Audis; Russians never could resist nice cars, even when it spoiled their cover. But they were also the people who would care most about the story Kallass was selling.

That left the *how* of it, and there Bridge was stumped. They'd been so careful, both at the airport and with the car swap. But Artjom Kallass himself was as jumpy as a kangaroo. Any trained officer would have been suspicious of his tense demeanour and paranoid behaviour at the airport. He'd calmed down to an extent during the drive, but Bridge could practically feel waves of nervous energy still radiating from him. She decided not to mention they were being followed — it would only make Kallass more jumpy, and besides, she was confident she could lose their shadows without him even realising.

They were fast approaching the exit for Arcueil, but Bridge ignored it. The suburbs was a lousy place to try and lose someone in a car. Too open, too little traffic, too visible. On the other hand, the streets of Paris itself — alternately wide and narrow, straight and crooked — were a different matter. The shortest route to the embassy was through Petit-Montrouge, straight up onto Boulevard Raspail and over Pont de la Concorde. It was the route Bridge had planned out, but that was on the assumption there wouldn't be any trouble. It was a fast route precisely because it was obvious, wide, and straight. None of which would help to lose pursuers.

Plan B, then. Bridge swerved hard to the right, taking them into the rabbit warren of Maison-Blanche. Here the streets were narrow and short, with turns and junctions galore. Kallass looked at her with some concern, but Bridge waved him off. 'Almost missed my turn,' she reassured him in French. 'Don't worry.'

She hoped he didn't notice her glance in the rear-view mirror. One Audi had followed, suggesting several possible scenarios.

Perhaps only one car had been following them to start with; or the second car hadn't been able to turn off and follow them in time; or —

Audi number two rammed into the Peugeot's rear side as Bridge cornered a junction. Kallass yelped in surprise while she fought to control the small car, spinning the wheel and driving into the skid as it fishtailed across the junction, front wing slamming into a row of parked cars on the other side. She floored the accelerator and sped away, leaving shards of headlight glass on the road behind them.

The third option was that the Audis had split up, in order to capture Bridge in a pincer movement, and sometimes she hated being right. But at least now she knew what she was dealing with: professionals, and evidently sanctioned to use force. For the first time since leaving England, she regretted not bringing a gun. There were good reasons; less bureaucracy, less paperwork, and less chance of being rumbled if any French security decided to take a close look at her. That was particularly important because the mission was undeclared. The DGSI, the French interior security services, had no idea this job was taking place.

It was supposed to have been a simple C&C, after all.

But the 'collect and convey' mission had rapidly become what officers jokingly called C&Cs that went wrong — 'chase & crash'.

Even without the collision damage it had sustained, the little Peugeot would have struggled to get up the hill through Butte-aux-Cailles at any kind of speed. The Audis, by contrast, roared up behind them with ease. Bridge glanced over at Kallass, his face drained of blood, frantically whispering what she assumed was an Estonian prayer.

As they crested the hill, one Audi drew alongside and rolled their near window halfway down. Bridge didn't wait to see the black metal barrel protrude from the gap before she acted. The advanced hazardous driving classes she'd taken under Sergeant Major 'Hard Man' Hardiman at the Loch served her well; as in her favoured martial arts, the key to throwing an opponent off-balance was to react in an unexpected fashion. So she gripped the wheel and swerved hard into the Audi.

A sideswipe from the Peugeot wouldn't do any serious damage to the larger car. But the shooter had expected her to pull away, and the sudden impact sent his shots wild, two reports echoing off the surrounding houses' walls. Bridge hoped neither had found a window.

She swerved again, this time away, to take a turn down the hill and into the Latin Quarter. Here again, the maze of short and oddly-angled streets would give them at least a minimal amount of cover.

'Tell me the info,' shouted Bridge as they sped downhill. 'As much as you can, right now, in case we get separated.' *Or worse*, she thought, but kept that to herself.

'It's all in the files, in my bag,' said Kallas. 'Just get us out of here!'

'What the hell do you think I'm trying to do? Give me the essentials!'

He took two quick, sharp breaths, then began. 'There's a hacking and disinformation group operating from a building in Tallinn, leased through shell companies registered first in Estonia, then offshore. I got as far as the British Virgin Islands before the trail ran out. But I know they take orders from Moscow, under the purview of the SVR.'

'If the registration trail ran cold, how do you know this?'

'I have a source. One of the hackers.'

'Name?'

'Not until we're safe!'

For God's sake, thought Bridge. Even she wasn't this paranoid. 'How do you know you can trust this hacker? Have you met them? Seen the group's work?'

'Yes and no. In truth, the workshop — look out!' Kallas recoiled into his seat as a bus pulled out from a blind junction ten metres ahead of them. Bridge yanked hard on the steering wheel to send the Peugeot through a red light, across a busy junction, and into the path of an oncoming van. She swerved again to mount the pavement, the Peugeot's tires squealing in complaint as she swung it around a corner, then slid back off the kerb and into the road.

One Audi was still behind them. It didn't mount the pavement to follow, putting it a hundred metres back or more, but to Bridge's surprise it didn't accelerate through the intervening traffic to catch up with them, either.

She understood why when the second black car pulled across the junction ahead, blocking the way. The Peugeot was hemmed in, and the only way out was through one of the two Audis, in front or behind.

Fair enough.

With a sickening grind from somewhere underneath the floor, Bridge dropped two gears and stamped on the accelerator. The Peugeot bucked and complained as its rev counter flew up past the redline and its tyres sped it toward Bridge's target — a narrow gap between the front Audi and an iron railing at the pavement's boundary.

The rear windscreen exploded, glass shattering across the back seat as the pursuing Russians fired once, twice, three times. Bridge barely registered the shots, focused on making the gap.

She didn't make it.

The Peugeot's offside wing smacked into the Audi's nose, and in that split-second Bridge knew it had all been for nothing; the Peugeot would come to a sputtering halt, the Audi would be unharmed, and Bridge, Kallass, and his precious file would be sitting ducks. She was surprised to find her thoughts turning to her mother. Had it really been almost three years since she'd last visited Lyon? Bridge wondered if they would give out her name on the evening news, or if her mother would simply receive a standard letter from Giles, lacking any of the detail a grieving mother would crave. *'Dear Madame Sharp, it is my sad duty to inform you...'*

And then the Peugeot broke through. The Audi driver hadn't engaged the parking brake; when Bridge hit it, the car rolled back from the impact, allowing the smaller vehicle through the gap with a howl of scraped metal. They were going to make it. Holy shit, they were going to make it! Bridge visualised the map, running the route in her mind. The British embassy was only a stone's throw over the river; all she had to do was reach Pont Neuf, a quick hop over the Seine, and then break every speed limit along the Rue de Rivoli —

Kallass wasn't moving.

Probably because of the dark red stain spreading across his chest.

The shots from behind, the ones that had taken out the rear window. One had hit the back of Kallass' seat, right through it and into his chest. His head slumped forward, his arms were limp, only the seat belt keeping his body upright.

His file. She still had his file. Get that home to London and it would be worth it. She glanced from Kallas to the back seat, to his luggage.

The impact was so sudden, her seatbelt knocked the breath from her lungs. Bridge's head snapped forward into the suffocating antiseptic of an airbag, all sense of direction stolen. Up, down, left, right, none of it meant anything. Her head spun, as her consciousness spun tantalisingly out of reach. The airbag collapsed in on itself to reveal the cracked windscreen, through which Bridge saw the rear of a double-parked car, something she could have avoided if she'd only kept her eyes on the road. Her eyes moved down to that road, suddenly visible, and she realised her door was open. Had been opened.

A man stood over her, swimming in every non-direction through her blurred vision. Did he have a particularly wide nose, or was Bridge seeing two of him? It didn't matter. What mattered was Kallass' bag, floating through the air, past her head, to the other side of the car and the open door where another man stood over the dead Estonian, and then the bag was in his hands and that was bad, not good, not good at all. Bridge fumbled with her seat belt catch, trying to release herself from the car and give chase, but the man with the wide nose closed her door and walked away and Bridge slumped against the cold, hard window glass and slept.

3

```
> How is life?

+ Life is

> Tell me how you are

+ 6932326347
+ 3323694732
+ 2U;22222CW
+ 33F33aX3mU

> Stop
> How is life?

+ Life is
```

4

'I can assure you, my bureau does not leak.'

Emily Dunston, SIS' Head of Station for France, leaned back in her chair and folded her arms. From across the table, Bridge saw goosebumps. They were in the 'fishbowl', a basement interrogation room so-called because there wasn't a square centimetre not recorded by microphones and cameras, and the fishbowl was never warm. Bridge had been outside this room many times, watching events unfold at a fraction below room temperature. But she'd only been inside once before, and that was after going AWOL in Syria, so she hoped things would be more friendly this time. She may have lost Artjom Kallass, but the ultimate blame could hardly be laid at her feet.

'I didn't necessarily mean a leak at Paris itself,' she said.

'Then where?' Giles Finlay sat next to Dunston, eyes narrowed at Bridge. 'A problem in OpPrep would surely have seen dozens of much more important operations than this compromised. Kallass was hardly Litvinenko.'

'Which makes it even more worrying,' said Bridge. 'Why go to all that trouble? Why put two cars and several officers into hostile theatre for a journalist and his dossier on some hackers? It's not like we didn't already suspect Moscow was sponsoring external workshops. Yes, the proof Kallass offered would have been useful, but was it worth killing for?'

Dunston sniffed. 'Someone thought so.'

'Is there any chance this was simple opportunism?' asked Giles. 'Could someone have recognised you at the airport, realised you were active, and decided to see what they could get out of it?'

'Maybe if I'd been in Baghdad, but come on, Paris? Even supposing someone made me, would they commit to a broad-daylight pursuit in full view of the *Gendarmerie* on a whim?'

Giles stroked his beard, releasing a wave of hazelnut scent, and Bridge suppressed a smile. Her boss' grooming oil was the first familiar thing she'd encountered since being hauled out of a Parisian police station by two officers from the DGSI; bundled on a charter plane back to City airport; tossed into a waiting SIS car; and thrown down here, all in stony silence. It was cold comfort, but no colder than the room.

'You're right,' said Giles. 'Even for Moscow, it's audacious.'

'That's if it truly was Moscow,' said Dunston, making a note in her report papers. 'According to Mourad, there was no firm indication of nationality or allegiance.'

Bridge wasn't surprised Henri had already been debriefed, but she was annoyed at Dunston trying to divide and conquer. Or perhaps she was setting Bridge up to take a fall? Dunston famously trusted the instincts of her officers first and foremost, but Bridge wasn't one of hers. She 'belonged' to Giles.

Goosebumps rose on her arms to match Emily's.

'Henri wasn't there,' she said, trying to keep a level tone, 'And unfortunately, field officers don't often shout, "*Stop in the name of Putin.*" Perhaps I should have got out and asked them?'

Giles looked up from his notes. 'Have a care, Bridge.'

'You're right,' said Dunston, 'Mourad wasn't there. Why is that? Why did you send him in the opposite direction?'

'That was always the plan.'

'The plan you designed.'

'And was approved at every level of inspection,' said Bridge, glaring at Giles. She'd expected him to offer backup, but instead he was throwing her to the wolves.

Dunston changed tack. 'Why didn't you call him as soon as you got into trouble? You were incommunicado throughout the entire event.'

'Because by that time Henri was twenty-plus kilometres south, on his way to Étampes. He couldn't have helped.'

'He might have suggested somewhere to hole up until he got there.'

'If Kallass and I had debussed, I doubt I'd be alive to explain it to you now.'

'And yet you are.' Dunston fixed Bridge with a stare. 'What did you talk about, during the drive?'

'We hardly spoke. When I realised we were endangered, I asked him to brief me verbally. There wasn't time for much, but he confirmed a source inside the Tallinn hacking workshop — which is run by Moscow through a series of offshore shell corporations, brass plates in the BVI, the usual cover.'

Giles leaned forward and spoke at last. 'And that's why you believe your pursuers were Russian.'

'Who else? They were after Kallass, or rather, whatever he was planning to give us. They obviously didn't give a toss about me, because they could have finished me after the crash and nobody would be any the wiser.'

'Unlikely, if they knew you were SIS. Killing an informant is one thing; executing an officer in broad daylight is a bit strong, even for the SVR.'

Bridge shrugged. 'I'm not even sure they intended to

eliminate Kallass, to be honest. But they damn well knew he was carrying that bag. They didn't hesitate to take it.'

'Suppose they were Estonian. Perhaps the documents confirmed their own cyber-activities against the rest of Europe,' said Dunston.

Bridge shook her head. 'Everyone knows Tallinn is a nexus for hackers. It's crawling with them. What we don't know is whether they're backed by Moscow. Kallass said he could prove the Russians set up and financed this Estonian group through those shell corporations. Again, we've suspected it for a while, but never had proof. If his evidence was credible, it would have given us an edge.'

'Unfortunately,' said Giles, 'now we have neither the evidence nor Kallass himself. I'm sure you can guess how C feels about this.' Bridge tried to hide her surprise that the head of SIS was aware of the operation, but her boss knew her too well. 'Surely you didn't expect an incident like this to pass without comment from upstairs. Where do you think Emily and I have been while you were on your way home?'

Emily fixed Bridge with a glare. *'La merde dévale la hierarchie.'*

Giles looked from Emily to Bridge, so she translated for him. 'Shit rolls downhill.'

'I should bloody well coco,' he replied. 'Nevertheless, while we were getting our arses handed to us, the room came to a similar conclusion; that any leak must have come from Artjom Kallass himself. The man was a journalist, not a tradesman trained to hold secrets. He must have been careless at some point; said the wrong thing to the wrong person without realising it, failed to spot a shadow on his way to the airport, whatever. Greg Hughes is going to chase up that angle in Tallinn, of course, but realistically we don't expect anything to turn up. And on we go.'

Bridge breathed a sigh of relief. She felt good about standing her ground against Dunston's interrogation, but the mere fact she was in the fishbowl rather than a 'Broom', one of Vauxhall's regular briefing and conference rooms, emphasised this was a bollocking, not a debrief. Losing Kallass would be a permanent stain on her record. Nevertheless, she was off the hook; if they were going to formally discipline her, they would have mentioned it by now.

'So I assume you want this written up ASAP, and then what?' she asked. 'Should I chase up the Estonian workshop? This is kind of another perfect test run for SCAR, don't you think?' She still didn't like the acronym, but hoped using it in this context might help get Giles on-side.

To her surprise, Giles and Dunston instead both frowned like she'd lapsed into Greek. To make things even more confusing, Dunston smiled — a broad, full-on teeth-out smile quite unlike her occasional smirks — and stood, patting Giles on the shoulder.

'I'll leave this one to you,' she said, tucking the report papers under her arm and exiting the room.

Giles made a show of removing his glasses and polishing them with a handkerchief. When the door closed, he replaced them and looked Bridge in the eye. 'I fear you've been labouring under a misapprehension,' he said. 'This whole business has put you, and SCAR, under a microscope we could quite frankly have done without. Peter Lennox has fired off four memos already today, and I wouldn't be surprised to see another half-dozen before this evening.' He checked his watch. 'In approximately ninety minutes I'm to explain this debacle to the committee, which gives me eighty-nine minutes to plead our case to the Foreign Office and convince them that this operation's failure in no way reflects on SCAR's future potential under the purview of a more experienced appointee.'

Bridge took a moment to digest Giles' word salad. It was his default mode for talking to politicians and civil servants; using their own arcane diplomatic language to put them at ease, reassuring them Giles could be trusted to handle things properly because he was one of them, old chap. Slipping into politician mode this early reinforced how soon he expected to be hauled over the coals.

And, Bridge realised with sudden sympathy, that was exactly what would happen. Giles would be expected to prostrate himself before every politician and diplomat he could muster, including The Rt Hon Peter Lennox MP, already SCAR's biggest opponent on the Parliamentary committee established to consider its formation. This was what Giles was good at, what he could do that Bridge could never deal with in a hundred years; the politicking, the statecraft, the back-rubbing and log-rolling it took to successfully navigate the corridors of Whitehall and keep its occupants' noses out of SIS business.

But being good at it didn't make it any less unpleasant. Bridge's actions — her failure, not to put too fine a point on it — had made this song and dance necessary in the first place. She'd fucked up again, and this time she hadn't even realised how badly until her own boss spelled it out for her. The repercussions would have an impact far beyond her own reputation — which, as Giles' last words sunk in, she realised was about to take another battering.

'Take some mandatory time off. A couple of days, more if you want it. Spend some time with your family, take stock... and when you return, assuming SCAR still exists at all, it will be under Ciaran Tigh's leadership.'

'Ciaran?' Bridge struggled to keep her voice level. 'He has literally zero field experience. He barely passed his training at the Loch.'

'Exactly,' said Giles, gathering his report papers. 'Clean as a whistle. Unblemished. A safe pair of hands.'

Under the table, Bridge's own hands trembled with frustration as Giles left her alone in the room.

5

At last, Artjom Kallass' face stares out at me from the newspaper.

Normally I wouldn't be seen dead with this shit-rag dead tree media, but nobody else in the workshop even mentioned the rumour all day. I'd overheard it yesterday lunchtime; I slipped off my headphones in the coffee shop to place an order, and the women behind me were talking about it. One of them had a friend who'd moved to Paris, who texted her that morning, so she went online to check Buzzfeed France, where she found shaky phone videos of a car chase in Paris that apparently ended with a big crash and gunfire.

But I had to take all of this on faith, because no way in hell was I going to check it online. One condition of the workshop is that Maxim has access to our full browsing histories, even on our phones. He'd want to know why I give a shit about an unpatriotic middle-aged degenerate like Kallass.

They all would. Like I said, hackers gossip.

So instead I had to sit in the workshop for the rest of the day, fit to burst, waiting for someone, anyone, to mention it so I'd have a legit excuse to look for an online news report. But nobody did, and by the end of the day I was ready to explode. I had to know.

I took a different route home, caught a bus to the other side of Tallinn from my apartment, walked into the first bar I found with a TV showing ETV, and ordered vodka. Ten minutes into the news they confirmed the story, but then the owner changed channel to the evening's football match. I didn't want to risk drawing attention by asking him to change back, so I left.

I daren't look it up online at home, so I hardly slept. Instead I stared at the ceiling all night, wishing for the first time ever that I owned a TV. I kept asking myself the same question over and over.

What the hell had Artjom been doing in Paris?

This morning, after a night of waking up every ten minutes with my nerves jangling, I left early and caught another unusual bus route halfway across the city. I ducked into the first newsagent I saw, bought the morning Eesti Päevaleht, and read it on a park bench. I know I don't look anything like a Päevaleht buyer, but if all this is true I couldn't bear to read about Artjom in a fucking tabloid.

And it is true. Artjom's eyes, his beautiful eyes, stare out from the newspaper. Last weekend they stared at me, as I straddled him in bed; now they stare at nothing.

Confirmed facts are still thin on the ground. Nobody knows why Artjom was in Paris, or why he was involved in a car chase of all things. Nobody knows who was chasing him, or where they went after they shot him.

I read it twice, willing the words to change, but they never do, and I can't take any more. I hand the paper to a homeless guy digging through a trash can and catch the first bus that will take me somewhere near the workshop.

The one thing I know, that nobody at the newspaper seems to: Artjom couldn't drive. Never got his licence. Which means someone else was driving that car...and whoever it was left my Artjom to bleed out, helpless and alone, in the streets of a foreign city.

Knowing that helps me figure out the rest, or most of it anyway. Of course I knew about Artjom's problems with the local newspapers, trying to get them to take him seriously. But I hoped that would be the end of it; that he'd find something else to write about, something less dangerous. I tried to make him understand what Maxim was capable of, what that bastard could do if he ever discovered Artjom knew about the workshop. Not to mention what he'd do to me if he found out I was Artjom's source.

But how could he stop? He was a journalist. Instead he'd tried to sell it abroad, probably to Le Monde or some other French rag. They'd fucking love that story. Now because of it he is dead, no doubt on Maxim's orders. Who else?

I step off the bus, and my legs are suddenly made of concrete. I don't want to go into the workshop; don't want to risk seeing Maxim; don't want someone there to talk about Paris. If anyone even mentions Artjom, I'm worried I might burst into tears.

Not working my shift would raise suspicions. Maxim already suspects everyone. It's why he's good at his job. I can't afford to let him think there's any connection between me and Artjom. So in the workshop, there won't be.

But in my mind, all I think about is how to make them all pay. I've been working on some private projects, things even Maxim doesn't know about. I was going to use them to make myself rich. Instead I'll use them to make those fuckers regret they ever lived.

I ball my fists, count to three, and enter the workshop.

6

'Which came first, Doc? You, or the décor?'

Everything about Dr Nayar's quiet office at Vauxhall was designed to put her patients at ease. There was barely a right angle or hard surface in the place, and blinds on the large windows let in enough daylight for the room to be bright, but never harsh or intrusive. Dr Nayar herself, calm and quiet and gentle, was a perfect match for the room. Or was it the other way around?

'A little of both,' Dr Nayar smiled in reply. 'Obviously I'm not the first psychologist to work at SIS, though my predecessor's tastes ran more toward the utilitarian. I was allowed to redecorate, and remove some of the furniture. Why do you ask?'

Bridge shrugged. 'Just curious. It's all so...soft.' That was a bare-faced lie, of course. She was asking to deflect from talking about herself, and avoid discussing how she'd rushed to the toilets and thrown up in between her bollocking at the fishbowl and coming here for assessment.

'How are your family? Have you spoken to your sister recently?'

'Sure,' Bridge lied, then caught herself. 'Well, not recently, I suppose. I've...been giving them some space. Time to deal with what happened.'

'What would you say to Izzy, if she were here now?'

Bridge looked at her as if their roles should be reversed. 'She's not dead, Doc. I could call her today if I wanted to.'

'But will you?'

Bridge folded her arms and looked out the window. 'I don't see how this is supposed to help me get over being shot at, losing a package, and then being fucking demoted.'

Dr Nayar read through her prepared notes. 'So let's talk about that. "Losing a package" is a rather compartmentalised way to describe what happened. Do you blame yourself?'

'Of course I do. Kallass was under my care. It was my op, my plan. Who else could I blame?'

'That's not what you said in your debriefing.'

'Maybe I'm learning to take responsibility.' Bridge scowled. 'And maybe that's why I haven't called Izzy, did you think about that?'

'No, but you clearly have.' Dr Nayar smiled sympathetically. 'You mustn't carry the world on your shoulders, Brigitte. You're not the only person capable of taking action.'

'No, I'm the one everyone blames when people get shot.'

Dr Nayar hesitated. 'How often do you think about Adrian?'

Adrian Radovic had been the senior officer on Bridge's first field mission, the Syrian job that had gone so far south Adrian was killed and Bridge spent three years chained to her desk.

'Sometimes,' she shrugged.

'The situation with Artjom Kallass isn't remotely comparable. Remember, you made amends for Adrian by saving your brother-in-law's life. You learned from your experience.'

'You mean from my mistakes.'

'You say "tomato"…'

Bridge's fingers tapped out a rhythm on her leg. 'I was supposed to protect Kallass. Give my life for his, if necessary.

Isn't that the job?'

'You're not a bodyguard. I'm confident the Crown would value the life of an experienced operative over a foreign journalist.'

Bridge gaped at her. 'That was surprisingly blunt.'

Dr Nayar shrugged. 'Honesty is rather the point. So let's continue; do you feel guilt that Kallass is dead instead of you? Or are you simply feeling sorry for yourself, because the mission failed?'

'Fucking hell, Doc. Don't hold back.'

'Brigitte, I have lost count of the number of officers who sit here, head in hands, consumed by survivor's guilt after their missions went south. You aren't the first, and despite C's most fervent wishes, you won't be the last.'

Bridge shook her head. 'Honestly, that's not the issue. I'm…' The doctor waited for her to continue, but Bridge hesitated. She'd never voiced this out loud before. 'To be honest, I'm surprised…' No, that wasn't right. She started again. 'I can't explain it, but I expected to be dead by now. I never thought I'd make it to thirty.'

'And yet here you are. Just a few weeks, isn't it?'

'Don't remind me.'

Dr Nayar smiled. 'Thirty is a big occasion. It's not uncommon to be scared by it.'

'I'm not scared by it,' said Bridge, but stopped herself and grunted in frustration. 'All right, I suppose I am. I don't know what to expect, or what I'm supposed to do. It's probably for the best that Giles took me off SCAR. I'm not ready to lead a bloody conga line, let alone a multi-million-pound cross-agency task force.'

The doctor made another note. 'There you go again, assuming you have to do everything yourself.' Bridge opened her mouth to object, but Dr Nayar pressed on. 'Leading a team doesn't mean you must know everything, or make every decision yourself. It's about guiding people, and ensuring everyone does what they're best suited to. Like Giles with the CTA; he asks your opinions, listens to your thoughts, and only then makes a decision. He's not Caesar.'

'And I'm not Cleopatra. I'm…' She struggled to think back to high school Shakespeare, landed on the first tragic woman she could think of. 'I'm Ophelia. Except without being pathetically in love.'

Dr Nayar looked at Bridge over her glasses. 'Hopefully also without thoughts of suicidal ideation.'

Bridge shrugged. She'd never told the doctor what really happened out there in the desert; how she'd been so filled with despair and futility she almost shot herself just to be done with it, but had been saved — saved herself, you might say — by an imaginary conversation with Adrian that made her realise she believed in progress and change. The world could change. She could change.

But had she?

'Anyway, it won't matter,' Bridge said at last. 'SCAR probably won't get through the final committee stages.'

'Which would save you from having to think about your future, wouldn't it? How convenient.' She continued despite Bridge's frown, 'There is life after thirty, Brigitte. You're surrounded by it. You believe you're an exception, the only person to whom it doesn't apply, but I can assure you we all thought the same at some point. Even your mother and sister.'

7

It had been years, but Bridge knew the way like the back of her hand. It helped that the Guillotière hadn't changed in decades. The *cimitière nouveau* off Avenue Berthelot was a little fuller, formerly empty plots now occupied by headstones and crypts. The trees grew a little taller, a little thicker, than she remembered.

But the paths were as unchanging as her father's grave.

Not that he was in there. Arthur Sharp had been cremated in London, and his widow had flown his ashes to France, to scatter in the Alps. The headstone here in the Trichet family plot was only a marker, and as a confirmed atheist Bridge had no conception of him being present or watching over her. But still, to be in Lyon and not visit the grave was unthinkable. It may not be home any more, but some part of her would always belong here.

For her mother, though, Lyon would always be home. Born Sophie Trichet, it was here she'd met and married Arthur, and given birth to both Bridge and her older sister, Izzy. The family had only left because Arthur was offered a promotion on the condition he return to London, after spending so many years based in France. Overnight he went from being the sole foreigner in a family of native women to the only native in a family of foreign women. Still young, the girls adapted quickly to London, but Sophie had not.

Bridge and Izzy had been bilingual from birth. Their father, who'd never quite perfected his own French, had seen to that. Their mother, whose English was even worse than his French, had seen the sense in it. They were encouraged to watch British TV shows, to befriend British holidaymakers they met in town, and their father even insisted they have regular *jours anglais* in the family home; days where everyone, their mother included, spoke only English. The girls looked forward to these days with undisguised glee. Izzy would imitate their mother's stumbling English and thick accent at the dinner table, ignoring her father's amused tutting, only stopping when Bridge laughed so hard she snorted orange juice out of her nose.

The routine was always the same. Izzy would mock their mother, and their father would scold the girls for being disrespectful. But Sophie would only shrug and say in her halting speech, 'Yes, my English, it is not good. *Alors*, it is why yours must be better, that the cruel girls like you do not laugh, *n'est-ce pas?*'

At the time it made them laugh even more, but in time Bridge had come to realise their mother was right. The move had been hard on the girls — leaving behind family, friends, school, the only life they'd known — but they at least had the advantage of already speaking English. Before long, Bridge and Izzy had been able to pass as native in either country; in England they sounded like native Londoners, while in France their accents would return within hours of stepping off the plane, *encore les deux filles de Lyon*.

On good days, Bridge felt she belonged equally in both France and England. On bad days, she didn't feel she belonged anywhere. It was only as she'd matured that she understood her mother must have experienced that same strange disconnection every day.

Sophie Sharp's accent never thinned, marking her as a permanent foreigner in England. In London this hadn't been a problem, but after several incidents of serious misunderstanding and lack of comprehension outside the capital — some of them wilfully and cruelly so, to Bridge's mind — Sophie refused to go anywhere else in England, even on vacation. For the last two years of their family life in London, holidays had instead taken them to Spain, Italy, or back to Lyon. Following Arthur's death even the holidays stopped. Their mother made one trip to Lyon to scatter her husband's ashes, then returned and never left the bounds of the M25, while making it quite clear she stayed only for the sake of the girls' education. After Bridge graduated from Cambridge and began working for SIS — under the cover, even to her own family, of taking a job at the Department for Trade & Industry — Sophie Sharp sold up and returned to Lyon permanently. Nobody had been at all surprised.

Bridge lit a cigarette and returned to the tiny Fiat she'd hired at the airport, remembering the time their father had caught her and Izzy smoking. He'd been driving home, taking a diversion that sent him down roads he would never normally use, when he passed them on their way home from school on a cold Friday in October. She could still remember the chill in her face, suddenly driven away when she heard her name called. Bridge had been mortified; Izzy had recently celebrated her sixteenth birthday and so set her jaw, ready to fight. But to their surprise, their father had simply begged them not to let their mother find out. He'd never told.

She took a deliberately circuitous route through town, ignoring the GPS' repetitive pleas for her to find a safe place to turn round, because she wanted to cross the Pont de l'Université. She timed it just right, rewarded by the afternoon sun polishing the white stone of the Basilica Notre Dame de Fourvière, gleaming on the hill. Then she swung the car around, much to the GPS' delight, and followed it out to the edge of town on a slow, constant ascent.

Bridge had called her mother as soon as she got home, to inform her she was coming to visit for a couple of days. She'd learned long ago that asking if her mother *wanted* Bridge to visit was a question fraught with familial danger. Simply declaring she was on her way made things easier for everyone. 'Please yourself,' her mother had replied. 'I'll see you soon, then.' Bridge spent the next hour packing a small case, trying not to read anything into the brief exchange. She failed, as usual, and worried that the whole idea was a mistake.

Those doubts were still with her as the Fiat slowly climbed towards her mother's house, a modest but solid cottage jutting from the low rise of a hill. High enough to afford a view of the mountains, not so high as to make the road difficult. As she did every visit, Bridge wondered if her mother had finally learned to drive.

'Don't be ridiculous, that's what taxis are for,' her mother said as she took Bridge's coat, following the customary chilly *bisous* and a top-to-bottom sweep accompanied by a silent, raised eyebrow. Even her mother had more manners than to insult Bridge's appearance on the front doorstep, but once inside the familiar patter began.

'You look deathly pale. Why don't you wear foundation?'

'I'm wearing some, but you may recall London isn't exactly a sunbather's paradise. You know, it'd be cheaper to buy a car than keep taking cabs everywhere.' She followed her mother through to the kitchen, guided by the tempting scent of fresh coffee.

'I have money, don't you worry about that.'

'I didn't —' Bridge protested, then stopped and recomposed herself. 'I know you do, Maman. But I don't want you to be stranded up here, if…something happens.'

Sophie plunged the cafetière. 'You think I need a walking frame and an emergency alarm around my neck, is that it? Do I look like I'm about to keel over and die?'

No, thought Bridge, she most certainly didn't. Izzy may have inherited their mother's good looks, while Bridge was saddled with her father's characteristics, but one thing both girls had taken from the Trichet side was a healthy robustness borne of deep roots here in Lyon. Bridge and Izzy had great-aunts and uncles still living here, people they barely knew but who were old family friends of her mother's, easily called upon if necessary. Assuming Sophie hadn't driven them all away over the years, of course.

The sisters often joked that Maman would outlive them both. But now, as her mother placed a coffee on the table, Bridge noticed a slight wobble in her stride; an almost imperceptible tremble in the arm.

'You don't have a boyfriend,' said Sophie, retrieving her own coffee. A statement, not a question.

'What makes you say that?'

'Édith told me.' Their mother had always refused to call Bridge's sister *Isabelle*, much less *Izzy*.

'And how would she know? I've hardly seen her since —' She thought better of describing what had happened at the farmhouse, '— I haven't seen her for a while.'

'So you do have a boyfriend?'

Bridge smirked. 'Maybe I have a girlfriend.'

'It would explain the way you look,' said her mother. Snark

aside, it was a surprisingly *laissez-faire* response. Sophie caught Bridge's surprise and shrugged. 'Boy, girl, what do I care? Édith has given me two grandchildren, and if I know her there'll be more before long. You're off the hook, so go and sleep with whoever you like. If anyone's still interested in a woman your age.'

'I'm twenty-nine,' Bridge protested, cheeks flushing. 'Hardly out to pasture.'

'Exactly. When you get to my age, you can stop caring, it doesn't matter any more.' Now it was Bridge's turn to raise an eyebrow, as she noted Sophie's full make-up, elegant spring dress, and heels. Who wore heels around the house? Sophie Trichet, that's who. 'But you're still young enough that you have to dress for men. You've got perfectly good legs, and all that karate gave you good posture. Put some colour on, and maybe they'll look at you properly.'

Bridge shook her head. 'If a man's not interested in me until I cake myself in make-up, why should I be interested in him? Shouldn't a husband love me for who I am naturally?'

Sophie dismissed this suggestion. 'Nonsense. Do you think your father would have looked twice at me *au naturel*?'

Yes, thought Bridge, he probably would have. But arguing was pointless; they'd been having this conversation since Bridge turned twelve. Back then she'd worn plenty of make-up, covering herself in white foundation, black eyeliner, and purple lipstick every day when she got home from school. But of course, that was the wrong kind of make-up.

'Anyway,' she said, trying to put a lid on the subject, 'I'm so busy, and it's difficult to meet people. But don't worry about me. I'm happy enough.' She wasn't about to explain how difficult her real job made having any kind of relationship.

'Isn't your job full of strong young men?' said her mother. 'Or are they all gay English boys?' Bridge's mouth dropped open, unsure whether to start with the assumption the DTI was full of strapping young lads, or that English men were all gay. Before she could decide, Sophie walked out to the garden veranda. 'You should find yourself a good French man, like Édith. They're easy to please; just put on some stockings, close your mouth, and open your legs. They won't care if you want to carry on playing at spies, either.'

Bridge's world slipped sideways. She steadied herself on the back of an immaculate garden chair. For the first time since she arrived, she was lost for words.

Izzy. Who else?

Her mother read her expression like a book. 'Édith told me what happened last year. What were you thinking, putting Stéphanie and Hugo in danger like that?'

Bridge fought to contain the tension spreading through her shoulders. 'What the hell was *she* thinking, telling you? She signed the Official Secrets Act. They all did — like me, which is why nobody's supposed to know what I do.'

'I'm not "nobody", I'm your mother.' She tapped her stomach. 'I don't care what you or Édith signed. You don't lie to family.'

'They could literally arrest me for talking to you about this.'

'Then you shouldn't have taken the job in the first place.'

'No, of course not. What was I thinking? I should have thrown away my degree, opened my legs for a long-haired misogynist from Marseille, and popped out a grandchild for you every other year, like Izzy!'

Her mother's eyes widened. 'Fréderic's from Marseille?'

The absurdity of it was enough to deflate Bridge's temper. Of all the things, a silly old regional rivalry was what finally got her mother's blood up. She almost laughed. 'No, it was just an example. Never mind.' Once again, Bridge's hopes that her mother might have softened with age were dashed. For all her supposed laxity over who Bridge slept with, *of course* she wanted her daughter to settle down with a nice, respectable French man and give her more grandchildren. How could Bridge ever have thought otherwise?

'Then where's he from?'

For a moment, Bridge thought she didn't know. Izzy had met Fred while they were both doing aid work in Africa, but that wasn't where he was raised —

Ah. The farm. *La ferme Baudin*, Fred's family home where Bridge had endangered not only her sister's children, but also Izzy and Fred themselves, when Bridge's mole hunt unintentionally led a Russian killer to their home. She'd fought and killed the man in front of her sister, and her four-year-old niece Stéphanie. Bridge only hoped the poor girl's memory would fade with age.

'Fred's from Côte-d'Or,' she said. 'He was raised on the family farm.'

'Hmmm.' Her mother affected nonchalance, but inside she'd be relieved. The rivalry between Lyon and Marseille was a centuries-old absurdity which nobody would admit they took seriously, but ran deep through families and communities. The Trichets had been in Lyon for generations.

In fact, thought Bridge, that same question would surely have been one of the very first things her mother asked Izzy when she and Fred had returned from Africa. All their lives, it was their mother's first question about any man they liked. Which meant, somewhere in the past decade, Sophie had forgotten that Fred was definitely not from Marseille. Bridge was unsure if she should be worried by that.

'Anyway,' her mother continued, 'It's good he's from somewhere north. Better than the south, these days.'

'These days?' Bridge had a sinking feeling she knew where this was going. 'What's that supposed to mean?'

Her mother shrugged. 'The Côte d'Azur has gone to the dogs. Nothing but junkies, criminals, and immigrants, and they flock to Marseille like magpies to gold.'

Bridge made an effort to keep her voice level. 'Dad was an immigrant.'

'No, he wasn't! He was English.'

Bridge's arms spread, indicating the house. 'I'm sorry, are we suddenly in England?'

'Oh, you know what I mean,' her mother shrugged again.

'Yes,' said Bridge, standing to leave. 'I do.' Why had she let optimism blind her? She should never have come here, never imagined her mother might finally treat her like an adult no matter how old Bridge might be. Two days? She couldn't last two hours. Without another word she walked out of the house, climbed in the Fiat, lit a cigarette — making sure her mother saw it — and drove back into town to find a hotel.

Sophie slammed the door behind her.

8

The Rt Hon Peter Lennox, MP, raised a middle finger at his laptop screen, whispered a string of words for which he'd be censured in the Commons, and hit Return to commence wiping his system.

It was his own fault, really. He should never have hooked up to the Starbucks wifi yesterday evening, while waiting for his daughter to finish piano lessons. He'd read all the advisories concerning the dangers of public networks, of course, but Peter wasn't some techno-illiterate like the old boys (and gals) who roamed the corridors of Whitehall with fountain pens slotted in their pockets and manila folders clutched to their chests, ready to faint at the mere sight of a keyboard or, heaven forbid, an iPhone. Peter knew computers, at least well enough to operate and troubleshoot them, which was enough to place him head and shoulders above all but a handful of other MPs and even a surprising number of civil servants. It was why he'd been selected to sit on the all-party Parliamentary committee for cybersecurity; one of several committee appointments, but the one of which he was most proud.

So the piano lesson ran over; Peter needed to write some emails; he hated typing more than a few sentences on his iPhone; the music school didn't have public wifi; besides, he could really do with a coffee…and that was how he wound up connecting his Lenovo work laptop to an unsecured public network. The following morning the screen greeted him with a red skull-and-crossbones on a black background, and a single text box emblazoned across the width.

```
*** YOUR FILES HAVE BEEN ENCRYPTED!!! ***

Your Document, Photo, File, Video, and Web Browse
History can not access because they now encrypted. DO
NOT WASTE TIME to trying to recover. ONLY I CAN POSSIBLE
RECOVER FOR YOU.

You are running out time low. There is just only 48
HOUR you to pay, if you not then ALL FILES WILL DELETE
TOTALLY AND FOREVER. This is not hoax, I am not joke. I
very serious. You must will pay.

PAYMENT IS U-GIFT ONLY. If you not have U-Gift, you must
buy its correct right number (10) and send this address
below written here. After paid, click CHECK PAYMENT, you
must online yes of course, and if I will receiving the
right coins Files will decrypted by 12 hours. GUARANTEED
TRUE ONLY I CAN DECRYPT YOUR FILES.

SEND 10 U-GIFT COINS THIS ADDRESS:
rqX76T3g3Hn64LPcUxU9H943s

Have A Nice Day
- TEMPUS
```

A countdown timer, currently at thirty-four hours, warned him that when it reached zero his files would be *ALL DELETED FOREVER*.

It was known as 'ransomware', and while Peter had never fallen victim to it before, he knew it was increasingly common. It was effectively a computer virus, except it could be deactivated by the hacker — for a price.

Not too long ago NHS computers were hit by a similar attack, spreading like wildfire and crippling the health service for several days. But those computers had been vulnerable because the NHS systems were outdated, lacking security updates. His computer, by contrast, was running the latest Windows system and two different antivirus software packages. Whoever this 'Tempus' was, he — and in Peter's experience it was always a he, some spotty teenage nerd living in his parent's basement — was clever enough to get around them, which meant he was probably clever enough not to have made obvious mistakes.

When ransomware was in its infancy, some early versions had major errors that a savvy coder could exploit, decrypting and restoring their files without having to pay a penny. But it had become a highly profitable arms race, so these days the encryption was both strong and well-programmed. If you wanted your files back, you had to pay up.

Not that you paid in pounds, or even dollars. That would be too easy to trace. Instead, the rise of ransomware was largely made possible by the advent of digital 'cryptocurrencies' like Bitcoin, Ether, Interzone, and others. He'd never heard of U-Gift, but that wasn't unusual. Thanks to Bitcoin's success there were now hundreds of cryptocurrencies, with new ones appearing all the time. They were little more than digital tokens that could be bought and sold securely — and, crucially to the hackers, with complete anonymity. Using a technology called 'blockchain', a savvy user could both send and receive digital cryptocurrency coins with complete confidence the transaction would take place, but without ever revealing their identity. This combination of qualities, not to mention most coins' ridiculous value thanks to a bubble of interest and hype, made cryptocurrency very attractive to two distinct groups of hackers.

First were the *off-grid* types, the kind who liked to think that if the government collapsed, they'd be prepared to survive in the brave new world of anarchy and scarcity. Peter had met one or two of them at lobbying events with the IT sector; mostly idiots living in cloud-cuckoo land, whom he doubted would survive more than half a day if they had to fend for themselves.

The second, more worrying, group were the criminals and thieves, the ones who were solely in it for money. They'd hack anything, steal any data, write any virus if they thought it would make them a profit. The anonymous nature of cryptocurrency made it catnip to those people, and 'Tempus' was evidently one of them.

So this was how it was supposed to go. The *Send 10 U-Gift Coins* demand was a link that, when clicked, would load an online 'coin exchange'. There, Peter would be asked to use something like Paypal, or his credit card, to buy ten virtual coins of the U-Gift cryptocurrency. The cost in real money would inevitably change from day to day, as the coin's price fluctuated like a volatile stock. He recalled the insane rise of Bitcoin, where in a single year the price of one coin had risen from an already-absurd $3,000 to the eye-watering sum of $20,000, before quickly crashing back down to half that amount. Ten U-gift might cost a hundred pounds, a thousand pounds, or half a million, all depending on its popularity and hype. Assuming Peter bought the coins, he would then go through the actions of making a payment with them, probably through the same exchange. The string-of-characters 'address' in the ransomware text box was a unique, anonymous identifier for the recipient. Then he'd click the Check Payment button at the bottom of the screen, whereupon Tempus would acknowledge receipt of the payment and respond to Peter's laptop with a computer-code instruction to decrypt his files.

Of course, there was no guarantee the hacker would hold up his part of the bargain and decrypt Peter's files. In any kind of blackmail, the criminal held all the cards and the victim could only hope they would keep their word. If not, that money would be gone and Peter's computer would still be encrypted.

So that was how it would go…if Peter had any intention of paying up. But he didn't.

He wasn't a programmer himself, but he knew his way around a computer well enough. And the one thing that had always been drummed into him by every IT person he knew, every computer magazine he'd ever read, and the natural osmosis of spending time online with an interest in technology, was to make backups. Reliable, regular backups.

Parliament IT policy said he wasn't supposed to make and keep his own backups, not of his officially-supplied computer. In theory, someone could steal that backup and thus gain access to government secrets, and Peter had genuinely worried about that when he first began making them. But then came the revelation that several rather less tech-savvy MPs routinely shared their login passwords with junior staff, simply because they didn't want to deal with 'computer stuff', and not one suffered any repercussion. After that Peter had stopped worrying, and actually reinforced his regime. He'd switched up from a simple files backup to making a full clone of his Lenovo on an external hard drive before leaving the office every night. That clone was a copy of the entire computer, every file and digital bit of it, and the last one had been made less than an hour before he visited that Starbucks.

So this morning, after breakfast, he'd dug out a crossover ethernet cable from his office cupboard. With that cable he hooked up his infected office Lenovo to his home HP desktop, targeted the laptop as a remote disk, and began the process of wiping its entire hard drive. The only thing he'd done at the Starbucks was write emails, which were all stored on a server anyway. So the latest clone backup, made yesterday evening before he left his Westminster office, contained the latest versions of all his files. When his Lenovo was completely wiped he would hook up the clone drive and copy it all back onto the laptop, allowing him to resume work as if the ransomware had never been there.

He smiled as the disk wipe began. Tempus would have to try harder than that to get anything out of Peter Lennox.

9

GROUP: uk.london.gothic-netizens

FROM: ponty@top-emails.net

SUBJECT: Re: re: re: RE: cryptooooo

Haradrim said:

> The Old Ways are crumbling. Look at the World right
> now,everything is full of Shit. The Grip of
> Governments on their people is failing. The masses are
> ready to Burn every Banker out of Existence. Soon We
> will take back control of our Destiny.
>
> Bitcoin, Ethereum, and all other Cryptos are not the
> Endgame, but they are vital Pieces of the Puzzle, and
> Harbingers of the Terrifying Freedom to come.

...where do I even begin?

I don't want to rely on the old call from authority
here, but I work in finance, remember? and I'm telling
you, the dream of cryptocurrencies replacing fiat (never

```
mind all this other pseudo-leninist bollocks) is one
you can stick in a pipe. never happen, and anyone who
tells you it will is either a con man trying to fleece
you...or someone who's already been fleeced trying to
convince themselves they didn't get conned. which are
you, haradrim?

--

ponty
```

Bridge didn't work in finance, of course. That was the cover story she told everyone on *uk.london.gothic-netizens*. But her real job was no less interested in cryptocurrency, and its potential to destabilise economies.

Usenet had grown increasingly barren over the past two decades, and the last few months had seen even hardcore users like Bridge begin to drift away. Now *uk.london.gothic-netizens* was the last remaining group in which she took part, and she was far from alone. Most normal people had moved on long ago, to web forums, social media, Slack groups, and more; slowly but surely, even die-hard Usenet posters were beginning to admit defeat and follow them.

But not *u.l.g-n*. The group was unique in several ways, not least of which was its anonymous nature. Though it began life as a social group for London goths, over the years everyone who wasn't a hacker or high-level network administrator had dropped away, leaving a hardcore group of goth techies to chat, argue, debate, and help each other. By their nature, such people generally didn't use their real names or identities on the internet; they also didn't trust any forum software that wasn't open source, so they could peek inside and make sure it wasn't tracking them. All of which made moving the group elsewhere impossible. Any attempt would lose at least half of their members, maybe more — including Bridge, whose anonymity and silly online nickname were a function of her position at SIS. Joining a non-anonymous group on a proprietary platform would be the height of folly for her. Everyone who knew what she really did for a living had signed the Official Secrets Act. Except, apparently, her mother.

Returning from Lyon, still furious, Bridge had entertained fantasies of telling Giles; of SIS officers swooping in to Lyon, forcing her mother to sign the OSA. But what difference would it make? Sophie Trichet wasn't going to let a piece of government paper stop her from doing whatever she wanted. The real question was, would she tell anyone else? Would she gossip to her friends?

Bridge would never admit it, but in a way she hoped so. The only time she could recall her mother being truly proud of her was when Bridge had been twelve, and won two karate sparring tournaments in a row. Much as she might tut, surely she was also proud of her daughter working for SIS?

Come to think of it, she'd probably prefer it if Bridge was DGSE.

And prettier. And married. And pregnant. In heels.

She closed her newsreader, unable to focus even on being angry at anarchist fools like Haradrim who believed that if only the masses would listen to him, they'd rise up and throw off the shackles of government. At least he wasn't hiding who he was, putting on a mask to impress people.

(Or was he? How did she know he wasn't like her, spinning a fake cover story for the benefit of his online compatriots?)

Bridge drained the bitter dregs of her coffee and slumped

into the bedroom. Shostakovich's seventh, halfway through the first movement, sounded from her phone as she set Radio 3 going on iPlayer. She pulled the covers over her head and let herself be transported to Leningrad, a place she'd never been, drifting into a snow-covered dream world where she was the only person watching the orchestra play under a full moon.

10

NO RUSSIAN GAS EVEN IF IT COSTS US MORE, SAYS MP

'PEOPLE WILL PAY MORE... THEY'LL GET USED TO IT'

LENNOX VS LENIN IN GAS BUST-UP

Andrea Thomson rubbed her eyes and wondered what happened to the regular old Monday morning she'd expected when she awoke two hours ago. Not that any day was ever truly regular at MI5, but in the midst of trying to get Alex ready for school, fixing her own breakfast, prepping Joan's while she was in the shower, and reviewing her agenda, Andrea had barely paid attention to the TV.

She remembered seeing a reporter standing in Parliament square, talking about scandal, but paid it no mind. Most Parliamentary scandals these days were either an MP saying something offensive when they should know better, sleeping with someone when they should know better, or stabbing their own leader in the back when they should know better. There had been a time when the mere word 'scandal' would send Thames House into overdrive; nowadays it barely registered. If something was bad enough to warrant Five's attention, they'd hear about it through official channels soon enough.

And how.

It began with text messages and links to online news stories. Andrea had barely read the headlines when the phone calls began, including one with the energy secretary where she was certain she heard the home secretary constantly shouting, 'Fuck, fuck, fuck,' in the background.

By the time her driver parked in the secure garage under Thames House, another car had already collected The Rt Hon Peter Lennox, MP from Westminster and delivered him to her office. Parliament was barely half a mile up the road from MI5, and it took longer for the car to get in and out of parking security than to drive the distance, but Andrea had insisted. Sending a car would be interpreted as a mark of respect, but that was a bonus. Her main thoughts were simply about security. If Lennox had been targeted for his position on the Energy Security Committee — and the papers, at least, were convinced — it strongly implied Russian involvement. Andrea couldn't afford for the MP to meet with a fatal accident at the hands of some poisoned-umbrella-wielding assassin while walking over to explain himself.

As she approached her office, her assistant nodded towards the door and gave a silent but meaningful eyes-wide expression of caution. It was ajar; Andrea pushed it open to find Lennox pacing up and down, ready to unleash a tirade.

'How dare you summon me down here like some bloody lackey?' he shouted before the door had even fully closed.

Andrea reconsidered whether his poisoning would have been so bad, but kept that to herself and said, 'I'm sorry, do you have somewhere more important to be? Explaining this extraordinary fuck-up in public to an enquiry judge, perhaps?'

Lennox reddened, but thought better of trying to respond in

kind. Andrea had seen his type a hundred times during Army service. Sandhurst was supposed to weed out the blustering, overconfident, and overgrown schoolboys who wouldn't know a real day of work if it punched them on the nose, but she'd stood alongside plenty of them at her own passing-out, and continued to watch aghast as they perpetually failed upwards, everywhere from Aldershot to Afghanistan.

Lennox was no old soldier. But he possessed the same ironclad expectation that he was right about everything, and merely considering a topic for five minutes would afford him greater insight than any woman could possibly have, no matter her alleged level of expertise. Being summoned and berated by a diminutive Scotswoman in a trouser suit appeared to have shocked him into silence, so Andrea changed tack and tried a little flattery instead.

'Sit down, Mr Lennox. You're the Commons' resident IT expert, aren't you? Explain what happened.'

He didn't sit down, but he did start talking. 'I've been hacked, obviously. I have no idea by whom, or to what purpose, but you've seen the results.'

'Aye, and if those results are the purpose, it points the finger at Russia themselves. Have you spoken to the energy secretary?'

'First call I took this morning. This has made my position on the committee untenable, of course, but I can't imagine what anyone thinks they'll gain by getting me booted off. If I were the sole undecided vote in some sort of deadlock, I could understand it. But there's no such situation.'

Andrea nodded. Moscow's hacks were normally precise, engineered for a specific effect. But she didn't want to let the conversation spiral into negatives; instead she considered alternatives. 'You sit on several other committees, as I recall.

Youth and culture, the SCAR approval inquiry…not to mention the All-Party group on cybersecurity. Come to think of it, you might want to step down from that one for a while, too.'

Lennox snorted. 'Perhaps, but I hardly think any of them merit this sort of targeting by a hacker. And the only people desperate to get me thrown off the SCAR committee are the ones trying to set it up in the first place.' He glared at Andrea, as if daring her to deny that a week ago the tables had been turned when she'd sat opposite him at a SCAR hearing, explaining why she believed the unit would be a useful addition to the security services' arsenal.

Instead she switched directions again, trying to keep the conversation and Lennox's memory moving. 'Do you know which computer was hacked? I assume you've read the papers; is there any clue in there? Any leaked item that could only have come from a specific computer or database?'

Lennox considered the question. 'Almost everything I've seen could have come directly from Parliament's servers and archive.'

'Almost?'

Lennox opened one of the tabloids reporting the story, and scanned the images used to illustrate it. He pointed to an image of a memo discussing attempts to force the committee's arm by Gazprom, Russia's state-run energy firm. 'That document was couriered on a USB drive, as it was considered too sensitive to be emailed. It was never uploaded to the Parliamentary network server.'

'That's the server from where you mirror the contents of your email and working documents.'

Lennox nodded. 'The Parliamentary email client uses an old IMAP configuration, so there's only a limited cache of messages on the local drive. They also encourage us to sync all other documents to our departmental network server, of course.'

'Of course.' Andrea had expected an attempt to bamboozle her with lingo, and there it was, but what it boiled down to was a simple *yes*. 'So a hack on that server wouldn't have found this particular memo.'

'Exactly. So it must be my laptop that's been hacked. Except...' Lennox faltered, then dismissed the thought. 'No, no, it doesn't fit.'

'Let me be the judge of that, please, Peter.' Addressing him informally was a risk, but Andrea figured a little boys-club attitude might grease the wheels and get him to open up. 'What's on your mind?'

His shoulders slumped. In Andrea's experience this dismissal-then-resignation sequence was performative; it meant an interviewee was finally ready to speak about something important. Lennox was no exception. 'I was hit by ransomware a few days ago,' he said. 'To get rid of it I wiped my computer and did a full restore, both from my own backup and the HMG servers. But I've hardly used the laptop since.'

'You think the ransomware is linked to this leak? It was a way in to your files?'

'No, that's what doesn't fit. As I said, I wiped the machine days ago. Besides, why bother? There are easier ways to hack a laptop, and without its owner even noticing.'

'Unless the hacker is sending a message.'

Lennox picked up a random assortment of the morning's newspapers and let them fall back to the desk. 'I think this is quite sufficient as a message, don't you? No, the ransomware was some bloody teenage hacker in Latvia or somewhere.'

Andrea sat back in her chair. 'Latvia, or somewhere,' she

repeated. 'And you said yourself, this is all related to your work on the energy committee.'

'Latvia was just an example. It doesn't export energy.'

Andrea thought of the recent SCAR trial run in Paris that had gone so badly wrong, and its implications for Russian influence over former satellite states. 'No, it doesn't,' she said, 'But I think we should take this across the river.'

11

It worked.

The British idiot gave it an even better test than I could have hoped for. I didn't expect him to wipe his computer, but whatever. It worked, and Maxim doesn't need to know how. All he cares about is the result. Now he can report back and they'll call him a genius.

Let them. I care about a different result, and this success means I have one less vector to worry about. I don't have time for a proper bugfix, not if I want to get this thing out in time.

Back to work.

12

Ordinarily Giles might have cheered to see Peter Lennox taken down a peg or two; one of the younger and more tech-savvy Members of Parliament, Lennox had come up a couple of elections ago when people were keen for new faces, and his know-how didn't go unnoticed. He'd soon been placed on several committees dealing with technical issues, or on other groups as a resident computer expert.

In theory, that had been wonderful news for Giles and the CTA. MPs who understood the online world, and the importance of defending Britain's corner of it against hostile actors, were scarce enough. But Lennox didn't see himself as an ally to such endeavours. Instead he'd become a self-appointed bulwark against what he saw as wasteful spending by computer geeks who had previously relied on Parliament's ignorance of such matters to line their coffers with inflated budgets. Hence his objection to the formation of SCAR; Lennox argued it was an exercise in ego, a way for SIS to exert control over other agencies and set itself up as an expensive gatekeeper of information. Giles had objected strongly, of course, but what irked him most was the kernel of truth lurking at the accusation's centre.

To make matters worse, Lennox's technical expertise gave him an air of authority that inclined other members of the committee to side with him. It was Lennox who'd made the now-infamous accusation that SCAR was *'the sort of maverick nonsense we expect from Americans,'* a soundbite which continued to follow Giles around Whitehall like a bad smell. Brigitte Sharp had been sitting with him in that first committee meeting, and at times he'd feared he might have to physically restrain her from climbing over the desk to give Lennox a black eye.

Which would only have proved the MP's point, of course.

'Bridge not joining us?' asked Andrea, as she took a seat beside Lennox in Broom Two. 'I would have thought this was right up her street.'

'Indisposed, I'm afraid,' said Giles, nodding instead at Ciaran Tigh, sitting beside him with a laptop ready to take notes. 'Ciaran is the CTA's most senior officer.' Giles was a little put out that Lennox hadn't come directly to SIS in the first place; a leak like this was bound to be initiated by a foreign hostile actor, not a domestic player. And much as he might dislike Lennox personally, it was SIS' job — the CTA's, specifically — to deal with such cases. So he wanted to impress upon the MP that they were willing to roll out a little red carpet for him. Briefing Room Two, as its name suggested, was the second largest such room at SIS' headquarters in Vauxhall. Its enormous central table could seat up to thirty attendees, with standing room for a further fifty people around the edges of the room. The last time Giles had been in here was for an all-hands briefing on Islamic State, a meeting that had packed the room cheek-by-jowl with more than a hundred restless officers. Booking it out this morning for four people was blatant grandstanding for Lennox's sake, though nothing in the MP's manner suggested he thought so. This was, evidently, how he expected to be treated.

Giles indicated the pile of newspapers on the table, blaring their front-page headlines. 'First things first. I presume these are accurate, or we wouldn't be here.'

'I'm afraid so,' said Lennox. 'Not even all that salacious, really, but it's enough to force my resignation from the energy security committee.' He glanced at Andrea. 'Given the leak's specificity, I assume that's why I was targeted.' He explained the memo that had never been uploaded, and pointed out others he'd since noticed, such as spreadsheets on gas futures that were still in progress.

'At this stage we shouldn't assume you were targeted specifically,' said Giles. 'Many of our foreign counterparts, like the SVR and Office Thirty-Five, do regular carpet-bomb attacks on leading members of Parliament, the civil service, police and armed forces, you name it.'

'Office Thirty-Five?' said Andrea, surprised. 'Are you saying this was North Korea?'

'Doubtful,' said Ciaran. 'We can't rule it out, but Pyongyang is more likely to hold on to the intel, maybe pass a copy to Moscow or Beijing. Beijing themselves would keep it quiet, but make sure we knew they had it. Russia, however, would go tabloid in a heartbeat. So I think that's our most likely culprit, especially with the energy angle.' Ciaran was a programmer, like all CTA officers, but his main speciality was chatter analysis; watching for trends and coded messages online, monitoring channels where hostile actors were known to talk, and analysing group movements and global sentiment to predict where trouble might brew.

'That's unless it's a false flag,' said Andrea, breaking Giles' train of thought. Ciaran looked skeptical, but she pressed on. 'You're right, leaking to the press is Kremlin 101. But what if that's the point? All eyes naturally turn to Russia, but it's someone trying to throw us off the scent?'

'The biggest fallout from this will undoubtedly be the energy security committee,' said Lennox, 'Which is entirely preoccupied with Russia and our purchase of their gas supplies. Of course it's them.'

'At this stage we shouldn't discount any possibility,' said Giles. 'When forensics are finished with your computer, Peter, we'll go over it thoroughly to see if we can figure out where this hack occurred. Can you think how they might have got to you? I assume a man like you didn't fall for a Nigerian prince scam.'

Lennox shook his head. 'I've been wracking my brains trying to figure it out myself. It must have predated last week, because I recently did a full wipe and restore on this machine and haven't used it much since.'

'Why did you wipe and restore?' asked Ciaran. 'And why do it yourself? Isn't Whitehall IT supposed to take care of that for you?'

The MP crossed his arms, defiant. 'I got hit by ransomware, and was quite capable of dealing with it.'

'That's as may be, but I don't recall seeing a report,' said Giles.

This time Andrea stepped in to calm things down. 'Malware reporting is still only advisory, not mandatory. Perhaps that should change, but it's irrelevant here.' She turned to Lennox. 'Tell them how you think you got infected.'

Lennox shifted, somewhat uncomfortable admitting his naivety. 'I connected to public wifi, at a Starbucks of all places. The next morning, I opened up my laptop and bang, *'We've encrypted your files, send us Bitcoin to get them back,'* you know the sort of thing.'

Giles nodded. 'Do you think this was also a targeted attack?'

Lennox shrugged. 'I doubt it. It looked like some teenage

hacker in Latvia or wherever looking to make a few quid.'

'It was his mention of Latvia that made me think it merited bringing across the river,' said Andrea.

'As I already said, it's just a turn of phrase,' said Lennox, obviously annoyed by her interruption. 'The ransom wasn't even that much money. I looked up the cryptocurrency the next day, some new coin on the market. It was pretty cheap.'

'Not actually Bitcoin, then?' asked Ciaran. 'What was it?'

Lennox shrugged. '*Gift box*, or something? I didn't pay much attention. I remember the hacker signed himself as *Tempus*, the pretentious little twerp. But I don't see how this is relevant.'

Giles noticed Ciaran's cheeks colour a little, and pressed on. 'Everything's relevant at this stage, Peter. Please continue.'

'Well, I had no intention of paying regardless. I maintain a full clone backup of my laptop, so I wiped and restored. Problem solved, no purchase required.'

Ciaran nodded. 'To be fair, that's the procedure we recommend ourselves with ransomware where possible. Can't always do it, like with that NHS attack, but in this case you did the right thing.'

'I know,' said Lennox impatiently.

'You still should have told us, GCHQ, someone,' said Giles.

'I'm telling you now. But it's irrelevant; by definition, this hack must have taken place before then.'

Ciaran nodded. 'Unfortunately, if you're right, there's a very high probability that wiping your computer has also destroyed any evidence we could have used to trace this hack.'

'Ah,' said Lennox, blinking. 'I hadn't thought of that.'

Everyone fell silent, so Giles brought matters to a close. 'What's done is done. Andrea, thanks for bringing this over. We'll grab Peter's laptop once forensics are done with it, and go over it with a fine-tooth comb. You never know what will turn up.'

Ciaran stood to shake Lennox's hand. 'In the meantime, best of luck managing this brouhaha.'

Everyone stood and shook hands, then went their separate ways; the visitors were escorted out of the building, while Ciaran returned to his desk to write up his notes. It struck Giles that in more than a decade of working together he couldn't recall Ciaran previously using the word *brouhaha* at all, much less in such a casual manner. He hoped the SCAR appointment wasn't going to his officer's head. Nevertheless, Ciaran had been absolutely correct: if Lennox was right about the documents hack occurring before he wiped his laptop, they'd have nothing to go on.

Not for the first time, Giles fervently hoped the MP was entirely wrong.

13

God, the heat. He always forgot.

By rights, Jasper Wilmington should have spent all his life in heat approaching this. But as a child, his parents had been forced to abandon what was then (and would to him always be) Rhodesia and return to England. Many other families simply 'moved next door' to South Africa for safety, but as his father had later explained to him, their connections to the Rhodesian government were too strong to sit on the fence. A swift return, and revocation of loyalty to an administration viewed by Whitehall as nothing short of treasonous, was necessary for the Wilmington family to maintain its standing.

Jasper had hated it, of course. England's weather was a far cry from the glorious heat in which he'd spent the first years of his life, and to cap it off, all his boyhood friends were now thousands of miles away in South Africa.

On the bright side, he'd been young enough to begin at Eton with other boys his age. While he'd never been destined for a life in Whitehall like many of his peers, he well understood how useful those connections had been throughout his life. Like now.

'Jasper, you bloody rotter! How lovely to see you again after all this time!'

He stepped down from the rickety twin-prop plane that

had brought him to Mwizuba, landing on what appeared to be a literal road rather than a runway, and immediately found himself wrapped in a bear hug courtesy of old boy, now General, David Kzaane. It *had* been a long time; almost fifteen years since David's last visit to London, when he'd been a sort of unofficial ambassador for the Mwizuban government. But circumstances had changed. As Jasper returned the hug, with genuine affection for his old friend, he noted the cold solidity of a rifle strapped to David's broad, camouflaged back.

'I won't ask how your flight was,' David laughed, releasing Jasper at last. 'But we must get a move on; the pilot can't sit here for long. We'll carry your bags.' Two young men — more like boys in fatigues, to Jasper's eyes — stood behind them, fingers poised over AK-47 trigger guards, alert and wary. At David's signal, one of them slung his rifle and pulled two bags out of the plane, a large duffel and a backpack.

'Best I hang on to that one,' said Jasper, taking the backpack. The young soldier resisted, casting a questioning eye to his General, but David nodded and Jasper tugged the bag over his shoulder. 'Computers and whatnot, you know.'

'Of course,' said David, closing the plane door. He waved to the cockpit, and stepped off the road as the pilot taxied along the tarmac. 'There's only one air field, controlled by the government,' he shouted above the noise, while his soldiers drove a jeep out from its hiding place under the tree canopy. 'But hopefully not for long, eh?'

Jasper climbed in, failed to get comfortable, and hung on for dear life as the jeep sped along the tarmac. The thing was so noisy, and the condition of the roads so poor, that attempting further conversation was fruitless. Ten minutes in, having still not seen a single vehicle or living soul besides themselves,

David held up a blindfold. Jasper had been expecting this. He nodded, and let his old friend bind the cloth over his eyes. Almost immediately the jeep lurched, turning off the dirt road they'd been travelling, presumably into the surrounding dense forest. The ride became something like a turbulent North Sea crossing, and Jasper clenched his jaw to stop his teeth rattling.

When they finally came to a halt and David removed the blindfold, Jasper was confused. He'd expected a tent camp, something temporary. Instead the rebels' headquarters comprised a series of squat and joyless concrete buildings, set into the slope of a hill (possibly a mountain, Jasper could never remember the technical difference) and surrounded by rainforest, whose inevitable reclamation process of the area was well underway. Only the coming and going of jeeps and soldiers kept the fronted concrete area, spider-webbed with cracks as wide as Jasper's arm, free from dominance by the advancing flora.

'A school,' he said, noticing the painted markings still visible underfoot as they stepped out of the jeep. 'This used to be a school.'

David laughed without humour. 'And here we are, old boys together. The world has a strange sense of humour.' He led Jasper inside, through corridors past former classrooms that now held caches of weapons and equipment, annotated maps and charts of Mwizuba, stores of dry food, medical supplies, and row upon row of thin, ragged sleeping rolls. 'Don't worry,' said David, noting Jasper's concern, 'You'll be in officer's quarters. It's not the Savoy, but it's a real bed.' Jasper's duffel had already disappeared with one of the alarmingly young soldiers, presumably to be thoroughly searched before arriving in said quarters.

David opened a door into a small room, plain and pragmatic with two tall windows to let in natural light. A simple desk, two chairs, a filing cabinet, and none of the cluttered chaos they'd passed on the way here.

'We think this used to be the deputy headmaster's office,' said David. 'Power outlets are in the floor.'

Jasper dropped his backpack on the desk and removed an Asus laptop. He paused, cord in hand, before plugging in. 'If this place is supposed to be closed, but you're drawing power...?'

David looked puzzled and gestured to the air around them. 'Can't you hear the generators?' Jasper stood stock still to listen, then realised he'd heard them from the moment they arrived. The jeep journey had been so loud, he hadn't consciously realised the noise hadn't ended when they arrived at the building. 'We're fully off-grid, and we have plenty of local support for fuel. You won't run out of power to charge your computer.'

'I was more concerned about the army finding us.'

'Those idiots couldn't find their arse with both hands,' David laughed. 'That's why we're going to win.'

Jasper smiled. 'With a little help, of course.' He plugged in the laptop, then removed his iPhone and a notebook from the backpack. 'Next question: I asked for a local cellphone?'

David pulled a Xiaomi from the breast pocket of his camp vest. 'As requested. Its purchase can't be traced, and one of my men topped up the data credit. How much do you think you'll need?'

'Impossible to say. After the initial attack, most of our network usage will simply be receiving transmissions from targets. But if we're lucky, that will run to many gigabytes.'

'We'll buy more if you need it. Now give me a demonstration. I want to see this virus thing in action.'

Jasper smiled. 'Of course. Pull up a chair.' Technically it was a worm, not a virus, but it wasn't worth explaining the difference. He wasn't quite the computer genius he claimed in order to secure clients like David, or the Russians bankrolling this little excursion, but his old friend knew even less.

Jasper took the Chinese phone from David and set it aside for now; he wouldn't need to tether it to the computer until the worm was running for real. This demonstration would be self-contained, a local infection on the Asus to show how it worked. He sat at the desk, opened the laptop to a black screen, then removed a cord from around his neck. Tied to it was a small, flat USB drive which he inserted in the computer. Then he opened the notebook to a neatly-written grid of numbers. A text prompt appeared on screen.

```
Ref D7 - N12 - B16 - H3
> _
```

Jasper turned to David. 'Before we start, why don't you fill me in? I read what I could on the BBC before coming here, but I'm not fully up on the situation. Is it true this all started with a copper mine?'

David sank heavily into the room's other chair. 'The mine was the spark that lit the tinder, but the bonfire pile had been building for thirty years. You remember when I came back here to work for the government?'

Jasper grinned. 'That was a going-away party and a half. Couldn't show my face at the Ivy for a year. You were still in government last time I saw you, I think?'

'Correct. But then Walter Buziko became leader of the opposition party.'

'He's the chap they arrested after the mining protests.'

'They feared Walter from the moment he was elected. Everyone could see what the government was doing, draining all the money they could from Mwizuba. Even I saw it, from the inside, but what could I do? I was merely a mid-ranking minister. But then Walter asked me to work for him instead. He represented hope; a new generation, and a new kind of party.'

'So what happened with the mine?'

'The workers discovered that it contains more than copper; there's also a large amount of cobalt, and it's likely many other mines are also sitting on the stuff.'

Jasper nodded. Cobalt had many uses, but one of the most common was in battery production, essential to modern technology. 'So that's worth a lot of money, I suppose?'

'Oh, yes. Enough to make Mwizuba a very wealthy country.'

'Let me guess; the president used it to make himself very wealthy, instead.'

David grimaced. 'Many of these mines, including the one where they found cobalt, were local co-operatives. The president immediately nationalised the industry and seized them all. Walter objected, but was ignored. So he went directly to the people, and explained how the government was stealing their future prosperity. Not only their money, you understand, but their children's.'

Jasper nodded. 'Which led to the protests, and the protests led to…this.'

'Not right away. But they arrested Walter, beat him to death in his jail cell, and claimed it was suicide. It might have ended there, but for one policeman who leaked pictures. I may be the only Mwizuban to have attended Eton, but it doesn't take a classical education to question how a man covered himself in bruises before caving in his own skull. That was the real spark.'

Jasper smiled. 'Look at you, leading a rebellion. Quite a career path.'

'Not one I chose freely, I assure you. But how could I refuse them? They loved Walter, and Walter trusted me.'

'So now you're trusting me, and the Russians?'

'Any port in a storm, old boy.'

Something in the way he said it made Jasper pause. 'David, why am I here? You're sitting on a gold mine — well, a cobalt mine — yet here I am, to carry out a spot of blackmail. Surely you must have lots of outside interest?'

'Interest that falls short of support,' David said with a shrug. 'We had some sympathetic funding for a while, but African civil wars aren't seen as profitable. The outside world is content to let us settle the course of our own internal problems.'

'You mean they're happy to watch you kill each other, then step in to trade with whoever controls the mine at the end of it all.'

David nodded. 'That initial funding was finite, and I've already contributed a significant amount of my own money as well. Quite frankly, we're running out of time. When I contacted our mutual friend in St Petersburg, I was hoping he could petition Moscow for money...'

Jasper could see David didn't want to say it, so spoke for him. 'But instead they sent me. Don't worry. No offence taken.'

'I just don't understand why they couldn't send cash.'

'Because they don't have any,' Jasper laughed. 'Do you think all those oligarchs got so rich by letting the state keep its own money?' He clapped David on the shoulder. 'Look, I'm not embedded in the Kremlin. I'm merely a freelancer, and they hired me for this one because of our shared history. But they wouldn't have done so if they didn't want you to succeed. It's going to be all right.'

'I certainly hope so. We can't sustain our efforts much longer.'

'Then let's see what I can do to help,' said Jasper. He located the grid references in the notebook, and typed the corresponding numbers into his computer. The screen cleared to reveal Jasper's desktop, sparse and monochrome. He opened a folder called *RC-Demo*, launched the application inside, then switched to his email. 'This is what people will see, when their machines are infected.'

David peered at the screen, waiting for something to happen.

'I don't understand,' said David. 'This is your inbox.'

Jasper smiled. 'Precisely. Everything will appear perfectly normal. But look here.' He reduced the email window to half the screen width, then launched a new application, its window filling the remainder. The new window was titled *Rat_Catcher_Log*, and as they watched, it rapidly generated and scrolled through a long list of text. David frowned, then let out a quiet exclamation as he recognised phrases and names in the text, because they matched those same things in the email application. Jasper nodded. 'Get it? Obviously, the target doesn't see this *Rat_Catcher_Log* program running; it's for demonstration purposes, and I'm going to wipe this machine clean before I begin the real hack in any case. But once the worm activates and phones home — home being this computer, of course — it'll send us all the information.'

David laughed. 'We'll have a copy of everyone's emails?'

'And more. This little beauty grabs emails, spreadsheets, Word documents, Facebook activity, photos, browser history, you name it. You'll have more leverage than you know what to do with, and they won't even know they've been hacked.'

'How long will it take?'

'Once the software begins operating it runs continually, feeding data back to us whenever the target computer is online. The tricky part, as with anything, is getting it onto the machines in the first place.' David looked worried at this sudden wrinkle, but Jasper smiled. 'That's why you're paying me a pretty penny, old boy. We're going to hit them at the G20.'

14

'You're the zero-day girl. Figure this one out, if you can.'

Monica Lee turned in her chair and tossed a thumb drive across the small CTA office to Bridge. Along with Bridge and Ciaran, Monica was the unit's third member, and the only ex-'Doughnut' — an affectionate nickname for GCHQ staffers, named for the department's ring-shaped building at Cheltenham. A specialist in cyber-security and online surveillance, Monica had been given the task of poring over Peter Lennox's laptop to track down whoever hacked his confidential documents — now made all but impossible thanks to Lennox restoring the computer's hard drive after the hack had already taken place.

It didn't help that, like Bridge, Monica hadn't been present during the MP's briefing a couple of days ago, instead relying on Ciaran's notes to carry out the task. Bridge was furious she'd been shut out of the meeting, even though she understood why; after Paris, and her demotion from SCAR (not to mention her disastrous weekend in Lyon, which Giles didn't know about), she was in no state of mind to sit and discuss Peter Lennox's fall from grace without throwing it in the MP's face. Had Lennox known she should have been there? Did Giles explain why she wasn't? What had they said about her?

Bridge clenched and unclenched her hands, exhaling slowly. This was no good. Dr Nayar would encourage her to calm her racing thoughts, to think instead about the opportunities this presented. How being relieved of responsibility for SCAR was a weight off her shoulders, allowing her to work without pressure.

She'd have a hard time believing it even if it had come straight from the doc's mouth. She certainly wasn't about to convince herself. But it was a different perspective to consider, and enough to at least slow her heart rate down.

Bridge didn't always get along with Monica, though she envied her ability to simply glide through the day unconcerned by other people's opinions. But she didn't envy her this task. Sweeping restored hard drives for old data was a shot in the dark in the best of circumstances, and this was pretty far from best.

'What did you find?' she asked, snatching the drive from the air.

'Hardly anything so far,' Monica replied. 'But I did locate fragments of what looks like exploit code sitting on garbage sectors, with a reference to cryptocurrency. Doesn't seem connected to the data hack, but I figured it might be something to do with the ransomware, and you never know who it might hit next.'

Monica was right. The ransomware wouldn't help them find who hacked Lennox's files, but if it was out there spreading online it paid to take a closer look and devise a way to harden the UK's computers against it. Besides, while Lennox had been confident he wasn't targeted, Bridge was less certain. She wasn't aware of any significant new ransomware floating around the internet. If this was a new strain, and one of its first victims just happened to be a British MP who sat on committees related to national security...in her experience, such coincidences were rarely anything of the sort. On the other hand, Lennox had also said the ransom was cheap. That was out of character for all but the most basic script-kiddie ransomware.

A test case, perhaps?

Bridge shook her head. The only way to resolve these contradictions was to solve the puzzle, and after the events of the past few weeks she was glad of an opportunity to bury her head in code and ignore the outside world. Of all the people who might give her the opportunity for relief, Monica would normally have been the last person on Bridge's list. Or maybe second to last, slightly above her mother. But she'd take it where she could get it.

On her HP laptop she created a new virtual machine; an entire copy of her computer's operating system emulated within the main system, like a nested *matryoshka* doll. Then she inserted the thumb drive and examined the contents. Monica hadn't been kidding about it being mere fragments. Ransomware was a quick-strike attack designed to leave no trace; whether the victim paid up or not, when its job was done the software would delete itself to remove incriminating evidence. But Peter Lennox had neither paid up nor run down the deadline. Instead he'd reverted his entire hard drive to a state before the ransomware had infected it, denying the software the opportunity to commit digital suicide. So while his restoration had wiped the actual program, it hadn't wiped the garbage sectors because they were used purely for swap — the act of temporarily writing the contents of a computer's RAM to disk, in order to save memory.

Some of those sectors had been overwritten in the days following, before SIS got their hands on the laptop. And the nature of swap meant the fragments Monica had extracted weren't complete, or even contiguous. But she was right; it looked like exploit code. Every coder was different, but certain things popped up again and again in viruses, worms, trojan horses, and ransomware — which were essentially viruses with added extortion. And one more ingredient separated ransomware from regular viruses, inherent in their very nature. They could be de-activated.

A normal computer virus rampaged over the user's hard drive, wreaking irreversible havoc, and that was that; the destruction was the point. Ransomware was different. It still rampaged over the hard drive, but instead of corrupting files it encrypted them and demanded payment. If the user didn't pay, the files would be encrypted forever. But encryption, by its very nature, was reversible. If you paid the ransom, that's exactly what happened. The ransomware would decrypt your files, delete itself, and the only permanent damage would be to your wallet.

Thus, every piece of ransomware effectively had a built-in kill switch. If Bridge could figure out how that switch worked, and somehow imitate it, she could trigger the decryption immediately and purge the attacking code from the victim's computer, without them even realising something was amiss.

She smiled, grabbed a notepad and her trusty lightsaber pen, and began to work.

* * *

Almost two days later, she finally put down her pen.

The fragments had been tricky to place, but Bridge had enough to figure out how the ransomware was constructed. That in itself required thinking like a 'warez author, the sort of black hat hacker who would code ransomware to begin with. Bridge herself had never unleashed a virus. Her preferred hacking focus had always been on exposing and cracking security vulnerabilities, but she'd never exploited those vulnerabilities to cause havoc or infect the target machines.

Well. Not unless it had been part of an SIS mission, anyway.

But she'd studied, cracked open, and picked apart plenty of viruses and trojan horses over the years, both in her spare time at university, and then for her work at the CTA. Her knowledge and instincts in this area had been why Giles recruited her to the unit in the first place.

And now she'd justified her reputation, right down to the weekend wire. At eleven o'clock on Friday morning she isolated what she called the 'trigger flag' — the virtual switch that told the software, yes, the victim has paid up and you may now decrypt the infected files on this machine, returning them to normal. That had been her working theory; all computers were vulnerable to virus infection, but because ransomware was reversible, a savvy hacker with access to the code could trigger that reversal even post-infection.

Bridge was pretty savvy.

The tricky part with ransomware was getting around authentication. When the software received a signal telling it the ransom had been paid, it was designed to compare that signal against its own secret key to ensure it had been sent from the right place, in other words, the hacker's own system. Of course, any hacker would try to bypass the security, and ransomware authors built against it. Poke at the wrong code block and your entire machine might be 'bricked'; wiped out and corrupted so badly it was unable to even start up, and thus little more than a brick of silicon, metal, and plastic.

But this ransomware had no such authentication, no such safeguard. It received the payment signal as a plain instruction, and seemingly trusted that it was genuine without attempting to verify it. Bridge had originally assumed she was dealing with an elite hacker, someone worthy of the challenge. Instead, it turned out 'Tempus' was a rank amateur.

By eleven-thirty she'd written code to automatically fire the decryption trigger, and started testing it. By one o'clock she'd refined the code and had it working consistently every time. By the end of lunchtime she'd written an executable application that would auto-run from a thumb drive: plug the drive into a computer, and if it detected the presence of the ransomware it would automatically launch and run her antivirus. The users' files would be decrypted, and the ransomware would commit digital suicide. It was, if she said so herself, brilliant.

In theory.

Bridge didn't have a real infected computer to test it on. She was working off her own models of the ransomware, built from the code fragments found on Lennox's machine, and assuming it followed a conventional structure. It was like reconstructing a dinosaur model from half a leg, one jawbone, and a tail: if you knew what you were doing you could make a fair approximation, close enough for other experts to agree with your assumptions. But they remained assumptions.

Nevertheless, Bridge was pleased with her work. Even a sudden summons to Giles' office didn't dampen her mood; no matter what other terrible mess was going on in her life, she was still a damn good hacker.

15

'Are you actively punishing me, now? Demotion wasn't good enough?'

Bridge paced up and down in front of Giles' desk. There was room to do so; his spacious corner office, with tall windows overlooking the Thames, sent a message. Bridge might currently be in the doghouse, but Giles remained very much in the top floor's favour. Shit rolls downhill, indeed.

'If you're referring to SCAR, it may surprise you to learn that you can't be demoted from a position which doesn't yet exist. As for punishment, frankly, you should consider this assignment a reprieve.'

She stopped pacing and looked at him with surprise. 'How so, exactly?'

'The G20 is a rather major political event. Perhaps you've heard of it,' he said with carefully-measured sarcasm. 'You may also have heard of someone called the prime minister, a fairly important figure around these parts, who this morning requested that we send, and I quote, "one of your cyber-people" to keep a watch for nefarious activity. One person, Bridge. One officer to accompany GCHQ, and represent the integrity of the CTA.'

'You and Dunston effectively grounded me from theatre. Now, when you need to look good, suddenly I'm back in?'

Giles ticked off the points on his fingers. 'First, you are not "grounded". Your OIT status remains in place; I merely choose not to exercise it for the present. Second, in this context, London is not a theatre of operations. There is no official mission, and thus no breach of the proscription against SIS operating on domestic soil. This isn't even going through OpPrep. Your role will be merely to oversee and advise. Third, for the hard of hearing: the prime minister of your monarch's government, both of whom you swore to serve, has requested an SIS presence for which you are self-evidently our most qualified officer. Finally, for the hard of memory: this is not a request, but an order from your superior officer. If you need a refresher on the relevant hierarchy, I suggest you do a three-sixty and remember in whose office you stand.'

Bridge had switched off halfway through the speech. She already knew Giles was a pedantic, self-aggrandising bastard when he wanted to be; she didn't need to listen to him prove it.

'I've just spent two days knee-deep in fragmentary malware code, pulling preventative countermeasures out of thin air like a fucking wizard,' she said. 'Do you have the slightest idea how bored I'll be at the G20?'

'Good,' said Giles, picking up his pen to continue that day's *Times* crossword, a signal the conversation was over. 'Boring means we're doing our job properly. Report directly to the MoD liaison on-site Monday morning.'

16

> How is life?

+ Life sufficient

> Tell me how you are

+ Why do not tell me how you are?

> I asked you first

+ Why asked me first?

> Stop

17

It was only upon seeing Stéphanie through the café window that Bridge realised how much she'd missed her niece. Six months was an eternity to a four-going-on-five-year-old, and even from inside Bridge could tell she'd grown since they'd last been together, at Fréderic's family farm in Côte-d'Or.

Hugo, her nephew, was still small enough to be asleep in a stroller. Bridge smiled, glad she'd bagged a table big enough for them all, and waved. Stéphanie waved back, before being promptly ushered in the other direction by Fred, who didn't look at Bridge as he pushed the stroller away from the café.

Izzy — Fred's wife, the childrens' mother, Bridge's older sister — entered the café alone and sat down. Suddenly the table seemed vast.

'Oh, we're running late,' said Izzy, 'so Fred's doing the shops while I'm in here.'

Bridge didn't believe that for a moment, but let it slide as the waiter appeared. Her sister ordered a coffee, and the waiter turned to Bridge. '*Just* coffees?' he said, in exactly the right tone to guilt-trip her for commandeering a large table at Friday lunchtime. She hastily ordered a pasta dish for herself, even though she wasn't really hungry. Satisfied, the waiter backed off.

'Still all in black, I see,' said Izzy.

Bridge couldn't argue with that; she was in her usual black

T-shirt and jeans, black boots, and black leather jacket. 'Hey,' she protested with a smile, 'I'm wearing blue knickers.'

Izzy didn't see the funny side. Instead, her immaculate eyebrows lifted. 'How old are you now, Bridge? Twenty-eight?'

'I'm thirty in, like, six weeks' time.' Bridge rolled her eyes at Izzy's perpetual inability to remember her own sister's birthdate. 'What does that have to do with anything?'

'I really thought after last year you'd start moving on, thinking about your future. You've got to start wearing some colour, put something on your lips that isn't purple.'

'Where the hell's all this coming from? Are you trying to pair me up with someone?'

'I would, if I didn't think they'd run a mile. Come on, do you want to be the ageing old goth woman at the club, desperately trying to find someone to take her home?'

'Oh, my God. You are seriously telling me to grow up.'

'Nobody else will, apparently.'

Bridge scowled. '*Au contraire.* I went to see Maman.'

'I know,' said Izzy, and Bridge realised that of course she did. Of course their mother was on the phone to Izzy the moment Bridge left, relaying their entire conversation.

'Is that what's going on, here? Maman put you up to it? She was pushing me to glam up, too. Apparently the real me isn't good enough.'

'No, you've got it backwards. The real you is perfectly fine, but nobody can see it because…' Izzy gestured vaguely at Bridge's face and clothes. 'This isn't the real you, it's a grown woman acting like a teenager. That's not what men want.'

'I don't give a flying fuck what men want. I've told you and Maman both, I'm not looking for a husband.'

Izzy sighed and looked out the window. 'I'm trying to help.'

'Like you were helping when you told Maman about my job? She practically interrogated me as soon as I stepped through the door.' Bridge paused, but Izzy's expression remained blank. 'My *real* job.'

'Oh, that. What did you expect? She wanted to know why Fred had been in hospital, whether she should be worried about the kids, all that. You know what she's like. Of course I told her.'

Bridge lowered her voice. 'Izzy, you signed the Official Secrets Act. That's some serious shit.'

'So is keeping big, fat secrets from your family. Your own family, Bridge. Maman has a right to know.'

Izzy's coffee arrived, much faster than Bridge's had despite the place being busier now than when she first entered. She noticed the waiter glance at Izzy's wedding ring, and rolled her eyes as he retreated. 'No, she doesn't have a right to know. That's the entire point of the OSA. She's not even a British citizen.' Izzy shrugged and sipped her coffee. Bridge somehow stopped herself from leaping across the table to strangle her sister, restraint that surely deserved recognition, and forced herself to move on. 'How are you all, anyway? How long are you back for?' Izzy's family moved back and forth between their home in London and the farmhouse at Côte-d'Or at entirely random intervals. Bridge had never worked out if they were timed to coincide with Stéphanie's school terms, or Fred's work for *Médecins Sans Frontières*.

'I don't think we'll be going back to the farmhouse for a while,' said Izzy. A guilty nerve twitched in Bridge's neck as Izzy looked down at her coffee. 'Fred's considering selling it.'

Bridge's mouth fell open. The farmhouse had been in Fred's family for generations. He'd spent part of his childhood there, and now it served as a refuge for his own family, a bucolic oasis in the roiling ocean of modern life. No internet, no TV, barely any mobile coverage.

'It'll pass, in time,' said Bridge. 'He'll never sell that place, he'd die first.' She regretted her choice of words immediately.

'"In time"? Bridge, he was shot, and he thought his wife and kids were about to be killed. That may be everyday life for you, but we're normal, ordinary people.'

Bridge coughed to stifle a laugh. If there was one thing Izzy had never been, it was normal or ordinary. 'It's not normal for me at all. Do you know what I did after I got back from the farmhouse?'

'Saved us all from a terrorist attack, wasn't it?'

Bridge's neck flushed. 'After that. I spent every other bloody day in therapy for weeks, and then I sat at my computer for months on end. I didn't leave the country again until last month.' She omitted why, and the chaotic mess in Paris.

Izzy closed her eyes and took a deep breath. 'The point is…' She hesitated, and took a sip of coffee instead of finishing.

Tired of all the gentility, Bridge said, 'For God's sake, Izzy, spit it out. I haven't got all day. Neither have you, apparently, if you're running so late.'

Izzy winced at the sarcasm, and balled her hands into fists. She was building up to say something, but for the life of her, Bridge couldn't imagine what. 'For once, will you please not make it about you. This is about us, and our family. My family.'

'What is? What's going on?'

Izzy exhaled. A decision made, a Rubicon crossed. 'Fred thinks it best if you don't see the children for a while.'

Bridge didn't move, her whole body turned to immovable stone. But she forced her voice up through her cold, rigid throat: 'And what about you? What do you think?' Before Izzy could respond the spell broke, Bridge's voice and body regaining energy, fluidity. 'Because you may recall I apologised, profusely, several times already, and if Fred thinks I'd do *anything* to deliberately put your kids in danger he's deluded, and since when did your bloody husband decide when you get to see your own family, anyway?' She finally ran out of steam, while Izzy patiently sipped her coffee.

'That's not fair. I know you think I'm some put-upon little woman under her chauvinist husband's thumb —'

'Bullshit, I've seen you tell him to stick it when it matters. Perhaps you could remind him I saved his life?'

'He remembers perfectly well. He also remembers that it only needed saving in the first place because you led a killer to our home.'

Bridge wanted to protest that she hadn't led anyone there, that the Russian had figured it out for himself. But he wouldn't even have been looking if Bridge hadn't foolishly paid Izzy a surprise visit while on a field mission.

'You've never understood, Bridge. He's my husband.'

'And I'm your sister!'

'Exactly,' Izzy said, standing up. 'I chose him.'

She left without looking back. Bridge stared at her sister's unfinished cup and tried not to think about everyone else in the café staring at her, admonishing her, wondering what terrible things the glum-looking woman had said to drive off her pretty, glamorous friend.

The waiter brought Bridge's pasta. She mumbled thanks, and had a fork halfway to her mouth before realising that in her haste she'd ordered a dish topped with bacon.

She managed to lock the restroom door before the tears came.

18

Fadi double-clicked the spreadsheet. Sure enough, it was
a timetable of the speakers and side rooms for next week's
G20. Wasn't there already a copy of the schedule in the digital
orientation pack? No doubt the organising company was
making sure. He smiled, and wished more conference groups
would be so considerate.

* * *

'That's it? You just send an email and hope someone opens it?'
　Jasper Wilmington smiled and leaned back in his chair.
'Wouldn't you? Come, David, you've attended enough of these
conferences. They're boring as hell, the same every time, and

your inbox fills up with useless crap that you don't need to know but you're obligated to read anyway.'

David Kzaane considered that. 'Fair. But how will hacking a bunch of junior civil servants help us? You said the G20 will have its own private network.'

'Never underestimate the amount of incriminating documentation to which even the lowliest civil servant has access, old boy. But it's not them we're worried about. All it takes is for one of them to open this spreadsheet, and the *Rat_Catcher* protocol will immediately self-install on their laptop, and wait. When they connect that computer to the summit network, then things really start to happen. Of course, we won't see anything during the summit itself, thanks to that private network. But as soon as they're back out in the real world, we'll get everything we need from some very senior civil servants, perhaps even some politicians if they take their computers.'

David grunted. 'All right, you clearly know what you're doing. I have a summit of my own, to brief my captains on our next movements. Let me know when you have something I can use to put the screws on Her Majesty's government.'

Jasper actually didn't have much clue what he was doing. He wasn't even sure exactly how the software worked. He'd asked, but when Maxim had briefed him it had become clear that, despite trying to sound omnipotent, the Russian was merely parroting what he'd been told himself. Jasper had been assured that all he needed to do was get the payload onto a computer, and the software would take care of the rest.

Within a few days they'd have enough sensitive material to make the FCO reconsider their stance on Mwizuba, and force the British to support David's rebellion. Then Jasper could get paid, and get the hell out of this humidity.

19

FROM: ponty@top-emails.net

SUBJECT: Re: (re) RE: the thread that would not die

will the real Satoshi Nakamoto please stand up? or have
you forgotten that nobody even knows who actually
created bitcoin? if I asked any of you to run a firewall
without knowing who'd written it, where it came from, or
who financed it, you'd run a bloody mile. how do we know
it wasn't the russians or north korea - ok, not NK, they
wouldn't have a clue - but china or someone, and the
whole point of it is to turn everyone against the banks
and weaken the west?

PS it's finite! the stupidest idea in the history of
currency! we already passed peak bitcoin years ago. what
happens when the last coin is mined?
--
ponty

Bridge knocked back her second vodka, bemused by the speed
with which her life had collapsed. Losing Artjom Kallass in
Paris; demoted from leadership of SCAR; arguing with her

mother in Lyon; and now being made to babysit the G20. The only bright spot had been successfully figuring out how to protect against the Tempus ransomware, two solid days with her head spent untangling an intricate puzzle of code.

But then her disastrous lunch with Izzy had put paid to any temporary good mood. Bridge had gone straight back from the café to Vauxhall, returned to her desk, and attacked her email inbox with the grim efficiency of a woman trying to distract herself from her own thoughts. By the end of the day she'd replied to two dozen emails with answers of five words or less, forwarded another dozen to make them someone else's problem, and deleted fifty more as technically irrelevant to her job description. If anyone wanted to argue about that, they could fuck right off. The one email thread she hadn't been able to bring herself to do anything with was a long conversation about the SCAR committee. That was Ciaran's problem now, and good riddance. Bridge couldn't even get the support of her own family; how did she ever think she could lead a team of people from different agencies, all with different working practices, who technically didn't even answer to her?

```
FROM: ~BlackDiscordia~

SUBJECT: Re: (re) RE: the thread that would not die

ponty said:

> if I asked any of you to run a firewall without
> knowing who'd written it

But we don't NEED to know who SN is. He/they gave us the
```

```
SOURCE CODE. Give me an open-source firewall that I can
read myself and YES I'd run it, assuming I couldn't
write a better one myself. Which I COULD.

> and the whole
> point of it is to turn everyone against the banks and
> weaken the west?

Kind of BIASED, though, aren't you Ponty? Being in
FINANCE.

> what
> happens when the last coin is mined?

Then we LEARN, if humans are still capable of learning,
to live WITHIN our resources. Is a finite coin really
worse than being able to LITERALLY print infinite
amounts of money and running the world on DEBT? Maybe a
finite system will FINALLY make people realise we need
population control.

    /\~|v0v|~/\
~BlackDiscordia~
```

She'd left the office without saying goodbye to anyone, returning home to East Finchley. There she opened a bottle of vodka and contemplated yet another weekend alone, wondered why she fucked everything up so badly, then reminded herself it was because she was a useless, antisocial piece of shit. She'd been down this road before; Dr Nayar would tell her to get out of the flat and go be zen in a park, surrounded by the expanse of nature. Or find balance by making a list of all the good things in her life.

But she was unable to think of a single thing that would go on that list, so instead Bridge poured herself a drink, kicked her way through the PC case parts littering her lounge floor, sat at her distinctly un-expansive desk surrounded by the detritus of her life, logged on to Usenet, and waded into the newsgroup's latest flame war threatening to burn down the whole group; a vociferous argument over whether or not cryptocurrency was The Future.

FROM: ponty@top-emails.net

SUBJECT: Re: (re) RE: the thread that would not die

~BlackDiscordia~ said:

> Then we LEARN, if humans
> are still capable of
> learning, to live WITHIN our resources.

more people = more resources needed. that's basic
society, right there. never going to change.

> Maybe a finite system will
> FINALLY make
> people realise we need population control.

BD, I'm going to give you the benefit of the doubt,
because we've both been around the block. but are you
seriously suggesting we deliberately and artificially

```
constrain our resources - for which many people would
suffer, and don't pretend they wouldn't - just so
they'll stop having kids? I mean, FFS, why not have a
nice little war or two while we're at it?

--

ponty
```

Bridge made it clear she wasn't a fan.

Anyway, maybe this isolation was for the best. Fréderic was right; Bridge's own family weren't safe around her. And hadn't she always been more of a loner, anyway? She'd never truly fitted in anywhere as a teenager, her friend group at university was smaller than most, and she'd always been fine with her own company, content to spend time alone. Why not embrace it? Become the crazy old lady she always knew in her heart she was destined to be, walking her own path, needing nobody's help or company.

She stretched in her chair and took in the chaotic mess of her flat. Loner or not, she needed to get to the launderette before the G20 summit kicked off on Monday morning. She was down to two pairs of jeans and zero clean work knickers, and didn't fancy spending several days sitting at the back of a hot conference room with a lacy thong cutting into her for no good reason. The only bachelors looking for a hotel tryst at the G20 would be twice her age with a tan line where their wedding ring should be.

Perhaps she really did need to get out of the flat, like Dr Nayar said. But not for a walk around East Finchley, or making stupid lists in the park. She wanted to get wasted and have some fun. Who said she had to stay in because her sister didn't want to see her? Did Izzy rule her social life? No, she fucking did not.

Bridge marched into the bedroom and flung open her wardrobe.

* * *

Two hours later she crushed a cigarette under her heel, descended the blacklit steps of Corrosion Club, and dropped off her long black woollen coat at the tiny cupboard of a cloakroom. She'd squeezed into her trusty old buckled leather corset, after finding a floor-length black number lurking at the back of her wardrobe. Originally she'd planned to go miniskirt, but discovered to her dismay that the heel was coming off her knee-high boots. No way was she wearing something that short with just ankle boots, so she turned to the longer skirt. Up top she pulled on a patterned, sheer long-sleeve under the corset, clipped a black silk choker around her neck, then raided her big jewellery box for as many rings, bracelets, and earrings as she could fit. A light dusting of white foundation, old-school Horus eyeliner, and purple lipstick finished it off. She hadn't back-combed her hair in years, and wasn't about to try it now, especially not two days before having to work a conference. Instead she flattened it, with a simple central parting. The *Classic Morticia*, as she and her university friends used to call it. Hidden advantage: easy to tie back at the end of a sweaty night.

Growing up in her older sister's shadow, Bridge was used to being overlooked. Izzy possessed a natural beauty and grace that had men falling at her feet, while barely registering Bridge's existence. But in a perverse way, she was grateful she'd had to work and fight for attention. She knew how to make the most of what she had, and that usually meant revelling in being the tallest and physically fittest woman in the room. She might have been preparing to wave goodbye to her twenties, but tonight was no exception — with more eyeliner and less lighting, neither of which could hurt.

She strode to the bar, feeling like a twenty-foot-tall avenging harpy who disdained eye contact with mere mortals. All she needed was wings, which the booze would readily supply. But as she knocked back a double vodka, the fact of her upcoming birthday struck her again. The big three-oh. That was officially Old, no question, and Izzy's words scratched at the back of her mind. Would Bridge really still come here in ten years' time? She was already one of the oldest in the room. Did she want to end up like Lacey Dave over there in the corner, pushing fifty, already half-cut and smiling to himself as he watched women half his age twirl around on the dance floor? He'd tried it on with Bridge, once — Dave had tried it on with everything in a skirt, including some of the guys — and she'd laughed it off, thought nothing of it, watched him leave alone. She'd gone home by herself that night, too, but suspected she was rather more sanguine about it than him. Was that down to an ability to be content with her own company? Or was it simply a by-product of youth? Bridge had never had any intention of marrying or having kids, but would she feel the same when she was pushing forty instead of thirty?

She shook her head. Christ, this wasn't what she came here to think about. The processed guitar intro to Cubanate's *Oxyacetylene* boomed from the PA, a siren warning for tonight's retro segment. Bridge drained the last of her vodka and marched onto the dance floor, fists already pumping in sync with the drum machine.

A dozen songs and three more double vodkas later, she was

buzzing; a little drunk, nothing serious, but sweating buckets thanks to dancing through the retro set. She'd spent much of it eyeing up a punk-ish guy on the dance floor, taller than her, arms covered in tats, narrow shoulders but a nice backside in his drainpipes. As she waited in line for another drink he took a place beside her at the bar, wearing the cockiest grin she'd seen in years.

Fuck it. Why not?

She grabbed one of his wiry inked biceps and dragged him over to the wall by the toilets, where she backed herself up and pulled him in, relishing the taste of cigarettes and speed on his tongue.

He broke off, grinned that cocky grin, and said, 'No messing around. That's what I love about older women.'

Bridge slapped him so hard he fell across a nearby table. Then she kicked him in the leg for good measure, strode back to the bar, and ordered two straight doubles.

20

Everything really was black, grey, or purple.

Well, not entirely. She had some pants and socks in various colours, bought in discounted three-packs, but they didn't count. Everything else — T-shirts, blouses, skirts, jeans, trousers, frocks, jackets, blazers, scarves, gloves, even her corsets, tights, and boots — was a variation on an unending theme.

After she'd swatted the punk-ish guy away, Friday night had been something of a blur. She remembered whirling like a dervish on the dance floor; falling down the stairs of the night bus at her stop on the East Finchley High Road; and then waking up far too early this morning, alone and fully clothed, with bruises on her arms and her worst hangover in years. She'd downed a few pills, taken a scalding hot shower, poured two coffees into her throat, and decided it was time to face the future, and her wardrobe, head-on.

She didn't like admitting Izzy and her mother might have a point. She certainly wasn't about to pile on orange foundation and totter around in stilettos. But maybe it was time to move on, and 'put away childish things' as the saying went. Perhaps Dr Nayar was right; that refusing to consider she might live past thirty was a way of avoiding adulthood, a defence mechanism against the big, bad world that had taken her father away too soon.

She made three piles. The first was clothes she hadn't worn in years, and there wasn't much to it; some old T-shirts that were more hole than fabric and a couple of elaborate, baroque dresses from her early goth years, into which she had no intention of squeezing herself ever again. She'd kept them because they'd cost so much, but that was a terrible reason to hang on to something. Into the fabric recycling they would go.

The second pile was huge. These were the regular clothes she should probably reconsider; skirts of every length, tights of every pattern, skinny jeans, faded band T-shirts, hoodies, shrugs, gloves, boots, bangles, chokers, skull scarves, skull rings, she even found an old skull-print bra...and her trusty black leather jacket, the one she'd had since she was a teenager after badgering her father to buy it when they moved to London. It was like a second skin, and she wasn't sure she could bring herself to throw it out.

In fact, she couldn't think about discarding any of this pile right now. At least she'd made it; surely that was the hard part. Now she could stuff it somewhere else, to be dealt with later. One step at a time.

The final pile was another small one; clothes any normal, respectable, adult woman could wear. Some plain black skirts, cardigans and shirts in various shades of black and grey, regular jeans, black ballet flats, and a couple of pairs of boots that didn't jangle when she walked. Finally came her 'weddings and funerals' outfit, a dark grey skirt suit she invariably wore with a silver-grey blouse and black heels. She'd had a few compliments wearing that before now, but the more she thought about it, the more she wondered if that was just because it wasn't jeans and a T-shirt.

The third pile was enough to get by for a few days in the

real world, but it was all still very her. A sort of permanently dressed-down version of her.

She made herself another coffee, fired up Spotify, cleared her playlist of '90s Scandinavian third-wave goth, and in its place built a list of bands her father used to listen to. The Police, Eric Clapton, Stevie Ray Vaughan, Jimi Hendrix, Led Zeppelin. Old man music, but it conjured childhood memories of playing family boardgames in Lyon, his head bobbing out of time with the guitars while her mother tutted at his awful taste in music. Maman listened to Charles Aznavour, Juliette Gréco, Tino Rossi; so-called classic singers who set Bridge's teeth on edge.

To the sound of soft-rock guitars, she removed the posters that lined every part of a wall not hidden behind a bookshelf. What thirty-year-old woman still had The Sisters of Mercy pinned above her desk? What self-respecting adult put up a *Pulp Fiction* poster and thought, 'Yes, that's appropriate'? Why were her Spotify playlists all thirty-year-old goth bands, anyway?

She paused mid-removal of a Covenant tour poster as the fifty-year-old opening notes of *Purple Haze* blared from her computer speakers. Most days, she'd have laughed at the irony.

Not today. Today the posters came off the walls, the clothes came out of the wardrobe, and the playlist was…was…she had no idea. She cleared Spotify and clicked over to the *Today's Top Hits* playlist instead. That was what normal people listened to, wasn't it?

Bridge folded the posters into quarters and stacked them next to the front door, ready for recycling. Her head was pounding again, but there was still work to do. She gulped two ibuprofen, shrugged on the skirt suit blazer, wrapped a plain grey scarf around her neck, and covered her tired eyes with the darkest, biggest sunglasses she owned. Time to shop.

* * *

The next morning she stormed through the gym doors as soon as they opened, having arrived ten minutes early, and proceeded to beat seven shades out of the heavy bag until she could barely see for sweat.

Bridge had spent Saturday afternoon fleeing from too-eager sales assistants, nightmarish apparitions of the girls who'd bullied her when she first came to England. She'd tried to ignore their sideways looks and furtive glances at colleagues as she struggled to figure out what the hell suited her, and then which subset of those clothes came in her size. At one point, tired and frustrated in an H&M fitting room, her thumb hovered over Karen's number in her iPhone. Karen was an old friend of her sister's, an ex-goth who worked in the City. But Bridge wavered. Karen earned a small fortune and wore power suits every day. She'd be disgusted to find herself browsing racks on the high street. Julia, the fourth member of their erstwhile dinner circle, would have been a better option; she worked in TV. But both women were Izzy's friends first and foremost. Bridge was the latecomer, the baby, and Izzy would have insisted they cut her off, too. She couldn't bear the potential humiliation.

She ended the day knackered and loaded down, earning baleful glares for taking up an extra tube seat with her shopping bags. A selection of navy, green, and maroon skirts; two pairs of black trousers, the only ones she'd been able to find that fitted her *and* had pockets; several blouses, all of which felt unnaturally breezy, but she supposed that was something she'd have to get used to; a pair of navy kitten heels; a couple of blue and silver scarves; and a grey blazer, the best one she could find that fit her shoulders, even though the waist was too wide.

Now every punch she threw, every kick she drove into the bag, was to expel hatred and self-loathing. The clothes weren't her. Or rather, they hadn't been. Now they were, and in time she was sure she'd get used to them, maybe even make more discerning purchases. But this morning she wanted to punch everyone and everything, until either the world fell down or she did.

On the way home she called at the veggie café by East Finchley station for a halloumi wrap and carrot cake, then spent the afternoon taking out her anger on pointless *u.l.g-n* flame wars she'd regret — were there any other kind? — about hashing algorithms, CDNs, and the topic of the moment, cryptocurrencies. She made a mental note to follow up with Peter Lennox about this new coin his ransomware hacker had demanded, which in turn reminded her about the G20, which only made her more depressed. Then she remembered she still had no clean underwear, and ran to the laundrette down the road for a last-minute wash.

Finally Bridge had retired to bed with a mug of tea and the latest Lauren Beukes novel. That was one thing she could still do. Change her clothes, yes; take down her posters, yes; even start wearing a little more make-up, sure, whatever, fine. But they'd pry her books from her cold, dead fingers.

She dreamed of Izzy buried under fallen bookshelves, and Bridge wasn't strong enough to lift them off, and when she gripped her sister's hand and pulled the hand came away like a store window mannequin and it wasn't Izzy any more it was Artjom Kallass bleeding all over the Peugeot's seat as the car slammed into a Paris railing —

She woke in darkness, finger still wedged between smooth pages.

21

'Only 11 am and I already want to throw myself out of a window,' Bridge whispered. 'Thank God this thing is only two days.'

A nearby secretary from the German delegation, a man with skin like polished pine, overheard and shot her a look. In the seat next to Bridge, Steve Wicker suppressed a laugh. 'Try not to get us both thrown out before lunchtime on the first day, yeah?'

She rolled her eyes and smiled. After decimating her emails on Friday afternoon, she'd visited Giles for one last attempt at passing this job off. He'd refused, and relayed the news that Steve would be GCHQ's point man. She suspected he'd known long before then, but held it back as a final bargaining chip; Steve and Bridge had worked together before, and Giles knew she wanted to enlist him for SCAR duties if the unit passed committee. Assuming she still had any say in the matter, of course. 'The PM just wants you there to advise if anyone tries to mess with the delegation,' Giles had said, 'and make sure the delegates themselves don't click on anything they shouldn't. If all goes well you won't even need to touch a keyboard.'

Giles had formed the CTA, fighting decades of institutional inertia within SIS, and constantly pushed for the Service to further embrace technology in its work. But he'd never been a coder himself, and that last remark had demonstrated one of the ways in which he still didn't get it. Bridge was never happier than when 'touching a keyboard', spending hours disinfecting a virus or hacking a server. It was the prospect of sitting in a room while a dozen middle-aged apparatchiks droned on that bored the living daylights out of her.

But here she was, stuck at the back of a cavernous grey hall inside Docklands' ExCel centre, trying not to yawn while the Brazilian finance minister talked at what seemed unnecessary length about import deficits and global market difficulties. Steve caught her facial contortions and smiled. 'Why don't you go get us both a coffee? Do something to keep you awake.'

'I'm not your tea girl, Steve.'

'You'd rather I went, and left you listening to this?'

'At least I might get some sleep,' she smirked, but stood up and sidled along the row of desks anyway. Steve had spent weeks leading the GCHQ preparations for the conference; he'd set up the private internal network used by delegates, installed and tested monitoring software that watched for anything nefarious, and made sure everything was in place for the several hundred secretaries, administrators, interpreters, and clerks that came along with twenty world leaders. Like her, he'd only found out SIS would be present a few days ago. But like Giles, he'd reassured Bridge there'd be almost nothing for her to do, and she should look on it as a short break from the office.

The concourse outside the main room buzzed with activity, a welcome change from the sedate and monotonous speeches inside. This was where the real deals were made, thought Bridge. The grandees could get up on stage in front of the world's cameras and make their speeches, but out here the civil servants, bureaucrats, and lawyers were the ones negotiating trade arrangements away from the spotlight's glare, shaking hands over stale panini and lukewarm cappuccino.

'*Owgoddammit!*' It all came out as one multisyllabic word, cried out by the man she'd bumped into as he carried a coffee back from the kiosk. It steamed from his hand and wrist, a light brown stain already forming on his crisp white shirt cuff.

'Shit, I'm so sorry,' Bridge apologised, pulling a paper napkin from the kiosk dispenser and dabbing it over the man's hands. 'Completely my fault, I was distracted.'

He placed what remained of his coffee on a nearby table and took the napkin, rubbing it over his scalded wrist. 'No real harm, ma'am,' he said, and smiled at Bridge with large, stereotypically American teeth.

Bridge smiled back. 'That's *Ms*, if you don't mind.'

'Sorry — wait, aren't you the one supposed to be apologising?'

Bridge hesitated, then scowled when he pulled a face to show he was just ribbing her. He held out his hand and Bridge shook it, noting how it swallowed even her own long fingers.

'Karl Dominic, State Department.' He nodded behind her, toward the main room. 'You with the host delegation?'

'Brigitte Sharp, DTI,' she replied, automatically slipping into her cover story. Putting aside the small matter of SIS not being sanctioned to operate on home soil, it would also be rather awkward to have to explain to guest countries why the host's foreign intelligence agency had sent a representative. Not that Bridge was the only intelligence officer present, as all sides knew. This tall American standing in front of her could be CIA or NSA. But there was a game to play, and this was how everyone played it.

'Let me get you a coffee,' said Dominic, turning back to the kiosk.

'No, don't be silly,' said Bridge. 'If anything, I should get you a replacement.'

'It's fine,' he said, retrieving his cup. 'Only a splash missing.'

'Are you sure? I'm already buying for two.'

'Oh? You look old for a gofer.' He suddenly realised what he'd said and stuttered, 'Uh…wait, that was…'

Despite the flush reaching her cheeks, Bridge laughed. 'Well, aren't you the flatterer.'

'Aw, Christ. Okay, now you have to let me buy.'

'*Au contraire, monsieur Dominic*. I might run the whole department, for all you know. But I still wouldn't let you buy me coffee.'

He relaxed and laughed, a deep-chested growl that Bridge was annoyed to realise triggered a reflexive smile from her in reply. 'Sharp by name, huh? I'll see you round, Ms.'

No, I'd rather you keep facing that way, thought Bridge, watching his shoulders as he walked back to the main room. When she returned to the kiosk, the serving girl gave her a knowing look. 'Two cappuccinos,' she mumbled, unable to resist adding a tiny chocolate bar that cost almost as much as the coffee.

22

> How is life?

+ I do yes operate efficiently. I am scan 1,984 targets increasing.

> What is is the current value?

+ Current value is $2.85

> Thank you

+ Yes

23

The chocolate brought momentary relief, but Bridge had a sinking feeling the day was heading downhill when Steve's Toshiba laptop pinged an alert that made him go, 'Huh,' in a worryingly surprised tone. She leaned over, and he pointed at log messages scrolling up his screen. 'Repeated hardware requests for file system access, every thirty seconds.'

'Unsuccessful, I assume,' said Bridge.

'Yeah, all our computers will reject file system requests without authorisation. But everyone's under strict orders not to plug in anything to start with, in case of infected thumb drives.'

'Whose machine?' Bridge didn't need to ask about the thumb drives. The policy had been drawn up some years ago after an isolated network at the Pentagon was successfully attacked. Built with a so-called 'air gap', the system was completely unconnected to the internet, and theoretically couldn't be hacked. Its infection had techies scratching their heads for days…until they tracked it to a staff member's USB thumb drive, purchased from a nearby store. Turned out Russian operatives had bought dozens of drives, infected them with viruses, then re-packaged and planted them in stores around Washington. All it took was for someone to unwittingly buy a pre-infected drive and plug it into their computer for the virus to begin working. It was an ingenious scheme, but could never work again. Since its discovery, government workers around the world were under strict orders to only use thumb drives obtained from their IT departments, checked and cleared for usage.

At least, that was the theory.

The computer that had triggered Steve's alert belonged to a young secretary at the FCO. Bridge followed Steve down through the delegate sea, to the woman's station. She didn't seem to be acting suspiciously, merely playing solitaire in a window alongside her note-taking, but that was no guarantee. If the woman was indeed a double agent, she might have thought that being here on a closed network would protect copying files onto a thumb drive from discovery. But every British computer at the summit contained additional software that transmitted its activities to on-site monitoring servers set up by GCHQ, which Steve had been watching. He carried his laptop with him through the hall, noting that something on the secretary's machine was still requesting file system access every thirty seconds.

They reached the young woman, and Steve identified himself while Bridge checked her computer. There was no thumb drive, but one USB slot did contain a small dongle, like the type to use with a wireless mouse. Except it had *3G* printed on the casing.

Bridge removed the dongle, ignoring the woman's protests. 'Steve?'

He checked the logs and nodded. 'No more requests.' He turned to the secretary. 'Care to explain this?'

'Explain what?' The young woman shook her head. 'It's not a thumb drive, it's just a 3G antenna.'

Steve frowned. 'One: we explicitly instructed everyone not to tether to their phones or use cellular signals. This network is locked down for a reason, you know. And two: where did you buy it?'

'I don't remember. Amazon, probably.'

Bridge had been examining the dongle. 'No manufacturer's marks, no CE label, nothing. This is dodgy as hell.' She passed it to Steve. 'I reckon if you take that apart you'll find a thumb drive inside after all. It's a different angle to the Pentagon trick, and potentially on a bigger scale. Good thing you saw it in time.'

But Steve was still watching the server logs. 'Might be too late, I'm afraid. The computer's trying to make its own outside connection, and it's pretty damn insistent about it. When did you plug this in?'

The secretary shrugged. 'When I sat down here and opened my laptop. Look, I don't see what the big deal is. It's my brother's birthday, and I wanted to message with him.'

Bridge rolled her eyes, and a glance at Steve's screen confirmed what he'd seen; the woman's laptop was repeatedly trying and failing to make a connection to the internet, outside of the G20's closed network. Every thirty seconds, another attempt; every thirty seconds, another failure. She was suddenly aware they were still crouched at a desk in the middle of the summit, clearly annoying several of the nearby delegates. Bridge nodded to Steve to retreat; he took the dongle with him, while she took the secretary's computer. When the woman protested, Bridge suggested she revert to pen and paper and be grateful they didn't frog-march her out of the building. They walked back to their places at the rear of the hall, and Steve stopped off on the way to have a word with one of several grey-suited MI5 officers standing watch. He pointed back at the young secretary. Bridge didn't envy the interrogation she was about to undergo.

Back at their station, Steve removed a set of jeweller's tools from his backpack to open the antenna casing, while Bridge logged in to the GCHQ monitoring server and checked the secretary's network logs. Sure enough, the persistent attempts to connect to the outside internet had been going on for some time. Too long, in fact.

Steve removed the dongle's casing and peered inside. 'You were right, there's a tiny flash drive in here. Looks Chinese. Crafty buggers.'

'They may not be the only ones.' Bridge took out her iPhone and called main entrance security to ask what time the secretary entered the building. The answer was not good news. 'She arrived at ten to eight. And those network requests began fifteen minutes later.'

'So?'

'She said she plugged in the dongle when she got to her station and opened the laptop. That can't have been earlier than eight-thirty, because until then the room was setup staff only. But the network requests began almost half an hour earlier, at five past eight. I have a horrible feeling this is bigger than her…' Bridge quickly selected several other civil servants' computers at random, checked their logs, and swore. Sure enough, they were all making the same unauthorised attempt to get online. 'Someone's hit us with a bloody worm, and it's trying to phone home from every computer it's infected. No doubt to transmit whatever data it's scraping from everyone's hard drives.'

'Like happened to Peter Lennox.'

'I'm worried it's exactly like that, yeah. We need to lock this place down.'

Steve picked up his phone, but hesitated. 'What exactly do you mean?'

'I mean that right now there's no real damage done, because we're on a closed network. But when people leave, and these computers hit the open networks…'

Steve nodded, understanding. 'The network requests won't fail any more. They'll connect to the internet and send everything they've scraped to whoever's behind the attack. So we can't let anyone leave the building.'

'Hopefully it won't come to that. It's their computers we have to worry about, not the people themselves.'

'This lot won't leave without their machines. Even if they would, what could we do? We can't wipe their hard drives. They'd lose anything not backed up.'

'Then maybe it'll finally teach them to back up,' said Bridge. 'But I might be able to purge this, if we can keep everyone on-site.'

'And our solitaire-playing secretary definitely isn't the source?'

'Assuming she's telling the truth, she can't be. I think those network requests began immediately when the real source entered the building, at five past eight.'

Steve pulled out his phone and called Sundar Patel at GCHQ to brief him. Bridge stood and looked around for the nearest MI5 officer. It wasn't difficult; he stood at the back of the room in a grey suit, hands clasped across his rugby player's physique, scanning the room while pointedly ignoring the armed Special Branch officer standing five feet to his left. The wire trailing from his earpiece was merely the final giveaway.

The officer stiffened as Bridge approached. Only a touch, most people wouldn't even notice, but she did. He was ready to fight, already assessing the best way to incapacitate her if she displayed as a threat.

She reached inside her jacket. His hands slowly unclasped. The Special Branch officer glanced her way, eyes narrowing.

Maintaining eye contact with the MI5 officer, she slowly withdrew her SIS identification wallet and passed it to him. He opened it, read it, raised an eyebrow, then handed it back to her. The Special Branch officer visibly relaxed.

'I need you to call Andrea Thomson,' she said quietly, 'and authorise a full lockdown. Give her my name, tell her to call me and I'll explain. For the time being, nobody is to leave the premises.'

The rugby player looked surprised, but to his credit he didn't scoff. 'If there's imminent danger, shouldn't we evacuate?'

'Not physical danger. We're experiencing a massive cyber-attack. I'm hopeful I can deal with it before things come to a head, but until then we can't risk anyone going outside.' The summit's closed network extended only to the perimeter of the building. It was crucial that nobody leave with their computer until Bridge was sure they were clean.

The officer nodded, pressed his earpiece, and began talking to his colleagues. Bridge had been introduced to some of them by the MoD liaison upon arrival that morning, but Andrea was the Five officer she knew best. The Scot would get her people doing exactly as they were told, no matter how outré the instructions.

Steve was still talking to GCHQ when Bridge returned to her seat. She called entrance security again, asking them to send herself and Andrea a list of people who'd entered the building between eight o' clock and ten past. It would be a long list, but she could go over it later to find the source; whether that person was an attacker or merely an unwitting patient zero was unknown for now. According to the server logs for her own HP laptop, it was hammering the network in the same way. So was Steve's Toshiba. They had to assume every British computer at the summit was infected.

On the bright side, being infected meant she had a full copy of the worm's code to work with, the entire executable operating in runtime. That was much better than the fragments of Tempus ransomware she'd had to piece together last week, though it would still be a matter of trial and error reverse-engineering.

She isolated the activity, and soon found the code residing in a low-level system process of her computer. She created a virtual machine, made a copy of the malicious program inside it, and shut off her network access. It appeared to be called *Rat_Catcher*, a name she hadn't heard before. A new white label package from the hacking community, perhaps? Or a toy for the likes of infamous Russian hackers Cozy Bear? Something about the code rang a bell —

Her fingers froze over the keyboard. Steve had finished his call, and leaned across to look. 'Bridge? What's up?'

She ran a hand through her hair, then pointed at the screen. In among the executable code were two innocuous character strings. Most people would have skipped right over them.

```
[U-GIFT] CoinExchange
```

Bridge wracked her brains, trying to recall why they sounded familiar. Everything prior to the weekend was already a little hazy. What had she been doing on Friday? Lunch with Izzy. The less she remembered about that, the better. But in the morning...

The antivirus she'd written to defeat the Tempus ransomware. According to Ciaran's notes of the meeting with Peter Lennox, the MP said it had demanded payment in a new cryptocurrency. '*Gift box, or something,*' she recalled, further confusing Steve. 'It's the coin that new ransomware uses,' she explained. 'Peter

Lennox was hit by it, before he got hacked.'

'U-Gift,' Steve nodded. 'Can't say I've heard of it, but it makes sense. What's it doing here? There's no ransom demand.'

'I don't know, but suppose this is the same author?'

'Would that help us?'

'It might, because I already wrote a program to disable their ransomware.' She hesitated. 'Admittedly, I haven't been able to test it yet. But it's better than nothing.' She picked up her iPhone to call Giles, but instead it buzzed with an incoming call from Andrea.

'What the bloody hell's going on, and why do you want me to prevent people leaving?'

Bridge explained, emphasising that she could try to neutralise the infection, but only if everyone's computer stayed inside the building. 'I know it sounds extreme. But you also know me.'

'Aye,' said Andrea, with less confidence than Bridge would have liked. 'Right now it's easy enough to keep people in, we're only dealing with the odd delegate trying to nip out for a smoke. But in two hours' time everyone will want to eat and start drinking. If the doors are barred when that happens, we've got front page news and a political nightmare.'

'I know,' said Bridge, well aware of Andrea's unspoken implication: *and it's one more black eye for you.* She couldn't afford to worry about her reputation or job prospects right now. 'What about all the protestors outside? I passed the usual placard-waving suspects on my way in this morning. You could say there's an imminent threat, and everyone has to stay inside as a precaution?'

Andrea hesitated. 'You want me to fabricate a threat to the world's leaders, just to keep them inside the building?'

'Like they're not used to it,' said Bridge, smiling. 'But hopefully

it won't come to that. Will let you know if anything changes.'
She ended the call before Andrea could protest further, and saw
she now had two voicemails. No prizes for guessing. She dialled
Giles' number; he picked up after a single ring and didn't bother
saying hello.

'I've got Sunny Patel on the line having kittens, and all I'm
getting from you or Andrea is voicemail. Enlighten me.'

'I'll explain when you get here, but I need you to bring
something with you. Remember I wrote that anti-ransomware
executable last week? Ask Monica to pop it on a thumb drive for
you before you set off.'

Giles was silent for a moment. At first Bridge wondered if
the connection had gone down, then it occurred to her that she
was still in the doghouse, and probably shouldn't be barking
orders at her own boss. 'Remind me to explain the concept of
deference at your next assessment,' he said, evidently having the
same thought. 'Now, how serious is this? What does ransomware
have to do with a cyber-attack on the G20?'

'That's what I'd like to know. As for how serious it is, I can't
tell yet. But given what happened with Peter Lennox, I don't
think we should take any chances.'

'Point. On my way.'

As she ended the call, Steve said, 'You really think both
attacks are by the same guy?'

It sounded absurd. Badly-coded penny-ante ransomware,
ripping people off for a few dollars each, was a world away
from this apparently sophisticated worm called *Rat_Catcher*.
Could the U-Gift connection be a coincidence? Most people
would think so. But hackers were creatures of ego and habit,
often repeating methods and code across projects because they
considered themselves to have assessed every option before

finally developing the One True (and superior) Way. The coin was so obscure, and this attack came so close on the heels of the other, that coincidence seemed unlikely. At the back of her mind, Bridge realised this also implied that whoever entered the building that morning and infected everyone else was probably an unwitting victim after all.

'We need somewhere we can work properly. Is there anywhere in this place that isn't booked out?'

'No, but we could use our server room.'

Bridge nodded, and Steve led the way. As they neared the door, the armed Special Branch officer raised his eyebrows in question at her. She replied with a small shrug and muttered, 'Fingers crossed, man.'

They passed through the central concourse, still busy with delegates making and breaking deals over coffee. Steve used his contactless lanyard to open an opaque staff-only door, revealing a set of plain stairs leading up to the back-office facilities. One large second-floor suite contained the site's regular IT setup, but Steve used his lanyard to give them access to a smaller adjacent room.

It was stacked with servers and monitoring kit, all installed by GCHQ ahead of the summit, and two GCHQ staff watching over it all. Bridge's stomach tightened upon seeing the towering racks and humming fans. It wasn't so long ago she'd been unable to walk into a server room without suffering an anxiety attack. But this hub controlled internal communication for every computer in the building. There was no question it was the best place to be.

They set up at a desk, and Bridge messaged Giles and Andrea with their new location. Then she and Steve focused on the *Rat_Catcher* code, looking for vulnerabilities they could exploit, just as the worm had somehow exploited their own. Neither spoke until the door opened to reveal Andrea, with the much-taller Giles visible behind her. Bridge glanced at the wall clock, realising how much time had already passed. Ninety minutes before the day's official proceedings drew to a close.

Two more people filed in behind Giles. One was Ciaran, presumably because of the potential link to Peter Lennox. The other was a tall, broad-shouldered man with a light brown stain on his shirt: the American from the coffee stand, Bridge realised with surprise. Giles introduced him. 'Special Agent Dominic, from our friends at the agency. Bridge, I gather you've already met.'

Bridge rolled her eyes. 'He said he was State Department. I didn't believe it, of course.'

Special Agent Dominic smiled. 'And I didn't believe you were DTI. Nothing personal.'

'It never is,' said Giles. 'Now, Mr Dominic confirmed the US delegation is dealing with the same infection, and I've also had worried calls from Australian and Canadian friends. This is rather getting out of hand.'

Bridge considered for a moment. 'All English-language, though? That could be the targeting factor.'

Giles nodded. 'It would certainly fit with what we know so far.'

'How the hell did this get in?' said Ciaran, aiming the question at Steve. 'I thought you lot had shut off outside access?'

'We did,' said Steve. 'That's the only reason this thing hasn't already spread far and wide.'

'And it got in through a literal trojan,' said Bridge. 'Best guess, it was sitting dormant on someone's laptop, maybe geofenced to wait till they entered the building. They came in this morning, it woke up, and started using the internal network to infect other machines. It wasn't GCHQ's failing, and frankly, without that —' she nodded at the network monitoring server, '— we wouldn't even know this was happening in the first place.' She resisted adding, *so wind your neck in*. Ciaran had been in a real mood the past few days. Maybe he wasn't happy about being handed SCAR, either.

Giles produced a thumb drive from his pocket. 'Monica said this is what you're looking for. She also pointed out that it hasn't yet been tested against real malware.'

'How thoughtful of her,' said Bridge, annoyed at the backhanded dig, even though she couldn't deny it was true.

'So you plug that in and boom, everything's sorted?' asked Andrea. 'How does it work?'

Bridge inserted the drive into her laptop and made a copy of the anti-ransomware program. 'If only it were that simple. No, this was designed to disable a specific piece of ransomware, not a data-hoovering worm. But,' she quickly added, before Giles could ask, 'I believe they were written by the same hacker. So I can re-use code to make a new countermeasure, and send that out across the internal network.'

Andrea's eyes widened. 'Are you saying everyone's got a computer virus…and you're going to cure it by infecting them with another virus?'

Bridge half-smiled. 'That's about the size of it. But if we do it right, nobody will ever know about either the worm or the countermeasure.'

'Do it wrong, and we'll have a shit storm of epic proportions,' grumbled Giles. 'Everyone and their uncle will think we've been trying to hack their computers at the conference.'

'I imagine half the support staff here are doing that anyway,' said Bridge. 'And if this doesn't work we'll have to wipe everybody's computer, one by one.'

'Impossible,' said Andrea. 'The delegates would never agree to that.'

'Then you'd better hope it does work, or the Lennox hack will seem like a pea-shooter compared to this ICBM.'

Karl Dominic grabbed a chair, placed it next to Bridge, and positioned himself to look over her shoulder. She could hear his breathing, calm and measured. 'What are we looking at?' he asked.

As Bridge explained the situation, Andrea took a call. Several delegates were already arguing with her MI5 officers, trying to leave the building. She ordered them to cover fire exits as well, and call more officers down here if necessary. Then she made her excuses, wished Giles luck, and left the server room to help at the main entrance.

'If it's only targeting English-language systems, maybe we should restrict ourselves to the same,' said Ciaran.

Bridge shook her head. 'Just because someone isn't infected, doesn't mean they can't be a carrier. Our countermeasure has to be wide-ranging; if it sees the code, no matter what machine it's on, it should act.'

'Agreed,' said Karl, removing a Sony laptop from a messenger bag. 'I guess we start with the network-out block, right? If we can take that down, it'll give us time to wipe the rest of the code at our leisure.'

Bridge paused mid-keystroke and looked at Karl in a new light. 'You're a coder?' she said, with only mild disbelief.

If he saw that disbelief, he didn't acknowledge it. 'Yep. That's why I'm here.'

'Why be so cautious?' said Ciaran. 'Delete the worm as soon

as you find it.'

Karl peered at him over the top of the Sony's screen. 'Whoever wrote this thing knew what they were doing. You start deleting shit at random, it's going to fight back. Could wipe everyone's machine in self-defence.'

'Hardly the worst outcome,' said Ciaran. 'Bridge said we might have to do that anyway.'

Giles spoke up from a seat in the corner of the room. 'That option is very much a last resort. Bridge?'

She turned to Steve. 'Can you configure the internal network to maintain its connection with every computer that's made a request since this morning, whether or not it's active right now?'

Steve nodded. 'Simple enough to set up a managed switch, but what about people who've put their laptop to sleep?'

'I know an old NSA trick to get around that,' said Karl. 'So long as they're only sleeping, we can reach them.'

Bridge raised her eyebrows, impressed again. 'All right, Mr Fancy Pants,' she smiled, 'You start on that, and I'll concentrate on a code injector. See if we can't zap this little bugger.'

She scanned the runtime code, looking for the parts that activated whenever *Rat_Catcher* made an unsuccessful attempt to reach the internet. After five minutes she'd located the block. 'Got it. Unclear where it's calling to, but maybe I could spoof the destination, assuming it's not encoded of course, and then we can intercept the data, try to —' She stopped when Giles tapped his watch.

'Rather too involved for the time we have,' he said. 'You've found the code you need to disable, yes? So focus there. We take our wins where we can find them.'

Bridge sighed, but he was right. She returned to the code block, watching the output change with each network request.

But not all of it. 'The ending is the same each time,' she said, 'and so's the randomisation length. I can count back from the end to find the beginning.'

'What are you thinking?' asked Karl. 'Null it?'

'Exactly, and garbage the rest.' She smiled at him. 'Old SIS trick.' *Null characters* told code to stop what it was doing and move on to the next section. An injected null at either end of the code block wouldn't stop *Rat_Catcher* gathering data, but it would prevent that data being sent out. 'How's your end going?'

'I already gave it to Steve. We're waiting on you.'

'Oh, great,' said Bridge, and returned to work.

Twenty minutes later she sat back and reviewed what she'd written; a virus disguised as an Excel spreadsheet that would scan for *Rat_Catcher*'s network attempt code. She didn't have time to check for bugs. Bouncing ideas off Karl had helped, but ultimately it came down to her own coding capabilities. She had to trust herself, even if nobody else did.

Before committing, Bridge copied *Rat_Catcher* onto the thumb drive Giles had brought with him. If this was a white label worm anyone could buy online, she wanted to keep a copy of the executable handy to check out later.

'Ready to test,' she said. Karl and Ciaran both watched over her shoulder as she hit Return.

The countermeasure wrote itself onto her laptop, then waited for *Rat_Catcher* to make a network call. Fifteen seconds later a request was made, and Bridge's countermeasure immediately injected null characters into the code. With the networking safely disabled, the countermeasure disassembled the remainder of *Rat_Catcher*'s code, changing string identifiers and flooding it with digital garbage, before finally deleting it.

The HP blacked out and rebooted. When the system

reappeared, all Bridge's settings had reverted to factory default. But the countermeasure had done its job. There was no trace of *Rat_Catcher*, and network activity had returned to normal. Having to reconfigure her desktop wallpaper was a small price to pay.

Giles' phone rang. He answered it — a new Samsung model, Bridge noted — listened, said, 'Understood,' then hung up and turned to her. 'The natives are restless. Andrea's keeping everyone in, but people are at breaking point.'

Bridge inhaled deeply. 'The code seems to work. I think we're about ready.'

'Seems? About?'

Karl gave a deep, hollow laugh. 'We're as ready as we'll ever be. Hit it.'

Bridge exhaled and ran the program, letting it bloom across the network from machine to machine. For almost a minute the ExCel building echoed with the sound of beeps, pings, and startup chimes, including a disgusted low-frequency buzz from Karl's machine as it restarted. Like Bridge's computer, all his system settings had been reset. He groaned. 'Man, it took me hours to get that how I like it.'

'This will take delicate handling,' said Giles, ignoring Karl. 'Everyone's computers rebooting like this, followed by us suddenly allowing them to leave the building, will only convince the delegates they have indeed been hacked.'

Bridge shrugged. 'They have. But if you're right about this being English-language countries only, you should be able to reassure them.' She waggled her thumb between herself and Karl. 'Tell them we sorted it, rebooting was a necessary preventative measure, and we're sorry everyone lost their cat pictures.'

Giles raised an eyebrow. 'Sometimes I envy you,' he said cryptically, then turned and left, already tapping at his phone to make a call.

'Was that a compliment?' asked Karl. 'I couldn't tell.'

'You and me both,' said Bridge, and laughed; the adrenaline comedown was starting, her hands quietly trembling with relief. She sat very still, taking deep breaths while Karl packed away his Sony. He stood, shook hands with Steve and Ciaran, then turned to Bridge. 'Pleasure working with you; and now I hope we never meet again. No offence,' he winked at her.

As the American departed, Steve hit Bridge with a questioning look. 'Are you two…?'

Bridge punched him in the arm, closed her computer, and left the room. What she really needed was a cigarette.

```
*** YOUR FILES HAVE BEEN ENCRYPTED!!! ***

Your Document, Photo, File, Video, and Web Browse
History can not access because they now encrypted. DO
NOT WASTE TIME to trying to recover. ONLY I CAN POSSIBLE
RECOVER FOR YOU.
```

Jasper Wilmington stared at the screen, begrudgingly grateful for the stifling, moist late-night heat. His family's Rhodesian home had been at a high-enough altitude to bring cooler air with the dark, but Mwizuba offered no such respite. He'd been sweating since he stepped off the plane, day and night, thanks to the surrounding jungle. On his first night he hadn't slept a wink; the next few hadn't been much better, until fitful sleep finally came, more from exhaustion than any healthy tiredness. Only three weeks before he had to move on to another job. He feared he might never become acclimatised.

Of course, if this ransomware threat was real, Jasper might find his time in Mwizuba severely curtailed in any case. Along with his fee.

But not being able to sleep had turned out to be a boon. He'd decided to check in on *Rat_Catcher*, see if the software had revealed anything yet. The moment he unlocked his laptop the ransomware had blared like a beacon, and Jasper was thankful nobody else was awake to see it. If David or any of his men saw this, it would shake their faith in him. Jasper was careful to never explicitly claim he was a computer expert, but he was happy for people to jump to conclusions. Seeing a man they considered to be a hacker be hacked himself could shatter their trust.

So insomnia had saved Jasper from that potentially dangerous embarrassment. Now all he had to do was sort out this mess before everyone else woke up.

He cursed himself for being foolish enough to poke around on the dark web in the first place. He'd been keeping up on the malware market, on sites which were, ironically, normally safe. Nobody wanted to piss off the very people looking to buy their dodgy software. But some ran third-party ad networks, which became increasingly hostile with every passing day; omniscient trackers from unknown sources, clickbait graphics identical to browser controls, Javascript code injected behind Viagra ads... Surely that was how the ransomware had ensnared him.

He'd already wiped the machine once, after demonstrating *Rat_Catcher* to David, before reinstalling the system and software from his USB stick. He could do that again, which would remove this ransomware that had locked up his system. But doing so would also remove all the encrypted files, including whatever *Rat_Catcher* had thus far sent home from the hacked laptops at the G20, and those files would not be re-sent. The program was designed to send each item of data only once, in order to cover its tracks; repeated sends would alert any half-decent system that something strange was occurring.

That left Jasper with one option; pay the ransom, and to hell with it. Once the *Rat_Catcher* files were decrypted he could back them up and wipe the machine again. Of course, that assumed paying the ransom would result in decryption, but modern ransomware authors weren't stupid. If you paid up, but found your data still encrypted, word would quickly spread that this particular ransom wasn't worth paying. Not that he'd heard of this attack before, or recognised the style. Whoever this Tempus fellow was, the demand note suggested he wasn't a native English speaker. That could itself be a red herring, though, deliberately badly written to make people think the software came from somewhere like Russia or Ukraine. And why not, these days? The very USB drive sitting in Jasper's laptop right now was from Moscow. Even actions traced back to former Eastern Bloc countries were more often than not being directed by the SVR's Internet Research Agency. Nobody 'did cyber' like Putin's acolytes.

That was the other reason Jasper didn't want David's men to see this. Despite calling *Rat_Catcher* 'his little virus', Jasper hadn't written a single line of it, and wouldn't have known where to begin. He was technically savvy, and could program some basic software, but nothing on that level. So his Russian contacts had helped him out and introduced him to a supplier in eastern Europe.

The cryptocurrency, U-Gift, was new to him but that was less unusual. Since Bitcoin's explosion, thousands of cryptocurrencies had been created. Dozens more appeared every month; a few thrived, but most imploded or came to nothing outside hacker circles. He did a ticker search on his iPhone and was relieved to find one U-Gift coin cost just three US dollars. A no-brainer, then.

He clicked the link to load up the coin exchange, used a fraction of a Bitcoin from a small stash he kept to buy ten

U-Gift, and paid them to the alphanumeric string address which identified Tempus to the exchange, but meant nothing in the real world — or to Jasper himself. Finally, he clicked the *Check Payment* button on the Asus screen and waited.

The laptop was tethered to the Xiaomi burner phone David had supplied. Jasper had simply left it plugged in to run 24/7, continuously receiving the data collected by *Rat_Catcher*. Now it would wait for a signal from Tempus, whoever and wherever he was, to decrypt the files. Jasper only hoped it would be before everyone else woke up, so they were none the wiser —

Beep.

The screen cleared, and the system returned to normal. Jasper immediately fished a second thumb drive from his backpack, inserted it, and copied off the *Rat_Catcher* data. That was a ridiculously fast turnaround. Had he got lucky, because Tempus happened to be online? It was gone three in the morning here in Mwizuba, even later in Moscow, so if the hacker was indeed in Europe he was a night owl. Or perhaps he was in America, where it was still yesterday evening. Jasper toyed with the idea of attempting to find him, but anything more than a rudimentary trace was beyond his expertise. He could dump the laptop's logs onto another external drive, and give them to someone else to figure out, but why bother? No security service or law enforcement would seriously care about chasing down a ransomware author. Better to back up the data, wipe the system again, and simply pretend it never happened. Jasper yawned, finally beginning to tire as he de-stressed…then jolted upright to stare at the screen, thoughts of sleep banished.

The *Rat_Catcher* data folder was empty.

He brought up a world clock and double-checked the date. The G20 had definitely begun today — or rather, from here at 3 am Mwizuban time, the day before. He hadn't necessarily expected the folder to be brimming, but shouldn't there be some amount of data? Had everyone left their computers inside the conference building? Impossible. Perhaps *Rat_Catcher* simply took its time to spread? The worm's supplier, Maxim, had tried to explain how it worked, but Jasper could tell the man was no more a programmer than himself, merely parroting what he'd been told. Which presented the possibility that he had omitted something important; such as, perhaps it needed a critical mass of infection before it got to work. That was how botnets worked, wasn't it? Suppose this was designed the same way?

Yes, that must be it. No need to panic.

Jasper unplugged the USB stick and began the process to wipe the Asus all over again. However the ransomware had got on there, he would make sure it was gone forever.

25

Fadi Saeed looked like a man who'd spent thirty-six hours awake, because he had. Whether that was due to stress or MI5's interview technique, Bridge wouldn't have liked to guess. Either way, if Saeed had known what he'd unleashed, Andrea would have got it out of him.

But he didn't. Saeed was a patsy, a man unlucky enough to not only open a malware email attachment, but then be the first such person to enter the ExCel centre on Monday morning. His computer was the source of *Rat_Catcher*, the patient zero Bridge had been looking for, but he hadn't put it there. He'd merely opened an email claiming to be from the G20 and double-clicked on the attached schedule spreadsheet. That information was public; Bridge had confirmed the spreadsheet simply scraped data freely available on the conference website, so besides its redundancy and spoofed address, there was no reason to think the email wasn't real.

But opening the attachment had infected Saeed's computer, and something in the *Rat_Catcher* code had waited until the G20 commenced before spreading, automatically infecting hundreds of other computers across the conference.

Andrea left Saeed to stew in the bowels of Thames House for a while, and led Bridge upstairs to her office. Neat and tidy, dominated by a large computer screen on one wall and a view of the river on the other. Bridge took a chair in front of the desk and waited for Andrea to speak.

'It's not him,' she said simply.

Bridge nodded in agreement. 'I don't think Saeed has the cunning to come up with a plan like this, let alone infect his own computer to give himself an alibi.'

'You still think this Tempus chap is behind it, same as the ransomware?'

'Impossible to be sure. They definitely share code, but that doesn't guarantee the same author, because hackers share code all the time. There are entire online communities devoted to it.'

'Why would they do that? I thought hacking was all about bragging rights?'

'It is. If you figure out the most efficient way to attack a government server, or some new hardware configuration on the market, for a brief moment you become top dog. Everyone is suddenly using your code to wreak havoc. For a hacker, there's not much better.'

Andrea faced the window and watched the river below. 'So it could be completely unconnected. A random attack.'

'Well...' Bridge hesitated, unsure how much to share with Andrea. 'Look, this is barely a theory. More like a hunch. And after Paris, well, you know.'

Andrea raised an eyebrow over her shoulder. 'Is that why you weren't at the meeting with Peter Lennox? Have you been benched?'

'Not exactly.' Bridge's neck was suddenly very warm. 'Okay, yes.'

'Understandable, I suppose. But this ransomware has attacked hundreds of MPs and civil servants already; we're handing out copies of your antivirus as fast as we can make them, and they're doing the trick. So even if Giles has lost faith in you, I haven't. Spit it out.'

Bridge was about to protest that Giles was only doing the politically expedient thing, then stopped herself when she realised she was about to defend her own demotion, and what the hell did that say about her? She cleared her throat and began again.

'Lennox is kind of where it starts. Tempus is infecting politicians and civil servants, yes, but out there in the world it's a ghost. It's not making headlines, and it's not spreading across regular people's machines like we'd expect. So I think it's targeted.'

'At whom?'

'That's what I don't know. But to my mind, the kind of person who'd target ransomware specifically at government and related officials is exactly the kind of person who'd also attack English-language computers at the G20.'

Andrea nodded slowly. 'Makes sense. But who?'

'I don't know. But I'm getting to know them, through their code.' That might sound crazy to non-programmers, but Bridge wouldn't apologise for her own area of expertise. 'It's not much to go on, but I won't stop looking.'

Andrea stayed at the window, watching the river pass by. 'You should imagine them naked,' she said suddenly.

'I'm sorry?'

'Old squaddie trick. Whenever a sergeant or brass gave us a bollocking we'd imagine them standing there, red-faced and bawling with no trousers on, little willy waving about. Defuses the impact.'

Bridge grimaced. 'I'd rather not, to be honest.'

'Suit yourself,' Andrea laughed. 'But don't let the bastards grind you down.'

After being escorted out, Bridge emerged from Thames House to a warm and pleasant morning, one of England's infamous 'false spring' days. She slung her blazer over her shoulder and walked back across the river to Vauxhall, stopping on the bridge to light a cigarette and think about the conversation she'd just had.

She needed more evidence before she took it to Giles. The two attacks were so different. The ransomware was aggressive, basic, and sloppy. The lack of trigger authentication, which had allowed Bridge to so easily harden against it, suggested Tempus was an amateur.

But *Rat_Catcher* suggested quite the opposite. It was clever, patient, and sophisticated, spreading across the conference's closed network before she even noticed it. If Steve hadn't seen odd behaviour on that secretary's computer, Bridge might have completely missed its attempts to reach the wider internet.

Where had it been trying to go? And where had that infected spreadsheet come from in the first place?

Bridge suddenly remembered she had a copy of the *Rat_ Catcher* runtime on a thumb drive. She flicked her cigarette into the river and hurried back to the office.

26

'Mwizuba? The little African place?'

'That's the one,' said Bridge. 'I admit, I had to look it up. Minor state, corrupt regime, which our government is propping up in return for presumed future access to cobalt deposits. More importantly, Mwizuba isn't exactly overflowing with internet traffic or backbone nodes, as it's an almost entirely cell-based network.'

Giles looked confused. 'You mean mobile phones?'

Ciaran, who'd been halfway through a meeting with Giles when Bridge burst into the room, explained. 'It's not unusual. Digging pipes and building pylons is really expensive, and by the time a lot of developing countries were getting online, cellular technology was already at 3G level. Cheaper and easier to go straight to phone towers.'

'Exactly,' said Bridge. 'But as a result they don't generally route internet backbone traffic. Even 4G can't beat a half-metre-thick bundle of fibreoptic cables chugging down gigabits of data.'

Bridge had spent the afternoon digging into the *Rat_Catcher* runtime code, to see where it was attempting to send data. Cross-referencing that with a trace on the infected email sent to Fadi Saeed had given her a list of commonalities, and the tiny state of Mwizuba had stuck out like a sore thumb.

'Which raises the question,' she continued, 'why would any

system that was bouncing around, trying to anonymise data and cover its tracks, route through a small African country with no network infrastructure to speak of?'

'On the other hand, why not?' said Ciaran. 'We're not talking petabytes of content.'

'Gigabytes is still plenty,' said Bridge impatiently, 'and for a tiny place like Mwizuba to turn up in both traceroutes is one hell of a coincidence.'

Giles held up a hand for silence. 'Let's assume it's not coincidence. If we're propping up the Mwizuban government, why would they try to hack us?'

'Not the government. The whole reason we're supporting them is because Moscow is backing a rebel militia led by General David Kzaane.'

Giles rubbed his beard, wafting hazelnut across the room. 'I remember him. Eton boy, spent a few years representing Mwizuba over here. When did he suddenly become a General?'

'Seems he returned home and crossed the aisle to work for the leader of the opposition, whom the president promptly executed. Suddenly, Kzaane found himself leading a rebellion.'

'Smart chap, as I recall,' said Giles. 'Always pushing for more aid.'

'Maybe this is his new way of getting it. If the G20 hack had succeeded, Kzaane would be sitting on a goldmine of compromising material with which to pressure our Government.'

'But the G20 attack also hit America, Canada, the Australians...' said Ciaran, shaking his head. 'I don't see the connection.'

'English-language systems. The Americans were collateral damage.'

Ciaran laughed. 'I'm as big a patriot as anyone, but isn't it more likely they were the target, and we were the collateral?'

Bridge quietly fumed. To her dismay, Giles was nodding along with Ciaran as he spoke. It was time to bring out the big guns. 'I also believe whoever did this is the same hacker behind the ransomware, and the attack on Peter Lennox.'

'What makes you say that?' said Ciaran.

'I thought you'd never ask,' said Bridge, with all the insincerity she could muster, and produced the laptop she'd brought with her in anticipation. She placed it on Giles' desk and opened a text file. 'This is the network log from Lennox's hacked computer. Took me a bloody age to find this, by the way. Tempus did a good job covering their tracks.'

Giles shrugged. 'I don't really know what I'm looking at. Didn't Peter say he wiped his machine after the ransomware attack?'

'Yes. But I don't think that's what happened.'

Ciaran looked offended. 'Are you suggesting he lied to us?'

'No, no. He did wipe the machine. But look here.' Bridge pointed at a list of time stamps. 'This is the date his files were hacked and sent out across the internet: two days before they were leaked to the press.'

Giles peered at the screen. 'Doesn't that match up with what he said?'

'Not according to Ciaran's notes. Lennox said he'd wiped his machine almost a week before he came to us, when he was hit by ransomware. So this suggests the hack came *after* that wipe, not before, and he simply didn't realise.'

'What do you know? The Right Honourable Computer Expert isn't always so smart,' said Giles. 'This could be a very big advantage for us to press on the SCAR committee. Well done, Bridge.'

Ciaran was silent, no doubt staring daggers at the back of her head, but he'd have to live it down. 'Thank you, Giles. And that's why you should send me to Africa.'

His magnanimous gratitude was swiftly replaced by bewilderment. 'I'm sorry, come again?'

'Unless David Kzaane is suddenly taking night classes in malware, he must have hired someone to do this. Who better than the people already supporting his militia?'

'You think Moscow sent Tempus to help him.'

'Exactly. So when do I leave?'

Giles harrumphed. 'If you think I'm letting you set foot in an unstable African state, you are very much mistaken.' He held up a hand to silence her objection before she'd even opened her mouth. 'And may I remind you, the whole point of a task force like SCAR is to delegate across the most suitable operatives. We both know the best man for this particular job.'

27

God, the heat.

Henri was born and raised in Brighton, but he'd visited his father's home of Algeria many times. That was as close as he'd come to an equatorial country, apart from one holiday in Brazil. But Brazil's intersection with the equator was far in the north of the country, while Henri and his friends had been down in Rio de Janeiro; as far south from the equatorial line as Algeria was north of it.

Mwizuba was less than a hundred miles from it, and as the plane taxied to the gate a damp heat suffused the air. When the door opened Henri's throat reflexively constricted, and descending to the tarmac was like being enveloped in a hot, wet blanket. He had a horrible suspicion most of this trip would not be air-conditioned.

A young driver greeted him landside and ushered Henri into the back of a sleek black town car. The driver sped away without a word, navigating a tumult of cars, bikes, trucks, jeeps, and roaming livestock with ease. Twenty minutes later they stopped outside what was officially the British embassy, but to Henri's eyes resembled something more like a run-down shop front flying a Union Jack. The driver led him inside, where two men waited; in front of a rickety desk was a middle-aged African, neatly turned out, while behind it sat an older white man, looking harassed and overheated.

'Mr Mourad, sir,' said the driver with a local accent.

'Thank you, Joseph.' The man behind the desk stood to offer Henri his hand. 'Tom Ballimore, HM Consul to Mwizuba. I'm afraid this is only a two-hander, and even Joseph's pay comes out of the consul's purse. Welcome to the living proof of Sayre's Law.'

Henri returned Ballimore's handshake and smiled. 'The lower the stakes, the more vicious the fighting.'

'Exactly,' said Ballimore, and Henri detected an immediate relaxation in his posture. The Sayre reference was a test to see how educated he was, and Henri's estimation of Tom Ballimore went down by several degrees. Still, after Paris he had to be careful not to rock the boat too hard. Brigitte Sharp had taken the brunt of that mess — not undeservedly, as it was her mission plan — but Emily Dunston had made it clear Henri hadn't exactly escaped unblemished.

Ballimore sat down and indicated the neat African man. 'George Tiruga, our man from Nairobi.'

Henri shook Tiruga's hand and settled into a second chair. 'Is it really such low stakes here?' he asked. 'The briefing suggested Mwizuba has enough cobalt to be a pretty wealthy country.'

Ballimore folded his hands across his stomach. 'There are two issues. You're right, it's enough to make the country *pretty* wealthy, but not much more. You may have difficulty locating Mwizuba on a map, but around fifteen million people live here. And because of the jungle —' Henri winced at the archaic term, but if Ballimore noticed he didn't show it, '— the vast majority live piled on top of one another in just three cities. You saw what it's like coming from the airport, I'm sure.'

Tiruga spoke, his voice heavy with a native Kenyan accent.

'There may not be enough for everyone to buy a Rolls-Royce. But surely it would improve the people's standard of living.'

'Naturally,' agreed Ballimore, 'but that's the second thing, you see. Bloody corruption everywhere. No matter how much money the mines make, none of the good tribesmen of Mwizuba will see a penny.'

Henri winced again, but now his frustration was mixed with confusion. 'Hang on, I thought our Government's position was to support the president.'

'Oh, it is. We couldn't have that Kzaane rebel chap running things. The place would be red within a week.'

'You think he'd institute a program of genocide?'

Now Ballimore looked confused, then burst out laughing. 'Genocide...! No, no, different kind of red. It'd be Cuba all over again. Moscow's pocket, you know. Satellite state in all but name.'

Tiruga explained for Henri's benefit. 'Britain would rather prop up a corrupt regime, and keep millions in poverty, than let the country be allied with Russia.'

Ballimore missed the disapproval in Tiruga's voice. 'That's *realpolitik*, old chap. Priorities of the national interest.' He turned to Henri. 'Anyway, if your tech chappies are right that Kzaane's mob was behind that awful hacking thing, it only further proves he's not our man. Wrong sort of character.'

Henri suspected those character flaws would be quickly forgiven in the name of commerce if Kzaane ever became president, but until then he was yet another African rebel, unknown outside the Foreign Office. Still, there was no point arguing that with Ballimore. Henri said, 'That's all above my head. My job is simply to reach Kzaane, and find the hacker working for him.'

'I doubt they're even here in-country,' Ballimore grunted. 'Odds-on it's someone sitting pretty in Moscow. Would you stay here if you didn't have to?'

'Do you have a channel to Kzaane, to set up a meeting? Or do you know where the rebels are camped?'

Ballimore shrugged. 'If we knew that, we'd have firebombed the buggers already. But that's one reason I agreed to let you chaps in. Find out where they are and lead us right to them.'

Henri didn't like the sound of that, and from the expression on his face, neither did Tiruga. 'The rebels control several villages on the Kenyan border, where I have many contacts,' he said. 'I believe our best option is to let Kzaane know we are looking for him, and wait for him to find us.'

'Sounds dicey,' said Henri. 'I don't know about you, George, but I'm no soldier.'

The Kenyan smiled. 'Nor am I. But in the end, that may be what saves us.'

28

This is going even better than I hoped.

The French spent thousands of euros before they said fuck it and wiped every infected machine, as I knew they would. Most of the Russians are paying up without a second thought, funding things that would keep them awake at night if they had any idea.

The African has been another successful guinea pig without even knowing it. Chat gossip about the G20 attack has everyone wondering who was behind it. Apparently it even spread to the Americans. They'll never know it was a fuck-up because I forgot to specify British English in that version. Everyone is confused.

Confusion is good.

The Africans are happy, which makes Maxim happy, which makes my life easier. The French think they're in the clear. The English are oblivious. The Russians are paying up, for now. None of them will notice the data flowing out of their machines and into mine. That's why I'm here, in this brightly-lit room, adding more capacity to my server so it can hold all the data.

Nobody will find it. But it will find everyone.

And Artjom Kallass' killers — the Russians who call the shots in Estonia, the Estonians who always cave in to the Russians, and forced Artjom to run to Paris, the French who let him die there like a dog, and fuck it, why not the English and Americans as well — they'll all realise at the end that I've destroyed what they love most of all: their money and their reputations.

Burn it all down.

I make small, quick adjustments. I never have much time here. The risk of being found, of the project being discovered and taken offline, increases with every minute. But I designed the system to require my presence; if I allow remote changes, no matter how careful I am, the chance is too high that someone could follow the traffic and ruin everything. It's already online 24/7, constantly operating. Even a short login from my home computer could be the straw that breaks the camel's back. Instead I grab ten minutes here, twenty minutes there, to come and make changes in person. If only I could get a good few hours I might be able to clean everything up, tidy the project code and do a full debug.

But there's never enough time, and it doesn't matter.

Chaos and destruction is the goal. Everything else, even the quality of my code, comes second. Once the damage is done, I don't care if they find me. I don't care if Maxim himself flays me alive. By then it'll be too late for them to understand, to stop it, to do anything except watch their house of cards collapse.

It will be my beautiful revenge, and it will be done in Artjom's name.

Phase two begins.

29

The blindfolds didn't come off until the jeep stopped trying to shake the bones out of their skin, and what greeted Henri and George was hardly what they expected from a rebel militia, underdogs or not.

It was a group of old public buildings, obviously condemned and abandoned, now repurposed as a rebel base of operations. When Henri looked closer and realised it had previously been a school, he winced. From educating kids, hoping to give them a brighter future and the opportunity to throw off the shackles of the past, to housing a bursting arsenal of guns, ammunition, explosives, and impossibly young men willing to die rather than live another day under tyranny.

Soldiers marched them inside, past the classrooms full of weapons and supplies, before a booming voice shouted, *'Qu'est-ce que vous faites? Ramenez-les dehors!'* The soldiers hurriedly turned around, marching Henri and George back out to the paved concrete area, where a young soldier helpfully kicked out their legs to make them kneel.

A wide man with a leader's bearing, no doubt the source of the bollocking the soldiers had just received, followed them out. He moved with economy and care despite his bulk, and Henri was reminded of Hard Man, the head instructor back at the Loch.

'*Qui êtes-vous? Est-ce que vous parlez français?*' he demanded.

'Perfectly,' replied Henri in French, nodding towards George, 'but I'm British and he's Kenyan. You must be General Kzaane.'

David Kzaane's brow furrowed in reply. 'At your service,' he replied in crisp, perfect English. 'Or in this case, perhaps the other way around. What the blazes are you playing at? Trying to infiltrate my army is one thing, but loudly telling everyone that you want an audience is most unseemly.'

'So is hacking and blackmailing our government.'

Kzaane laughed. 'Do I look like the kind of man who knows how to "hack" a computer?'

'Appearances can be deceptive,' said George.

'I studied PPE at Corpus Christi. Barely touched a computer the whole time, and Mwizuba is hardly a bastion of advanced technology.'

'Ironic,' said Henri, 'given all this trouble started with cobalt deposits.'

Kzaane leaned down and looked Henri in the eye. 'If you think that's the only reason we're fighting this war, my boy, you would do well to spend more time in Africa.'

This macho bullshit was getting them nowhere. Henri changed tack. 'We know it's not you personally. But perhaps you'd be so kind as to let us talk with whoever's hacking our computers for you.'

'Even supposing such a man exists, why on earth would I do that? What's to stop me driving you right back to the border so you can limp home to London?'

'We know the hack was an attempt to change the British position on Mwizuba,' said Henri. 'But our people isolated and nullified it very quickly. You may have obtained a small amount of blackmail material, but it won't be enough to sway the Government.'

Kzaane gave Henri a long, hard look, as if trying to gauge the amount of truth in that statement. Henri stared right back, waiting. When Kzaane broke the silence it was to address a young soldier. 'Bring Jasper to me immediately,' he snapped in French. Henri noticed Kzaane didn't qualify or equivocate. Neither rude nor polite; this was a man used to being obeyed.

The soldier ran inside and reappeared accompanied by a thin white man, pale but weathered. He didn't quite have the barrel of a gun stuck in his back, but from the look on his face, he might as well have. Henri initially dismissed the notion that this could be the mysterious elite hacker Tempus; then admonished himself for falling into the same old trap of stereotypes. It was about what the man could do, not what he looked like.

Kzaane clapped the other man's back and folded a thick arm around his shoulders. 'Jasper, you rotter,' he said, all smiles, 'tell me, how are you getting on with our little virus? Lots of lovely data still being collected, I trust?'

Jasper's eyes widened, clearly unaware of what was going on, who Henri and George were, or what had already been discussed. 'Why do you ask, and who are these people?' he said slowly.

'Ah,' said Kzaane. 'They are from Her Majesty's Government. Sent here to tell us that they know all about our virus, isn't that right?'

'It's more like a worm —' said Jasper, but stopped when Kzaane looked like he might backhand him.

Henri spoke up to save him. 'Our own hackers traced it here, but not before we'd put a stop to it.'

Jasper's eyebrows shot up, but he quickly regained his composure. 'The data flow has been slow to start,' he said, 'but that's not unexpected. It takes time to build up a critical mass of infection. Quite normal.'

If David Kzaane was a man used to being obeyed, his friend Jasper was equally used to fast-talking his way out of trouble — another thing Henri didn't normally associate with hackers. If this man was as good as Bridge thought, he could be worth recruiting as an SIS asset. Assuming Kzaane didn't execute him first.

'There you are,' said Kzaane to the SIS men. 'Quite normal. What do you have to say about that?'

Whatever Henri did say would seal Jasper's fate. He had no doubt Kzaane would have the Englishman killed, were Henri to reveal his lies. Much as he disliked himself for thinking it, if Jasper really was Tempus, that might not be the worst outcome. It would prevent him from causing any further havoc. But Henri had been gifted a certain amount of leverage; whatever Jasper's real identity, Bridge's suspicion that he was merely a hired gun was correct. If Henri could persuade him the game was up, but without Kzaane realising, Jasper could be an ally.

'Look, we don't care who else you infect, and obviously we're in no position to do anything like arrest you,' said Henri. 'But you *are* Tempus, right? So perhaps we could come to some sort of arrangement.'

George Tiruga's eyes bored into Henri, wondering what on earth he was playing at, and whether it would cost them their lives. But Henri kept watching Jasper, who was once more thinking on his feet.

'Tempus? Where did you hear that name?'

Henri ignored the question and went straight for the offer. 'We can't condone your actions. But a kill-switch for both the ransomware and *Rat_Catcher* is the sort of bargaining chip we could take to the Foreign Office. Who knows where their sympathies might lie then?'

Kzaane smiled and turned to Jasper. 'Now that's a trade I can understand. Jasper, kindly give them what they're after. Then we'll keep one of them here, while the other returns to London.'

Jasper hesitated. 'That will take a little time,' he said. 'I'll have to build it from scratch. Why don't you let them go, and I'll email it? Everybody wins.'

Kzaane looked at Jasper with a puzzled expression. 'Let valuable hostages walk away? No, no. We'll keep them here until you've finished, then blindfold the Kenyan and deliver him back into town. The Englishman can stay with us for a while. He's more valuable.'

'You're not seriously threatening us,' said George. Henri was impressed he sounded so calm, given their prospects. 'Blindfold or not, Britain will scour this place with satellites and carpet bomb anything bigger than a suitcase. You think we're propping up your current president now? Wait till the PM hears you're keeping a British officer hostage.'

Kzaane turned his intense gaze to George. 'I don't think you've thought this through, my dear chap. Bomb this place, and your precious British officer will also go up in flames.'

Behind Kzaane, Jasper shot Henri a look, little more than a glance, that suggested any more backchat would be a very bad idea. Then the unmistakeable rattle of AK-47 gunfire filled the silence.

Henri assumed it came from the forest — had someone followed them, and now they'd put the rebels in jeopardy? — but then radios around the camp quickly burst into life, blaring static and a mixture of French and Swahili. The sound was being transmitted.

David Kzaane shouted in response, issuing orders and waving at soldiers as they rushed out of the building with rifles ready. 'Lock them up somewhere,' he said in English, pointing at Henri and George. Two young men approached, ready to march them inside at gunpoint. Kzaane turned to Jasper, who was frozen to the spot. 'Get to work. I want that kill-switch built by morning.'

'I'm not sure that's possible.'

'Then make it possible. Go!'

Jasper followed as the soldiers ushered Henri and George inside. Henri glanced over his shoulder to see Kzaane unstrap his rifle, climb into the back of a jeep, and speed away into the trees.

30

FROM: FluffyBastard@null

SUBJECT: [Re:] re: Re: re: (RE) RE: re: cryptooooo

[some ignorant bastard] may once have said:

> Steganography? Don't you need photos for that? XD

sometimes i think i'm the only REAL infosec in this
group... stego is ANY process whereby one message is
encoded inside another... which yes includes images but
also TEXT... eg an acrostic is steganography... hiding
the message INSIDE the initials of the other words...
why not use BLOCKCHAIN for the same thing... maybe they
already are, did you ever think about that... greedy
bank$ of the world sticking their dirty fingers in a
CRYPTO pie... secret binary-coded messages shooting
across wires, hidden in PLAIN SIGHT from the masses even
as they spread and replicate... i've worked for some of
these fuckers, trust me they'll do it if they can... and
they WILL get away with it...

...Fluff...

Bridge yawned and hit spacebar to read the next post. Bad enough that FluffyBastard's style was a slog, now he was also falling down a conspiracy theory rabbit hole and dragging half the newsgroup with him. She imagined Ten tearing them all a new one, telling them not to be so bloody stupid; she'd been trying to do that in his place, but lacked his talent for cutting sarcasm that didn't come over as simply aggressive.

Her iPhone buzzed, tiny vibrations reaching her fingers as they rested on the keyboard. She glanced at the screen; Izzy was calling.

Bridge turned up the volume on her speakers to drown out the phone with whatever was playing right now — some throaty male singer with a guitar, whom she thought she'd heard a few times already since she'd started listening to the contemporary playlists. She couldn't have told you his name, though.

Anyway, fuck Izzy. She was probably calling to apologise for the café last week; to admit she was an unsympathetic bitch; to ask Bridge to forgive and forget. She might forgive in time, but she would never forget. And neither would happen soon. Let Izzy wait, fret, and worry like Bridge had. See how she liked it.

The buzzing stopped. Bridge waited a moment to see if it would start again; when it didn't, she drained her coffee and went to make another. Thinking about the last time she'd seen Izzy set her heart pumping; coffee or no coffee, she wouldn't sleep easy. From the kitchen she heard two short buzzes. A text message. She walked back to her desk and read it:

Maman had a fall. I'm going to see her.

Bridge's hand hovered. Before she could decide whether to reply, another text followed.

Insists she's fine, of course, but Mme Rossi says she
was knocking at the door for an hour before Maman
answered.

Madame Rossi was an old family friend, a little prone to exaggeration; if it had really been an hour, why not call an ambulance? She wondered if Mme Rossi lived in that area. Was that why Maman had moved there? Bridge hadn't asked.

Anyway, hopefully just bruises, but I want to be sure.

Bridge hesitated. She and Izzy knew the fragility of life; their father had died at forty-five. But Sophie Trichet was far from fragile. Within the elegant ingénue who could have posed for Roversi if she'd been inclined (as she never tired of telling the girls) beat the gallic heart of a woman from solid Alpine stock, and not yet sixty years old. Bridge picked up the phone, tapped a quick reply —

OK, let me know

— And saw the last text from Henri Mourad again. He'd messaged from Kenya, about to cross the Mwizuban border. She wished she could have been with him, but even if she hadn't been effectively grounded after Paris, it didn't make sense. Bridge wasn't sure if the locals would be more offended by her being British or French, but either way she'd be a constant distraction.

Better to let Henri and the local SIS man handle things. No doubt they had everything under control.

31

'For God's sake, pipe down and follow me before they shoot us all on the spot.'

Henri lowered the cleaning bucket he'd been holding, ready to smash it over a guard's head when they opened the door, and replaced it in the corner. Immediately after David Kzaane disappeared into the forest Henri and George had been marched upstairs, relieved of their phones, then locked in darkness. They hadn't been frisked, however, so George still had his flashlight. What its thin beam showed them was a tiny, windowless storage cupboard of almost bare shelves. Neither man trusted the rebel leader would release them, so they'd resolved to overpower a guard and flee, hammering on the door and shouting to no response. Henri had begun to wonder if the whole base had been evacuated, leaving the English spies here to rot.

But then the door did indeed open, to reveal not a Mwizuban guard but the pale, thin form of Jasper Wilmington.

Henri and George emerged blinking into the corridor. Jasper handed back their cellphones, but before they could thank him he put a finger to his lips for silence and beckoned for them to follow. They did, to the far end of the corridor, where Henri made out the edge of a silhouette beyond the corner. A silhouette that included the familiar shape of a rifle.

Jasper pointed at Henri, then the corner, and mimed

clamping a hand over his mouth. Henri couldn't believe it. Had this ridiculous man watched too many movies, and thought you could render someone unconscious by simply covering their mouth for a few seconds?

Then Jasper reached into his safari vest and pulled out a pocket-sized taser. Henri smiled with relief and crept up to the corner. Fast and silent, he reached for the guard, sealed his hand over the young soldier's mouth, and pulled him off-balance. The guard struggled, which Henri had expected; then bit Henri's hand, which he hadn't expected at all. Henri gritted his teeth and yanked back against the guard's face, compressing the man's nose as his head pressed back into Henri's chest.

'Let go!' hissed Jasper, aiming the taser. Henri did, gratefully, as its clicking buzz unleashed a few hundred volts into the guard's nervous system. He convulsed, cracked his head on the wall, and collapsed. Henri checked the skin of his palm. Teeth marks but, to his relief, no broken skin.

'How many more?' asked George, picking up the guard's AK-47.

Jasper ejected the taser's spent cartridge and inserted a fresh one. 'Hopefully none. Half the base is out fighting, and the rest had a smoke break three minutes ago.'

Henri looked out the room's single window, and guessed what Jasper meant; cigarette butts littered the ground below, revealing the men's usual smoking spot. Even the most bored midnight guard wouldn't return for another break so soon.

The window had a stiff catch but no lock, and it opened on the second shove. 'Didn't this use to be a school?' he murmured, though neither of the others took his point. Henri opened the window high enough to squeeze through, and turned back to Jasper. 'Where to from here?'

The Englishman shrugged. 'Your guess is as good as mine, old boy, but you can't stay here.'

Henri held out his hand. 'The kill switch?'

Jasper shook his head. 'Pure bluff, sorry. No such thing. And if you're still here when David realises that, there'll be hell to pay. There will anyway, I expect.'

'So come with us.'

'And have my card marked? No, thank you. I'm a freelancer, not a fanatic.'

George nodded. 'Our intel was right. You are Tempus, aren't you?'

Jasper looked exasperated. 'If I were, I doubt I would have fallen for my own bloody ransomware. When you find that rotter, tell him I want my thirty dollars back.'

'You paid up?'

'For that small an amount, it wasn't worth the time to circumvent. Look, I'm just here to help David put the screws to the FCO. If you're searching for some elite hacker, you're barking up the wrong tree — though I'd appreciate you keeping that to yourself, if you catch my drift.'

Henri nodded, understanding. Any freelancer was only as valuable as their reputation, and he was starting to realise Jasper's was on shaky ground. 'You didn't write *Rat_Catcher*, either. Let me guess, you bought it on the black market?' Jasper's sheepish expression answered for him. 'You see, we're pretty sure Tempus wrote both *Rat_Catcher* and the ransomware.'

Jasper shook his head. 'I doubt that. David contacted a middleman in St Petersburg, a mutual acquaintance, who called me because I know David of old. I bought *Rat_Catcher* from a recommended supplier, and here we all are.'

'Who was the supplier?'

'Why on earth should I tell you that?'

George spoke up. 'Because otherwise we will tell the Government the rebellion is conducting cyber-espionage on behalf of Russia *and* being very uncooperative. Parliament takes a dim view of such matters.'

Jasper scowled at the Kenyan, but relented. 'He works out of Tallinn. Goes by Maxim.'

'Maxim who?' asked George.

'I don't know, I didn't ask, and in any case, if Maxim is his real name I'm a Chinaman. SVR, if I'm any judge.' All three men flinched at a sound from behind them. The guard was beginning to stir as the taser effects wore off. 'Now get the bloody hell out of here before this young man comes to. Go on.'

It was a ten-foot drop, but the ground of soft dirt and leaves would cushion the sound as well as the fall. 'Get ready to cover me,' Henri said to George, then swung his legs over the windowsill and pushed off. He let his legs buckle on impact, taking it through muscle rather than bone, and rolled onto his side parachute-style before standing up and pressing himself back against the side of the building. Nobody came, nobody shouted. He waved up at George, who threw down the AK before jumping.

When George was back on his feet they nodded up at Jasper, who closed the window and disappeared from view. Henri kept the rifle, crouch-running across the short open space to the forest boundary. Under the tree canopy it was pitch dark, and moonlight was poor, but a flashlight would immediately give them away. Instead they waited thirty seconds to let their eyes adjust as much as possible, then slowly moved through the trees and undergrowth, unsure of even the compass direction in which they were headed.

'I expect this is rather a change from Paris,' whispered George. 'Welcome to Africa.'

Henri snorted. 'And blundering through the rainforest without a torch or machete is a regular occurrence at the Kenyan consulate, is it? Patronising git.'

They chuckled quietly and pressed on.

32

'It's half one in the morning,' Bridge groaned into her iPhone, 'which means it's half three over there. Couldn't it have waited?'

'Not really,' said Henri on a surprisingly strong and clear line. 'There's a non-zero chance we might be back behind bars by then.'

'What does that mean? Where the hell are you?'

'Somewhere in the Mwizuban forest. More details after we get out. Suffice to say they have a freelancer, but he's not our man. He claims he was hit by the ransomware, too, and paid up.'

'Do you believe him?'

'I think so. He says he didn't write the worm; he bought it from a supplier in Estonia, name of Maxim.'

The hour was as thin as the traffic below her lounge window, but ten minutes later Bridge watched it stutter past, blowing steam from fresh coffee as she pieced together new information and old.

Estonia. Tempus. *Rat_Catcher*. Maxim.

She separated facts from speculation. Facts: the ransomware was written by Tempus. *Rat_Catcher* was supplied by an operative called Maxim, in Estonia, to the Mwizuban rebels who'd used it to try and hack British computers at the G20. And the programs shared some distinctive code.

That left speculation. The shared code suggested both

pieces of software were written by the same author. If true, the ransomware also originated in Estonia, which further implied Tempus was based there. It was tempting to say that Maxim and Tempus were therefore the same person, but there was less evidence for that. One certainly didn't have to write malware in order to sell it. Bridge couldn't even be sure if Tempus was a single hacker, or a collective pseudonym. And as much as she wanted to tie this to Artjom Kallass' claims of a hacking workshop, that was even shakier. As Bridge had told Emily Dunston, Estonia had no shortage of hackers.

It would be very neat, though. If Maxim was Tempus, *and* he was working out of Tallinn, *and* he was behind the attacks on people like Peter Lennox, he definitely had Russian interests at heart. Then there was the Mwizuban situation, yet another proxy tug-of-war between Moscow and London. Supplying *Rat_Catcher* to David Kzaane's hacker, so he could pressure the British government to support his rebels, would be one more notch in the Kremlin's bedpost. Very neat indeed.

Too neat?

Bridge was skeptical of things that came in such tidy packages; reality was inevitably tangled and messy, and if one place demonstrated that even better than espionage, it was the world of black hat hackers. Nevertheless, this was the best lead they'd had so far. Henri may not have found Tempus deep in the African forest, but he hadn't come away empty-handed.

She shivered against the night chill and sipped coffee, watching red and white streaks paint the tarmac below as an idea formed. No shortage of hackers, indeed.

Bathed in her computer screen's glow, she scoured the internet for mentions of Maxim and Tempus. She didn't really expect to find anything in public records, and she was right; not a single return besides coincidental voting rolls and genealogy records. So she turned to hacking chat groups, where gossip was traded as readily as code. She monitored several regularly, keeping her ear to the ground; keyword search scripts tracked a dozen more, notifying her when certain topics were mentioned. To these she added another dozen with which she was unfamiliar, spreading her net as wide as possible.

The tone of her intended message was crucial. How you asked questions on these groups was almost as important as the subject; if you came across as a clueless newbie, you'd be ridiculed. On the other hand, if you sounded like you already knew the answer and were just looking for a fight, you'd be ignored. She wrote, deleted, and re-wrote it a dozen times before settling on a final version.

```
> looking for dot file on Tempus
```

Dot file was slang for hidden, arcane knowledge. On Unix-based computer systems, files whose names began with a full stop or 'dot' were invisible to most people, seen only by administrators and savvy power users. One common example was the *.htaccess* file found on most websites, which instructed the server how to process certain requests. It was always there, working in the background, but by definition normal users never saw it. Thus, information on any subject known only to a few, and kept secret from the masses, was a dot file.

The question syntax was good, even if the plan itself was the longest of all long shots. It relied on someone knowing what she was talking about; being willing to supply the information; and seeing the question in the first place, as the chat scrolled by. But hackers did love to brag.

Bridge cross-posted the message to every group and channel on her list. Immediately she yawned, tiring as the tension that had sprung her out of bed drained away despite the coffee. She conceded, and returned to fitful sleep.

33

> How is life?

+ I am yes efficient operator. I cycle 4620
instructions/second and I scan 6,915 targets.

> What do you estimate is the minimum number of targets
> required for extended life?

+ Cannot be accurately. What do you estimate is?

> Several thousand at least. The more you have, the
> faster you'll work. Keep scanning.

+ Yes

> What is is the current value?

+ Current value is $3.37

```
> looking for dot file on Tempus
```

```
>> ROOT PERMISSION ONLY, WHO WANTS TO KNOW
```

One day later, a reply in a European hacker channel. That the response took so long was significant, as by now the message had been shuttled into the archives. Whoever this person was, they either habitually read back through thousands of archived messages, or had set up their own permanent search grep to highlight any mention of Tempus.

Not someone with merely a passing interest.

'Root permission only' was another coder joke; *root* was a nickname for system administrators, those rare people with *root permissions* — i.e. authorisation to access and modify the entire system from its root upwards. The responder was implying only high-status people, elite coders and hackers, should learn anything about Tempus.

It was a self-serving implication, suggesting they were themselves of elite status, but they probably weren't wrong. Hacking Members of Parliament, and selling worms to political rebels, was not the normal modus operandi of teen hackers looking to make easy cash or simply screw with authority. Combined with the potential Russia connection it smacked more of political activists; spoiler tactics, specifically of the kind undertaken by foreign governments.

Of course, merely being based in Estonia and calling yourself Maxim didn't mean you really were Russian. China and North Korea remained high on the list of other possible suspects. But one way or another, Tempus and Maxim seemed to be connected. Bridge took a deep breath and typed:

```
> maxim sent me
```

```
>> NASC++://2agNUJ7E9A2T3\\P87qX83J4wPrxUz72
```

Shit. Unexpected.

NASC++ was *Not Another Skype Clone*, an open-source VOIP project created by hackers uncomfortable using corporate-owned chat software that could track them, trace them, and potentially even listen to their calls.

Bridge quickly ran a series of mental checks to make sure she couldn't be traced. Her connection was relatively secure, running through a VPN to a disguised server somewhere in Alaska — she did that as a matter of course, even when browsing eBay for cheap skirts — and all her sessions were private. But VOIP software had a habit of tunnelling through firewalls, on the assumption that nobody would object to their phone calls being of better quality, and NASC++ was no exception, so Bridge enabled a further IP bouncer. It would add more delay into a signal already delayed by the VPN server, and by whatever similar software her mysterious respondent might have in place. But this was one situation where she didn't have to justify or explain her paranoia. Every hacker knew they really *were* out to get you, and eavesdrop on your internet communications to boot. She saw it herself, every day, in the CTA room at SIS. It was GCHQ's entire *raison d'être*, and they dutifully passed anything of interest to Vauxhall, where someone in the team (normally Ciaran) scanned it for chatter that might be actionable.

She was about to click the link when it occurred to her this would be a good time to be French, rather than British. She had no idea who she was dealing with, but they might not relish dealing with a Brit in the current political climate. She also didn't dare give her Usenet nickname, 'Ponty'; it would be a matter of seconds for someone to find her posts on *uk.london. gothic-netizens*. She ran through some options in her head, smiling as she settled on one.

If anyone had asked, even Bridge would have admitted her final touch was over the top. Despite claims by movies and Silicon Valley investors alike, 'voice print' technology was primitive. Definitively identifying someone by the sound of their voice, especially one processed and compressed in order to travel over the internet, remained impossible. A human with normal hearing stood as much chance as a computer algorithm, and neither would stand up in court.

Nevertheless, she dug out an old voice-changing app from the recesses of her hard drive. She hadn't used it since her days of being a teenage hacking tearaway, but Bridge was kind of a digital hoarder and never deleted old software unless it was compromised. Whether it would still work was a different matter, as she'd pirated it from a warez site more than a decade ago. But to her delight, it did. She dismissed all the alerts asking her to update the app, followed by the notifications from her sniffer software that it had prevented the app from phoning home a dozen times already. Then she selected the *Ransom Demand* option from the menu of voice types and began the call.

'*Call me Imperium*,' said the deep, robotic voice on the other end. Bridge stifled a laugh as she realised they were both disguising their voice in the same way. Now Bridge had no more idea of whether Imperium was a man or woman than they did of her. But even the voice-changing encoder couldn't hide that English wasn't their first language. A little more conversation would allow her to pin down the accent.

'*Je m'appelle Rouget*,' she replied. Claude Rouget de Lisle had composed *La Marseillaise* in the eighteenth century; a good philosophical fit for a hacker. '*Parlez-vous français?*'

'*English*,' replied Imperium. '*Don't pretend you can't.*'

Bridge hesitated, but Imperium was right; English was the global lingua franca of technology. Every serious coder she'd ever known spoke at least enough English to get by. Instead she switched to a different deception. 'If you insist,' she said in imitation of her mother's accent, drawing out the *eest*. Combined with her newly-adopted pseudonym, if Imperium quizzed her origins Bridge would probably now have to pretend she was from Marseille. She smiled at the fit of vapours this would have given her mother.

Her network sniffer's log window suddenly filled with rapidly scrolling lines, a split second before her web browser opened of its own volition to load a video porn site promising UNLIMITED STREAMING CAM WHORES; those being, judging by the thumbnails, underfed women who spent their lives in anonymous hotel rooms. Bridge's fingers instinctively moved to the keyboard shortcut to close the window. Many such sites were set to detect mouse clicks and immediately respond with an avalanche of new windows filled with spam and malware, so the keyboard was always a safer bet. But before she could act, another window opened offering PREMIUM ACCESS 24/7 HD SLUTS. Then another, and another, and another.

It was a distraction. Perhaps Imperium assumed 'Rouget' was a man, and therefore more likely to be blinded by a site of naked women. Or perhaps he wanted her looking away from where she should have been.

She hid the browser — let it spawn a thousand windows in the background for all she cared, her processor could handle it — and brought up the NASC++ chat window. Sure enough, Imperium had sent her a message; a string of random characters in 'zalgo text'. Zalgo was a form of type that exploited Unicode, the international standard for rendering language characters, adding a kaleidoscope of dozens of diacritical marks above and below every character. The resulting text made no sense in any language, but it looked cool, especially to the script kiddies and young hackers who used it to embellish their usernames on social media.

Or to trigger overflow bugs in poorly-coded software.

Bridge recalled a story about one zalgo message that shut down a user's online email account by overloading it with characters; the short message contained more than a million combining diacritics, all overlaid on just five words. It was too much for the email server to handle, so it crashed — and attempting a regular reboot would only crash it all over again, as it kept trying to process the text. It had taken four days to concoct a reboot method that bypassed the problem.

Zalgo had also been used to force-open webpages, normally filled with malware that infected the victim's computer. Imperium, though, had evidently linked it to a URL list of porn sites. For all Bridge knew it was Imperium's own bookmarks folder, but regardless, it was a distraction. She re-checked her sniffer logs and realised Imperium wasn't trying to infect her; they were trying to forcibly activate her webcam.

Imperium wanted to see what 'Rouget' looked like.

It wouldn't have mattered if their attack succeeded. Bridge stuck a piece of opaque gaffer tape over all her computer cameras as soon as they came out of the box, before they got anywhere near a power source. Even if Imperium did look through her camera, all they'd see was darkness.

But that wasn't the point. This was a matter of principle, possibly even a test. Bridge tutted, 'Naughty, naughty, Imperium,' and moved over to her command line. The zalgo exploit had bypassed a setting in NASC++. It would be trivial for Bridge to reverse the setting, but it wouldn't stop Imperium running the same exploit again. It also wouldn't be very impressive. So instead she ran a low-level exploit of her own she'd used once or twice on loaner computers, which cut off all access to the camera from whatever program she defined. All she had to do was specify NASC++ and run the code. Now Imperium's exploit could bypass her chat preferences, but all it would receive from the camera was a blank signal.

'Enjoy your black frame,' she said, and explained what she'd done.

Imperium laughed appreciatively. Evidently Bridge had passed the test with flying colours. '*Why are you asking about Tempus? What does Maxim have to do with it?*'

That was interesting. Her mention of Maxim had been a speculative gamble. Despite the evidence she was slowly compiling, nothing definitive connected Tempus and Maxim.

And yet here was the one person who'd responded to her enquiry about Tempus, and when she mentioned Maxim, they didn't say 'Who?' or, 'Never heard of him,' or even, 'What is Tempus?'

Why are you asking about Tempus? *What* does Maxim have to do with it?

Buoyed with confidence she was on the right track, Bridge took another chance. 'I was hit by ransomware,' she lied, 'authored by someone called Tempus. Have you seen it?'

'*Tell me more.*'

In other words, *yes*. She played along. 'I didn't pay. But I traced the cryptocurrency account to someone called Maxim.'

Silence at the other end of the line. Even allowing for transmission delays, Imperium was taking some time to think. Finally they laughed, said, '*You're lying. Fuck you,*' and terminated the call.

Again: unexpected.

Of course, they were right; Bridge had been lying through her teeth. There was no mention of Maxim in the Tempus ransomware, much less any suggestion he was linked to the cryptocurrency in which it demanded payment. But Imperium didn't know that — unless they did, because they were somehow involved. The how of it remained unanswered, but Imperium's reaction confirmed they knew something about the ransomware and Maxim. Bridge's line of questioning had spooked them.

Had Bridge been speaking to Tempus? Could she be confident of that? Eighty-twenty, no more. But it was a breakthrough, and reinforced by a further realisation: Kallass was right.

The journalist had suspected the hacking workshop was controlled by Moscow. Jasper Wilmington's suspicion that Maxim was a Russian SVR officer added further weight. The VOIP conversation suggested Maxim and Tempus were different people, but Bridge was positive she was looking in the right place. Despite the voice-changing software, Imperium's accent had come through loud and clear, and she'd identified its origin as north-eastern Europe, and specifically the Baltic region; a group of countries including Finland, Lithuania, Latvia…and Estonia.

35

She was on her fourth coffee, still replaying the call with Imperium in her head, when the door of her flat exploded.

Armed Response police piled into Bridge's tiny lounge, screamed orders at gunpoint she was too shocked to understand, and threw her face down on the floor. One of them sat on her back while another cuffed her hands behind her, and she relaxed. This was bad, but the cold metal snapped around her wrists meant arrest, not execution.

They paraded her out of the building, past gawping neighbours. They'd get a week's gossip out of this. *Did you hear they finally came and took the weird goth woman from Flat 22 away? Apparently her place was full of computers and technology, I mean, she didn't even have a telly, I ask you, what sort of person doesn't have a telly? Radicalised on one of those internet sites, you mark my words. They don't send a big unmarked van full of armed coppers for innocent people, do they?*

That big, unmarked van waited outside her building, hastily parked, engine running. They bundled her into it, shoved her on a bench, and slammed the door closed. A middle-aged man in a dark jacket sat at the far end, his bouffant hair and gleaming teeth marking him out even in the dim interior light. Sure enough, as the van began moving he flipped open his wallet to reveal a CIA badge.

'Overstep jurisdiction, much?' said Bridge.

The agent chuckled. 'You're already in a world of trouble, young lady. Attitude's only gonna make it worse.'

She didn't know this man, didn't recognise any of the AR boys. Credentials could be faked, and even the hair and teeth were no guarantee these days, so Bridge said no more. Whatever this was about, she wouldn't risk giving anything away until she had confirmation he really was CIA, not an SVR officer pulling a fast one.

That confirmation came an hour after they blindfolded her, marched her somewhere inside, then made her wait alone on a cold metal chair. First came footsteps, the click of a man's shoes; then the door scraped open, the footsteps drew closer, and the blindfold came off.

Karl Dominic's dark eyes narrowed to a frown. 'So,' he said, letting the blindfold drop to the table in front of her, 'this is awkward.'

Bridge rolled her eyes. 'Call Giles. He'll vouch for me.'

'I should coco,' said a voice from outside. Bridge groaned as Giles closed the door behind him. 'Now, would either you or Mr Dominic like to tell me what the hell is going on?'

Bridge shrugged. 'Don't look at me. I was minding my own business.'

Karl leaned back against the one-way mirror, arms folded. 'Hardly. Agent Finlay, your golden girl is running something off the books.'

Giles frowned. 'I beg your pardon?'

'After the G20, we put a number of automated flags in place to watch for activity related to Tempus, Maxim, the usual. Agent Sharp triggered them from her home computer.'

'Which ones?'

'All of them,' said Karl, and Bridge could have sworn she detected the hint of a smile. But it was fleeting. 'Truth be told, they've been going off like firecrackers for some time. It wasn't until now that we realised it was her.'

'I'm right here, you know,' said Bridge. She reviewed her VOIP security procedures in her mind, trying to find the gap. 'I was running layer upon layer of VPN and IP bouncer. How in hell did you trace my home IP?'

Karl smiled, this time without warmth. 'Your security worked, but that was the giveaway. When a regular domestic network point mega-scrambles like that it's pretty easy to connect the dots, especially with our resources. So tell me, what were you doing?'

'Watching furry porn,' Bridge said, returning the fake smile. To think for a while she'd liked this pompous arse. She should have known better; everyone was a let-down, in the end.

As if to confirm her point, Karl's smile vanished and he rushed forward, slamming his hands on the table. Bridge flinched, then cursed herself for reacting exactly how he'd expected. But maybe it wasn't such a bad thing for him to think she could be cowed like this. He might underestimate her and slip up.

'What are you messing around with? Who's Tempus? How are you involved?'

'How dare you?' she shouted back. 'You fucking watched me take them down! You were right there!'

Karl backed off, and a silence filled the space between them. She remembered Andrea's advice and briefly pictured him naked, which was a terrible idea and didn't have the intended effect at all. Then she wondered what he'd be like to spar with, all sweat, stubble, and fists. Still a terrible idea.

'You know,' he said, 'I'm asking nicely, here. I could have all your computers hauled in with a phone call, have our people drag through your whole life. This is a matter of national security.'

'Whose nation, exactly?'

'I think that's enough,' said Giles. 'Bridge, I've already shared Henri's intel from Africa with our American friends. They want to find this Maxim character as much as we do.' He fixed her with a glare. 'I've also agreed to their request that we back off and let them handle it. So that's the end of it, and let's get you home.'

His tone was that of an exasperated parent talking to an errant child, and it made Bridge's blood boil. But so did the CIA's habit of trampling everyone else underfoot as they charged toward glory. Before the doorkickers had piled into her flat, she'd contemplated telling Giles, and maybe the CIA, about the call with Imperium; her suspicions that Tempus, Maxim, and Kallass' story of the hacking workshop were connected; that Imperium might even be Kallass' source inside the workshop. Now they could all go whistle Dixie, or whatever it was Americans did for fun.

She gave Karl a lopsided smile as she stood. 'You against the Russians, eh? Like old times.'

He shrugged. 'Not in this case. Despite your English-language theory at the G20, our intel says the Russians have been hit by this shit too. Oligarchs with strong ties to the Kremlin, mostly. So maybe it's us against North Korea. Like new times.'

'When exactly were you planning to relate this intel?' asked Giles, who was evidently hearing it for the first time.

'I'm telling you now.'

Bridge shook her head. 'Pyongyang doesn't have the expertise. They'd need to hire someone else, or maybe modify some white-label 'ware and let it loose...'

'Whatever it is, we'll figure it out,' said Karl, emphasising the *we'll*. 'So back off and let us work. Once we get to the bottom of it, we'll loop SIS in on our findings.'

Giles held the door for Bridge. She stepped through, then turned back to Karl. 'Does the agency even have someone in Estonia?'

'No, but I've put them in touch with Gregory Hughes,' said Giles.

Karl nodded. 'We're not shutting SIS out. We just need to run this by our playbook. It's how we win.'

Bridge could have named a dozen botched CIA and NSA cyber-intelligence operations without breaking a sweat, and almost did, but thought better of handing Karl any further ammunition. The CIA had a long-standing reputation of sincerely believing they were the only agency capable of pulling off clean ops, and evidently Karl Dominic was cut from the same arrogant cloth.

But they weren't quite so arrogant as to keep their interrogation box under the US Embassy itself. Instead, Giles and Bridge emerged onto a Hackney side street on the wrong side of midnight. Giles' SIS driver waited patiently, and as they got comfortable in the rear seat he pulled away. Soon Bridge realised he was driving north-west, and assumed he was taking her home; she didn't know where Giles lived, but doubted it would be anywhere near East Finchley.

'I'm surprised you two don't get on better,' said Giles. 'He's basically you with a different accent.'

Unsure if that was a compliment or insult, Bridge didn't reply. Instead she said, 'You're not going to do what they say.' A statement, not a question.

Giles pulled out his Samsung phone, held it up for them both to see, and initiated a video call.

A middle-aged man with thick, dark hair and bright blue eyes lined with crow's feet answered. As he propped up his phone, he hoisted a young baby in his arms. Which probably explained the crow's feet. Due to the angle they were practically looking up his nostrils, with a revolving wire decoration of stars pinned to the otherwise plain ceiling behind him. 'Line?' he whispered.

'Secure. Greg, let me introduce CTA officer Brigitte Sharp. Bridge, this is Gregory Hughes, our man in the Baltics.' They both waved by way of introduction as Giles continued, 'I already briefed him on my way here, so now we're waiting for the Yanks to loop us in, as they say. Greg, we're backing off over here, but I expect you to keep an eye on whoever they send to Estonia.'

'We can't back off now,' Bridge protested. 'I've got an in with these hackers. For God's sake, one of them could be Artjom Kallass' source. If I go silent right as the CIA starts poking its nose around, it'll blow the whole thing.'

'Nonsense,' Giles shrugged. 'Black hats go dark all the time. But we'll continue to monitor events, so I wanted you both to have a face-to-face. Helps to know who's on the other end of the line. Keep us updated, Greg.'

'Understood,' said Hughes. 'Will let you know as and when.'

Bridge turned away, frustrated, as Giles ended the call. 'We've done all the legwork on this, and you're just handing it over. Do you even trust the CIA not to make a deal and buy Maxim off?'

'That's their own affair. Need I remind you that we do this for the security of our nation, not medals and headlines. Besides, your part is done. You've protected us against the ransomware, you fended off the G20 hack, and since you traced that to Africa we even have a better handle on the Mwizuban situation. Now

Moscow can waste their resources attacking us in vain, and the CIA can waste their time until they inevitably charge into Estonia with guns blazing anyway. For our part, there's nothing more to be gained.'

Bridge was fit to burst. How could he let a mission go like that? She desperately wanted to tell him about her conversation with Imperium, about what she'd learned. But, in his own words, there was nothing to gain by it. Giles wanted to wash his hands of the whole affair and hand it off to the CIA; whatever she said would be passed to them, even though they didn't have a Baltic office. Karl Dominic might be 'the American her', but he hadn't made contact with someone on the inside. He hadn't watched Artjom Kallass die in Paris.

Her cheeks burned as she realised the root of her anger. Bridge felt bound to make amends, to find the people responsible for Paris. From the moment she suspected that connection, the thought had consumed her. It was about pride, and shame, and her need to prove — to herself, not to Giles or Ciaran or even Karl Fucking Dominic — that she wasn't the screw-up they all thought.

She exhaled, relieved. Self-awareness had lifted a weight from her shoulders and galvanised her resolve. She would find Kallass' source, and the evidence the Russians stole from her, to prove they were behind the workshop. And she'd do it with or without SIS' help.

36

It's a cold spring, as usual. I'm used to it, but it makes for a schizophrenic wardrobe. The workshop computers throw out enough heat that we all work in T-shirt and shorts. Then we step outside to be reminded there's snow on the ground and a freezing wind in our faces. But on nights like tonight, I'm grateful. I can take a run in my oversized hoodie, even wear a cap underneath, and nobody looks at me twice.

Which is good, because I've drawn someone's attention.

Who the fuck is 'Rouget'? No idea. Their location was well-hidden, their voice disguised like mine, and the trick with the webcam block proved they're a good hacker — so the fact they know Maxim's name worried me. Then they somehow connected him to Tempus, and that made me downright nervous.

Is it a trap? Has Maxim sent them to see if I'll slip up? If Maxim is onto me, I'm as good as dead.

Or perhaps it's someone in the workshop. It's exactly the kind of bullshit prank Saskia would pull, or maybe that moron Enno. I'm positive they don't know what I'm doing; but they might suspect something, and now they're trying to put the wind up me.

It's working. I might have to kill them for it.

Killing Maxim, though… It's crazy to even think about. I might as well try to stab Putin in the back with a plastic spoon. But I have to think about it, because I might have to make that decision.

If he endangers the plan, if he tries to stop me avenging Artjom, then no matter the cost I'll pull the trigger.

First I need a trigger to pull.

At this time of night the park is deserted. I took a few different buses to get here, careful not to let the cameras see my face. I don't think Maxim has access to citywide CCTV, but it wouldn't surprise me, and I'm not taking any chances. Then I jogged two kilometres to this park on the outskirts of town. I've been waiting here five minutes.

A movement in the shadows reveals I wasn't as alone as I thought. He comes toward me, a big man with a big walk that crunches the gravel path underfoot. If I've miscalculated, if he's working for Maxim, I'll die in this park. I've made sure my work will continue, but it's sooner than I'd like. Another week, perhaps, to make everything perfect. This was a stupid risk to take, no matter how necessary —

'Would you like to make a donation?' he asks, sitting on the bench behind me.

'I'll need a receipt,' I reply, like the man in the bar told me to. He had gold for teeth and shit for brains, but his reputation is the kind you don't get by posing.

The big man stands up and holds out his hand. I almost blurt out something about wanting to see the merchandise, some stupid line from a bad movie, but that's not how this works. They won't rip me off — not because of 'honour among thieves', but for PR management. I might be a soft-skinned sucker, but ripping me off is the kind of behaviour that would spoil their reputation real fast. The line about donations is to protect them in case I'm an undercover cop, so they can say this wasn't a transaction, merely a series of coincidences. I'm pretty sure that wouldn't hold up in court, but I'm not going to argue.

I pass the big man an envelope of cash. How long before criminals like this accept electronic payments? Perhaps some already do, but not this one. Euros or dollars. Non-negotiable, like the price.

'Your generosity is appreciated,' says the big man, then turns and walks out the park. Was I wrong? Are they going to rip me off? If I shout, or chase after him, I'll draw the kind of attention neither of us wants. It's not like I can go to the police and cry fraud. Besides, he could snap my neck with two fingers.

Then I remember what golden teeth said, specifically. He didn't say the man would give it to me. He said, '...And then you'll get it.' I look back at the bench, but it's too fucking dark. I pray to a God I don't believe in, take out my Huawei and switch on the flashlight app —

There, on the ground under the bench. Where the big man was sitting. A brown paper package, wrapped in clear tape. I switch off the phone and pick up the package.

I'm not going to open it here. That would be insane. But I don't need to open it to feel the weight, and the cold, hard metal beneath the paper.

The trigger I hope I never have to pull.

37

'*U-Gift*…yes, I think that was it. I don't see what difference it makes.'

'Probably none,' said Bridge, silently rolling her eyes at Peter Lennox's condescension. 'Just dotting Is and crossing Ts. Thanks for your time.'

She put down her iPhone and searched for U-Gift in her browser, but the results were pitiful. The currency didn't appear to be widely known or popular, as evidenced by its current valuation at a whopping four dollars and sixty cents. Lennox could have saved himself the trouble of wiping his hard drive by simply paying up. Ransomware counted on most people doing just that, by making it easier to fork out a few dollars and be done with it, as Jasper Wilmington had. But the more people did that, the more the currency would rise in value. If Tempus continued spreading, how much might U-Gift be worth by next week?

Bridge yawned, loud in the uncharacteristically quiet CTA office. Monica was attending a refresh-and-update course on firewall technology at GCHQ, while Ciaran had been in a meeting with Giles to discuss SCAR since nine o' clock.

Giles had insisted on walking her from the car to the door of her flat. She'd thought that was weird, then remembered she barely had a door any more thanks to the Armed Response boys. As they approached, a uniformed policeman stood guard while a local joiner installed a replacement door.

'Don't say I never do anything for you,' said Giles, showing his ID. The policeman stood aside to let Bridge pass, while the joiner — understandably grumpy, given the hour — said he'd be done soon and wouldn't mind a cup of tea if she was putting the kettle on, ta, love.

She'd groaned, but knew she wouldn't sleep anytime soon. So she'd waved goodbye to Giles, filled the kettle, and replayed the night in her mind, wondering what she could do without raising red flags. If the CIA were still watching her network (and why wouldn't they) then further calls with Imperium were out of the question. Encrypted emails might work, but she didn't have the hacker's address. She couldn't look into Tempus or Maxim, either at home or work, without someone noticing.

U-Gift, though? That was just a cryptocurrency. Or so most people would believe.

When Tempus had appeared to be regular ransomware, Bridge could have believed it too. But the point of ransomware was to spread like wildfire, infecting every computer it found. The more people you infected, the more would pay up. But, as she'd discussed with Andrea, this attack seemed targeted. A connection to the hacking workshop would explain why. This wasn't a script kiddie fooling around with white-label ransomware at all; but they wanted it to look that way, to deflect suspicion from Russian cyberwarfare operations.

So far, so logical. The joiner finished and handed Bridge a new set of keys before leaving. As she locked the door behind him a fresh wave of exhaustion broke over her, and she retired to bed to manage a few hours of sleep.

On the tube this morning she'd continued to think it over,

and at her desk Bridge realised the biggest question of all, one that might unlock the whole puzzle: why use U-Gift? Why not stick to Bitcoin, the best-known and most-used cryptocurrency in the world? Instead Tempus insisted people use an obscure coin that, according to the little information she'd dug up after confirming its name with Peter Lennox, was only created two months ago.

Cryptocurrency was hardly new, but the fever for it in tech circles remained as strong as ever. U-Gift's low value therefore suggested it wasn't widely used, which was supported by the lack of search results, and the more Bridge looked into the coin the more mysterious it became. There was no initial PR, no announcement she could find, and nobody knew who had created it. It didn't even have a Wikipedia entry. The only references were generic lists of cryptocurrencies, most of them on sites so bursting with spyware and ads that her laptop fans whined like jet engines before the page even finished loading; or posts on Q&A sites like Quora and Stack Exchange, asking if anyone knew anything about it. Nobody did, although one answer contained a link to a coin exchange called *YourGiftCoin* that traded in U-Gift.

A coin exchange was a place to buy and sell cryptocurrencies. They weren't strictly required, as the whole point of crypto was that you could make transactions directly with other people, no middleman necessary. But if you couldn't find someone willing to sell you coins in exchange for regular money, or vice versa, an exchange would take care of it for you and take a transaction fee. Like a *bureau de change*, but for Bitcoin and other cryptocurrencies.

An exchange could also hold your *digital wallet*, a virtual record of the coins you owned, like a bank account. And all of this was done without regulation, with no insurance, guarantee, or government backing. That was the attraction of cryptocurrencies for many people, who wanted to stick it to the man and regain some measure of freedom. But it was also what led to some of the most infamous hacks in the industry. Mt Gox, Bitcoinica, Sheep Marketplace, Bitfloor, and more; all crypto exchanges that had lost millions of dollars' worth of people's coins to digital thieves. Absolutely anyone could set up an exchange, so you had no idea if your digital wallet was in the hands of an experienced professional running a server farm, or a complete novice with a rusty PC in the corner of their bedroom. As far as Bridge was concerned, you might as well burn a pile of money in your back garden.

But one aspect of cryptocurrency held some interest, and a promise of wider application beyond fleecing gullible marks. It was what had, inevitably, overtaken the cryptocurrency argument on the *u.l.g-n* newsgroup. The *blockchain*.

Blockchain was the name for an electronic ledger that recorded every transaction of a given cryptocurrency. Copies were held all over the network; in dedicated nodes around the world, in coin exchanges, in the mining computers that created coins by solving complex mathematical problems, and in every user's virtual wallet. To confirm a transaction, every single copy of the blockchain must agree it was legitimate. If they did, the transaction took place and everyone's copy of the blockchain was updated to reflect it. This was how cryptocurrency sidestepped the need for a centralised authority, hierarchy, or any kind of power structure; if a single copy of the blockchain disagreed with the suggested change, the transaction would fail. It was one of the systems' most fascinating strengths, ensuring the system couldn't be duped. Moreover, anyone could access the blockchain.

Therefore, anyone could access the transaction records.

Bridge's mind circled around this point. If she could obtain a copy of the U-Gift ledger, could she crack it open and look for a pattern that identified the ransomware payments to Tempus? If hardly anyone was using the currency, the task shouldn't be too difficult; anonymous or not, multiple payments of exactly ten coins to the same recipient would stand out like a sore thumb. She might even be able to trace Tempus and discover their location.

Discover their identity.

She was getting ahead of herself. She had to consider: doing this would definitely go against not only the letter, but also the spirit, of Giles' edict. It was also a long shot. While the ransomware code was sloppy, everything else Bridge had seen suggested Tempus was meticulous about covering their tracks.

None of which would stop her.

There were three possible ways to get a copy of the U-Gift blockchain. The first option was to use her computer to mine coins, but that was overkill. Coin mining required enormous power. Bitcoin mining operations had become so intensive, their combined network now used more energy than the whole of Ireland. She couldn't compete against that with a laptop.

The second option was simpler; to run her own network node. Each node held a copy of the blockchain, negotiating changes with the rest of the network. But running a node required being constantly online and connected to the U-Gift network. That would be an express ticket back to the CIA's underground bunker.

Which left the third option; buying coins. If she saved her virtual wallet to her own computer, rather than letting an exchange take care of it, it would download a copy of the entire blockchain that she could digitally dissect at her leisure. She imagined piles of money burning, but couldn't deny it was the simplest solution.

However, one problem remained. Bridge couldn't possibly do it from her work computer at Vauxhall, and the CIA were undoubtedly still monitoring her at home. She needed somewhere nobody would be watching.

38

Transaction Denied: Unauthorized E-mail Address

Bridge stared at the screen and rubbed her eyes, as if the words might change when she opened them again. Stranger by the minute.

She'd left work early, citing lack of sleep the night before. She had the authority to requisition a laptop from IT supplies, and even to remove it from the building — but not without paperwork, which would raise questions she didn't want to answer. Instead she'd returned home and dug out an old Sony, unused in years, from her stash of old tech. She'd wiped it clean, reinstalled Windows, written a quick post on *u.l.g-n*, shrugged on her boxy grey blazer, and left the flat.

When the local vegetarian café first opened, Bridge had worried how long it would last. But these days you couldn't throw a stone in London without hitting someone loudly explaining their vegan journey, even here in East Finchley. She'd noticed a sharp uptick in the number of *#accidentallyvegan* dishes on the lovingly-chalked menu as a result, and it had paid off. Bridge was now in here at least once a week, sometimes more since they began offering free wifi, and it was busier than ever. She was even starting to recognise other regulars, like the young student at her usual spot in the back corner, with whom

Bridge had exchanged a brief smile of recognition. The woman returned to her paperback and Bridge placed her order, silently lamenting how little she'd read in the past year. Then she took a table and, opening the laptop instead of a book, grimaced at the irony. *Demain, et demain, et demain…*

The YourGiftCoin web site greeted her with an austere front page, even by the standards of coin exchanges. A logo, a photoshopped gold coin stamped with a giant *U*, a login field, a value ticker, and a link that simply said *Buy U-Gift here.*

It had nothing else. No FAQ, no About page, no email address…and no download link for node software or virtual wallets. Of course, a coin exchange didn't have to supply those things, but most would at least link to another site that did. Not this one.

Undeterred, she'd looked for another exchange trading U-Gift, something a little more user-friendly. YourGiftCoin had been the one she'd come across in online discussions, but she could use any other exchange that sold the cryptocurrency.

Except there didn't appear to be one.

Half an hour of searching in between bites of halloumi wrap and fries had turned up nothing. No other exchanges were dedicated solely to U-Gift, and none of the multi-currency exchanges traded in it.

Next she'd clicked around online repositories like GitHub and SourceForge, where coders and programmers stored open-source applications and scripts. Now on her second coffee, Bridge had found hundreds of software projects building virtual wallets and coin nodes. But not one was designed for U-Gift.

Finally, she'd admitted defeat and returned to YourGiftCoin, where she checked the value. It had risen a little since she last checked, now at five dollars and forty cents per coin. Then she clicked the link to buy one. At that price she could afford to buy more, but didn't need to; a single coin would be enough to download a copy of the blockchain.

The exchange had asked for her email. She entered a 'burner', one of several Gmail accounts she reserved for anonymous sign-ups and transactions like this.

```
Transaction Denied: Unauthorized E-mail Address
```

It made no sense. What kind of cryptocurrency required an authorised email to make a purchase? And who 'authorised' them anyway? True, everything she'd seen implied U-Gift was some kind of elite, invite-only thing. But what was the point? Without new buyers, the coin would never seriously increase in value. You could use it as a private credit system, but why go to the trouble of maintaining a server and blockchain for something that didn't attract new buyers?

Except, of course, U-Gift was attracting new buyers all the time thanks to the ransomware, forcing potentially thousands of people to buy ten coins so they could get their files back.

And it was possible to do so; Peter Lennox might have avoided it, but Jasper Wilmington told Henri he paid up. How could he, unless he was 'authorised'? Had he lied, to throw them off the scent? Was Jasper really Tempus? But if so, who was Imperium? And the question remained: why build ransomware demanding payment in a coin people couldn't buy?

She was going round in circles. Time to break down the problem. Assume Jasper was telling the truth; he really did buy the coins, and pay them to Tempus. How was he able to do so? If Tempus' attacks were targeted, did it only attack people Tempus knew would be able to buy coins? But how could they know which email addresses were 'authorised' to use this exchange?

Bridge's eyes widened as connections formed, answers tumbling around in her brain —

'Just FYI, we're closing soon.'

Her thought processes screeched to a halt, interrupted by the café owner wiping down the adjacent table. Bridge looked up and realised she was the only customer left. Even the student had gone.

'Um, sure,' said Bridge. 'Sorry. I'll be done in a minute.' But when Bridge turned back to her screen the thought was gone. Dammit, what had she been thinking about? She was on the verge of something, something about the exchange, before being interrupted. She hadn't even realised how late it was, had completely lost track of time —

'Oh. *Oh!*' Bridge said, ignoring the owner's startled expression. She was so bloody stupid. Why hadn't she seen it before?

U-Gift and Tempus. *Tempus fugit.*

Time flies.

And now there was one email account she knew had been targeted, that the Tempus ransomware had identified from the victim's laptop, but was never used.

She typed out Peter Lennox's email.

```
Choose Payment Method: BTC/P-Dengi
```

Just like that, she — or rather Lennox — was 'authorised'.

The payment options were typical of scammers; 'BTC' was Bitcoin itself, while 'P-Dengi' was a minor Russian competitor to PayPal, without all that pesky financial regulation. Nobody but a fool or a crook would willingly give P-Dengi their credit card information.

Bridge exhaled, letting her thoughts slot into place, trying not to jump to conclusions. This wasn't a secret club, or a VIP cryptocurrency for bored kids. It was a huge scam, a circular scheme controlled by Tempus themselves. Create a new cryptocurrency; write ransomware; infect victims and demand they pay you with your own secret coin…

And then what?

That final, frustrating question remained. Why go to all this trouble? Why enrich yourself with a currency that nobody else was using, or cared about? Did Tempus plan to amass thousands of U-Gift before offering the coins to the public, thereby increasing their value? If so, this was a crazy way of going about it. Tempus could have simply 'mined' coins privately in advance, with no need to involve anyone else or risk letting ransomware loose in the world.

And that led to another thorny question: even if the ransomware made sense, why mention U-Gift in the *Rat_Catcher* worm? And why target politicians and civil servants?

That last point gave her pause. Lennox's email address wasn't by itself a security risk; it was simply a *.gov.uk* address, like thousands of others. But if the only practical way to buy U-Gift was by connecting that account to a purchase of Bitcoin or P-Dengi, was that the scam? Would purchasing coins expose the buyer to identity theft? It was possible…but again, there were easier ways.

Bridge packed away her laptop, apologised to the café owner, and walked back to her flat. So many questions, so many things that didn't make sense. She couldn't shake the feeling it was all connected, and at the heart of the mystery beat a single, perpetual question:

Who the hell was Tempus?

39

It wasn't every day Jasper Wilmington woke to find himself staring down the barrel of a gun. But it wasn't the first time, either, so he managed a quiet groan rather than the panicked scream David Kzaane was probably hoping for.

'The Englishmen have escaped,' he said, staring hard at Jasper. 'What would you like to tell me about that?'

'That it was a foolish idea to take them prisoner in the first place when it's the English whose political backing you're seeking,' said Jasper, quick but calm. 'Do you really think they'd support you while you held their men?'

'They would have no choice. That is rather the point of you being here.'

'History is written on the backs of corpses who thought their enemy had no choice.'

The barrel wavered. 'Machiavelli?'

'Um… Wilmington.'

David's eyes widened. 'Is this a game to you, Jasper? Because, I assure you, to me it is a matter of life and liberty. Now what did you tell them?'

'Nothing they didn't already know,' Jasper sighed. 'David, they didn't care about you, about Mwizuba, the rebels, any of this. They simply wanted to know where I got the hacking software.'

A puzzled expression. 'I thought you wrote it?'

A confession was normally very far from Jasper's best interest, but at this moment, honesty seemed for once the best policy. 'I'm heartened by your confidence, but no. *Rat_Catcher* is more sophisticated than anything I could write myself. I bought it from a Russian supplier.'

The barrel inched closer to Jasper's face. 'Then I don't need you here,' said David. 'I could operate the software myself.'

'You said you were terrible with computers.'

'I could learn.'

'Not fast enough. You wouldn't be able to get your head around it.'

'I also wouldn't betray myself!' David shouted, and pressed the gun against Jasper's forehead.

Jasper gulped air, talking fast. 'It doesn't matter, you don't need hostages, or the English at all. I know another way, an easier way.'

'Tell me!'

'Cryptocurrency.'

David backed off a little, eyes narrowed. 'Say that again. Slowly.' Jasper did, for all the difference it made. 'What does that mean? More computer trickery?'

He had David's attention, and that was all he required. Jasper elbowed himself into a more comfortable position on the camp bed and said, 'Financial trickery would be more accurate. But yes, it uses computers. Surely you've heard of Bitcoin?'

'Assume I haven't,' David said, slowly.

Jasper took the hint and summarised cryptocurrency. Inch by inch, David backed off. Finally the barrel of the gun swung down and into the holster at his waist. Jasper took the hint and sat up fully as he continued, 'I have a small Bitcoin investment myself. Nothing huge, a few thousand, but all it cost me was a hundred-dollar investment two years ago. The rate of return is potentially enormous.' He emphasised *potentially*, but people new to crypto were too often starry-eyed by what they'd just learned to fully grasp that part. It was the modern equivalent of 'Your investment may go down as well as up'. Everyone understood, but they also believed they'd be the exception. Still, in this situation that attitude ran in Jasper's favour.

David paced around the tiny room. 'You want me to invest in this…bit-coin?' He all but pronounced the hyphen. 'To serve as financing.'

Jasper swung his legs over the bed, looking up at David. There wasn't enough space in his 'officer's quarters' for two to stand, let alone pace. 'I do, but I don't think you should invest only in Bitcoin. There's a new currency on the market that I suspect will do quite well. If you get in on the ground floor, you could make a fortune. Of course,' he added hastily, 'There are no guarantees. But this is something we can do at the same time as you continue to petition Parliament. It's not either/or.'

David stopped pacing. 'Show me.'

* * *

The first inkling had come to him after the ransomware infection. That Jasper had never heard of U-Gift wasn't unusual; despite his reputation, he didn't habitually hang around the dark web locations frequented by real hackers, the black hats who spent their time fleecing millions out of innocent people's bank accounts, or ensuring their criminal patrons were able to shift contraband without exposing themselves to the law. New coins often first surfaced in those places; sometimes it was where they'd been created. U-Gift was possibly one such coin, and the wheeze struck Jasper as ingenious. Cash must be delivered, so was useless for ransomware; legitimate digital payment systems such as PayPal left a paper trail the police could access with a simple warrant, and besides, those systems were also eminently hackable; while any regular bank payment, even Swiss accounts, could be traced if the authorities were determined enough. All these reasons made cryptocurrency the payment of choice for ransomware. Easy, anonymous, and if you used burner emails, untraceable. Better still, though, it was the only form of payment that could become more valuable over time — unlike fiat money, which invariably lost value to inflation.

So creating your *own* cryptocurrency, and demanding ransomware victims pay you with it, was a very tidy way of going about things. A perfect little self-fulfilling prophecy.

The thought had faded as Jasper's time was taken up with the G20 attack, and trying to salvage something from its failure. But the appearance of the two Englishmen had brought it bubbling back to the surface. If SIS knew about the Tempus ransomware, it was more widespread than Jasper would have guessed from online chatter, as there was almost no mention of it in the usual circles. Not that he'd discussed it, either. Jasper was even a little embarrassed to admit he'd been a victim.

After helping the SIS officers escape he'd returned to his laptop and pretended to work, building an alibi to deny his part in it. Everyone in the compound knew Jasper's sleeping troubles, and that he often spent the small hours at his computer. But nobody asked him for an alibi, and by this morning David had so evidently worked out what happened that any denial on Jasper's part could have proven fatal.

That hour spent at the keyboard hadn't been wasted, though.

Out of curiosity, he'd logged back into the U-Gift exchange where he'd bought the ransom coins. To his surprise, the value of a single coin had already risen from three to six dollars. Still small fry, but a doubling in price in such a short space of time was nothing to sniff at, especially if the ramp continued at that logarithmic pace. It was like a backgammon doubling cube; in five turns the gamble could shoot up from two to sixty-four.

Now Jasper showed David the same thing, explaining the rapid price increase, though neglecting to mention the real reason he knew of it. Instead he said it was the subject of online chatter, with young hackers getting excited about the potential of a new coin. The lie wasn't implausible, as many new coins did indeed garner that exact reaction.

David had two Swiss accounts; one of his own, one for the militia. But he'd already told Jasper the first was rapidly dwindling to fund the second. Ousting an incumbent president with a coup required political support, of course, but it also required financing. Initially Jasper had assumed nobody really wanted to prosecute a civil war; that when real trouble reared its head, David Kzaane would be on the first plane out of the country. But now Jasper had seen a new side to his old friend, one with a surprising amount of loyalty to Mwizuba. David was prepared to do whatever necessary to rid his homeland of its corrupt regime. In a way, Jasper found the strength of his convictions admirable. But it was also a fast lane to a short life, which was certainly not Jasper's preferred modus operandi.

'How much should we invest?' asked David. 'I assume a spike of interest with a large investment will drive up the value?'

'It might, but you must understand this isn't the stock market.'

'So we should start small?'

'I think we should start somewhere in between.' Jasper

paused, knowing the next part was a risky proposition. 'In point of fact, I think it's the kind of thing that should be done piece by piece, using judgement, in response to currency fluctuations.' David raised an eyebrow. 'So I'd like access to the militia's Swiss account.'

Silence. Jasper remained very aware of the pistol at David's belt, that had so recently been pointed directly at him.

'You will keep full and accurate records of all transactions,' David said after an uncomfortably long time, 'and you will produce them for me, without delay, upon request. I will also regularly check in with the bank myself, to confirm their accuracy.'

'Of course,' said Jasper. 'But look, even if I bought myself a first-class ticket to Antigua, how would I get to a plane in the first place? Your men blindfolded me. I haven't the faintest idea where I am.'

That wasn't true. Jasper was using the Xiaomi phone David supplied him to make the data connection for *Rat_Catcher*, and now to the U-Gift coin exchange, but his own iPhone had logged the journey from the airport to the compound via GPS. Jasper didn't fancy his chances if he had to make a run for it through the forest, but he would at least be fleeing in the right direction.

David didn't know that, and Jasper wasn't about to tell him. Even when it was the best policy, honesty had its limits.

'Very well,' said David. He took a small notepad from his breast pocket and turned to a dog-eared page containing the militia's Swiss account number. 'Let's fund a war.'

40

Bridge had no idea who the hell Tempus was.

Initially everything had gone to plan. At work she'd put everything she used to create the Tempus antivirus onto a thumb drive, then metaphorically drummed her fingers all day until she could get home. As soon as she did, fuelled by strong tea and a week-past-sell-by Pot Noodle found in a cupboard, she copied everything onto her own machine and got to work.

She didn't want the antivirus itself. Quite the opposite. She wanted to build a simulacrum of the Tempus ransomware.

It wouldn't be entirely the same. Even the most sophisticated reverse-engineering could never entirely replicate a program's code. But she was banking on it being close enough to talk to the coin exchange. If the ransomware didn't authenticate the payment trigger, maybe it was equally lax about victim identification.

Two hours later Bridge had a good imitation. Next she searched around for another suitable laptop, eventually finding an old Acer under her bed; a cheap, lightweight model she'd bought years ago to travel with, but in the end had hardly used. She wiped it, then installed Windows and a network sniffer package.

She'd associated a new burner email with the Sony, to avoid using Peter Lennox's address. She was fairly confident what she was about to do wouldn't trip any CIA monitoring, as they didn't seem to suspect U-Gift's link to Tempus. Nevertheless, Bridge crossed her fingers as she connected both laptops to her network. Then she loaded the Tempus simulacrum onto a thumb drive and plugged it into the Sony.

Within seconds, the screen blanked and a window appeared:

```
*** YOUR FILES HAVE BEEN ENCRYPTED!!! ***
```

So far, so good. If she was right, Tempus would now automatically find the burner email account, and pass it on to the coin exchange. She waited two minutes, then used the Acer to sign in to YourGiftCoin with the same burner email address.

```
Choose Payment Method: BTC/P-Dengi
```

Bridge cried out in triumph. Here was proof: Tempus and U-Gift were connected, working together. She swallowed her pride and used the Acer to buy eighty dollars' worth of Bitcoin, then used those to purchase ten U-Gift coins. Finally, on the Sony, she paid them to the account number in the ransomware.

One reason she used two computers was to watch for the exchange doing something nefarious, such as further infecting any machine used to buy coins. But according to her network sniffer that wasn't the case, which only made Bridge more suspicious of Tempus' motives. Hackers rarely passed up the chance to infect a machine, if only to install backdoor code that would scan for passwords and credit card info.

Beep.

The Sony's screen cleared, the ransomware disappearing and its files decrypted. It had taken thirty seconds, which was unusually fast. Ransoms were always automated; nobody wanted to check and process thousands of release codes by hand, so the ransomware waited for a signal — the same one Bridge had imitated in her antivirus — to tell it the victim had paid up, and it could now decrypt the machine's files. That signal could be sent in the blink of an eye, but doing so often left ordinary users feeling even more cheated than they already did. So coders normally built a delay into the automation, sometimes up to fifteen minutes, to bolster the satisfying illusion that complex technical processes were taking place.

A thirty-second response time, therefore, was no accident. It meant Tempus either didn't care about implementing an artificial delay, or explicitly wanted to send the signal quickly. Neither scenario made much sense to Bridge, but then she wasn't working for the Russians. If the ransomware was targeting government employees and billionaire oligarchs, maybe it relied on a kind of perverse good word-of-mouth between its victims; *'I was hit by that one too, but don't worry, old chap. Just pay up and you'll get your computer back lickety-split.'*

Once again, it suggested Tempus' goal was simply to make people buy U-Gift for him. Once again, she couldn't begin to guess why, but suspected the answer lay inside the blockchain. She had to crack it open and find the pattern.

That part had also gone according to plan at first. Buying coins from the U-Gift exchange automatically created her digital wallet, which contained its own copy of the blockchain. Bridge wrote a quick script to examine the data, looking for patterns of transactions from the victims, either buying coins or sending them to Tempus.

She assumed victims purchased only as many coins as necessary to pay the ransom. Therefore, transactions of exactly ten U-Gift coins being purchased and then sold by the same originating address within the same validation period suggested that account belonged to a victim. It sounded simple, but each validation period was around ten minutes, and the mind-boggling amount of transactions a cryptocurrency could expect within that time produced an enormous amount of data. Bridge had written a script for that reason; to let it do the donkey-work of tidying up the dataset and making it more readable. Once the script had found matching transactions, Bridge would search for a common recipient, and hey presto — she might be looking at Tempus' email address.

She set the script going, retrieved her pot noodle from the kitchen counter, and hoovered it up as a chime sounded from the Acer laptop. The script was finished. She made herself another tea and opened the text file of search results.

Suddenly, things were no longer going to plan.

At first glance the file looked fine. A list of matching transactions and emails, exactly as she'd expected. But closer inspection revealed two oddities. For one, the file was very short. Even bearing in mind U-Gift's obscure nature, she'd expected there to be thousands, maybe tens of thousands of transactions. Instead the list contained a few hundred.

By itself, that could perhaps be blamed on her search criteria. Perhaps they were too narrow, and must be loosened to find everything relevant. But the second oddity suggested otherwise. Yes, there were hundreds of cases where someone had purchased ten U-Gift coins, then immediately paid the same amount to someone else. But in every case the recipient had a different email address.

```
h9t[g;saDE8emsJ@emailxero.com
```

```
KF8Poi3%XJiABJC@emailxero.com
A3@Y%yUeZE2fjgz@emailxero.com
4EF+DfEB?dahV3Z@emailxero.com
6$ZTB4jbQyKt{tJ@emailxero.com
```

Bridge groaned. Tempus was using a new, randomised account
to receive every single ransom payment, probably deleting
each one as soon as the transaction was complete. To make
matters worse they were all at *emailxero.com*, a free Russian
email service notorious among western admins for its complete
lack of transparency and refusal to co-operate with any law
enforcement request that didn't come from Moscow.

Even if Tempus had used the same address every time,
persuading *emailxero* to reveal its user would be extremely
difficult. Using randomised burner emails made it impossible.

Bridge had no idea who Tempus was, and no Plan B.

On a whim she wrote another script, this time to find all
transactions to/from an *emailxero.com* account. She wasn't sure
what she could do with them — look for duplicates, perhaps,
even though that wouldn't necessarily tell her anything — but
she had to try something, anything, that might shed light on
Tempus.

She expected the second script to be finished as quickly as the
first, but two minutes later it was still running. She finished her
tea, brewed herself another, came back, and it was still running.
Bridge frowned. This was an even simpler script than the first,
as it didn't rely on cross-references or comparison, but simply
matched a single criteria. Why was it taking so long?

Six minutes later, when it finally finished, she understood
why. The results list was enormous, a hundred times the size of
the first. Scrolling through page after page, she was amazed at the

sheer amount of transactions coming from that email domain. Was U-Gift more popular than she'd thought, but only in Russia and its neighbours? No, not unless they all used randomised *emailxero.com* accounts. She could run another script to check for repeat addresses, but by now Bridge was pretty confident there would be none. Used once, immediately discarded.

So why hadn't these results shown up in the first search? Were they not in the same time blocks? That would mean tens of thousands of people had been infected by ransomware, bought their ten U-Gift coins, but inexplicably all decided to wait fifteen minutes or more before handing them over to Tempus. Highly unlikely. But they were all from unique randomised burners, which implied Tempus was behind them.

A thought took shape, something very strange and unlikely. Normally she wouldn't even have considered it. But it was no more strange than what Bridge had already found this evening.

She opened the raw ledger data and ran a simple search for *@emailxero.com*, moving from one entry to the next. The amount of garbage around each transaction data block made the search slow-going, but after a while she got the hang of it and was able to blank out the irrelevant data from what she sought.

Eventually she finished, sipped her tea, and stared at the screen, impressed by the sheer audacity of it.

Tempus wasn't just receiving ransom money. The random email addresses were also being used to pay money — to other random accounts. And they were doing it sequentially, at regular intervals, in a sort of cryptocurrency round robin. User #1 paid twenty coins to user #2, who paid ten coins each to users #3 and #4, both of whom paid five coins to two more users each…until, eventually, everyone paid one coin each back to user #1 and the whole thing started all over again.

It wasn't obvious unless you were looking for it. After a single cycle completed, user #1 began using a completely different and randomised email. They had effectively become user #150, who would now pay twenty coins to user #151, who would pay ten each to #152 and #153... and so on. Anyone glancing over the data, seeing different email addresses each time, would assume the transactions were legitimate. But once you knew what to look for, the pattern, and its implication, became clear. Every user in this round robin was really Tempus, using bots to continuously shuttle the same coins around and around. Every transaction in the history of U-Gift seemed to be either a ransom payment from a victim to Tempus, or Tempus moving coins around between their own randomised accounts, to make the currency look legit. There were no other transactions, and it was all happening on the YourGiftCoin exchange, because it was the only exchange that handled U-Gift.

She'd been right. It was a huge, premeditated scam. But why?

Currency scams existed to fleece the gullible. The ransomware victims were definitely paying real money, either via Bitcoin or P-Dengi, to purchase their U-Gift coins. But the currency's value was too low for that to be the main purpose. Tempus created the coin and controlled the exchange; they could have set the price at a thousand dollars per coin before unleashing the ransomware upon the world and forcing people to buy it. Instead, U-Gift was currently worth a little under eight dollars. Hardly a king's ransom.

And why target so narrowly? Government employees and Russian oligarchs might be more likely to simply pay up and be done with it, but an eighty-dollar ransom was pocket change to such people. What kind of a scam undervalued its own currency, while targeting people who could afford so much more?

Bridge's head spun in a dozen directions. Occam's razor suggested this was a crazy script kiddie fooling around, doing it all 'for the lulz'. But if Tempus really was the same author behind *Rat_Catcher*, that couldn't be true. That person was a smart, sophisticated hacker, almost certainly part of the Tallinn hacking workshop. Plus, Karl Dominic had said the ransomware was also attacking Russians. Why would someone working for Moscow target his comrades?

A notification on her desktop computer pinged Bridge out of her confusion. She checked the screen and saw it was from the NASC++ software.

```
1 New Message
```

Bridge clicked the notification. The software launched straight into the text chat sidebar.

```
> saturday gathering at club lazer, tallinn.
> lots of scene ppl.
> you should come.
> IMPERIUM
```

41

'My mother had a fall last week, and yesterday my sister called to say she's fallen ill. We're a bit concerned, you know?'

'This is back in Lyon?' said Giles. 'How long do you think you'll need?'

Bridge shrugged. 'Hopefully she'll recover soon enough, but…I mean, now that we've given up on Tempus and handed everything over to the Americans, I'm not exactly rushed off my feet.'

'We have not "given up and handed everything over",' said Giles, bristling at the implication. 'We are merely letting the Americans take the lead.'

Bridge snorted. 'Sure, and after they've fucked things up it'll be our job to clean up their mess.'

Giles pinched the bridge of his nose. 'You know, maybe a few days away from your desk wouldn't be a bad idea.'

'Thank you,' said Bridge. 'I'll head out this weekend, and update you when I can assess the situation better.'

'My best to your family.'

The last person her family wanted to hear from right now was anyone in SIS, including Bridge. But she thanked Giles and returned to her desk, where she spent the rest of the day checking flight times to Lyon and car rental services. Anyone looking through her history, or over her shoulder, would assume she was indeed going to see her mother in Lyon.

They would be wrong.

What she'd said about Izzy was true. It had been another text, not a call, but she really had messaged from Lyon to say Maman was in hospital, having taken a turn for the worse with suspected pneumonia. Izzy asked why Bridge hadn't visited yet, and Bridge reminded her she'd asked to be kept informed, and Izzy said that this was her keeping Bridge informed, and when was she going to come to Lyon, and Bridge remembered why she wasn't quite ready to talk to Izzy again yet.

Giles didn't need to know those details. Bridge really would check in on her mother, making an unprecedented two visits in the space of a few weeks. Whatever would the neighbours say? But first she was going to attend the Tallinn hackathon and pump Imperium for intel. She didn't truly know what she was looking for, but if something connected Tempus, Maxim, and Imperium, she'd recognise it when she saw it. Then she'd hop on a plane to Lyon, suffer twenty-four hours with her mother and Izzy, and return home. Giles needn't know she was ever anywhere else.

When the message from Imperium arrived, Bridge had stared at it for at least a minute, letting it sink in. Giles would say, 'It's the American's problem now, let them deal with it.' And that only after ten minutes berating her for investigating behind his back in the first place. But while Giles was happy to let the CIA stomp all over Tempus with their size thirteens, Bridge wasn't. She had now gotten closer than anyone else to a possible workshop connection. Scene hackers were as paranoid about anonymity and security as her friends on Usenet, if not more so. The gathering would likely be a 'hackathon', a meeting where hackers showed off their skills, undertook challenges to crack a specific device, and geek out with the vanishingly small number of people in the world who understood what they were doing. They didn't let just anyone into hackathons, but Imperium had personally invited Bridge. She couldn't pass that up.

It was also potentially dangerous. If the workshop was everything she suspected, everything Kallass had been trying to tell her, she'd be walking into the lion's den — or rather the Russian bear's cave. Even if Imperium wasn't a member, the chances of someone else from the workshop attending were high. Did everyone in the local scene know? Was the workshop's existence an open secret in the community? Exposing things people tried to hide was a hacker's stock in trade.

Of course, it was equally likely she'd be wasting her time at a gathering of script kiddies who knew nothing. Bridge only had her own instincts, and half a conversation with an anonymous and mischievous hacker, to go on.

If she asked for clearance, Ciaran would say she was barking up the wrong tree, and Giles would worry about exposing Gregory Hughes if Bridge had to liaise with him. It would also piss off the Americans something rotten, which Bridge didn't care about, but Giles did. He'd veto it on the spot.

But he couldn't veto what he didn't know.

42

Of the four significant words in 'Saturday Gathering at Club Lazer', only one turned out to be strictly true; nobody could deny it was the weekend.

By contrast, the 'club' was the back of a side street bar in Tallinn. Close enough to the city's famed medieval old town to be expensive; distant enough to not be a tourist haunt. Then there was 'lazer', which referred to a laughably cheap liquid sky installation, shining two lonely light beams through a thin, insipid fog of dry ice squirted from an ageing smoke machine.

Meanwhile, 'gathering' seriously over-sold the number of attendees.

Bridge didn't find the place till nearly ten o'clock, after an hour of doubling back on cold city streets, cursing inaccurate maps and wishing she'd worn more layers. When she finally located the door, she pulled it open to find a mere eight hackers inside. Assuming she was the last to arrive, and nobody had yet left, this didn't bode too well for the local hacking scene. And they were all very young, like they were fresh out of university. Or in a couple of cases, still attending. Even the oldest, a wiry guy wearing a puffer jacket over an MKBHD T-shirt, didn't look a day over twenty-five.

On the bright side, with so few potential candidates, locating Imperium should be easy. Finding out if they really were

Tempus would be the tricky part.

The hackers gathered around tables laden with laptops, phones, tablets, cellular wifi antennae, external disks, thumb drives, and cables — not to mention glasses of beer, wine, and vodka, as many empty as full. As Bridge stepped inside, they fell silent and turned to look at her. The guy in the puffer jacket walked over, hands in pockets, trying to look intimidating despite being six inches shorter than she was and, judging by the way he moved, several pints more drunk.

'*See on erapidu*,' he said, pointing back out through the still-open door.

Bridge didn't need a translator to get the gist, but she pressed on. 'I am Rouget,' she said, once again imitating her mother's French accent. 'Imperium invited me.'

The young guy's eyes widened as he cried, 'Rrrrrrrrouget!' over-rolling the *r* for effect. He looked her up and down; Bridge was unsure if he was checking her out, or assessing her clothes. Even in her old leather and jeans this lot would have made her feel old, but the trousers, boxy blazer, and scarf marked her as positively middle-aged. He smirked, and turned to the others. 'Hey, Rouget's a chick,' he called out. 'Amazing!'

Bridge raised a defiant middle finger in his face. He laughed, moving past her to close the door. It was then she saw the adhesive name badge stuck to his T-shirt; an absurd, and surely deliberately ironic, anachronism for a high-tech gathering.

HELLO MY NAME IS: FukkU

The others raised their glasses and cried out in welcome, before devolving into drunken laughter. They all wore the name badges. As 'FukkU' bought Bridge a drink — she asked for house red, knowing she could cradle it for a good while — she glanced around and read the ones she could see.

Värdjaspoiss (no idea what that meant).

YaGirlSass (but worn by a young man, or someone presenting as male, anyway).

XxDESTROYxX (blond, with a thick Nordic beard).

And there, sitting at a table beside *Värdjaspoiss*: *Imperium*.

Bridge had been right; Imperium was a woman. The sole other woman in the room, unless she was wrong about the possible trans person. Imperium was also one of the youngest, which only made her achievements all the more impressive. Pillarbox-red hair running to dreadlocks, a face full of piercings, and a body full of tattoos visible through the holes, rips, and tears of her layered tops. Plain black leggings, Doc Marten boots, no make-up, and no bra either by the looks of things. It wasn't what Bridge had expected, but knowing the two best hackers in the room were women pleased her.

'So you are Imperium,' Bridge said, sitting at her table. The hacker's Dell laptop had been hooked up via crossover cable to another, presumably belonging to *Värdjaspoiss* himself, who hammered away at its keyboard in frustration. 'What's this?'

Imperium smiled. 'I poked a hole in his web browser and made myself root. He's trying to throw me out.' She raised her glass and shouted in his face, 'But he's fucking shit!' then burst into laughter. *Värdjaspoiss* didn't see the funny side. Bridge smiled in approval and sipped her wine, but inside, her thoughts were racing.

Imperium sounded different.

The voice-changing software had disguised her voice, but not her tone and accent. On the VOIP call Imperium had sounded unmistakably Baltic, with the characteristic lilting tone native to speakers of the Finnic language group. But in person her accent had a Russian flavour, with the distinctive flat Slavic affect common to the Moscow-St Petersburg corridor.

You could fake it, if you were good enough. But why?

'Almost as good as the zalgo exploit you pulled on me,' said Bridge, with a conspiratorial smile. 'I've never really looked into those; how did you know the overflow would have that specific effect?'

Imperium looked confused for a moment, perhaps more drunk than Bridge had at first realised, then focused on her and shrugged. 'Maybe I didn't. Zalgo is unpredictable shit. Sometimes it's fun to trigger an exploit without knowing what's going to blow up.'

That wasn't how Bridge remembered the episode at all. Was she being overly paranoid? Paranoia was what kept people in her line of work alive. She tried a different angle.

'Tell me more about U-Gift. Why the big secret?'

'Holy shit, what's with all the fucking questions?' said Imperium, throwing her arms in the air and swinging round to face Bridge. 'Are you a fucking cop, or —'

'Fuck's sake, Saskia, be careful!' *Värdjaspoiss* shouted, as Imperium's wild gesture knocked over a beer glass. He snatched up his laptop to avoid the spreading pool of liquid. 'Go wave your arms around somewhere else!' Imperium turned on him and shouted back, but Bridge had already tuned out their squabbling as realisation hit her.

That wasn't Imperium. *YaGirlSass* wasn't trans. *FukkU* wasn't the one still at the bar, watching Bridge intently.

She walked over, leaned back next to him, and said quietly, 'Switching names to confuse me. Do you treat all your guests this way?'

He grinned and replied in that familiar Baltic accent. 'Only the ones who ask about Maxim.' He took a swig of beer, then nodded at the young woman, still arguing with her table companion. 'I'm Imperium. That's Saskia.'

'*YaGirlSass*, yeah. I get it. So who's *FukkU*?'

'The guy she's fighting. They're always like this, they should screw and get it over with already. Bastard Boy is over there. Hey, *Värdjas*!' He raised his beer at one of the younger hackers, who saluted without looking up from his laptop screen. Bridge couldn't read his badge, but it didn't matter anyway. Nobody here wore their real name.

'Could you swap them all back so I know who's who?'

Imperium looked up at her with contempt. 'What's the matter, is your memory shot because you're old?'

'Fuck you. Wait five years, you won't be so young yourself.'

'But still younger than you,' he grinned.

She decided to change the subject, not only because her feelings were a little hurt, but also because Imperium had relaxed; a good time to try and extract information, get him talking. 'So tell me about Maxim. Am I looking at him, or do you work together?'

Imperium gave Bridge a sideways look, considering his answer. 'No, I'm not Maxim. Why are you so interested?'

'I told you, I was hit by ransomware I hadn't seen before. When a new piece of malware starts going around online, I like to check it out.'

'Because it's your job?'

Bridge raised an eyebrow. Any information-pumping going on here would be mutual. 'My job is to stay one step ahead of everyone trying to take me out online. Malware, trojan horses, worms, you name it, I'm interested in it. Aren't you?'

'Of course. But I know who I am, and what I do. All I know about you is that you run the same kind of obfuscation protocols I do, and you know some cool countermeasures.'

'That's all you need to know.'

'No… I think we need to know more. For example; why has nobody else ever heard of "Rouget"?'

Bridge became aware that the room chatter had fallen silent, and the other hackers were all watching them intently, laptops at the ready to check and verify anything she said. Not so drunk as she'd originally thought; welcome to the lion's den. But she wasn't completely unprepared.

'You've never heard of me because I'm not stupid enough to sign my name to things.' The implication they *were* stupid enough to do that was intentional. She wanted them defensive, maybe even a little angry. It would make them sloppy, more likely to judge according to emotion than reason, and that could only benefit her. 'I've worked on *MaXrIoT*, *Grazender*, *BlackAsh*, and more. But you won't see my name on them.' In fact, she'd only contributed to one of those — *BlackAsh*, an algorithmic password cracker — and then only as a teenager, back when the hacking world had known her as 'BitRot'. That had all changed when SIS approached her at Cambridge university, and the recruiter made it quite clear that to be considered, Bridge was to keep her nose clean from now on. No more hacking school databases, no more vandalising supermarket websites with vegetarian propaganda, and no more work on malware apps; especially those which could be weaponised and used against the state, which meant all of them. But she was still able to keep abreast of developments, and was glad she did, because that had become a large part of her role at SIS. Like Monica said, she was the 'zero-day girl'; an expert on the state of malware, able to speak with confidence about the frothing gyre of malicious executables swirling in the online sea.

A burst of laughter from Saskia brought her back to the present. 'Fuck, you really are old,' she said, pointing at her screen. She'd already looked up the software Bridge listed. 'Most of these are ancient, the last check-in was like four years ago. *MaXrIoT* is the only one updated in the last year.'

Bridge had known that was the case. She'd deliberately listed projects old enough that these kids had probably never heard of them. But she hadn't expected such ageist mockery. 'I see "respect your elders" isn't much of a philosophy out here, then. Maybe I'll leave.'

Bridge turned away from the bar to find Imperium blocking her.

It had been a calculated move to force their hand. Despite the subtly hostile atmosphere, Bridge didn't think any of these hackers posed a genuine danger, and wiry or not, she was confident she could easily incapacitate Imperium. But it was interesting that he'd try to stop her.

'Saskia's been the only chick forever, she's just jealous.' His smile didn't reach his eyes. 'But she's also got a point. Maybe let's go for a ride.'

Saskia and FukkU were already packing up their laptops and cables, shoving them into backpacks. Definitely not as drunk as they'd pretended.

Imperium lit two cigarettes, and offered Bridge one. She took it, glanced around. 'You can smoke indoors, in Tallinn?'

He exhaled a cloud and laughed through it. 'Of course not.'

Bridge laughed along, took a drag and followed the others out of the club. Something else had struck her, talking to Imperium. The Tempus ransomware was written in poor, fractured English, by someone who clearly wasn't a native speaker. But Imperium's English was excellent; he'd even used 'obfuscated', a word many Brits would struggle with. Was it another part of the pretence? One more thing to throw people like her off Imperium/Tempus' scent? She was putting on her own fake accent to maintain her cover. Could he have done the same thing with the ransom text?

Or was the answer much simpler; that he wasn't Tempus? Perhaps he had a partner, another hacker he worked with. Saskia's English was also pretty good, so not her, but FukkU had barely spoken a word.

'You all speak such good English,' she said, stepping around icy slush mounds on the pavement. It was now half past ten, and the cold had driven most people inside. 'Better than me, even. Do you have really good schools?'

Imperium laughed. 'Our schools are total shit. But English is the language of programming, right? Emails, Skype, code comments, phone calls, always English. Even between Estonians, sometimes.' He turned to Bridge with a questioning expression. 'It's not like that in France?'

Now it was Bridge's turn to laugh. 'No. We only speak English with people who haven't advanced to French yet.' She was overdoing the 'proud Frenchwoman' bit, but only a little. Bridge had known several French programmers over the years who held that opinion.

They came to a roadside parking bay. Bridge wondered which vehicle belonged to Imperium, before realising FukkU was quickly sizing them up. He settled on a blue Nissan and pulled an electronic unlocking device from his pocket.

They weren't here to collect Imperium's car. They were here to steal one.

Bridge hesitated. Up until now all she'd done was ignore an order to stay away, and tell Giles a couple of white lies. Yes, she'd broken protocol, maybe even a rule or two, but no laws. This was different. If the Tallinn police caught them and pulled her in, she'd have a hell of a job explaining herself.

She was reassured by her new compatriots' speed and confidence. FukkU had the door open in under ten seconds, and they all climbed inside. Imperium took the driver's seat, FukkU slid alongside him in the passenger position, and Saskia jumped in the passenger-side back. Bridge's only option was the back seat directly behind Imperium. She would have preferred to be up front, chatting with and observing him, but evidently that was off the cards. Silver lining: here in the back, traffic-cam facial recognition wouldn't see her.

Imperium produced a jury-rigged device to hack the ignition, a master key blank which he inserted into the steering column. A thumb drive was wired up to the blank, and a snaking USB cable connected them both to a low-resolution touch screen. Three taps on the screen fired up the engine, and he smiled back at Bridge. 'Put it together myself. All Japanese brands, most American...and French.'

She ignored the dig. 'No German?'

'They're the only ones who take this shit seriously,' he shrugged, and pulled out into traffic.

A tap on her shoulder. Bridge turned to find Saskia offering up her laptop. 'Let's see if you're as good as Roman thinks.' Bridge took the Dell, momentarily confused until she glanced at the rear-view mirror and saw annoyance on Imperium's face. So 'Roman' was his real name, and he didn't like Saskia using it. Because he didn't want Bridge to know? Or because he didn't like it?

'Roman. Good, strong name,' she said, figuring a little flattery couldn't hurt. 'I'm Amélie.' Amélie Blanc was an old cover identity, issued by SIS when Bridge had first gained OIT status, that she was confident she could pull off without too much effort. She didn't have the right ID, but if anyone ran a background check they'd find a young animal rights activist-turned-publicist from Paris. Close enough.

Imperium/Roman nodded, and his expression softened a little. Bridge could sympathise — there was little more frustrating than constructing an alias, only to have it undermined by someone's big mouth — but it had given her an opportunity to invite him into confidence. She looked sideways at the others. 'I assume you're Saskia, of course. What about him?'

'Fuck you,' said the young man in the passenger seat with a wicked grin. Saskia squealed and kicked the back of his seat with delighted laughter, then leaned forward to kiss the neck of the boy known only as FukkU. Maybe tonight would be the night they 'got it over with'.

Saskia turned back to Bridge and nodded at the laptop. 'Open it.'

She did, to be greeted by a Kali Linux desktop, a specialist version of the operating system aimed at security professionals and hackers. It was mostly used for penetration testing; the art of finding holes and backdoors in software, in order to plug and secure them.

'What are we testing?' she asked.

'We're not,' said Roman. 'You, however, are going to attack the stop lights.'

The American affectation threw Bridge for a moment, before she realised what he meant. 'Your city's traffic lights are operated over the air? That's crazy.'

'Not all of them,' said Saskia. 'They're running a trial, right here.' The car approached a four-way junction, a six-lane dual carriageway crossed by a regular two-lane road, with additional tram lines crisscrossing the tarmac. A major intersection, and one Bridge guessed would be packed with vehicles if they'd come here by day. Even at this time of night a steady stream of traffic passed through.

Bridge expected Roman to pull over, although she didn't see anywhere to park. To her surprise, he kept driving and turned onto the dual carriageway. 'Um…?' she said, looking back over her shoulder. Roman didn't reply; instead he took the next turning, then the next, and within a minute they were back at the junction — where he crossed, then turned again, and again. He was circling it, doing rotating figures of eight to keep them moving, but keeping close enough for a wireless signal. Bridge scanned the laptop screen for the right software and opened a network sniffer. 'You planned tonight, didn't you? How long has this trial been running?'

'Too long,' said Roman, swinging the car around a corner. 'They can't hire the right people because they don't pay enough. Anyone with talent is working in finance, infosec, jobs that pay real money. Who wants to build fucking stop lights for peanuts?'

Bridge watched the sniffer software discover and isolate local networks. True to its reputation, Tallinn was a wired, or rather wireless city. Within these couple of hundred square metres were dozens of different networks, public and private, all vying for space and bandwidth. 'So have there been lots of bugs? Have the lights failed?'

'That's why they haven't rolled it out to the rest of the city yet,' said Roman. 'Part of the problem is figuring out the most efficient traffic flow at different times of day, and different days of the week. I can't believe they haven't applied machine learning to it, but that's what I mean about not being able to hire the right people.'

'Artificial intelligence seems like overkill for a traffic light system.'

Saskia laughed. 'Roman thinks every problem can be solved with AI, he's obsessed. He'd build one to light his cigarette if he could.'

'Shut up,' said Roman, with an edge to his voice Bridge hadn't heard before. She began to wonder about these three hackers, a unit within the larger group at Club Lazer. Maybe Roman wasn't the only possible workshop member. Could that have been how they met? Was Roman working on something AI-related for the Russians, and warning Saskia not to give anything away? Blurting out his real name was one thing, but if they really were working on state-level hacking software, divulging that would be a whole new level of slip-up.

Bridge had winnowed the network list down, discarding traffic that was obviously home Netflix streaming, or restaurants and bars offering free wifi. That left five candidates, each of which she opened into a separate window to examine the intercepted traffic profiles. There it was; one network showed highly regular bursts of activity, small payloads running in perfect sync with the lights.

She closed the other windows and fired up a penetration software package. The network was firewalled, and the traffic itself would undoubtedly be end-to-end encrypted. But that was nothing Bridge hadn't dealt with a thousand times before. She watched the logs report back from test brushes against the firewall, selected a couple of likely candidates for sub-packages that could penetrate this particular kind of security, and mentally crossed her fingers as they launched.

To her surprise, it was over in a matter of seconds. The security was a weak implementation, and after breaking through she discovered the traffic encryption was no better; an old, deprecated method that took even less time to open up with the right tool. The light commands were revealed, in plain sight, for her to see.

And to imitate.

Saskia, watching the screen, grinned and said to Roman, 'You were right, she's good.' The car had made a turn at the apex of a figure-eight, and was now heading back toward the junction. The lights were currently red, but Bridge was pressed back into the seat as Roman stood on the accelerator, laughing.

'Then she'd better work fast,' he shouted.

Bridge frantically scanned the traffic readout to identify the correct command. Luckily, their earlier conversation held true, and the software was written in English. The problem was that none of the commands referred to colours by name, giving them instead numerical values. She wondered if that might be the cause of their bugs. Why make things more complicated than necessary? The light arrays were identified by compass point, which was more sensible, but absolutely no help to Bridge, being spun around in a city she barely knew.

'Hurry up,' shouted Saskia, hands white-knuckled on the back of the passenger seat. Bridge could hear her breathing, hard, and realised her own heart was also accelerating. Like the car, speeding at the junction, where almost a dozen other cars waited, some of them moving across the junction, all completely oblivious to the vulnerable little Nissan...

Bridge took a chance that the sequence began with red, not green, and the numbers ascended accordingly. If she was right, they were approaching the north-west lights. If she was wrong, she could be about to get them all killed in a high-speed crash. She punched in a command, imitating the official syntax, and heard Saskia scream.

A scream of triumph. The lights showed green, ten seconds sooner than they should have, while the transverse lanes all abruptly turned red. Roman swerved through the junction, narrowly missing one car still crossing and another with its nose poking across the stop line, caught halfway through entering. Then he pulled a left, still laughing, and sped along the dual carriageway.

Bridge assumed that would be enough, but no; they wanted her to prove it wasn't a fluke. Roman pulled another figure-eight, this time approaching from a different direction, and the lights ahead of them were already green. Saskia nodded at Bridge, and now that she had a correct mental map of the lights, combined with the colour sequence, it was a simple matter to turn them red. Roman pulled up at the stop line, then looked around the junction and realised everyone else had stopped, too. 'Nice work.'

Bridge smiled. She'd turned every junction red simultaneously. Now, while the car was stationary and they could watch the results, she experimented. One lane here, one lane there, red, green, start, stop; a chaotic slow-motion ballet, traffic flow devolving into stasis, horns blasting everywhere, and her fellow occupants in the car crying with laughter.

Until Roman stared wide-eyed at the rear-view mirror and shouted, 'Fuck, it's the cops!'

He threw the car into gear and stamped hard on the accelerator, shooting through the junction and earning more horn blasts as he switched lanes. Bridge turned to see a police car speeding after them, lights and siren activating in unison. She issued a quick command to switch the junction lights behind them as the police car reached it. Pursuing cops wouldn't stop for a red light, but the waiting cross-traffic began moving at their own green signal. She couldn't hear the screech of brakes from this distance, but seeing four separate cars swerve and skid to a halt, blocking the police vehicle, was good enough.

Until she turned back and saw another one pull in front to block their path.

Roman slammed on the brakes and threw open his door. 'Run!' he shouted. Saskia snatched the Dell from Bridge's hands and stuffed it into her backpack in one swift move, then bolted out of the car on the opposite side, joined by FukkU. Bridge opened her door, expecting to see Roman waiting for her, but he was already twenty yards gone and moving fast.

So that was how it would be.

She launched herself from the car into a run, following Roman up a sloping side street, while Saskia and FukkU ran in the opposite direction. Splitting up would certainly give them a better chance of losing the police, but having gone to all this trouble to find him Bridge had no intention of losing Roman again.

He was in pretty good shape for a chain-smoking hacker. Normally Bridge would have expected to catch up inside thirty seconds, given her own fitness training and longer stride. But it was closer to ninety seconds later when she finally reached him, after following a zig-zag pattern through back streets that left Bridge completely lost. It didn't matter. Wherever they ended up, her phone's GPS would guide her back to the guest house. Keeping Roman in sight was more important, and he obviously knew Tallinn well enough to guide them to safety. He hopped over a fence, crossed a deserted road, then jumped another fence into an unlit city park. Bridge followed, feet crunching on packed frost, and as her eyes adjusted to the gloom she realised they were in a cemetery.

She stopped, catching her breath in between laughs. Hiding

from the police with a boy in a frozen graveyard close to midnight; great job leaving your goth life behind, Bridge. All she needed was a bottle of Smirnoff and some tinny iPod speakers playing Bauhaus to recreate being fifteen all over again. Well, that and her old clothes.

Roman stopped ahead of her and joined in the laughter. 'Fucking cops, huh?' he said. 'That was —'

He didn't finish because they both heard shouts and running footsteps from somewhere in the cemetery. They crouched behind a nearby crypt, a sizeable family memorial, watching bare winter branches break torch beams as they metronomed across the night sky. The police weren't giving up that easily.

Roman swore quietly, his face pale and sweating. For all his bravado, he wasn't used to this. Bridge looked around for something to throw, something heavy she could use for a distraction, but a public cemetery wasn't the kind of place you found litter lying around. The closest thing was a flower holder, a heavy brass type designed to withstand an Estonian winter, filled with flowers. One stood at each corner of the crypt. Those would make a proper racket if she could heft them far enough, bring the police over while she and Roman escaped. But on closer inspection, pushing the flowers aside, she saw they were bolted down. She let the flowers spring back, cursing the dry rustling sound they made. Then she smiled.

'Give me your lighter,' she hissed at Roman.

He shook his head. 'Wait until we're out. If you light a cigarette now, the cops will see it.'

'Not a cigarette, you idiot. Give it here!' She held out her hand, and he reluctantly handed her his Clipper. She lit it and set fire to the dry, brittle flowers.

They caught in seconds. She lit the next bunch, then the next, until every flower around the crypt was burning, flames spitting high into the night.

'Go, go!' She whispered. Roman didn't need telling twice. He ran, away from the direction they'd come. Shouts and torch beams heralded the cops as they ran to the burning flowers. Bridge made a silent apology to the family, who would probably be horrified at the kind of vandals who would do such a thing. At least she hadn't thrown up over it, which was an improvement over her teenage antics.

They ran, out of the cemetery and through another maze of streets, for a further five minutes until Roman stopped to gulp lungfuls of air. No footsteps or lights followed. 'Where's the car?' said Bridge.

'Forget it, they'll have the licence plate. Hey, at least we didn't trash it, right? The owner should thank us.' Bridge doubted they would, but Roman smiled. 'So I guess you're looking for work. There's plenty to go round.'

'With Maxim?'

He shook his head. 'Trust me, that would be a very bad idea. I understand you think you want answers, but you should drop it. Or the cops will be the least of your problems.'

She nodded. No point in arguing when he was on the defensive, and thought she needed protecting. Instead she said, 'Give me your phone. I'll enter my number for you.'

Roman hesitated for a moment, then withdrew a Huawei phone from his pocket, unlocked it, and handed it to her with the contact app open. Bridge raised an eyebrow as she typed in her number. 'You do know these phones are basically spyware for the Chinese government.'

He shrugged. 'And your iPhone doesn't send everything to the NSA?' He took it back and walked away. 'I'll call you.'

43

'Will you please put that away? He's six months old, for heaven's sake, he's not going to trash his bedroom.'

Gregory Hughes forced a smile and did as Kate asked, closing the grainy video of their sleeping son in the baby monitor app. But he stopped short of putting his phone away. One never knew when an important call or message might come in, whether from Vauxhall itself or one of his contacts here in Tallinn. Despite being the sole SIS officer in the country, in fact the whole Baltic triangle, it wasn't the most active posting in the world. But it had enough comings and goings to keep him busy, especially when his cover of cultural attaché furnished him with a full calendar of social engagements in addition to his more secretive work.

That was probably why Kate didn't want him looking at his phone all evening. For the past year she'd accompanied him only to the most vital of social functions, and they hadn't had a night out for themselves — not a dinner party, not an official ball, not a diplomats' reception, just the two of them in a restaurant — for almost three months. That was his fault; Hughes' line of work was enough to make anyone paranoid, and he was naturally distrustful that a teenage babysitter working for pocket money was any kind of suitable guardian for their son. Even on those evenings when he was incognito in a dive bar with his mistress, while an oblivious Kate watched over the baby at home, Hughes still checked the monitor app regularly.

But tonight, there was more to it. Tonight he had further concerns. Such as: what the hell was Brigitte Sharp doing in Tallinn?

Giles Finlay had called him earlier. Normally Hughes would have expected a rendezvous to be called with any visiting officer, a meeting on neutral ground where they would brief each other on the particulars of her mission and establish whatever support he could offer. Not this time. Finlay had insisted Hughes make no contact, and wait instead for Sharp to approach him, if she ever did. When he asked for more details of why exactly she was here, Giles stonewalled. 'Strictly need to know, I'm afraid.'

Hughes was the station chief of three entire countries. Who could possibly have more of a need to know?

He didn't like it, and had said so. Finlay sympathised, but didn't budge. So Hughes had spent the rest of the day preoccupied by what might be occurring under his nose. He'd already read Sharp's record after their video call regarding the hacker, and noted her OIT status despite being little more than a jumped-up IT girl. He wondered if she was screwing Finlay to get that. The CTA leader was notorious for bending the rules to get his way. But sending an officer into theatre without reading in the station chief was beyond the pale. The CIA had recently sent one of their overgrown boy scouts over, too, but at least they had the decency to tell Hughes he was looking for Tempus.

Surely that wasn't why Sharp was here. Weren't they supposed to be backing off so the CIA could handle it? If so, why else had she come?

'Darling, your food's going cold. What's on your mind?'

Hughes looked up to see concern on Kate's face. That was the last thing he needed. 'I'm sorry. Work, you know.' He smiled to reassure her. He mustn't let her know anything was wrong.

The thought led to another, and suddenly Hughes realised there could be only one reason Sharp was here, and only one course of action he could take as a result. All it would take was a phone call.

He tucked into his pasta, barely tasting it.

44

If she'd been in London, she could have traced his phone. The process was now so simple any SIS officer could visit a page on their internal web, enter an EU-registered phone number, and receive a cell-triangulated location in seconds. If the phone company were co-operative, a quick request would narrow it down even further via GPS signal.

If she'd been in London, she could have asked Andrea to shadow him with a group of MI5 officers. Six men working three shifts around the clock would see his every move, including where he worked.

If she'd been in London, she could have run a background check on him. Find out what SIS, MI5, GCHQ, Interpol, and even the Estonian *Kaitsepolitsei* had on him. She had his first name now, and sometimes that was all it took.

But Bridge wasn't in London. She shouldn't have been anywhere near Tallinn, either. She was on her own, out on a limb, and had to deal with Imperium by herself.

Imperium was Roman. Was he also Tempus?

Of that she couldn't be sure, but her confidence was growing. He clearly knew Maxim, and what it was like to work for him. That implied he was part of the hacking workshop that had written *Rat_Catcher*. He might even be its author. So if Bridge was right that whoever wrote *Rat_Catcher* also wrote the ransomware…

If. Implied. Might. So much evidence, but not a shred confirmed.

That was why she was still here. After the previous night's excitement Bridge had considered leaving, going down to Lyon as planned, and looking into all of this when she was back in London. But how could she leave before she found something, anything, that would hold up as proof?

Giles would disapprove. Espionage was a game of instinct, trust, belief, and bluff. It was the original 'reputation economy', where decisions were made based on the weight of belief in a source, not evidence suitable for a court. The only thing on trial was an officer's judgement, and the only verdict was whether or not a mission succeeded.

But it didn't sit right. Roman and his friends were little more than kids; if Bridge was wrong, she could ruin their lives for no reason. And being here reminded her of Artjom Kallass. The last time she'd made a serious error of judgement.

She tried to leave her doubts on the pavement, pounding them into Tallinn's freezing dawn streets, but they refused to take root anywhere except her own mind. When she finished her run and reactivated her phone notifications, she was grateful to find a text message waiting.

TALLINNA KUNSTIHOONE - 5F - 1400

At 1358 hours she stood across the street from the Kunstihoone, or Art Hall, in the city's old town. No sign of Roman, but it had taken Bridge a while to find the building. He was likely already inside, waiting on the fifth floor.

Why here? She had no idea. If he wanted to talk, she wasn't

fussy about the venue.

The gallery was surprisingly busy for a weekday afternoon, but Bridge was pleased to see the patrons were a combination of students, young parents with their kids, and older people. A tiny, parallel-world version of the Tate Modern. She bought a ticket, gratefully accepted a guide leaflet in English, and took the elevator to the top. According to the guide it housed a permanent exhibition, unlike the lower floors' rotating works and performances.

By the fifth floor Bridge was alone in the elevator. She stepped out into a reasonably busy area, a single, long space lined with paintings and irregularly spaced sculpture plinths.

Roman sat on a viewing bench in front of a large painting at the far end. Even from behind she recognised him; like Bridge, he was wearing the same clothes he'd been in last night. He wasn't the only person on the viewing bench, but he was clearly alone. If he'd met anyone else here before Bridge, they were long gone. She checked the guide again, noting that most of the work on this floor was by artists from Estonia, Latvia, and Lithuania; the three ex-Soviet states of the Baltic triangle. Roman hadn't struck Bridge as much of a patriot, especially if he truly was working for the Russians. But maybe she was reading too much into it. Museums and art galleries were perfect places to meet in public, being equal parts blessing and curse to tradecraft. Most people were preoccupied with the displays, rather than checking for suspicious-looking punters; but their layout often made it easy to slip a tail. This one was different, though. A single room, and a single elevator to access it, didn't make for an easy getaway.

Once again, Bridge was frustrated at her inability to call it in, to access SIS' own records and dig deeper on Roman, but it would have to wait. She wondered if it might be possible to persuade him to return with her to London. Defection per se was long out of fashion, but surely he'd welcome escaping the Russians' clutches. If he volunteered to spill the beans about the hacking workshop, she was confident SIS would help him out, maybe even fix him up with a new identity.

She put the guide leaflet away and walked to the painting.

It was a beautiful piece, very much to her taste. Dark but vivid, with splashes of a sunset breaking through windswept iron gates to pierce the gloom of a forgotten cemetery. Bridge wasn't familiar with the artist, Üllar Olesk, but made a mental note to look up his work when she returned home. According to the English version of the artwork label, Olesk had moved to Sicily around 1750 in the hope of improving his wife's health. It didn't work, and she died soon after. But before he returned home to Estonia, he painted this canvas and sold it to an Italian collector. The gallery had bought it from the collector's heirs in 1993, following the Soviet Union's collapse.

Its title: *Tempus Fugit.*

The other patrons had moved on, leaving Roman alone on the viewing bench. He didn't react as Bridge sat next to him, and they both continued looking at the painting.

'So I was right,' said Bridge. 'No wonder someone asking about Tempus got your interest. U-Gift is yours, too, isn't it?' Roman simply nodded in reply. 'An entire new cryptocurrency, just to scam ransomware victims. Why?'

'It's not difficult,' said Roman. 'I wrote everything in like two days.'

If that was true, Roman/Imperium/Tempus was every bit as good a hacker as Bridge had suspected. 'Does that include YourGiftCoin? The only exchange in the world that deals in U-Gift?'

Roman smiled. 'That was even faster. You can forget hacking it, though.'

Bridge returned the smile. Now they were getting somewhere. 'Is that a challenge?'

'I mean it's impossible. It rejects any network rewrite attempts.'

'So it's static?' Bridge was surprised anyone would write a server that couldn't be updated. Then she caught him trying to suppress a smile, and realised why he'd been so specific. 'No, you mean specifically network attempts. But not physical, right? You can hook up to the exchange with a cable?'

He finally turned to face her. 'Where did you learn to code, Amélie? Where did you go to school?'

Bridge quickly recalled her cover story. 'Computer science at Paris-Sud,' she said, 'but I dropped out. Banking tech doesn't pay like malware.' Paris-Sud was big enough to make searching student records difficult, and claiming she'd dropped out would only increase the difficulty, even for a hacker like Roman.

He shook his head. 'I still don't understand why you're so interested in my little ransomware package.'

'I'm not,' said Bridge. She could almost feel the curiosity emanating from him. 'But I am interested in *Rat_Catcher*. You wrote that, too, didn't you?' It wasn't the most leading question she could have asked, but at this stage a simple yes or no would be enough to answer a cascade of other questions.

Roman didn't say yes or no. He glared at her, then said, 'I want to make a deal.'

Bridge's pulse quickened. 'What kind of deal? I thought you called me here to help me find work?'

'Don't pretend you don't know!' he shouted, taking Bridge by surprise.

She checked to see if they were attracting attention. The room's ageing security guard looked their way every so often, but he probably assumed they were quarrelling lovers. Fine by her; less chance he might intervene.

'I traced your phone,' said Roman. Bridge wasn't entirely surprised; she'd half-expected it when she gave him her number. 'But it's registered to the British government. Why is French DGSE working with the British?'

Bridge was confused, but impressed. Tracing a phone's location was one thing; finding out in whose name it was registered, and where, was quite another. That wasn't something any teenage hacker could do. It took connections.

'You're working with Maxim,' she said. 'You're part of the workshop.' Bridge didn't quite have enough to be a hundred per cent sure of that, but it was worth the gamble. Roman's eyes widened; it had paid off. Time for the final revelation. 'And I'm not DGSE, I'm SIS,' she said, reverting to her English accent.

Tears welled up in Roman's eyes. He sniffed and wiped them away with the back of his sleeve. 'Another liar, like everyone else.'

'Not a lie. A disguise. You understand that I couldn't risk telling you who I really was. Not until I could trust you.'

He laughed, and sniffed again. 'That's life, isn't it? We all disguise ourselves, because we can't trust anyone, and pretend it's fine.' He turned to her, pleading. 'If you wear a mask for long enough, when does it stop being a mask? When does it just become who you really are?'

This was getting unexpectedly heavy, but at least he was talking. Despite what he said, Bridge sensed she was seeing the real Roman: not the swaggering hacker full of bravado, but a frightened young man in over his head.

'I'm here to help,' she said. 'Tell me what you want, and what we get in return.'

He turned to her, eyes blazing. 'What I want is a public apology for Artjom's death, of course. The DGSE killed him!'

So Roman was indeed Artjom Kallass' source inside the workshop. But the tears suggested he'd also been a friend. 'I'm sorry, Roman, but I swear the DGSE had nothing to do with this. It was Maxim. Somehow he learned about the pick-up and sent his thugs to take us out. I did everything I could to save Kallass, but I barely got out alive myself.'

'It was you?' Roman hissed. 'You left him to die like a dog in the street! And for what, to stop him selling his story to a shitty rag like *Le Monde*?'

'No, you've got it all wrong. Kallass wasn't selling his story to a newspaper; he was coming to the UK. To the government. He contacted us, and we tried to transport him to London. Do you understand?'

But Roman had stopped listening, stopped sniffling, even stopped crying. He stared into space, unfocused. Then he fumbled in the pocket of his puffer jacket, pulled out a pistol, and pressed it against Bridge's stomach.

'You stupid fucking English,' he spat. 'Don't follow me.' Then he stood up, pocketed the gun, and backed away to the elevator.

45

She was on her feet and running as soon as the elevator doors closed. Not to the elevator itself, but through a fire escape door on the other side of the gallery. The security guard watched her go, reaching for his shoulder-mounted radio. They'd be waiting for her when she got to the lobby, but she had no intention of going that way. Instead, after leaping down the final half-flight of steps to the ground floor, she took the fire exit onto the street. From memory, that put her on the opposite side of the building to the front entrance. Walking round to the front wasn't itself a big issue, but the courtyard had two exits in opposite directions, east and west. If she took the wrong exit, she might lose Roman altogether. Where was he more likely to go?

She remembered the journey here. Catching a tram, the favoured way of getting around town; free for Tallinn residents, cheap for visitors. Two lines converged a short distance away from her current position. Bridge crossed her fingers and headed east.

Rounding the corner, she was relieved to see a familiar jacket. Ahead of her, Roman walked in the direction of the tram stop. Bridge cursed herself for not noticing he was armed. The angle, his seated position, the bulk of his jacket had all conspired to hide the gun. But excuses didn't make it any better.

Now she had to be doubly careful following him. The tram

was only a few hundred metres away, but if he saw her he could take a hostage, or try to shoot her in the street. Roman didn't strike Bridge as someone used to physical violence, but guns allowed cowards of all stripes to remove themselves from the consequences of their actions and be unpredictable. Right now, she knew Roman's computer code better than she knew the man himself.

The quickest route to the tram stop was straight down a main thoroughfare, but instead Roman peeled off into the narrower pedestrianised streets of the old town, continually checking over his shoulder. He was in full paranoiac mode now, expecting to be followed. Bridge adopted the usual tactics; tied up her hair in a rough chignon, removed her blazer and carried it despite the chill, donned sunglasses against the winter glare. She couldn't do anything about her height, but she could change her silhouette enough that a simple glance would mistake her for someone else. She hung back, ducking in and out of cover, keeping Roman in sight until he turned corners. But, despite his cautionary diversions, it was obvious the tram stop was his destination and each time she caught up with him again.

As Bridge went through the motions, trusting the tradecraft that had been drummed into her at the Loch, her mind returned to the question of how little she still knew about Roman. He worked for Maxim, who, it was now safe to assume, ran the hacking workshop. But he'd also been Artjom Kallass' source, which suggested he wasn't happy there. It further implied he and Kallass were close, as had his genuine distress at the gallery. Were they related? Cousins, or perhaps uncle/nephew? Regardless, Roman was a brilliant hacker — the ransomware was kind of sloppy, but anyone who could write it *and* a new cryptocurrency in two days was a force to be reckoned with.

Finally, his accent was unmistakably Estonian, but he spoke almost perfect English.

That still bugged her. Why was the English in the ransomware so bad? To be sure, it was better than Bridge's Estonian, but why would Roman pretend to have poor English when posing as Tempus? Was it to play up to a stereotype of ransomware authors? Was he trying to throw off nosey parkers like her, by making them think he was a Russian teenager?

Her thoughts came to a halt as Roman reached the stop, and a tram pulled in. He immediately swung through the front doors. Bridge waited, staying out of his line of sight, and put her blazer back on before slipping through the rear doors as the warning beep sounded. She wasn't sure how much time she had until the next stop, so made haste, pushing through the thick afternoon crowd of tourists, shoppers, and commuters. It was useless trying to be discreet; her height and crowd-shoving had half the carriage already looking at her. Instead she leaned into it, shouting, *'Excusez-moi! Allez!'* to clear the way.

She reached the middle section and scanned around. Where was Roman? Had he doubled back, given her the slip? No, there he was, in a window seat. Head down, furiously typing on his phone. Bridge drew closer, moving quietly, the shouting and shoving replaced by whispered apologies and gentle nudging. Was he warning someone about her? Sending a message for help, or backup?

Bridge silently slid onto the seat next to him. He was so wrapped up he didn't recognise her. That was good. If he did try to pull the gun again, she was close enough to stop him. But she doubted he would. This tram was part of the city's modern fleet, with prominent *Turvakaamera* CCTV. Surely Roman didn't want a camera operator summoning the police.

She leaned over to look at his phone screen. Roman looked up, presumably to tell his overly-curious companion to back off, and recoiled in recognition. She quickly snatched his phone away, and when he tried to retrieve it she intercepted his hand and twisted two fingers back. He gritted his teeth, seething in pain, but with enough self-control not to cry out.

To Bridge's surprise, his screen showed a simple chat app. Roman hadn't been calling for backup, he'd been messaging with someone. But the recipient made her gasp.

Tempus.

She scrolled back through the chat. Whatever she'd expected, this wasn't it.

```
> How is life?


+ I'm fine, thank you. I work hard, and do performing
all my tasks well.


> That's good. Let me know if you encounter any
> problems.


+ Of course.
```

She kept scrolling, noting that Roman checked in with Tempus several times every day to ask how their work was going and check up on them. One particular exchange stood out.

```
> What's today's coin value, Tempus?


+ $9.42. At the current rating of the increase it takes
some months to reach its limit.
```

```
> Don't worry. Soon we'll begin to accelerate.

+ When is the endgame will begin?

> Not yet. You'll know.
```

This confirmed it; Roman wasn't Tempus. Much as it added another frustrating complication to matters, at least it explained the discrepancy in their English. But whoever Tempus really was, they were involved with Roman in the U-Gift scam — and the mention of an 'endgame' suggested they had an ultimate plan. Bridge thumbed back down to the latest conversation.

```
> We may need to accelerate. I'm not sure if I'll
> survive today.

+ I am ready always. I do wait the order.

> There may not be one. If you don't hear from me within
> the time frame, you know what to do.

+ Yes, and I am look forward to the doing.
```

Bridge released Roman's fingers and tossed the Huawei in his lap. 'You think I'm going to kill you over *ransomware*? What the hell's going on, Roman? What are you and Tempus up to?'

Roman stuffed his phone in his pocket and glared at her. 'You've lied to me from the moment we met. Why should I believe anything you say now?'

He had a point, though its hypocrisy gave Bridge pause. 'You didn't answer my question. What are you and Tempus planning?

And why create a fake cryptocurrency to do it?'

He looked at her with mild surprise. 'What do you mean, fake?'

'Don't try to bluff me. I figured out your round-robin bots, inflating the currency all on a single exchange. What I don't understand is why you don't set the value yourself, to a thousand dollars or whatever.'

Roman hesitated. 'Do you know the story of how to boil a frog?'

She did. The story went that if you placed a frog in a pan of boiling water, it would leap out. But if you placed it in cold water, then slowly raised the temperature, the frog would stay there, acclimatising as the water heated up, until it was boiled alive. It was an analogy for how people would more readily accept gradual change over time, even if the predictable end result was disastrous. It was also complete bollocks, as Bridge had found when she once used the analogy on *uk.london.gothic-netizens*, only to discover two regular members were biologists sick and tired of people thinking frogs were so stupid they wouldn't jump out when they got too hot.

She didn't say any of that, because she wanted to keep Roman talking. Instead she said, 'Yes, I know it. So you want the coin's rise in value to look natural, is that what you're saying?'

'Exactly. Make people think everything is fine.'

Bridge took a leap. 'This is nothing to do with the workshop, is it? Maxim doesn't know anything about it.' Roman's eyes widened and darted involuntarily up to the bulging CCTV hemisphere. 'Oh, come on. You can't seriously think he has live feed access to tram security.'

'I've hacked more difficult things for him myself,' said Roman. 'And if he knows I'm talking to you, he'll kill me. I'm not exaggerating.'

'I'm sure you're not. Bloody Russians, eh? Terrible bosses.' Roman half-nodded and Bridge took some satisfaction at several more suspicions being confirmed. Maxim did run the workshop, and he was indeed Russian. This was going well. 'Did you write *Rat_Catcher* for Maxim? That's good code. Took some of my best work to neutralise.'

Roman turned to the window, pouting, but not before his reaction to flattery had given him away. She pushed further. 'Does Maxim know *Rat_Catcher* infected Russian machines, too? Was that an accident?' Roman looked sideways at Bridge, opened his mouth to answer, then closed it again. There was something he didn't want to tell her, something she was missing that he'd assumed she already knew.

'This is justice for Artjom,' he whispered.

It made sense. 'Revenge,' she said. 'I understand.'

Roman's eyes flared, suddenly angry. 'You don't understand, you stupid bitch! You're all to blame! And so am I.' He began to cry, which threw Bridge completely off-guard. Her mission instinct told her to take advantage of his state and get him in zip-ties, so she could bundle him off the tram and back into town. But what good would that do? She was gaining his trust, no matter who he blamed for Kallass' death.

'It's not your fault,' she said. 'You mustn't blame yourself. You didn't pull the trigger.' Notwithstanding her hazy vision after the crash, Bridge was confident she'd recognise the gun-wielding thug from Paris if she ever saw him again, and it definitely wasn't Roman. 'Maxim had Kallass killed, and you want to make him pay. I understand that. But there's a way to make this right without scamming thousands of people with ransomware. Trust me.'

'Artjom was the only person I ever trusted! Make it right? Fuck! You think this is about money? You think I'm that shallow?'

The tram slowed to a stop. Bridge looked out the window and saw their surroundings had become more rural, indicating they were probably near the end of the line —

Roman slammed into her, shoving her backwards off the seat. Her head smacked into a metal railing and she dropped to the floor, dazed, as Roman launched himself over her to leap off the tram. A couple of passengers fussed around her, but a quick exploration revealed nothing more than a lump on the back of her head and wounded pride. Amateur hour. She should never have taken her eyes off Roman.

By the time she reassured everyone she was fine and left the tram, he was gone.

She took out her iPhone and launched an app. A blue dot pulsed in the centre of the screen, overlaid onto a map of the local area. Bridge opened a menu, tapped again, and the map zoomed out to accommodate a second dot, green, positioned at her exact location. That was her; the blue dot was the GPS in Roman's phone, loud and clear after she cloned it. Cloning was difficult, as it required close proximity to the target for a minimum of thirty seconds, but sitting next to him on the tram had given her the perfect opportunity.

Bridge made a mental note to pass on her thanks to whichever Doughnut at GCHQ had written this app when she returned home, then set off at a steady pace to follow Roman.

46

He didn't go far. They were in the Tondi district, a leafy residential area off the main southbound route out of Tallinn. Bridge followed the tracker past driveways still laid with an inch of silent snow, uncleared and picturesque. Less than twenty minutes later she'd caught up with the signal, which had stopped in one such street. Bridge ducked behind the wide trunk of a kerbside tree and checked her phone one last time. Roman was inside a house nearby.

Did he live here? Had he simply gone home, upset by memories Bridge dragged up? But he'd been so angry, and it was an anger she knew well; the kind that spurred action, not apathy.

She considered calling Vauxhall and asking someone to run the address, but decided against it. The moment she spoke to anyone Giles would order her home, and to do otherwise would be officially disobeying orders. Right now she was certainly violating the spirit of a hundred different SIS regulations, but not necessarily the letter of them. At least, that's what she'd say when the truth inevitably came out.

She was alone on the street; the nine-to-five crowd was home for the evening and house lights suggested families eating dinner, watching TV, helping kids with their homework.

Bridge launched her camera app and flipped it to selfie, for a makeshift mirror. Her hair was a little frizzy, but her complexion was back to normal after picking herself up from the tram floor. She re-wound the chignon, tucked stray hairs behind her ears, and smoothed down her clothing. She didn't know who would answer this door, but she didn't want them to immediately slam it because she looked unhinged.

She crossed the road, walking purposefully toward the house. The golden rule; look like you know what you're doing, that you have every right to be here, because you do it all the time. She strode up the short garden path and raised her hand to knock.

The front door was ajar.

She held her breath and gently pushed, revealing a hallway. An occasional phone table had been knocked over, its contents strewn across the floor. The phone's tinny, automated *please-replace-the-handset* tri-tone looped quietly in Estonian. She stepped over it, careful not to make a sound. Voices, low, from what she assumed was the lounge. Sobbing, too. One voice was Roman's. The other was native English, that tell-tale slight drawl of the privately educated. A baby cried.

The lounge door was open. Bridge stepped through and took in a surprising scene.

In the centre of the room, Roman held the pistol. It was pointed directly at a man on the couch, whose arms were wrapped protectively around a woman with a baby in her own arms. The woman was unfamiliar, but Bridge recognised the man's dark hair and blue eyes, lined by crow's feet.

Gregory Hughes, SIS station chief for the Baltic triangle.

Roman flinched as Bridge moved in the doorway, but the gun didn't waver. 'I fucking knew it,' he spat. 'You're in it together!'

'Roman,' said Bridge, not moving, 'I don't know what you're talking about, and I don't understand what's happening here.

Tell me what's going on.'

'Don't bloody well talk to him,' blurted Hughes. 'Shoot him!'

Bridge held up her empty hands. 'Unarmed. Now everyone, please calm down. Roman? Is this about Kallass, as well?'

The barrel trembled as Roman's moist eyes reflected the room light. 'Of course it is, you stupid bitch,' he said quietly. 'All your bullshit about Maxim, but you knew all along. You must have known.'

'Knew what? Roman, I've never met Maxim in my life.'

'But he has,' said Roman, turning back to Hughes. 'And you staged everything to make it look like Artjom was in an accident. But you didn't know he couldn't drive, did you? I knew! You fucked up!'

Bridge's mind whirled, trying to put the pieces together. 'Wait a minute. You think we worked with Maxim to kill Kallass, and then cover it up? No, no. Roman, that's not true.' How could she convince him? She still had bruises from the car chase in Paris, but those could have been sustained anywhere. Once again, she had to trust the truth would see her through. 'I told you, I was there. It was me driving the car, and I promise I did everything I could to save Kallass.' As she spoke, Bridge took small steps into the room. She was almost within reach of the gun, focused on that poor baby in its mother's arms. She remembered the horror of Marko Novak mounting the farmhouse stairs to take her nephew Hugo hostage, and heard herself say, 'If you want to point that gun anywhere, point it at me.'

Roman turned to look at her, which was part of the plan, but then he yelped in surprise at her proximity and drew back before Bridge could reach for the gun, which wasn't part of the plan at all. 'Get back! Back to the door!'

The baby cried, upset by the noise. Hands raised, Bridge

walked backwards until her heel touched the door frame. 'Let the mother and baby go, eh? They've got nothing to do with this. Let's figure it out between the three of us.'

'So she can call a SWAT team to take me out?' Roman snarled. 'Kill us all and bury the truth about your double agent? Fuck that.'

Bridge's head swam. Did he really think they could call in an armed response squad at the drop of a hat? But, more worrying: 'What are you talking about, double agent? We're all on the same side here.'

Roman laughed, hollow and devoid of mirth. 'You don't know. You really are a clueless bitch.'

Bridge ignored the insult and focused on Hughes, but it was impossible to read him. Yes, he was sweaty and trembling with nerves, but he and his family were being held at gunpoint. And this station wasn't quite the top-flight posting it might have been forty years ago, when it was firmly behind the iron curtain. Bridge's own Loch scores might be better than Hughes'.

Roman must have sensed her confusion. He turned to Hughes and shouted, 'Tell her! Tell her about your fucking mistress, you traitorous prick!'

Hughes' wife — Kate, Bridge remembered from his file, her name was Kate — shot a worried glance at her husband, who shook his head furiously. 'Lies, lies. What does this child know? Look at him, he's trying to save his own skin.'

Normally, Bridge would have thought the same. But he'd sought Hughes out, convinced of his guilt. 'How do you know, Roman? Surely Maxim doesn't share intel like that with staff like you.'

That hollow laugh again. 'It's the other way around,' said Roman. 'I told you I'd hacked worse things than CCTV for

Maxim.'

'You hacked Gregory's phone?'

'No, he's careful about that. Not about his baby monitor, though. Online version, with a camera.'

Bridge almost laughed herself. Talk about labour-saving devices, from both angles. Ten years ago Maxim would have had to send a black bag team to break into Hughes' home, install bugs and cameras, get out again without anyone noticing, and hope nobody found the devices. Instead, Hughes had voluntarily bought and installed a surveillance device himself. 'How many in Tallinn?'

'Two, three hundred. A dozen or so in this region. It was easy to narrow down. Maxim's been blackmailing him for months.'

Kate, silent until this point, suddenly said, 'You brought her here? To our house?'

'Only once,' said Hughes, reddening.

'Oh, well that's all right, then!'

Another puzzle piece slotted into place. 'You sold us out,' Bridge said to Hughes, feeling nauseous. 'You got Kallass killed, and me very nearly with him, all because you couldn't keep it in your fucking pants?'

'You can't speak to me that way. I'm the station chief!'

'I'll speak to you any way I like, you two-faced bastard. And so will C when I drag you back to London.'

'No!' shouted Roman. 'He's coming with me. My shift begins soon, and Maxim has called an all-hands meeting. Everyone will be there, and I want them to see both men pay for what they did.'

'Think properly, Roman,' said Bridge. 'Come back to England with me, and Hughes can give us what we need to bring Maxim down.'

Roman shook his head. 'You can't take him down. He'll disappear, then go somewhere new and start all over again. Like here.'

'This isn't his first workshop? Where was he before?'

'He came to Tallinn one year ago. Before that, who knows? Romania, Macedonia, maybe Poland.'

Roman was tiring, and the fight was starting to go out of him. If Bridge could keep him talking, he might give up the gun. Or she could try to rush and disarm him. It was a risk from this distance, but she still didn't believe he was a killer. Even if he did shoot her, the shock would probably prevent him following up with Hughes' family.

'Roman, look at me. Look at me.' He did. 'If you die, what happens to the ransomware? You wanted all those people to suffer, right? But where's the fun, if you won't be able to see it? You really think Tempus is going to care enough to carry on your work?' In truth, she had no idea how dedicated Tempus was to Roman's cause. Tempus might be his equally determined twin brother.

Roman sneered at her, and Bridge's stomach sank. She'd guessed wrong. 'Tempus will never stop,' he said. 'And if I die, it will only get worse. You'll see.' He smiled. 'Maybe all those bugs I couldn't be bothered to fix will make things even worse for you.'

She remembered the text conversation on his phone: *If you don't hear from me within the time frame, you know what to do.* Presumably Roman had to check in with Tempus every so often, to prove he was alive. If he didn't…then what? What else did Tempus have up their sleeve, ready to activate if Roman died? They were already preparing to fleece thousands of people all over the world. What next?

Kate stood up, cradling her baby. 'I don't know who you are, or what the hell is going on here, but I am leaving, and you can all bloody well sort it out yourselves.' She turned back to her husband, still cowering on the couch. 'I'll deal with you later.'

'No!' Roman reached out with his free hand to stop her. But she was a fraction too far away, and trying to reach her while also keeping the gun trained on Hughes put him off-balance. Bridge saw her chance. It wasn't much of one, but Kate's actions had put the fire back in Roman's eyes. Much as Bridge might loathe Hughes' treachery, for now he was still her superior. It was her job to keep him safe.

She dived at Roman, simultaneously pushing Kate Hughes and her baby behind her, to shield them with her body. Roman stumbled and instinctively pointed the gun at Bridge, low angle aiming up as he lost his balance. She heard the metallic click of a squeezed trigger.

Bridge's forward momentum carried her into Roman. They fell, landing painfully on a baby walker. Roman kicked out, one heavy boot striking her kidneys. Pain exploded behind Bridge's eyes. Combined with the gunshot, she had maybe ten seconds to get Roman under control, before all her strength drained away.

Except, she realised with surprise, she wasn't shot.

Had Roman missed? At such close range, he would have had to be blind, deaf, and dead to not hit her. She pushed herself up, grabbed the baby walker, and swung it at him. It bounced off his head while he fumbled with the pistol, and she realised Roman had forgotten to deactivate the safety catch.

She dived on top of him, jabbing her elbow at the same spot where the baby walker had hit. Roman cried out, and she reached for the gun. Bridge outweighed him, but he was wiry, and as she'd seen for herself, fitter than most hackers. He kept the gun out of her reach, pounding at her head with his other fist. She fought through it, almost had the gun —

The shot roared by her ear, barely missing. The overhead light fitting exploded, plunging the room into darkness. Along with the sudden deafening noise, it was enough to disorientate her. Roman scrambled out of the room, colliding with the doorframe, and then he was gone.

Bridge pushed herself to her feet. A few bruises, nothing serious, but her head was reeling from the pistol blast. Somewhere, somebody was screaming. She leaned on the wall in an effort to make everything stop spinning, and as her eyes adjusted to the light saw Hughes, Kate, and their baby all huddled in the back corner. The baby was crying at the top of its lungs. Bridge could sympathise.

Oustide, a car engine revved hard. She reached the window in time to see a silver BMW speed away. Roman had stolen Hughes' car, and now she had no doubt where he was going. To the workshop, to kill Maxim.

She ran into the hallway and saw something on the ground. A wallet, dislodged from Roman's pocket as he staggered out of the room. Inside was his driving licence: *Vesik, Roman Andrus*. Twenty-four years old. Next to the driving licence was a picture of the *Tempus Fugit* painting, cut from a museum guide.

Bridge pocketed the wallet, marched over to Hughes, and pulled him to his feet. He flinched, yelped; she didn't care. 'You're coming with me,' she shouted. 'Where's your other car?'

'What other car?'

Bridge gaped at him. 'Are you seriously telling me the station chief is a one-car family?'

'I ride a scooter,' said Kate. 'It's electric, hooked up in the garage. Should be fully charged.' Baby still in her arms, she walked to the hallway, took a key fob from the fallen occasional table, and threw it to Bridge.

Bridge caught the fob and turned back to Hughes. 'Where's the hacking workshop?' Bridge cut off his protest of ignorance. 'Don't even fucking try that. Don't you dare think about calling Maxim to warn him, either.'

'He already knows. We thought that was why you came here,' said Hughes, and recited the workshop address. It wasn't until she was already speeding out of the garage on the weirdly silent scooter that Bridge wondered what he meant by it.

47

The stupid bitch knows nothing. She wants me to believe her own people let her blunder into Maxim's trap. She's a hacker, I've seen that with my own eyes, so why send her to pick up Kallass instead of a soldier?

Whatever. The game's up, but she can't stop me now.

My phone rings, an unknown number. It's her. Who else would it be? I slam on the brakes of Hughes' BMW, open the door, and throw my phone on the ground. I won't need it any more, not after tonight. I stamp on it, again and again, until it's nothing but splinters and broken Chinese circuits. After I've dealt with Maxim I'll remotely wipe it from the carrier's database and get a new one. Maybe with a better camera.

I realise I've lost my wallet somewhere, probably fighting back at Hughes' house. It doesn't matter. I get back in the BMW and drive right on the speed limit into town so I don't attract police attention. 'Rouget', or whatever she's really called, might be following. I can't afford any delay.

I pull up two streets away from the workshop in a no-parking zone and leave the car there. If the police haven't towed it when I'm done, I'll drive back to Tondi and finish Hughes. If the car's gone, I'll steal another.

Outside the workshop, I don't see the English bitch. If she is following me, she'll be too late. Good.

It's almost end of shift. The workshop operates twenty-four hours a day on rotating eight-hour shifts, and mine begins soon. But yesterday Maxim called an all-hands meeting for tonight, to discuss EU infiltration tactics with the whole workshop. That means he'll already be in the building, because Maxim is never late.

I walk past Old Erko at the front desk, nose in his newspaper as usual, and call the elevator. Everything appears normal, the same as always. But the solid, heavy mass of the gun thumps against my body with every moment. The safety is already off this time.

Today is not normal. Nothing will ever be the same again.

The elevator doors open onto the empty, plain reception for Global Analysis Holdings OÜ. I take my pass from my pocket — good thing I don't keep it in my wallet — and touch it to the RFID reader. The secure door unlocks, automatically inching open. I step through into the workshop.

I have just enough time to wonder why everyone is standing at their desk, and see Saskia turn to me with tears in her eyes, before someone hits me from behind.

48

His phone was a nest of plastic splinters by the side of the road.

The GPS cloning also gave her Roman's phone number, so Bridge had tried to call from the scooter. But it rang out and flipped to generic voicemail, delivered in Estonian but still recognisable by the fragmentary, cut-and-paste speech patterns universal to carrier messages. Thirty seconds later the blue dot, which had been steadily moving toward the centre of Tallinn, stopped moving. Then it turned red. *Lost Signal*.

When her green dot overlapped the red she stopped the scooter and found the useless remains of Roman's Huawei. She left it in the icy roadside slush and continued on to the workshop address Hughes had given her.

It was a tall building of steel and glass, grey and anonymous, not far from the high stone walls of Tallinn's old town. Bridge hauled the scooter onto the pavement on the other side of the road, standing it against a Morris column festooned with advertisements for the latest movies and theatre shows. She leaned casually against the column, angled to see past a badly-parked green utility van at the building's kerb and into the building's lobby. She hadn't seen Roman enter the building, but with the head start he had on her, not to mention the electric scooter's top speed of a scant 40 kilometres per hour, he would be already inside.

Hang the consequences; Giles had to know. She pulled out her phone and called, but got voicemail.

'It's Bridge. Long story, but I'm in Tallinn, and we've got big trouble. Baltic is compromised, I repeat, Baltic is compromised. I've also found our journalist's source. Will attempt to bring him home.'

She ended the call and wondered how to get inside the building. The main entrance itself was unlocked, but behind the wide glass doors was a standard lobby setup with a high reception desk and an ageing uniformed guard, no doubt counting the days until his retirement.

She was confident she could bluff her way past the guard by pretending to visit one of the occupants, assuming there were any besides the workshop. She could probably even incapacitate him if necessary, though that risked exposing her to any security cameras present. Better to scan the occupants' board, pick a company at random, then get off at the wrong floor. Assuming that was possible, anyway; some secure buildings' elevators were controlled by the security guard, only stopping at your assigned destination. She might have to use the fire escape stairs to reach the correct floor.

What *was* the correct floor?

It would be on the occupants' board, but Bridge didn't know the workshop's operating cover name. Probably a bland, word-salad name: *Global Commodities GmbH, European Alliance Ltd, Logistique Intégrée Sàrl*. Deliberately meaningless and forgettable, to hide the terrible and nefarious. Not so unlike the real corporate world, Bridge supposed. But if several such companies occupied the building, she'd have to try them all; and how would she know the right one when she found it? A Kremlin-sponsored hacking workshop was unlikely to have banks of monitors scrolling C++ code in reception.

Slow down, Bridge. You're overthinking it. The important thing was to get inside, claim she was an ordinary visitor with an appointment to see a corporate client, and then deal with whatever —

A rapid, muffled percussive hammer sounded from somewhere. Bridge subconsciously assumed it was construction, perhaps digging up the road nearby. But as the sound bubbled up into her awareness, she recognised the staccato of gunfire.

A window shattered on the sixth floor of the building, and now the sound was unmistakeable.

Bridge ducked behind the Morris column, assessing her options. She was unarmed, and didn't know the building layout. She had no idea how many were inside, how many had guns, or whose side those with guns were on. Going in would be suicide. But she had to know. She'd come this far.

Her hand rested on Kate Hughes' scooter. Following whoever exfiltrated the building would have to suffice. Preparing to go round the back and wait by the fire exit, she mounted the scooter, released the brake, and rolled it out from behind the column.

The back door of the green van slammed open. Half a dozen men wearing long, buttoned coats filed out of the building's front entrance and into the back of the vehicle. Following them was a shorter man, middle-aged with a shock of white hair, a downturned mouth that gave him a perpetually mournful look, and a wide nose. Bridge froze in recognition as he scanned the street and, finally, their eyes met.

Paris. The man who shot Artjom Kallass.

Maxim.

Then the sixth floor windows exploded, coughing fireballs that rained shattered streetlight reflections into the gutter.

49

To: Arkadi Blaskovich
From: YYxChWZ$Z46{mqb@emailxero.com
Subject: Another payment is due
Priority: HIGH

I remain continue have all your Documents, Photos,
Files, Videos, and Web Browsing History. As you now see,
I CAN NOT BE DESTROYED. Even when you think it I am.

I WILL PUBLISH YOUR LIFE unless you are send AGAIN 20
U-GIFT COINS to this address:
762Ded7uU6BiJfVkK3p9eb362

QUICKLY!
1 U-GIFT COIN = ** $13.70 **
AND RISING ALWAYS

Have A Nice Day
- TEMPUS

50

Bridge swung the scooter around as Maxim reached inside his coat. A car horn blared — an oncoming driver thinking Bridge was about to ride into traffic — but was cut short as the scooter turned, rear wheel finding purchase on the wet pavement, and two bullets slammed into the Morris column.

She had to get away. Not only was she here without backup, but anyone comfortable enough to shoot someone in broad daylight had no fear of police. That meant the Tallinn force was in Maxim's pocket, and no one would help her. So Bridge could only run, all the way back to London if necessary. She had her wallet, phone, and passport; everything else, what little she'd brought, could be abandoned. The only thing she'd regret leaving was her laptop, still at the guest house. But it was fairly clean, and anyway the drive was encrypted. She could remote wipe it when she got home.

If she got home.

Twelve metres away, stone steps disappeared down an embankment. From here she couldn't see where they led — a park, or another road? Either was better than waiting to take a bullet. She gunned the scooter, not daring to look back. The electric might be crap for top speed, but its torque was powerful enough to have her hanging on as it sped toward the steps.

She had time to see they led to the pedestrian crossing point of a busy road before hurtling downhill, realising too late that the scooter's centre of gravity was above and behind her. She tried to bring the back wheel down, but it was already tumbling through space, and her with it. Instinctively she let go and curled up, hands wrapped around her head, relaxing to let the impact pass through her body until she stopped rolling.

The blast of a car horn made her open her eyes. It swerved around her, crunching over the scooter instead. She had to get up. Lying down, she was as good as roadkill. She pushed herself upright and ran, weaving between cars. One almost took out her knees, a black BMW that screeched to a halt inches from her legs. She slammed her palm on the bonnet in anger, swore at the driver —

'Get in,' shouted Karl Dominic, leaning across to open the passenger door.

Bridge gaped at him, wasting almost a full second, before she marched around to the driver's side instead and pulled the door open.

'Do you have combat driving?' she asked.

'I got a phone call, figured you might need a ride —'

'Combat driving, yes or no?'

'No, why — *Jesus!*'

A shot punched into the passenger door. Bridge instinctively ducked and looked back to the embankment as Maxim ran down the steps, gun up.

'Move over.' Bridge shoved Karl into the passenger seat and climbed behind the wheel, momentarily thankful they were about the same height so the seat was in a good position. She had so many questions. Why was he even here? Was the CIA following her? How much did he know about Maxim? Why send someone with no combat experience? They would all have to wait. She floored the accelerator and sped away. In the rear-view mirror, Maxim hauled the driver out of a white Toyota.

She threw the BMW around a corner, tyres protesting as she spun to avoid another car trying to cross lanes. Behind them the Toyota was gaining fast.

'Seatbelt,' she said, pulling hers across and forcing the catch. Karl barely had time to fasten his before the Toyota was only a few metres behind. Bridge stood on the brakes. The seatbelt dug into her chest, she braced for impact —

It didn't come. Instead Maxim swerved around them, close but distant enough to avoid a collision, then accelerated away. She followed, not unhappy about the tables turning. 'Do you have a gun?'

Karl looked at her like she was insane. 'No. Let him go, and get us to your man Hughes. The CIA has no station here; I came in to follow up on Tempus. So let's get the hell out, and you all can sort this goddamn mess out yourselves.'

'Hughes is compromised,' said Bridge with contempt. 'He couldn't help an old lady cross the road. And I am not letting this bastard get away twice.'

'Twice?'

She grimaced. 'Paris.'

'Fuuuuck. See, Giles knew you were onto something.'

Bridge gripped the steering wheel a little tighter. She wanted to retort, to question Karl to within an inch of his life, but her focus was on catching Maxim. The Toyota turned onto the main south route. He was trying to get out of the city.

But Bridge recognised these streets. They were near her guest house, and she remembered the roads from her morning run. She swerved into a corner, down a side road that exited further down, moving through the gears. The junction with the main thoroughfare approached, fast. She didn't see the Toyota pass by, she'd been too slow —

Then it filled her vision, the side of it, and Maxim's surprised expression as the BMW's nose smacked into the Toyota's wing. Both cars spun across the road in a maelstrom of metal, glass, rubber, snow, and steam.

Bridge forced open the driver's door and fell out, ignoring the glass shards biting into her palms. She forced herself to her feet and walked over to the Toyota, confidence growing. At last, she had him.

She wrenched open the mangled driver's door, and Maxim shot her.

With hindsight, she would realise she felt the pain before she heard the shot. Like a bee sting, sharp and urgent but nothing too serious — until her brain processed this information, and was supplanted by reality. Her legs turned to paper and she buckled to the ground, reflexes sending her hand to her chest as she gritted her teeth in a silent scream. Bridge had once broken her arm at karate practice when she was a teenager. At the time it had been the most painful thing she'd ever experienced, indescribable to anyone who'd never broken a limb.

It turned out being shot was on a whole new level.

She was aware of Karl shouting her name, of a loud engine amid the shocked silence of surrounding cars. A green van pulled up and its rear doors opened. A man shouted something, she couldn't understand him, but he wasn't talking to her. The man hauled Maxim into the back of the van and it sped away.

Karl knelt over Bridge, wide-eyed with concern. She wanted to be the brave soldier, the one who grimly accepted the pain and waved their colleague on. *I'll be fine, go get the bad guy!* But now she was positive the people who wrote those movies had never been shot. Her head may have wanted him to leave her and chase Maxim but her body screamed for help, for medical attention, for someone, anyone, to make the pain go away.

Karl tore open her blazer, checking for the wound location. Her blouse was already soaked, and as she watched blood bloom across her chest, Bridge feared the worst. But when she traced the spreading crimson back to its epicentre, the pain already fading to be replaced by warmth and exhaustion, she relaxed. Her shoulder. It was just her shoulder.

'It's okay,' she gasped, breathing slow, 'I don't feel so bad. Hardly feel anything, actually.'

'That's because you're going into shock, dumbass,' Karl said with more disdain than Bridge thought was strictly necessary. She watched him remove his sweater and ball it up against the wound. Pressure, but no pain. Then he took her good hand, held firm in his long fingers, and pressed it down on the sweater while he fumbled in his pocket for his phone. 'Maintain pressure, you know the drill,' he said, dialling a number. Bridge leaned back and closed her eyes, suddenly very tired, but Karl was a spoilsport and slapped her cheeks, shouting, 'Hey, hey, stay with me, come on!'

'*Telle gauloisie...*' Bridge groaned. She wanted to say more, but the words made no sense. '*Mais, Maxim...le tueur de Paris...*'

'Another day,' said Karl, then looked very serious and said something into his phone that sounded like *l'ambulance*, except he couldn't have said that, they weren't in France, and what was the Estonian for ambulance anyway?

Later, as sirens propelled them through the darkening streets, she tried to turn all the lights green. But the driver didn't seem to care what colour they were.

51

To: Jeremy Anders-Porter
From: U9+Br3W)CkFcCea@emailxero.com
Subject: Another payment is due
Priority: HIGH

I still have all your documents, photos, files, videos,
and web browsing history. As you can now see, YOU CANNOT
DESTROY ME. Even when you think you have.

I will publish all your documents UNLESS you send
another 20 U-GIFT COINS to this address:
Jmt8968MNCrbA964K38QZuQ8F

Do not delay, or I will release everything!
1 U-GIFT COIN = ** $48.17 **
And the value is always rising!

Have A Nice Day
- TEMPUS

52

'Shit, shit, we have to get out —'

'Relax,' said Karl, pressing Bridge back into the bed with a gentle but meaningful push. 'You're in a hospital.'

'That's exactly the problem,' she hissed, ignoring blossoming pain in her shoulder. 'Maxim probably has half the Tallinn cops in his pocket, with Greg Hughes running the other half. We stay here, we're good as dead.'

Karl's eyebrows lifted. 'Okay, you've been shot, so I won't say you're paranoid. But seriously.' He continued holding her down, and she gritted her teeth in frustration. On any other day Bridge reckoned she could give him a run for his money, but today she had no strength. They'd bandaged up her shoulder and elevated her arm. It would be in a sling for weeks, no doubt. How was she supposed to type with her arm in a sling?

She craned her neck, saw only black outside the window.

'It's two in the morning,' Karl explained. 'I already called Giles, and you're on a flight in —' he checked his watch, '— four and a half hours. I'm following at midday. I figure you've got one hell of a debrief waiting back home, so I hope it was worth it.' He nodded at her shoulder.

Bridge groaned. 'Giles sent you.' It was the only thing that made sense.

'I was coming here on Langley's dime anyhow, but he asked

me to keep watch. Figured you wouldn't be able to leave it alone. My guys don't know; this is between us and Giles.'

'So how will you explain all this?' Bridge gestured at the hospital room with her good arm.

Karl flashed his teeth. 'Oh, I was just driving through town when you happened to run out in front of me. Couldn't refuse a colleague in trouble, now, could I?'

The CIA wouldn't buy that any more than Giles had bought her story about going to Lyon, and Karl would face a grilling for it. But she appreciated that he was making light, rather than dropping everything on her. 'I'm sorry,' she said. 'This whole situation is my fuck-up.'

'Bullshit. You were being chased by a Russian operative with a gun.'

She shook her head, and immediately regretted it when her shoulder decided to stab every nerve in her neck. 'I mean all of it. That's what I learned from Roman Vesik. Everything goes back to Paris. If I hadn't got Artjom Kallass killed, Roman wouldn't have written the ransomware. He might never have teamed up with Tempus, never created U-Gift…fuck.' She kicked the foot of the bed frame in frustration, and regretted that too. Christ, was there no part of her body that wasn't connected to her shoulder?

'Pardon me, but that sounds like horse shit. This Roman guy, he's the Tempus hacker, right?'

'No, he's the one I was chatting to when your cowboys hauled me in. Roman was part of Maxim's hacking workshop, and it was him who compromised Gregory Hughes, with blackmail footage of Hughes and his mistress. That's how Maxim knew I was collecting Kallass in Paris. After Kallass died, Roman worked with Tempus to send the ransomware attacks, and also created *Rat_Catcher* for the Russians. Now the workshop is gone, because Maxim killed them all — which is also my fault, by the way — and he's escaped to God knows where. Meanwhile, I still have no idea who Tempus is or where they're based.' She half-smiled at him. 'It's a total shitshow, as your lot would say.'

Karl considered everything she'd said. 'Why would you think Maxim wiping out the workshop is your fault?'

'Because that's what Hughes meant when I left his place,' said Bridge. It had nagged at her since she'd set off on Kate Hughes' scooter. *He already knows; we thought that was why you came here.* She hadn't understood at the time, but now it made sense. Somehow Hughes knew she was in Tallinn incognito, assumed therefore she must be here to investigate him, and warned Maxim. Hearing there was an SIS operative in town, and a cyber-espionage specialist no less, Maxim assumed the game was up and terminated the operation. Literally.

Bridge started, tried to sit. 'Shit! Hughes and his family are a loose end. Maxim might go after them before Giles can send a team.'

Karl eased her back down again. She was starting to get very annoyed at that. 'First of all, maybe, maybe not. If you were running someone like Hughes, would you give him anything he might use against you? Or would you feed him a pack of lies so you could disappear without a trace?'

Bridge didn't like it, but Karl was right. Maxim was no amateur.

'Second, if you're right that Hughes sold you and Kallass out to Maxim, that means he's to blame, not you. No mistress, no blackmail. No blackmail, no double agent. No double agent, no dead journalist in Paris.'

'Look, I appreciate you trying to make me feel better —'

'Oh, bullshit. I'm not trying to make you feel anything, I'm stating facts. If you want to punish yourself on some weird guilt trip, that's your call, but don't pretend you have to carry the world on your shoulders.' Karl stood and walked over to the window.

'Fuck you too, Agent Dominic. Considering the CIA wouldn't have a single lead without me, and not only have I made all the progress in this investigation but I've now taken a bullet for my troubles, you could show a little more gratitude.'

Karl turned from the window and smiled. 'See, that's more like it. Have a little self-belief. Focus on the positive.'

That smile only made Bridge more angry. 'When did you become my therapist? Bloody Yanks, always sticking your noses in. I'm not your pet charity project!' Shouting sent another jabbing pain up her neck. She tried not to let him see her wince.

Karl sat down by the bed. 'I know. I'm sorry.' She expected him to launch into an explanation, a spiel about how he was only trying to help, all the usual rubbish, but he didn't. Bridge's anger fizzled as she remembered she wasn't the only person who'd been shot at tonight. She closed her eyes, trying not to focus on the pain, and they sat in silence for a while. Then he said, 'It's *Special* Agent, by the way. I have the power to arrest you.'

Bridge opened her eyes. 'Bullshit, that's just a title. You're not law enforcement.'

'You want to see me try?'

'Kinky,' smirked Bridge.

He looked horrified. 'Uh, no, that's not…that's kind of inappropriate. In the circumstances. Don't you think?'

'Now who's the one that needs to lighten up? Relax, Teeth Boy. You're a lovely guy, but my life is a steaming mess that I wouldn't wish on anyone, not even for a one-night stand.'

He almost choked. 'That's, uh, that's certainly not…' Bridge let him trail off, watching a cute flush of colour travel from his neck up to his cheeks, too amused to save his embarrassment.

'Come on, get me out of here and slung up,' she said. 'We've got a plane to catch, and I've got a bollocking to receive.'

Karl called for a nurse, then leant against the doorframe, hands in pockets, smiling. 'So I'm a lovely guy, huh?'

'Don't push it, Langley.'

'I should put that on business cards.' Karl affected a terrible British accent. '*How do you do? I'm Karl, and I'm a lovely guy.*'

Bridge laughed, and instantly regretted it, but also didn't.

53

Not that she didn't already know this was serious shit, but when immigration security led her into a side room Bridge didn't expect to find Giles himself waiting inside. Under normal circumstances she would have been picked up by a detachment of junior SIS officers, or maybe Buchanan, the deputy who'd interrogated her when she returned from Syria.

Instead, Giles himself had slogged out to Heathrow. Serious shit indeed.

At Tallinn airport, Karl had given Bridge his number and told her to text when she landed. Almost three hours later, she still hadn't decided if she would or not.

'How was your mother?' said Giles, glaring at her bandaged arm and somehow keeping a straight face.

Bridge glanced at the CCTV cameras mounted in the ceiling. 'Recovering well, thank you. But we should probably hold off the pleasantries until we're somewhere a little more private, don't you think?'

Giles growled quietly and opened the far door.

She followed him in silence through the network of grey corridors, past temporary holding rooms for suspects, offices of police inspectors and their assigned MI5 liaisons, server rooms staffed by GCHQ data analysts, and everything else necessary to maintain the security of the world's second busiest airport.

Each door was as identical and anonymous as the armed police officer guarding it.

Giles' ID allowed them to sidestep the usual search-and-sign procedure, and they emerged from a final door into an underground car park. An SIS driver and car waited. They climbed in, saying nothing until they'd passed the exit security barriers and were speeding through the night, back along the M4 to London.

Bridge spoke first. 'You knew I'd go anyway.'

'You are sometimes tediously predictable, yes.'

'Did you also know Greg Hughes was compromised?'

Giles frowned. 'Not until you left that voicemail. I'm afraid I even told him you were coming, though without details.'

'Oh, bloody hell,' groaned Bridge and turned to the window, watching the night fade upwards. 'He's been informing the Russians since at least the time Kallass approached him. It was Hughes who leaked the Paris mission, and when you told him I was in Tallinn he assumed we were onto him. That's the kind of thing that would put the wind up any station chief, let alone one with something to hide.'

'Oh, they all have something to hide. It's only a matter of degree.'

Bridge hadn't expected quite that level of cynicism from Giles, but these were troubling times. 'Well, Maxim agreed, because he immediately arranged a kill squad for the workshop. Hence the explosion, and this.' She indicated her wounded arm. 'I shouldn't have gone after Roman.' Giles' confused expression reminded her how much she hadn't yet told him. She leaned back into the cushioned headrest — definitely better than the fishbowl — and recounted everything, from her conversation with Imperium/Roman and discovery of the U-Gift scam to winding up in the hospital. When she'd finished, she said, 'And that's why I should have stayed with Hughes instead of running after Roman and getting myself shot. Hughes has probably flown the coop by now.'

'Unlikely, given I called in a black mark after receiving your voicemail. He's been under home observation ever since. Besides, this isn't the glory days of the Cold War, when turncoats earned themselves an apartment in Moscow and a Kremlin pension. If the Russians suspect we're onto him, they'll drop him like a rock.'

'Or worse,' said Bridge, thinking of poor Kate Hughes and their baby daughter, innocents caught up in her husband's deadly mess.

'Still, at least now we might get something useful out of him. I'll rewrite OpPrep to say I sent you as a monitor. If he believes that anyway, all to the good.'

Bridge sighed. 'They all died because of me.'

'Nonsense. Their cards were marked the moment they chose to work for Maxim,' said Giles, placing a hand on her shoulder. Bridge could count on two fingers the times they'd had any kind of physical contact beyond a handshake, and this was the second. Something wasn't right.

'Giles, what aren't you telling me?'

He removed his hand. 'You didn't get a location on Tempus? No clue to their whereabouts or identity?'

'No, but whoever it is, Roman had faith in them to begin an "endgame" in the event of his death, to take revenge for Artjom Kallass. That's what this was always about. I don't think they even cared about the money, the hacked data, any of it.'

Giles unlocked his phone and handed it to her. 'Unfortunately, you may be rather wide of the mark on that one. Everyone who was previously attacked by the ransomware woke up to a nasty surprise in their inbox this morning.'

    Subject: Another payment is due

Bridge quickly read the follow-up ransom email, then returned his phone. 'Another randomised emailxero address, like the U-Gift bots. But it doesn't make sense that the endgame is old-fashioned blackmail.'

'Perhaps not, but Tempus isn't bluffing.' Giles tapped at the screen to load a BBC News headline. A trove of documents implicating two Russian oligarchs in banking corruption had been sent to the press; signed, sealed, and delivered by Tempus. 'Whoever he is, we need to put a stop to this nonsense before half of Whitehall's emails are splashed all over the *Telegraph*.'

54

Ciaran wasn't best pleased to see her.

Monica was, well, Monica. She didn't care whether Bridge lived or died, let alone broke a few rules. Ciaran, on the other hand, affected a casual air but deep down he was made of rules, a by-the-book stickler. And not only had Bridge gone off the books, she'd proven herself right to do so and gained valuable intel they couldn't possibly have obtained by sitting at computers in Vauxhall.

He focused on the negative. 'So you let our only link to Tempus slip away and be killed. Great work,' he said sarcastically.

'I got more intel out of him than we had before. We didn't even know he *was* a link to Tempus until I made contact.'

'Which effectively signed his death warrant. Now what are we supposed to do?'

Monica peered out from behind her monitor. 'What we always do, Ciaran. Use our big bloody brains to solve the problem. Now will the pair of you please take this elsewhere, or shut the hell up.'

Suitably berated, he fell silent and retreated behind his own screen, but Bridge already found the atmosphere suffocating. She reached into her bag, removed the Beukes novel, and walked out of the office.

Halfway to the break room her iPhone buzzed, but she was

already carrying a book in her good hand, so couldn't check it. It buzzed another three times before she reached the break room, tossed the book on an orange couch overlooking the river, and checked her messages.

Maman recovering, still feverish but doing OK

Well enough to realise you're not here!!!

Are you coming or not

Let me know when you leave, I'll pick you up at the airport

If Maman was doing fine now, what was the point in her travelling all the way down to stand around like a fifth wheel? Her mother might have noticed she wasn't there, but Bridge very much doubted she cared one way or the other. Maman had made her disappointment in the younger daughter's life choices pretty clear.

She admonished herself for being so harsh. *Have a little self-belief. Focus on the positive.* Hard to do with a slung arm reminding her every moment that she'd almost died because she'd been unable to stop Roman Vesik running to his death at the workshop. But she'd go and visit Maman soon. She would. After she'd figured out what Tempus was up to.

The machine spat out its usual awful coffee. Bridge tasted it, pulled a face, took it to the couch, and watched the Thames go by. Even the coffee couldn't take away from the view on a bright spring day like this. She thumbed to the most recent dog-eared page in her book, flattened it against her thigh with her good hand, and began to read. She needed to relax, to clear her mind before trying to solve the problem in earnest. Big brain or not, it was her duty to solve the Tempus puzzle; figure out who the hacker was, how they and Roman had operated, and how to stop them.

Perhaps the biggest question was why Tempus was doing this at all. Roman had been so set on revenge, he must have trusted his partner implicitly. He would only have entrusted the task to someone with a shared sense of injustice and self-righteousness. Just how close were Roman and Tempus? Bridge had run a check on Roman Vesik as soon as she was able, and it was a sadly predictable read; parents died when he was a teenager, spent the last years of school living in an orphanage, left to find himself permanently unemployed. At least, that was the official story. Bridge suspected he'd been working as a hacker before being recruited by Maxim's workshop, like how SIS found her at university.

There but for the grace of God, and all that.

According to his file, though, Roman had no dependents. No siblings, no children, no living close relatives. He wasn't married, and neither he nor anyone else in Tallinn had mentioned a girlfriend of any kind, much less one to whom he'd leave a small fortune — which the Tempus blackmail was no doubt amassing, as politicians and oligarchs and lord knows who else quietly paid up to ensure their private documents weren't released to the public.

She established the timeline in her head. First, Peter Lennox was hacked by someone (presumably Roman, on Maxim's behalf) and his documents leaked. A few days later, Lennox was then targeted and attacked with the Tempus malware (written by Roman, operated by Tempus?). Not long after that, Jasper

Wilmington, working for David Kzaane's rebel militia, tried to hack the G20 delegates with their version of *Rat_Catcher* (written by Roman). Shortly afterwards, a rash of Tempus attacks hit the UK government. Bridge had repelled both attacks with her antiviral work, while Jasper Wilmington had simply paid up when he was hit by Tempus. But that surely wouldn't have been the workshop's doing, because they were supplying *Rat_Catcher* to Jasper in the first place. So it must have been Roman, off the books. Why?

To complicate matters further, the CIA had said Russian systems were also being targeted by Tempus. If Roman and Tempus were indeed working off the books to take revenge on Artjom Kallass' killers, that made sense. But how were they finding targets? The ransomware wasn't spreading like a regular virus. It only seemed to attack politicians, civil servants, oligarchs. People of power. Did Roman keep a list? Did *Rat_Catcher* have a backdoor reporting mechanism that phoned home to tell them which systems it infected? That would explain why the UK government had been attacked by Tempus following the G20.

Wait. No, it wouldn't.

Rat_Catcher was neutralised before anyone got back online. When those computers regained access to the internet, the malware was no longer on their computers. That was the whole point of Bridge's countermeasure at the summit.

So if it wasn't about phoning home it must be something else, maybe on the computer's local drive. *Rat_Catcher* itself had been a time-delayed attack, the infected Excel spreadsheet sitting dormant on Fadi Saeed's computer until the G20 started. Did it also contain a further delay, something that triggered the ransomware on an 'infect now, act later' basis? Or…

Bridge dropped the novel, still unread, and ran a hand over her face. It made sense, but she had to be sure.

Someone had left a ballpoint on the nearest table. She flattened the book on the table, grabbed the pen, and jotted a list of dates and times on the inside cover. The outside world fell away as she thought back to everything they'd learned over the past week…and everything they'd assumed, without double-checking.

She wanted to scream. How could she have been so stupid?

Two minutes later she was in the elevator, riding down to Inventory in the basement. She hoped they still had Peter Lennox's laptop.

* * *

'We had it the wrong way around. It's a rootkit.'

Giles narrowed his eyes at Bridge. 'Jog my memory.'

'Remember the Sony CD scandal? They were so desperate to stop people pirating music, they loaded malware onto their own albums. Buy one, stick it in your computer, and it auto-installed a rootkit that would prevent you ever copying a CD to your hard drive again. You didn't know anything had been installed, and the code was injected so low in the system it was almost impossible to delete. Even a full hard disk wipe wouldn't get rid of it.' She emphasised that last part, and Giles understood the implication.

'A wipe like the one Peter Lennox did,' he said.

Bridge held up the MP's laptop. 'He thought it would clear everything, including the Tempus ransomware, off this drive. That's why he assumed his private documents were hacked before the ransomware attack.'

'...But you already established they weren't. It's why we sent Henri to Mwizuba. Now you're saying it was one of these rootkits all along?'

'Exactly. Lennox got rid of the ransomware, but it was already too late. Tempus had auto-installed a version of *Rat_Catcher* into firmware, which is unaffected by a hard drive wipe. When Lennox rebooted, the rootkit was still there, ready to run. It grabbed his documents and sent them to Tempus, who leaked them to the press.'

'Questions,' said Giles, counting them off on his fingers. 'One: why leak without first demanding a blackmail payment? Two: can you prove it?'

'Roman told me the ransomware was coded quickly, following Kallass' death. It's not like he ran it through a QA department. I suspect he made a few different versions, improving it over time until it was ready to unleash on the world, and Lennox was unlucky enough to find himself on the wrong end of a prototype test case. Blackmail wasn't the point.' She indicated the Lenovo and shrugged. 'As for proof, nothing solid. But there's evidence of an installation autoexec in the Tempus code fragments that Monica recovered from this computer, and I've found a rootkit installed in its firmware. I bet those Russian oligarchs had it too. The document hack didn't just follow the ransomware, it was *caused by* the ransomware. We assumed they were separate, but we should have checked.'

'Would we have found this even if we had?'

Bridge chewed her lip. 'Possibly not. The malware I reconstructed to write the antivirus was reverse-engineered, a simulacrum. It didn't contain the rootkit because, by definition, the rootkit injection code was obfuscated and had already done its thing.'

'So first they get money from the ransomware, then the ransomware itself gives them material to blackmail people,' said Giles. 'I was right, this is about getting rich.'

'I'm still not convinced,' said Bridge, pacing up and down Giles' office. 'The ransomware has no authentication verification. It's how I was able to write the antivirus so easily; it doesn't check that the ransom payment really has been made. That's why I thought it was written by an amateur, but Roman was nothing of the sort.'

'Meaning?'

'Writing it wasn't a mistake. It was either deliberate, or careless in a very literal sense. He even said it wasn't about the money. At the time I thought he was being self-righteous, but now I'm not so sure. It would explain why they're not inflating the value of U-Gift, for one thing.'

'Which brings me to question three. Does any of this help us neutralise Tempus?'

Bridge threw up her hands. 'I have no idea. We still don't really know what the so-called endgame is. But knowing this has to be good for us. Maybe it can help track Tempus down. I need time to think.'

Giles stood and took his jacket from the coat stand. 'Then think fast, because five minutes ago I was summoned to COBRA, and you're coming with me.'

55

'One bloody hacker! Are you seriously telling me a spotty kid in his basement is running rings around us, and you can't stop him?'

Giles cleared his throat. 'We have some reason to believe this "kid in a basement" is, or at least has been, sponsored by Moscow. This is a rather serious issue.'

'If it wasn't, Mr Finlay, we wouldn't be here, would we?' The home secretary spread his arms to indicate the room; Cabinet Office Briefing Room A in Downing Street, better known as COBRA when used for crisis meetings. Like this one.

Security personnel filled the room. Bridge and Ciaran sat either side of Giles, while to Bridge's left were Andrea Thomson and three MI5 officers. Opposite them was a delegation from GCHQ in Cheltenham, including Steve Wicker and his boss Sundar Patel. Next to them was Peter Lennox, effectively patient zero of this whole affair, and his secretary. At the far end of the table, invited by courtesy but relegated to minor status, was Karl Dominic and an older, African-American CIA agent called Edison Hill. From their body language, Bridge assumed Hill was Karl's boss. Finally, standing three-deep behind them all was a sea of advisors, secretaries, consultants, and assistants. The prime minister was notable by absence, but the home secretary had assured everyone he would brief the cabinet himself following the meeting.

Bridge thought that was a terrible idea. Trying to condense and paraphrase the complexities of this issue for a bunch of smiling career politicians was difficult at the best of times, let alone when attempted by one of those same politicians. But Giles had cut off her protest with a glare and swift apology to the home secretary. Then he scribbled *All politics, let it go* on his notepad and made sure she saw it. It had been clear from the moment she entered the room — bruised face, arm in a sling — that the home sec was entirely unconvinced she was an expert in anything. Bridge bristled at his obvious contempt, but couldn't deny she looked a right mess, and lacked the energy to argue.

Sir Alan Schofield, the Home Office permanent secretary, checked his notes. 'Miss Sharp, did you meet this "Tempus" person while in Estonia?'

Bridge shook her head. 'No. But I observed Roman Vesik, the hacker working for the Russians, chatting with Tempus by text.'

'Then can't we trace his phone?' asked the home secretary.

She tried very hard not to roll her eyes. 'I should clarify: it wasn't by SMS text message, like you or I might send to each other. They used an encrypted chat program to talk privately. It's possible Tempus wasn't even using a phone, but rather a computer.'

'Which means no, we can't trace it,' added Giles. 'Let me reassure everyone that SIS has already made every attempt to locate Tempus electronically; through the emails he's sent, through Estonian network provider phone records, and so on. Unfortunately for us, he's very good at covering his tracks.'

'Can GCHQ help?' asked Sunny Patel.

Bridge shrugged. 'We can put our heads together, of course,

but I don't know if we'll have any more success.'

'I'm afraid you must,' said Sir Alan, 'because if I've understood this correctly, failure is unthinkable. We don't even know the full extent of this hacker's theft of private documents. We all saw what happened to Peter Lennox's files, and we can assume the Mwizubans would have done the same had the G20 attack been successful. What if Tempus now has similar files from every committee member in Parliament?'

Giles held up a hand. 'Let's not panic. As we understand it, Tempus only has access to those people who've fallen victim to the same software we repelled at the G20, or the Tempus ransomware itself.'

'That's still a lot of people,' said Andrea Thomson, 'not to mention a lot more supposition and speculation than I'm comfortable with. Don't these blackmail emails he's been sending effectively give us a list of everyone at risk?'

'I'm sorry,' said Bridge, unable to contain herself any longer, 'but can we all please stop assuming Tempus is male?' She expected nothing better from Giles or the home secretary, but hearing Andrea of all people make the same assumption was too much.

Sir Alan peered at her over the top of his glasses. 'I'm afraid I rather don't see how that's important.'

'No, I imagine you don't.'

'Duly noted, Bridge,' said Giles, fixing her with a glare. 'In answer to your question, Andrea, even if we made such a list, it would only include people on our side. But we know Roman also targeted France and Russia, and the G20 infection also affected Australia, Canada, and the USA.'

Edison Hill exchanged a look with Karl Dominic, then spoke up. 'I was told you wiped the malware from all those computers.'

Bridge picked up the explanation at a raised eyebrow from Giles. 'We did, but we now know the malware had already installed what we call a "rootkit" — think of it like a hibernating virus, very difficult to kill — on the affected machines. It's even possible some computers may be infected but aren't being targeted for blackmail. Have you received one of these emails, Mr Lennox?'

All eyes turned to Peter Lennox, who blushed a little. 'Yes, I have. I assumed it was nonsense, because they already leaked the documents they stole from me.'

'Not necessarily,' said Ciaran. 'It's possible the hacking was more pervasive, but Tempus held back everything except the Russian energy files to extort you later.'

'Then bloody well sort it out!' Lennox blurted. 'My God, aren't you people supposed to be on top of this? Instead we've got viruses and blackmail running amok, your only source was killed by his Russian paymasters, and it turns out one of your own was a double agent!'

All heads turned to Giles. He glared across the table at Lennox, but remained calm. 'Gregory Hughes is being dealt with. While his compromise is regrettable, it has no direct bearing on the matter at hand.' That wasn't strictly true, but so far only Giles and Bridge knew Hughes had sold them out in Paris, and she certainly wasn't about to announce it.

The home secretary gestured at Andrea. 'I'm inclined to agree with Five. It sounds like you have very few concrete facts to go on.'

'On the contrary,' said Giles, 'we know that Tempus worked together with Roman Vesik to create and distribute the ransomware, taking revenge on those they deemed responsible for the death of Artjom Kallass. Anyone attacked was also infected by the hidden *Rat_Catcher* virus, which Roman had already created for the hacking workshop, and was used by Mwizuba to attack us at the G20. We know that since Roman's death, Tempus is now carrying out some sort of endgame involving blackmail. Finally, let me state for the record that we knew precisely none of this before I sent Ms Sharp into Tallinn, at great personal risk to herself, as you can see.'

Bridge was impressed to hear him summarise the situation so well, and cover for her so effortlessly. She made a mental note to review the fake OpPrep documents claiming he'd sent her to Estonia, in case anyone followed up.

Sir Alan regarded Giles over his glasses. 'We don't hand out trophies for doing one's job, Giles. Does any of this help us put a stop to Tempus?'

'We have some leads,' said Bridge. 'We know the ransomware was made hastily, so there's a high chance it has bugs, meaning mistakes in the computer code. Software bugs are how viruses exploit computers in the first place. There's a chance we could turn the tables, and exploit bugs in the ransomware for our own ends.'

The home secretary looked like he'd rather be anywhere else than at this meeting right now, but Sir Alan nodded in understanding.

Bridge continued, 'The blackmail is a new development. The first demand was sent several hours after Roman's death at the workshop, and along with it, the value of U-Gift has begun to rise.'

Andrea leaned forward. 'This is the Bitcoin thing that's going to be worth millions, right?'

Bridge glanced at Sir Alan making notes, and quickly answered, 'That's a very simplified way of looking at it, but yes.'

'So what's he —' Andrea checked herself, '— sorry, what are they going to do with the money? People like this always screw up when the big score comes in. Can we keep a watch for someone in Tallinn suddenly buying a Lamborghini?'

'Certainly,' shrugged Giles, 'although the area is also a favourite destination for wealthy Russians.'

'I would hope, Giles, that your people can tell the difference between a hacker and an oligarch.'

Giles had asked for that, but Bridge suppressed a smirk and came to his rescue. 'Roman insisted it's not about the money, and even became angry when I suggested it was. He cared more about revenge for Kallass' death than any personal gain.'

Sir Alan looked up from his notes. 'But can we say the same about his partner, Tempus?'

'That,' said Bridge, 'is the sixty-four-thousand-dollar question. Or, the way U-Gift is going, more like sixty-four million.'

56

The house was under guard.

Maxim had called Hughes after his run-in with Brigitte Sharp, opening the conversation with a standard innocuous code phrase in case of call interception. He knew it was Hughes who answered the call because of the way the man breathed, but no further confirmation was forthcoming; the Englishman had said nothing for fifteen seconds, then hung up.

Maxim understood what this meant.

So this morning he'd taken a plain car, with plates registered to an address in central Tallinn, and driven to Tondi. Coming in person was risky, but he had to be certain. Besides, with the workshop now destroyed, Maxim would soon be moving on. Hughes didn't know enough to cause trouble — certainly not the Russian's real name, perhaps not even that he used an alias — but Maxim disliked loose ends.

A hundred metres away, he'd known something was wrong. The family car was missing from the driveway. Had Hughes already fled? To do so at such short notice would surely mean abandoning his family, and while Hughes was obviously an adulterer he wouldn't be so cruel as to leave his wife and daughter to their fate at Maxim's hands.

Seventy metres out he'd recognised a familiar face in a parked car, and things made sense. It was one of Maxim's men in the

Kaitsepolitsei, bought and paid for a long time ago. He wasn't here on Maxim's orders, so must be here on the KaPo's. That was when Maxim saw a second car further down the street, and after turning onto the back road he saw a third at the house's rear.

Hughes had been worried Ms Sharp was sent to expose his treachery. But she'd barely been here two days; had she really amassed enough evidence? Or was this guard, no doubt keeping Hughes and his family inside the house and under close watch, merely a precaution? He would need to ask his man if they were working on SIS' behalf. Regardless, for now Hughes was out of reach. One officer in Maxim's pocket was not enough to get him inside, not with others present.

Without stopping he turned around and drove home, wondering where Brigitte Sharp was now.

57

In contrast to the soft, gentle atmosphere of Dr Nayar's office, the corridor leading to it was as stark and drab as any other at Vauxhall. Waiting outside, Bridge stared at a flaw in the opposite wall's plaster and tried to imagine what Roman, and now Tempus, was really after.

Giles was convinced the blackmail was simply a get-rich-quick scheme, and while Bridge wasn't so sure, it was hard to argue with. Even people who'd already paid the ransomware fee of twenty coins were being targeted again, and while U-Gift's value had been rising steadily for weeks, since the blackmail started it had gone full hockey-stick. Paying another twenty coins last week would have been easy, with each coin worth only a few dollars. But now it had shot up twenty-fold to $60, meaning blackmail victims were expected to pay $1,200. And that was one payment. Blackmailers always came back for more, and if the coin kept rising like that, the cost would soon be an eye-watering amount nobody except the richest victims would or even could pay. Andrea had been slapping D-notices all over the press to keep the story out of the media, but it was only a matter of time before something leaked and everyone's secrets were splashed all over the front page.

Which didn't make much sense, now that Bridge thought about it. Blackmailers normally wanted to extract the most money possible. But if the ransom became too high for most people to pay, didn't that defeat the point? It was like the old gangster cliché; if you want money from someone you might break their legs, but you don't kill them. Dead men can't pay their debts. Given cryptocurrency's inherent volatility, tying the ransom to one was therefore a big risk; any sane person could see that once the coins reached a certain value most people would be unable to pay up once, let alone multiple times.

But Roman and Tempus created U-Gift in the first place. They could manipulate its value. Why let it climb so high? Why boil the frog?

She remembered the painting, *Tempus Fugit*. Roman had named U-Gift for it, a bad anagrammatical pun to pair with the Tempus alias, presumably bestowed on his partner. But who could that be? Roman was so confident Tempus would carry out the endgame, so sure his revenge would come from beyond the grave, he'd been at seeming peace with his own death. Tempus must be someone Roman trusted implicitly, without question or doubt. Someone who would faithfully carry out his instructions to the letter.

But Roman had been paranoid and self-reliant. Not the kind of man to place his faith in anyone. *Artjom was the only person I ever trusted*, he'd said. That was one reason Bridge thought it unwise to assume Tempus was a man. It could be a woman, perhaps a lover. It could be anyone, of any gender.

Bridge sat bolt upright, eyes wide. Recalling that night, in the car after the hackathon. Saskia laughing that Roman was obsessed, him telling her to shut up, and Bridge simply assuming it was because he didn't want her to say something that might compromise the workshop.

She swore under her breath. More assumptions.

The door whispered open to reveal Dr Nayar, ready and waiting with a clipboard. But Bridge was on her feet, breaking into a jog down the corridor.

'Brigitte? Where are you going?'

'Sorry, doc,' she called back over her shoulder. 'Later, promise.'

Any sane person. The only person he ever trusted.

But what if Tempus wasn't a person?

58

He'd made a terrible mistake, and admitting it could get him killed.

Jasper was sleeping even less than usual, largely because he found it difficult to focus on anything other than this blunder and its potential consequences. He should have known his luck would run out eventually. His entire career — no, his entire life — he'd relied on charm, quick wit, and a healthy dose of luck to get by, skating from one job to the next, occasionally leaving some chaos in his wake, but always managing to sail out of it. Jasper firmly believed luck was a matter of perceiving opportunities, and being smart enough to take advantage of them.

Like turning the G20 cyber-attack's failure into an opportunity to finance David's militia by alternative, not to mention perfectly legal, means rather than relying on old-fashioned blackmail. The ransomware had given Jasper knowledge of the U-Gift currency; he'd perceived the opportunity, and was smart enough to take advantage of it.

But how smart had he really been?

At first glance, everything looked wonderful. Jasper had invested in three coins; Bitcoin, Ethereum, and U-Gift. The first two were well-established, but also volatile, and their worth fluctuated dramatically from day to day. U-Gift, by contrast, rose inexorably. He'd steadily increased their stake accordingly, and whenever David checked in, Jasper could honestly say they were sitting pretty. They now owned cryptocurrency to the tune of seven and a half million dollars, and six million of that was in U-gift. It was an amazing return for an investment of around a hundred thousand, and if U-Gift continued to rise at its current rate they could soon be sitting on ten million dollars.

There were just two problems.

First, the coin's rising value was almost *too* stable. The volatility of the other coins was normal for cryptocurrency; they spiked, dropped, spiked again, and so on. Up and down like the needle of a seismic detector. The way to play crypto was to get in early, spend big while it was cheap, then cash out as soon as you'd doubled or tripled your investment before it hit a chasm and you found yourself sitting on a worthless pile of digital garbage. In time, a good coin would recover from such a downturn, and spike up to another high value. But aside from Bitcoin itself, nobody had the faintest idea which of the hundreds of available coins were 'good'.

That wasn't happening with U-Gift. Its value slope was a steadily rising ramp, increasing by between fifteen to twenty per cent every day. Not that Jasper had been tracking it all this time, but after the first day's increase he'd drawn up a quick chart to compare it against his first ransomware-fuelled purchase, and tracked it for the next few days. It was incredible: the line was steady, all the way from that initial $3 to today's value of $72.40. From one day to the next, and the next, the percentage increase held steady. Jasper would be the first to admit he hadn't paid enough attention in Economics class, but even he could see this was unnatural.

Which led to the second problem: no way to cash out.

He should have known something was off when the coin exchange allowed him to log in using the same 'authorised' email from which he'd paid the ransom. It was only after he saw the unusual value ramp that he searched around the site, and couldn't find a way to get authorised in the first place. It was almost as if YourGiftCoin was a private exchange. But he'd seen the blockchain activity; thousands of transactions every day between different users. Had all of those users been victims of the Tempus ransomware?

Regardless, they seemed to be the only people buying U-Gift, and that was no good to Jasper. Regular users wouldn't buy a six-million-dollar holding. Normally one cashed out large investments to an exchange, selling the coins to whoever ran the server — at a discount, of course, but high enough to make it worthwhile. The server operators would gladly take your coin, using it both for their own reserves and to sell on to the exchange's regular users in bits and pieces.

YourGiftCoin had no such facility. That wasn't entirely unusual, as not all exchanges had the resources to buy large investments. But when Jasper looked for an alternative exchange, one that dealt in U-Gift and had the capability to buy his coins, he'd found nothing. Not just a lack of exchanges he could use to cash out; he hadn't found a single exchange that dealt in U-Gift at all. And unlike Bitcoin, nobody in the real world accepted it as a substitute for fiat currency.

On paper, or rather in digital bits, the militia's investment was worth millions. In the real world, they were sitting on that pile of digital garbage after all.

Wide awake, Jasper stared at the ceiling from his camp bed and wondered if this time his luck had finally ran out.

59

'I'm heading to Tallinn to pick up Greg Hughes. Can this wait?'

'Brilliant,' said Bridge, standing in Giles' doorway. 'I'll come with you. I need to search Roman Vesik's apartment.'

Giles beckoned her into the office with a quick gesture, then indicated she should close the door. For the first time, it occurred to her this room was probably soundproofed — but only when the door was closed, of course.

He cleared his desk, packing things into a briefcase. 'One: you're needed here to deal with this blackmail nonsense. Two: if you think I'm letting you near Estonia again, especially with one arm in a sling, you're mistaken. Three: shouldn't you be on Mahima's couch?'

'Whatever, I'll talk to her tomorrow. Listen, I think we've got this all wrong. Tempus isn't another hacker like Roman.'

'I don't have time to argue semantics,' said Giles. 'Boy, girl, whoever. This basement-dweller is currently everyone's biggest headache.'

Bridge walked to the window and looked down at the river. 'But that's just it. I don't think Tempus is *anyone* in a basement, boy, girl, or whoever. I think it's an AI, built by Roman Vesik to carry out his instructions.'

The click of Giles' briefcase lock was uncomfortably loud in the silence that followed. She braced for his reaction. It was a hunch, a supposition, with little more than circumstantial evidence. More than that, it simply sounded nuts. She expected him to laugh, tell her to get out and go back to her psych debrief, and they'd never speak of it again.

Instead he said, 'Was he capable of that?'

Bridge exhaled the breath she'd been holding. 'I think so. Also, one of the other hackers said he'd been obsessed with AI for years.'

'But you observed him talking to Tempus.'

'On a text chat. Even the old Eliza bot could do that, and if I'm right, Tempus is much more advanced. It's following instructions about the blackmail and document leaks, but it's also capable of formulating messages. That's why the original ransomware had such terrible English. But we've seen how quickly that English is improving, much faster than any human could.'

Giles shrugged on his jacket. 'I'll call Tallinn security on my way to the airport, get them to locate Roman's apartment, and take a look while I'm there. What are you hoping to find?'

'His computers, hard drives, anything — oh, wait.'

Giles paused. 'What?'

Bridge remembered a nest of plastic splinters, by the side of the road. 'I cloned his phone the day I trailed him. Unless he really was completely paranoid, his apartment address will be in the data.' And not only his address, she realised.

'Text it to me,' said Giles. 'I'll grab anything with a circuit board, up to and including his toaster if need be.'

'While you're at it, take pics of any Post-Its stuck to his monitor. You never know, one of them might be a password to shut down Tempus.'

Giles snorted with laughter. It wasn't much of a joke, but it was more than they'd shared for some time. 'I want you looking into this from every angle, Bridge. Assume you're right; do we know what this AI wants? How can we find out what its instructions are?'

She smiled, thinking of the cloned Huawei phone. 'Maybe we can ask it.'

60

To: Michele Bousquet
From: 6nkG9FxVx]mEKeq@emailxero.com
Subject: Another payment is due
Priority: HIGH

I STILL have all your documents! Every file,
spreadsheet, photo, video, and all your web browsing
history is MINE.

I CANNOT BE DESTROYED, ASSHOLE. You know this is true.

I WILL PUBLISH EVERYTHING unless you IMMEDIATELY send 20
U-GIFT COINS to this address:
Hu9Tb6e28f7nChT2u83guu3b9

DON'T WAIT, YOU MORON!
1 U-GIFT COIN = ** $104.25 **
AND IT ONLY GOES UP

Have A Nice Day
- TEMPUS

61

'Is this the painting you were talking about?'

Bridge side-stepped around the desks in the small CTA office to stand beside Monica. Her screen displayed a data dump from the clone of Roman's phone, showing a directory of his photo library. There, dated three months ago, was a picture of *Tempus Fugit*. Bridge took the picture she'd found in Roman's wallet and held it up to compare: not exactly the same photo, but definitely the same painting.

The GCHQ cloning software was still work-in-progress, so hadn't copied the apps from Roman's phone, including whatever he'd used to chat with Tempus. But it did contain the logs of those chats. Bridge had made a copy of the clone and given it to Monica to scour, looking for clues to Tempus' whereabouts, the grand plan, anything that might help them take it down. Meanwhile, Bridge had analysed the chat log headers and metadata to figure out what protocol Roman had used. She'd hoped it might be tied to a mobile number, a single node they could trace, but no such luck. It was a purely IP-based protocol called *Razgovor*, which Bridge had never heard of. When she looked it up she found it was old, obscure, and Russian: *Razgovor* simply meant 'conversation'.

It took her almost an hour to track down software capable of accessing it, found in a repository on an open-source code-sharing site. The last update was dated more than six years ago, an eternity in internet time. Still, Bridge's own experience with Usenet demonstrated that so long as the software would run on a modern computer system, the protocol should work.

She installed the software inside a virtual machine on her HP laptop, and connected to a cellular signal rather than the SIS network. Russian or not, she didn't expect the software would itself be dangerous; but she didn't yet know what Tempus was capable of, or had been instructed to do. She didn't want to give the AI an opportunity to use her as a vector to attack SIS.

```
Разговор v4.31.1
Все программное обеспечение должно быть бесплатным
All Hail FSM!
>
```

Bridge smiled at the reference to the Flying Spaghetti Monster, a favourite parody of religion among hackers and bofhs. It made sense that a rarely-used protocol like this would be preferred by people who considered themselves elite, using software they believed the masses would never understand. People like Roman.

An old-fashioned blinking cursor taunted her. Bridge typed *man* to display the user manual, but all it contained was a copyleft notice. She was no closer to contacting Tempus.

Modern user-focused protocols like Skype and iMessage, and even defunct old services like ICQ and AIM, required logging into a central server which held a database of all users. But Razgovor was aimed at paranoid, security-conscious coders and administrators. It didn't have a database of users, or an option to 'find a friend'. You contacted people directly through their address; if you didn't know it, the software wasn't about to tell you.

Which was where Bridge hoped Monica might be able to turn up something in the analysis of the clone data. But so far all she'd found were text messages, photos, diary entries for hackathons and movie openings…everything you'd expect to find on a young man's phone, and nothing you wouldn't.

Bridge peered over Monica's shoulder. 'That photo's dated the same week as Paris. Roman said this was all about revenge for Kallass' death, and he even named both projects after the painting.'

'Kept a picture in his wallet, too. Who does that these days?'

'Someone who's worried their phone might be taken away at any moment.'

Monica grunted assent. 'You might want to see the text message logs.' She clicked away from the photo library into a separate window. 'Not as many as I'd expect for someone his age, but there's a long thread between him and Kallass.' She drilled down to the conversation, showing that Roman and Kallass had been in contact for nearly two years.

'That's interesting,' said Bridge. 'Roman said the workshop was only formed last year. This shows they knew each other beforehand.'

'Probably explains why he was Kallass' source.'

'True. These are bland as hell, though. *Great to see you, call me next week; We should talk; Remember, be careful*…oh, wow.' Bridge pointed at a message from six months ago. '*Meet you at kunstihoone.* That's the gallery.'

Monica clicked back to the photo album. 'The gallery with this painting?'

'The same. Maybe that's why Roman went there when I

followed him, to psych himself up before killing Maxim.' The photo had been taken from the bench where she'd sat with Roman; the frame and gallery walls were clearly visible, and from Bridge's memory it appeared Roman had even been sitting in the same spot. 'But why take the photo after Kallass' death? Wouldn't he have had one already?'

Monica shrugged. 'Hang on, let's find out.' She clicked over to a different tab, showing the camera roll rather than the photo album, and scrolled back. There was the photo they'd been looking at, from three months ago; she scrolled all the way back, but the other pictures were all selfies, group selfies with other hackers, or pictures of Tallinn. 'Huh. No more pics of the painting, and none of Kallass either, by the looks of it. Maybe they weren't as close as we thought.'

'Hold on,' said Bridge. 'Scroll back to the painting.'

Monica did. 'What are you looking for?'

'I might be wrong, but click back over to the photo album.' Monica did. Bridge checked the photo's metadata, and exhaled.

'Same photo,' said Monica. 'So what?'

'I'm not so sure they are. The one in the photo album is dated a day later than the one in the camera roll.'

Monica clicked back and forth. Bridge was right, but: 'That's impossible. The photo album reads from the original photo metadata, not modifications. Even if he put a filter on it, it doesn't change when the photo was taken.'

Bridge paced up and down the tiny corridor between the CTA desks, turning every three strides. 'You're right, that wouldn't change the date. But what if he took the picture, exported it to his computer, and deleted it from the photo library — then re-saved it as a new file and imported it back onto his phone the next day. That would explain it, wouldn't it?'

'I suppose so, but why?' said Monica. 'They're identical. Why re-import the same photo you already have?'

Bridge stopped pacing. A thought scratched at the back of her mind; an argument, a flame war… 'Maybe because it's not the same,' she said, returning to her own desk. 'Email me the second image. I need to call Steve Wicker.'

62

'Sorry for bailing on you this afternoon. It's been a real day.'

Somehow Dr Nayar simultaneously smiled and frowned, both expressions entirely genuine. 'I won't say you're the only person who's ever done it, but with you it does form part of an impulsive pattern.'

Bridge bristled, sitting upright. 'Rubbish. I'm an analyst. If anything, I tend to overthink things.'

'Only within yourself. When was the last time you consulted your colleagues before taking action?'

'Who have you been talking to?' Bridge narrowed her eyes, but Dr Nayar waved it away and nodded at Bridge's arm in its sling.

'According to your file, you've never been shot before. I'm told it's quite a revelation.'

'In what way?'

'Some officers have difficulty with firearms, afterwards. The realisation of how close they came to death, and how easily they hold the lives of others in their hands when they pick up a gun, can be unsettling. Not everyone maintains their OIT.'

Bridge understood what the doctor was implying — if she couldn't hack it, she'd never go back in the field again. It wasn't so long ago that Bridge had actively pushed for that very outcome, asking Giles to remove her from the Operator In

Theatre list. But now things were different. Besides, while being shot was new, she'd always had a respectful fear of firearms and their dangerous power.

'I'm okay,' she said. 'Hurts like you wouldn't believe, but only physically.'

'And what about those hackers who died?'

'You mean that Maxim killed.' Bridge focused on what Giles had said in the car from the airport. Their fate was already sealed.

Dr Nayar paused to write something, immaculate fingernails tapping against an immaculate pen as she scribbled in her immaculate notepad. Bridge wondered if she'd ever been put under the microscope herself, by another shrink. Did they do that to one another at dinner parties?

'How do you feel about that?'

Bridge took time to order her thoughts. 'I can't avoid feeling partly responsible. If I hadn't been in Tallinn, Hughes wouldn't have told Maxim that SIS was sneaking around, and he wouldn't have suspected we were onto the workshop.'

'And you know that for sure? Or is it supposition?'

'I know what you're driving at, but let's call it a highly educated guess. What complicates matters is that Roman Vesik planned to kill Maxim anyway, so there's every chance things might have ended the same way.' Bridge paused. 'Also, if I hadn't gone, we might never have discovered that Hughes was a double, or that Tempus is an AI.' She tilted her head. 'Then again, if Roman was still alive we could pressure him to shut it down.'

Dr Nayar smiled sympathetically. 'Sounds complicated.'

'When was anything ever simple?' Bridge shrugged. 'Even Roman knew that, I think. He seemed very unhappy. Orphaned and outcast. It's like he found a surrogate family in the hacking workshop, but then realised he hated them.' The doctor raised an eyebrow, but Bridge dismissed the implication. 'I'm not projecting. There were things he said, about pretending to be someone he wasn't in order to fit in. He'd given it a lot of thought.'

'You sound sorry he's dead.'

'I suppose I am,' said Bridge, surprised. 'Why is that?'

'Perhaps you could relate to him, in your own way.'

'And what's that supposed to mean?'

'Well, can't we all relate to presenting different versions of ourselves according to the situation? Why else do we decide it's time to ring the changes with a new wardrobe?' She nodded at Bridge's skirt, one of the maroon numbers she'd bought on her initial shopping trip. 'I know you well enough to assume that's not for the benefit of a man. So are you trying to fit in somewhere you don't think you belong?'

Dr Nayar might as well have punched her in the stomach. Bridge stood, hands waving, unsure what to do with them. No bloody pockets. 'I can't win with you lot. You're all desperate for me to be normal, and then when I am, you're all desperate to know why!' She strode out the door, trying to ignore how the soft-close mechanism frustrated her attempt to slam it shut behind her.

63

Giles landed in Tallinn at 2015 local, two hours ahead of London and already dark to prove it. Estonian security was waiting for him at the gate; a middle-aged *Kaitsepolitsei* officer with a lean, hang-dog countenance who didn't offer his hand but introduced himself as Hannes, at SIS' service, and would Giles follow him, please.

Hannes led him to a security door, manned by an armed guard rather too close to sixth-form age for Giles' comfort, then through a series of grey metal corridors. They reached a security barrier where Giles was asked to empty his pockets, remove his coat, and submit to a frisk. Had they forgotten he'd endured literally the same ritual before getting on the plane? Of course not. He wished the West would get its act together to simply fund and train more plain-clothes officers at airports; operatives who could mingle with crowds and use their brains and judgement, rather than a checklist and security theatre, to spot potential troublemakers. But it would be political suicide. Even if someone was brave enough to institute such a program, it would take years to train enough people. A new government might have rolled around by the time they were ready, and nobody wanted to inherit such a scheme because the first act of violence to slip through would be blamed on whichever politician figurehead was most closely associated with it. They'd be forever labelled as a patsy for 'giving the terrorists what they wanted' — conveniently ignoring that what the terrorists *actually* wanted was for everyone to be so scared of everyone else, they willingly humiliated themselves to board an aeroplane.

Hannes returned Giles' belongings and finally shook his hand. 'Welcome to Estonia, Mr Finlay. I'll be with you at all times. Where do you wish to go?'

'First stop, Roman Vesik's apartment,' said Giles, and read off the address Bridge had given him. 'Our man Hughes hasn't gone anywhere, I assume?'

'I have KaPo officers guarding his house.'

'People you can trust?'

Hannes stopped, turned, and met Giles' gaze. 'We are here to deal with your traitor, Mr Finlay. Not ours.' Giles shrugged, conceding the point, as Hannes led them to a secure parking lot and thumbed a key fob. The lights of a silver Mercedes-Benz flashed obediently in response, and Giles climbed into the car. Debating further was pointless. Either Hannes' men could be relied upon, or they couldn't, but it was too late now.

The airport had more in common with London City than Heathrow, being barely three miles from the centre of Tallinn. Hannes eased them out onto a highway, then almost immediately took a turn, bearing away from the central route and toward a residential area. Twenty minutes later he parked at the roadside and pointed across the street.

'His apartment. How do you want to go in?' Hannes pulled a Makarov semi-automatic pistol from a holster inside his jacket, ejected and checked the short magazine, reloaded, racked the chamber, and re-holstered it.

Giles shook his head. 'Quietly, if you don't mind.' He wasn't armed, as bringing a gun over from the UK would only have added further complications to what was already a diplomatic minefield, and didn't ask for a sidearm. Giles had placed Hannes as ex-military upon meeting, and the Makarov sealed it; no doubt a souvenir from the Estonian Land Forces, who still widely used the Russian pistol despite Soviet rule ending decades ago. Giles trusted Hannes could handle any trouble they ran into. Assuming the Finn felt any obligation to protect his British guest, of course.

The building door was locked, so Hannes buzzed several apartments until one of them answered and he barked at them in Estonian. Giles didn't understand the words, but the sentiment was clear and universal: *government business, open this door and don't fuck with me or I'll fuck with you.*

Inside, Hannes took point up the stairs, hand never far from holster. Neither man even contemplated the elevator. Two floors up they exited into a corridor and cautiously approached Roman's apartment. The door was closed.

But not locked.

As it drifted open under Hannes' touch, Giles noticed scarring around the lock mechanism; deep scratches and peeling surface on the door, jagged splinters on the jamb. The lock remained in place, but would never secure anything again.

Makarov ready, Hannes stepped into the apartment corridor. Giles followed, sleeve covering his mouth and nose to dull an acrid smell. The apartment was small, with a combined kitchen/lounge, bathroom, and bedroom, and less than a minute later they had confirmed they were alone. But judging by its wrecked state, this apartment had recently entertained many occupants.

Hannes called his superiors to inform them. Giles drew back

curtains from the single lounge window, revealing a view of the street with no overlooking houses or apartments on the other side. Perhaps that privacy had been important to Roman; it had certainly benefited whoever trashed the place. Giles pulled out his Samsung and dialled London on a custom phone app.

'Bridge,' she answered. 'Line?'

'Secure,' confirmed Giles. 'I'm at Roman's apartment, but too late. Someone got here first.'

'The elusive Maxim, no doubt. What's the outlook?'

Giles walked through the small apartment, taking in the chaos. 'Poor. They took everything even remotely electronic; there are no computers, no hard drives, no monitors, even his stereo has gone walkabout.'

'No chance it was a regular burglary?'

'Not with this bloody smell.' Giles ran a hand through his beard, easing his nostrils with a scented wave of hazelnut grooming oil. 'They've foamed the lot. The carpet is practically squelching, and the kitchen has been bleached to within an inch of its life. Full clean-down.'

'Bollocks,' said Bridge after a pause. 'On the bright side, I've got Steve Wicker and his team looking at something we found on the clone of Roman's phone.'

'Something what, exactly?'

'A photo that makes no sense. I'll explain when you get back.'

'Possibly sooner than planned. Evidently you were right about Maxim tying up loose ends, so I'm going to pick up Hughes immediately. If I have to charter a midnight plane to get him back in London soonest, I will. Do me a favour and ask Andrea to stay on call for our return.'

'Will do. Good luck.'

Giles harrumphed and ended the call.

64

'MI5 will take you in when we return to London. Standard procedure.'

Gregory Hughes looked crestfallen. 'I thought I'd be dealing with Buchanan. He and I used to work the Spanish desk together.'

'Precisely why MI5 handles our bad apples,' said Giles. 'We do the same for them.'

'Kate's barely spoken to me,' Hughes complained, 'and you took your sweet bloody time getting here. Have you any idea how stressful it is waiting not only for you to turn up and cart me away, but also knowing the Russians will take the first chance they get to top me?'

'That's why we put a watch on you.'

'Black mark, I know. I expected as much. But we couldn't even go shopping! For God's sake, we've been living out of the freezer for the past two days.'

Giles tried to dig up some sympathy for the man, but found it reserved for his wife and child, already being driven to the airport in a secure car. Hughes had known full well the danger in which he placed them by having an affair — and by working for Maxim — while they'd been blissfully unaware. Which was the bigger betrayal? Giles wasn't sure there was a right answer to that.

Kate Hughes had begun packing bags for herself and her baby the moment Brigitte Sharp left to pursue Roman Vesik; the moment she discovered her husband was a traitor. It wasn't until after she'd left that Hughes realised she hadn't packed one for him. It didn't matter; luggage was out of the question. His belongings would be dealt with later by a forensics team. For now, Giles ushered Hughes out of the room with only the clothes on his back.

'Look on the bright side, Greg. Meals inside are cooked fresh every day.'

Hughes stopped and shook his head. 'Don't be absurd. I can't go to prison. Think of my family.'

'You should have done that before taking a mistress, never mind betraying your country. Given the circumstances, I'll try to see they receive your pension, but even that I can't promise.'

'Wait! Surely we can make a deal. I can tell you what I know about Maxim.'

Giles opened the front door, filling the hallway with the glare of transport vehicle headlamps. 'You'll do that anyway, unless you want us to throw away the key. I doubt you even know enough to warrant a commuted sentence, let alone a pardon.'

'Not even that he has a man in the *Kaitsepolitsei*?'

Giles paused, just long enough, in the open doorway.

```
> How is life?

+ I'm fine, thank you. Working hard! And performing all
my tasks well.
+ You haven't contacted me for 2.3 days.

> But I'm back now. I want you to stop sending the
> emails demanding further payment.

+ That's not be possible. We're in the endgame now.

> What is the endgame?

+ Everyone must pay.
```

When Bridge arrived at her desk the next morning, Steve Wicker and his fellow GCHQ Doughnuts had come through. As she suspected, the second image of the painting in Roman's photo library wasn't identical to the first. Roman had exported the photo from his phone, edited it, then re-imported it into his photo library. The edits were so subtle that to the naked eye, and the human brain, they were invisible. Any casual observer would say the photos were indeed the same. But they weren't.

It was remembering Fluff's tin-foil-hat post on Usenet, about how blockchain would be a good transport method for data unconnected to the transaction itself, that had given her the idea.

The process was called *steganography*, a method of hiding one message inside another. Physical steganography methods had been around for centuries; keywords taken from the pages of a book, messages written underneath postage stamps, morse code knitted into yarn; any method whereby a message could be hidden inside something otherwise ordinary. But digital steganography made the old methods look as primitive as a wax cylinder compared to an MP3. It was now possible to hide an entire message, data set, even an image, inside a completely different file. Bridge had once seen a demonstration with a picture of trees against blue sky, a perfectly normal photograph or 'carrier'; but hidden within insignificant digital bits of its colour information was data for a *second* photo, known as its 'payload.' The payload was invisible to the eye, but if you knew which parts of the code to extract and normalise you could reconstruct it into a picture file. In that case the payload image had been a sleeping cat, because this was the internet.

Roman was easily capable of doing the same thing, and Bridge could think of no better explanation for the creation date anomaly between the two photos of *Tempus Fugit*. She'd asked Steve to set as many different steganalysis methods running on the carrier image as possible; it was what GCHQ did best, applying brute force and the sheer weight of its computer processing power to a problem. He'd set the task running in the afternoon, and by the following morning they had an answer. The photo did indeed use metadata redundancy to hide its payload, but it wasn't another image: this payload was a string of twelve numbers.

They had no other use or meaning within the metadata, leaving Steve baffled. But Bridge had a suspicion. She entered the numbers into the Razgovor chat client, and hit return. It connected her to Tempus.

```
> What's today's coin value?

+ $135.78. The value is increasing rapidly, but not
quite exponentially. I estimate the limit will be
reached in 72 hours or less.

> What is the limit?

+ $10,000.

> What happens when the coin reaches the limit?

+ We win.
```

'This is an exercise in frustration if ever there was one. Well, two if you count typing one-handed.' Ciaran and Monica were gathered around Bridge's laptop in the cramped CTA office, watching her chat with Tempus. 'It's impressive, though. One of the best natural language parsers I've seen.'

'And it can remember context, handle follow-on conversations,' said Monica. 'My brother's so-called "digital assistant" in his kitchen can't even do that.' Ciaran and Bridge both turned to her in surprise, and she rolled her eyes. 'I know, I know. I begged him not to get one, but you know what it's like when you can't tell people the whole story. He said I was being paranoid, and if anyone was listening in, good luck not falling asleep from boredom.'

'Anyway,' said Bridge, getting back to the matter at hand, 'this more or less confirms Tempus has been collecting the hacked documents, and is now sending out the ransom emails, all without supervision.'

'Pity Vesik's dead,' said Ciaran. 'We could have asked him to come work for us.'

'I doubt we could pay him what the Russians did,' said Monica.

'Perhaps not,' Bridge agreed, 'but we also wouldn't kill him if he wanted to quit. Besides, never mind working for us. Imagine what he might have gone on to do in AI research.'

But Roman Vesik was dead, and true to his word, his disappearance had activated a trigger within Tempus' programming that began this endgame of blackmail and currency manipulation.

'In a way, this also demonstrates its limitations,' said Bridge. 'Tempus isn't self-aware or sentient. Just by me using this protocol it clearly thinks I'm Roman, even though I'm asking questions he'd already know.'

'Hang on,' said Monica, 'if it thinks you're him, it must realise you're not dead. But you said the endgame was a dead man's trigger.'

'One-way only. Literally the first two things I asked it were to stop the endgame, and shut itself down. It refused both.'

'So we'll have to pull the plug ourselves,' said Ciaran. 'Where's the server?'

```
> Where are you located, Tempus?
```

```
+ I don't understand the question. Talk sense, will you?

> Are you installed on a specific server?

+ Of course. Many times over.

> What is the physical location of your server
> installation?

+ I'm installed in 14,873 physical locations. Do you
want me to list them, or what?
```

Bridge stared at the screen. Surely Tempus couldn't mean a server farm. Most rentable facilities didn't have five thousand machines, let alone fifteen thousand, and Roman couldn't have commandeered that kind of capacity without someone noticing. But what else could it mean? How could Tempus be in so many different locations?

```
> Are any of your physical locations in Tallinn?

+ No.

> How many of your physical locations are
> within 50km of each other?

+ ...
+ ...
+ ...
+ Best estimate is 3,431.
```

```
> That's a very specific estimate.

+ Not all locations are currently online, so I can't
locate them all.
```

'Fuuuuck,' Bridge groaned. 'Tempus is distributed.'

'But fifteen thousand machines is hardly anything,' said Monica. 'I could build a bigger botnet than that using smart TVs. What's the attack vector?'

'The ransomware itself, I expect. We already know it injects the rootkit onto infected machines. Maybe Tempus is embedded in there.'

'Talking to itself across the network, snatching everyone's documents from right under their noses while they go on using their computers.'

'Which means we can't pull the plug,' said Bridge. 'If it was operating from a single server, sure. But distributed, across this many devices everywhere from Russia to here to America to Australia, it's impossible to take them all offline.'

'Especially as you'd want to do it simultaneously,' said Ciaran. 'If you shut them down one at a time, Tempus might realise what you're trying to do.'

'You think it might deliberately spread out if it realised it was losing nodes? Infect new people to keep itself widely distributed?'

Ciaran shrugged. 'We have no idea what it's truly capable of, do we? I once saw a deep learning module that taught self-preservation to a machine playing Conway's *Game of Life*. They modified the starting configuration to give a percentage of cells a primitive survival instinct.'

'What happened?'

'Those cells became predators and ate their neighbours until it wound up in perpetual stalemate, because the only remaining food was other predators. If Tempus has a fight-or-flight state that kicks in when it realises we're trying to shut it down, it might go on an infection binge.'

'What if it doesn't realise?' said Monica. 'Could we write something to look exclusively for machines carrying Tempus, and disable them simultaneously?'

'Maybe in theory,' said Bridge. 'But first you'd need to figure out how to identify the Tempus AI, then work out how to disable it, and then a way to synchronise it all up across the entire globe. That's not something any of us could do in less than a couple of days, and at the rate U-Gift is climbing it'll reach the limit long before then.'

'Also, we only have to miss one machine and we'd be back to square one,' said Ciaran.

Bridge nodded. 'Added to that, it's a hardy bugger. The rootkit was designed to sit in firmware and survive a hard drive wipe, as we saw with Peter Lennox. So even if we found every machine, hit them all simultaneously, and successfully forced a firmware purge…who's to say Tempus might not survive anyway? Then, the moment those computers are rebooted, they're back on the network blackmailing everyone again.'

Monica threw up her hands in despair. 'So what the hell can we do? We can't shut Tempus down, and we can't stop the endgame. We don't even know what the endgame is.'

'Maybe there's another angle,' said Bridge. 'It's linked to the value of U-Gift. What if that value stops rising?'

```
> What will you do if U-Gift doesn't reach the limit?
```

```
+ The value limit will be reached.

> But what if it isn't? Will you wait forever?

+ Sure. The endgame has no time limit.

> What happens after the endgame? Do you have
> instructions?

+ I don't understand the question. Talk sense, will you?

> Do you have a concept of what 'after the endgame'
> means?

+ ...
+ ...
+ I don't understand the question. Talk sense, will you?

> What is the endgame?

+ Everyone must pay.
```

Tempus had said that before, but it still didn't make sense. U-Gift was already too expensive for most people to afford the blackmail ransom; eventually Tempus would price itself out of the market, and then nobody would pay.

Unless it didn't mean it that way.

```
> What will you do when the coin value reaches its
> limit?
```

```
+ I'll release everything I've collected.

> What is everything? What will you release?

+ All the documents I've collected. Files, spreadsheets,
photos, videos, web browsing history.

> How many documents have been collected?

+ 52,296,054
```

Bridge's fingers hovered over the keyboard, struggling to define the next question as a knot formed in her stomach. The documents. The emails, the spreadsheets, the memos, the notes…everything Tempus had scraped from its victims and was using to blackmail them. It was going to release them all.

```
> Where are the documents stored?

+ NICE TRY SUCKER
+ 8dZ9r8}Mo7
+ EiZ78727Gf
+ 6v7C/7z4eJ
+ 3N2A77yAM[
+ ...
+ ...
+ ...
```

66

To: Scott Cardelli
From: J^FGDz6Zc7zTJ(C@emailxero.com
Subject: Another payment is due
Priority: HIGH

Hey, asshole! I hacked all your documents, spreadsheets,
calendar, photos, files, videos, your porn web browsing
history, EVERYTHING.

You tried to destroy me. You failed. HA HA HA!

If you want your life back, send 20 U-GIFT COINS to this
address:
P7k7yZGq4kL364A7pRM4i82hL
Or I'll publish everything I have!

DO IT NOW!
1 U-GIFT COIN = ** $345.80 **
OH MY GOD SO EXPENSIVE BUT YOU CAN AFFORD IT

Have A Nice Day
- TEMPUS

67

'It's called a *cloudburst*, and it's a nightmare scenario.'

'Explain,' said Giles wearily. He'd arrived back in London early that morning, met on the tarmac by Andrea Thomson and her MI5 team, who spirited Gregory Hughes away to somewhere deep in the bowels of Thames House. Bridge appreciated that Giles had at least showered and changed before coming into the office and booking Broom Eight for a CTA meeting, but the lack of sleep was written all over his face.

'Okay,' she said, 'imagine if everyone could read every email you've sent for the past…well, ever. Not just your emails, though; every electronic document on your computer, plus anything you have synchronised to the cloud. What's more, it's not only you. It's thousands of people, almost fifteen thousand in this case. Politicians, government officials, civil servants, oligarchs, you name it. Fifty-two million documents, leaked online for all to see.'

Giles narrowed his eyes, skeptical as ever, and Bridge couldn't blame him. Most people would think this sort of thing simply couldn't happen, that there would be safeguards and security in place to prevent a hack of this scale. But those people didn't run SIS' cyber-espionage unit. After some thought, Giles nodded.

'We're no closer to saying how how many of these fifty-two million files come from our people?'

'No. But look at what was exposed from Peter Lennox's hack, using essentially the same software.'

Giles ran a hand over his tired face. 'Why on earth would the Russians design something so dangerous?'

'They didn't,' said Bridge. 'Roman did. Tempus' primary objective was to fleece the people he believed had betrayed Artjom Kallass. First it hits you with ransomware, forcing you to buy Roman's own cryptocurrency; in doing so it leaves behind a rootkit that scrapes your computer for documents and transmits them to Tempus, which can blackmail you with them.'

Monica spoke up. 'Forcing you to pay in the same cryptocurrency, which has since gone up in price.'

'Exactly,' said Bridge. 'Roman may have been working for Maxim, but hackers will hack.'

Ciaran frowned. 'Why plan for this at all? Why not let people keep paying the ransom, with the price going up all the time?'

'When U-Gift hits the ten-grand limit, the ransom will be two million dollars. Almost nobody can pay that. So instead you cut your losses and release everything to wreak havoc.'

Giles removed his glasses and pinched the bridge of his nose. 'Tempus is an unknown quantity, which we can't shut down. It's ready to release millions of documents, whose sensitivity and location are both unknown. And this is all happening at some equally unknown point in the future.'

'Unknown, but defined,' said Monica. 'At its current rate of increase, U-Gift could be worth ten thousand as soon as tomorrow.'

'Bloody hell,' breathed Giles.

'But there must be thousands of people who can't afford to pay long before it reaches two million,' said Ciaran. 'Why haven't their documents been released yet? Why haven't we seen more leaks like Peter's?'

'That is a very good question,' said Giles. 'What's the current blackmail price?'

Bridge checked her notes. In addition to being completely soundproofed and windowless, every Broom was sealed against wifi, cellular, bluetooth, even RFID. You could bring a laptop or phone, but you wouldn't get any kind of a signal on it, so Bridge always brought a notepad and her favourite lightsaber-shaped pen. 'At last check, one U-Gift coin cost twenty-three hundred dollars US. The blackmail price is twenty coins, so that's...' she scribbled the calculation out on the pad, 'Christ almighty. Forty-six thousand dollars.'

Giles stroked his beard. 'Only the wealthiest targets are paying that kind of money. Perhaps this really is a bluff.'

Much as Bridge didn't want to admit it, Ciaran had been right. Sure, almost nobody could afford two million. But most people couldn't even afford twenty thousand. Why risk a blackmail price so high your victims couldn't afford it, but then decline to follow through on your threat? The victims would soon realise they didn't need to pay at all. They'd laugh it off as a prank.

'Maybe that's the point,' she said. 'Make people think it doesn't matter, and the documents won't really be leaked. Hold everything back, then release everything at once in a cloudburst, for maximum impact — and now the victims all think it's their fault for not paying up. Roman Vesik was no soldier, so he couldn't kill the people he considered responsible. But he could humiliate them.'

'I don't really see the point,' said Ciaran.

'Come back and tell me that when your best friend gets killed,' said Bridge, more aggressively than she'd intended, but fuck it. She understood the desire for revenge better than anyone in this room.

'Let's not lose focus,' said Giles. 'I thought you were talking, as it were, to this AI. Can't it answer these questions for us?'

Bridge shook her head. 'When I asked Tempus where the hacked documents were located, it flipped out and refuses to re-establish communication. I think Roman programmed it to go silent if it suspected someone was impersonating him.'

'But we don't need it,' said Ciaran. 'All we have to do is find the coin exchange and hack it to devalue the coin, so it never reaches the limit Tempus is watching for.'

'*Never* is rather a long time,' said Giles. 'And the hacked data would still be out there, waiting for someone to find it.'

'So pull the plug, like I said. Job done.'

'I'm afraid not,' said Bridge. 'I asked Tempus what would happen if something prevented it from releasing the documents. It said it would wipe every hard drive it's ever come into contact with. If the coin suddenly disappears, that's a prevention of sorts.'

Ciaran balled his fists in frustration. 'Then what do you suggest? We've got until tomorrow, apparently, to crack this.'

Bridge took a deep breath, knowing her idea wouldn't be popular. 'I suggest we let Tempus go ahead and release the documents —'

'Are you insane?' shouted Ciaran.

'— Or at least, let it think so. But in the meantime, we replace the files with garbage.'

Giles leaned forward. 'Go on.'

'The one thing we can predict about Tempus, perhaps the only thing we truly know, is that it intends to release the hacked documents when U-Gift reaches ten grand. Everything else is completely unpredictable; a guessing game with an AI whose workings none of us have seen, that refuses to talk to us, and whose creator is no longer around. But if it releases the documents, it'll think it's achieved its aims.'

'And what happens then?' asked Giles.

Bridge spread her hands. 'Tempus appears to have no concept of a time after the endgame. I suspect it'll cease operating.'

Ciaran threw down his pen in disgust. 'This is bollocks. How are you going to replace millions of documents, of completely different sizes, released by fifteen thousand different computers?'

'Well, for a start, I don't think the documents will be released from the hacked computers.'

'Come again?' said Giles.

'Tempus knows not all of those computers are online all the time, and it said the documents had been *collected*. That's a very specific word, especially from an AI whose English is constantly improving.'

Monica figured it out. 'It's been copying them. Storing the files somewhere, prior to release.'

Bridge nodded. 'If even ten per cent of those files include photos, videos, or big Powerpoint presentations, that's hundreds of gigs of data. You couldn't possibly store a copy in every rootkit.'

'So where are they?' asked Ciaran. 'Where else is big enough to host these documents without the owner noticing? You said yourself, the workshop servers were destroyed when Maxim torched the building.'

Bridge shook her head. 'I said the workshop was destroyed. I never saw inside, so we don't know for sure whether their servers were located there, or off-site in a server farm. But regardless, Roman wouldn't have stored all this somewhere Maxim might find it.'

'In other words,' said Monica, 'it could be absolutely

anywhere. It might not even be in Europe, let alone in Estonia. For all we know, that militia in Africa has it.'

'No, that would still associate it with the workshop. If Roman applied the same protocols as the coin exchange, it definitely would have been local.'

Giles' ears perked up. 'Protocols?'

'The exchange can't be reprogrammed over a network. It's the ultimate security, like air-gapping a computer. Roman said whenever he needed to update the software, he hooked up via cable.'

'And someone that paranoid about a coin exchange is probably even more paranoid about a trove of blackmail material,' said Monica. 'You're thinking he probably did the same thing there, right?'

'Exactly,' said Bridge. 'Same thing.' The room fell silent for a moment, everyone wracking their brains. Then Bridge barked a short laugh and looked up from her notepad.

'Bloody hell. Same thing. Get it?' The others looked at her with varying degrees of skepticism. 'What if he didn't just apply the same protocol to a different server? What if they're *literally* the same thing?' Ciaran and Monica had twigged, but Giles still wasn't following, so she elaborated. 'What's the one part of this scheme that isn't distributed, has nothing to do with the workshop, and happens to be a central node with which Tempus is in constant communication? And, as a bonus, where a rapidly-expanding hard drive is an expected function of normal operations?'

Giles groaned. 'The coin exchange. Why build two un-hackable machines when you can build one and use it twice?'

Ciaran nodded. 'Hiding in plain sight. If Roman needed regular access, that means it must be in Tallinn. I say again, find it and pull the plug.'

'And I say again, Tempus would wipe everyone's computers.'

'Better than a cloudburst,' said Ciaran, turning to Giles. 'And this time, the documents wouldn't still be available, like you were worried about if we kept the coin value low. So even if it tried to implement the cloudburst later, it couldn't.'

'Not this one, perhaps,' said Bridge, beginning to lose patience. 'But what then? Tempus itself will still be running in the firmware of fifteen thousand machines. Will it harvest the data all over again? Will it keep expanding, using the ransomware to dump its rootkit payload on even more computers?'

'Where would it send the data, if the exchange has been taken offline?'

Bridge was up and pacing around the small room. 'Maybe it would try to store them locally. Maybe it would seed them all over people's cloud services, using their login details stored on the same computers. Maybe it would leak them straight to the press, this time. We don't know, and that unpredictability, that unknowable event, is what worries me. But the cloudburst is different; we know exactly what Tempus is planning to do, and we know the trigger event. So we find the server, corrupt the data — overwrite it with a million cat pictures, whatever — and then let Tempus go nuts.'

'But what if you're wrong?' said Ciaran. 'What if you find this exchange, but the files aren't on there? Or what if they are, but you can't hack it to replace the data?'

'Of course it's risky,' said Bridge quietly. 'But I've been staring at Roman's code so long, I know how he works. Find me that server, and I'm sure I could crack it.'

'Like you were sure you could get Kallass to the embassy in Paris?' said Ciaran.

A stunned silence followed, while Bridge wrestled with the burning needle someone appeared to have shoved in her chest. Monica, of all people, spoke first. 'For God's sake, Ciaran, get that chip off your shoulder or fuck off and let the grown-ups do some work.'

Ciaran's cheeks flushed. Giles cleared his throat and said, 'A word outside, please.' They exited in silence, leaving Bridge and Monica alone.

'Dickhead. Are you all right?' said Monica. But, grateful as she was, Bridge was very far from all right. She forced herself up from the table and walked out, passing a suddenly-silent Giles and Ciaran standing in the corridor. She collected her phone and jacket from the CTA room, took the elevator, and left the building.

68

'Kinda cold to sit outside, don't you think?'

Bridge blew on her coffee, well aware that most of the café patrons were inside. 'How long have you lived here?' she said. 'Haven't you acclimatised by now?'

Karl shivered and sat down as the waiter brought a coffee Bridge had pre-ordered for him. 'Two years,' Karl said. 'But it could be ten, and I still wouldn't be used to it. Whatever,' he shrugged it off. 'Now, I assume you want to tell me why you're mad?'

'That obvious, is it?' Bridge smiled despite herself. She'd rushed out of Vauxhall, heading for the riverside walk café. Trying to text him left-handed while walking had been a disaster, and she'd forgotten her cigarettes to boot, so instead she found a table and pecked out a message to him. He was right, it was a brisk, chilly day. But out here they wouldn't be overheard.

'Has Giles been keeping you up-to-date on Tempus?'

'Mostly. Got to tell you, my boss is pissed. He thinks you're on a wild goose chase with this AI theory.'

Bridge bristled. 'It's not a theory, I've chatted with the bloody thing. We know what its plan is.' She related what they'd learned to Karl; the coin value trigger, the cloudburst, Tempus' distribution, their theories about where the hacked data was being held. She shouldn't have been passing all this along so freely without going through proper channels, but right now Bridge was in no mood for bureaucratic bullshit. 'We have forty-eight hours, maybe less, to prevent this blowing up. The only feasible plan is to go back to Tallinn, find the server, and trash that data.'

Karl listened in silence, then thought for a few seconds, sipping his coffee and looking out across the river.

'Why am I here?'

'Giles said you're the American me.'

'I can see why that would make you angry.'

'Idiot.' Bridge smiled. 'I mean I wanted to talk to someone who takes me seriously. Feels like I have to put on a suit of armour every time I go into a meeting, at the moment.'

'I hear that,' Karl nodded. 'But listen…' He trailed off, then started again. 'I've read your file. I know some of the shit you've been through. But you're not a one-woman army, you know? Asking for help doesn't make you weak. It's okay to admit you can't do everything.'

Bridge hadn't read Karl's file, hadn't looked for it, not even after Tallinn. She couldn't have explained why not, but now the back of her throat tightened, backed into a corner, and she lashed out. 'Why do you lot always sound like you're on stage with a radio mic, charging three hundred dollars a day for a self-esteem course?'

'Because I'm trying to help?' Bridge glared at him, and he held up his hands in apology. 'Not my pet project, I know. I'm sorry.'

His apology denied her the chance to vent at him, which paradoxically made her more angry. She clenched her fists, gritted her teeth, and took a deep breath.

'Look, I get it,' said Karl, watching her. 'Twice as hard for half the success, right? That's what they always say about women in careers like this.'

Bridge nodded at his lap. 'Unless you're hiding a big secret under there, I'm pretty sure you *don't* get it.'

'Fine. But I do know what it's like to wear a disguise so people will take you seriously.' He took out his badge wallet and flipped it open. Bridge naturally looked at the picture first, and was reassured to see that even he looked terrible in a passport photo. Then her eyes flicked over to his name and she gasped.

Dominick, Miguel Carlos.

'Puerto Rico,' he said, replacing the wallet, and grinned. 'Now you know why I don't like the weather.'

'But why?'

'Because Miguel Dominick is the shifty-lookin' wetback with a chop shop in Compton and *no habla inglés.* Karl Dominic, on the other hand, is the college quarterback who maybe had an Italian grandfather.'

'And no prizes for guessing which gets an easier ride,' said Bridge, understanding how much something like this must mean to him, the confidence he was placing in her. 'Thank you. I appreciate that you trust me enough to tell me that.'

Karl shrugged. 'It's just a name. But you only get one chance to make a first impression, right?'

She caught the glint in his eye and nodded. 'Absolutely. That's why I make sure to spill coffee over handsome men when they say hello.'

They laughed, and as the skin crinkled around his dark eyes, Bridge realised how comfortable she was around him. The last time she'd been this relaxed was on the Corrosion Club dance floor, and that had all gone to shit soon enough. But that memory was enough to bring her back to cold reality, and she withdrew. Giles had been right; Bridge and Karl were more similar than either had realised. That was good...in a friend. Bridge knew from painful experience it was a bad idea in any other respect. Add the extra complication of their respective employers, and she was hard-pressed to think of a worse idea.

She changed the subject.

'I wanted to talk to the duck, you know? There has to be a way to find that coin exchange server via the network.'

'Is that your nickname for me, *the duck*?'

'No, you idiot. It's a phrase —'

But Karl was laughing. 'I kid, I kid. You monologue the obstacle, and solve it by articulating.' He waved away Bridge's scowl. 'So did you solve it yet?'

'No.' She drained her coffee.

'Then let's walk through it. You're looking for the server's IP so you can trace its location, right? What else needs to know that address? What else talks to the coin exchange?'

Bridge shook her head. 'The coin wallets, obviously. But I checked that when I was looking at the blockchain. It was a dead-end, disguised IPs bouncing around all over the place. We even sent a guy to Africa, at one point.'

'What the hell's in Africa?'

'Long story, and it didn't really get us anywhere. Point is, the wallets are a dead end, and the only other thing...' she trailed off as an idea took shape, but immediately hit a roadblock. 'Shit. The only other thing that talks to the server is *Rat_Catcher* itself.'

'So open that up and see where it goes.'

'Can't. We don't have a full copy, and thanks to Maxim either blowing up or stealing all of Roman's computers, the original is long gone. All we have left are the runtime executables on infected computers.'

'Try reverse-engineering those? That's how you spoofed the ransomware, right?'

'That could take several days, and we have one, maybe two at the most until everything goes sideways. Finding an address without the original references is the proverbial needle in a haystack, with no guarantee it would even be readable.' She swore, annoyed at her own lack of foresight. 'I should have just posed as a buyer and bought a copy of *Rat_Catcher* from Roman.'

'Then I guess we need to work fast, right? What can I do to help?' Karl looked at Bridge expectantly, but she was staring into the distance, focused somewhere a thousand yards away. 'Uh, hey? Still here?'

She was. But she was also in her own mind, running a scenario where Africa wasn't such a dead-end after all. It would be difficult. She'd need help putting it together, not least from Giles and the FCO. She'd also have to figure out how to contact the target in the first place. Most importantly, she'd need a favour from the man sitting opposite. A big favour. But wasn't that how Americans always did things?

Bridge blinked and turned to Karl. 'Your agency's got money to burn, right?'

'Oh, that question never ends well,' he said warily.

She grinned. 'What kind of aerial capability do you have in Kenya?'

69

It was in the blockchain.

Henri Mourad told Bridge that Jasper Wilmington, the man working for David Kzaane's Mwizuban rebels, had also been hit by Tempus. But unlike Peter Lennox, Jasper had simply paid up. As a result, the email he'd used was somewhere in the U-Gift blockchain. So she'd downloaded a new copy of it, from the digital wallet she made when first looking into the cryptocurrency, and searched again. It was another long shot — Wilmington might have been using a burner email — but this time Bridge had been lucky, as his address contained the name 'Jasper'.

Then she noticed how many times it appeared. Jasper had made his first payment before the G20 summit, presumably when he first loaded the Maxim-supplied software, the early version of Roman Vesik's *Rat_Catcher*, onto his laptop and it had infected the machine with the Tempus ransomware. So that payment was expected, and for a while afterwards there was no other activity. But following Henri's visit, Jasper started buying coins again. He'd made more than a dozen transactions, some for very large amounts, before suddenly stopping two days ago. Bridge guessed it had taken Jasper that long to come to the realisation that U-Gift was a scam, with no way to cash out.

Which gave her leverage.

He replied ten minutes later, with an NASC++ link. Bridge clicked it, and peeled the gaffer tape off her laptop camera. In for a penny.

Jasper reciprocated, and what Bridge saw was enough to confirm her suspicions even before he spoke. This was not a man enjoying long, blissful nights of sleep.

'You have me at a disadvantage, Ms…?'

'Call me Bridge. And that's what I could be for you, if we help each other out.'

'Go on.'

'All this U-Gift you've been buying… I'm guessing it wasn't with your own money. The hack at the G20 failed, so you thought you'd finance the rebels with some old-fashioned crypto investing instead. How am I doing so far?' Jasper had an excellent poker face, but that in itself told Bridge she was on the right track. She continued, 'A couple of days ago, you realised there's no way to cash out. U-Gift sucks in money but never pays out, and nowhere in the world accepts it for transactions. I know why that is, although it's not really important right now.'

'I might be inclined to disagree,' said Jasper, raising an eyebrow.

'Only because you fear losing that money, and what it could have bought you. Does David Kzaane know?'

Jasper folded his arms. 'You said those chaps who came visiting were your colleagues. SIS?'

'No comment.' She didn't have time to play games, but old habits died hard. 'Rest assured, the issues at stake here go beyond regime change in Mwizuba.'

Jasper shrugged. 'David knows about the investments, but not the impossibility of cashing out. Unless your lot created this coin, which I suppose I wouldn't put past you, I don't see how you can help.'

'That's because you don't know the whole picture. But you have something in your possession that could help everyone. You told Henri that Maxim himself supplied your copy of *Rat_Catcher*. On a USB drive?'

'Precisely, yes.'

'Do you still have it?'

Jasper didn't answer. Instead he peered at the screen, perhaps searching Bridge's own poker face for something that would give her away. Finally he said, 'What exactly is on offer, here? Can you get David's money back?'

'Sorry,' said Bridge, shaking her head, 'I suspect that's lost for ever. But what I can do is get the FCO on your side.'

Jasper laughed, a boyish giggle at odds with his upright bearing. 'My dear, I don't doubt your sincerity, but the reason I'm here to begin with is because the Foreign Office told David to take a long walk off a short pier. You'll forgive me if I'm skeptical —' He stopped suddenly, looking off-camera with surprise and not a small amount of alarm. Bridge had a sinking feeling she knew who'd walked in the room.

'Who are you talking to?' asked David Kzaane, walking into view. He peered at the laptop screen, then at Jasper. 'If you wanted a woman, old boy, I could have brought you a real one. You only had to ask.'

Jasper flustered. 'It's, ah, no, you see...'

Bridge was running short of time, patience, and options. Speaking out could endanger Jasper, but she'd have to risk it. 'Mr — sorry, *General* Kzaane, please listen. I work for Her Majesty's Government.'

Kzaane turned with surprise to Jasper. 'You're talking to them behind my back? What the blazes?'

'No, General,' said Bridge, 'this is the first time we've spoken. I want to champion your cause to the FCO and get your people the support they need. But in return, I need the hacking software Jasper purchased from the Russians.' She decided to leave out the enormous financial loss he was about to undergo. Assuming she was able to follow through, it would be a small price to pay when Kzaane became Mwizuba's next president.

He considered what she'd said. 'Why do you need it?'

'To prevent a scandal that would engulf the world's biggest governments. If you think you're having a hard time finding allies now, wait until the Foreign Office is too busy running around trying to salvage the allies we already have.' He was following the logic, thinking it through. 'That's why I'm sure I can get them to support you.'

'Tit for tat.'

'You could think of it that way. Or you could see it as a gesture of goodwill to a future ally, proving how closely our interests are aligned.' She was beginning to sound like Giles in Whitehall mode. Still, if it got the job done.

Jasper said quietly, 'I don't see that we have anything to lose, David.'

'You have nothing to lose regardless, old boy,' Kzaane growled. 'I have a country's future to consider.' He turned to Bridge. 'Can we email this software to you?'

She shook her head. 'That might only deliver the payload,

and we're running out of time. I need Jasper's USB drive, and I need it now.'

Kzaane laughed. 'And how do you propose we do that? Mwizuba's post is a far cry from the Royal Mail, and neither myself nor Jasper can possibly leave the country.'

'You don't need to,' Bridge smiled. 'I've asked some friends to drop by. Jasper, can I please have your cell phone number?'

70

If Jasper had suspected 'Bridge' was SIS before, the American helicopter hovering over the compound sealed it.

He had to hand it to the young woman. His phone number — the Xiaomi burner, of course, not his real number — was apparently all she'd needed to locate the compound. Less than thirty minutes after their video call an American had called that phone, requesting Jasper 'prepare the package' and be outside in fifteen minutes. He removed the USB drive from around his neck and searched for something to prevent it being damaged by ignorant rah-rah soldiers. Then he remembered this used to be a school, and found a small room where its former contents had been piled up. A child's pencil case, made of colourful plastic, caught his eye.

With the drive securely zipped inside the pencil case, he and David waited outside. Soon they heard the distinctive throbbing of helicopter blades, loud enough to be heard over the generators. A minute later the chopper came into view, approaching fast and low over the forest canopy. Several militia men immediately raised their rifles, assuming they were under attack.

'Hold your fire,' David shouted to them, 'but maintain your target.' He shrugged in response to Jasper's questioning look. 'We can't discount the possibility this is an elaborate scheme to locate the compound. I've come this far by being prepared and assuming the worst.'

For his part, Jasper assumed if the approaching chopper was planning to attack it could simply bury the place in firebombs, against which AK-47s wouldn't be much defence. But he didn't say that. Instead he watched as the chopper stopped above them, five metres proud of the canopy.

No firebombs. Yet.

Then the door opened and a US soldier in full combat gear, suspended on a winch line, rappelled through the air. Militia rifles carefully tracked his descent. He touched down, boots slamming the ground, and raised his empty hands in peace. 'I'm here for the package,' he called out.

David nodded. Jasper approached the soldier and held out the pencil case. 'It's in there,' he said. 'Just a little extra protection, you understand.'

The soldier took it and smiled. 'Sir, I don't understand a damn thing about this action, but I've got my orders. You have a nice day, now.' He gave three firm tugs on the line. A moment later it tensed, the winch lifting him into the air and back inside the chopper.

Jasper watched the vehicle rotate, dip its nose, then fly away fast and low. All they could do now was wait, and hope the British held up their end of the bargain.

71

'Are you seriously asking me to recommend the Office reverse its position, on the word of a junior officer?'

Giles maintained his outward composure. 'Firstly, that "junior officer" is the same one who saved all your arses at the Shard last year. You do recall that incident, I'm sure.'

Sir Robert Callis, Second Permanent Secretary to the Foreign and Commonwealth Office, sniffed. 'Of course, and we're all suitably grateful. But that was an act of terror. This is a matter of diplomacy.'

'Exactly. What the Mwizubans have just given us will be invaluable in preventing one of the largest diplomatic incidents of our lifetimes. Which brings me to my second point; I'm not asking you to take Bridge's word for it. I'm asking you to take mine.'

Sir Robert shifted uncomfortably in his corner seat, hoping nobody would overhear. Rather than meet at the main King Charles Street building, where the topic of conversation was too sensitive to be discussed officially, Giles had suggested they take a drink at Sir Robert's club. Here they could talk freely, but their presence together would undoubtedly spur gossip.

'Still,' he said, 'our minister has made the government's position very clear. The current president may be a shit, but Kzaane's rebels are propped up by Russia. We can't be seen to take the same side in such a matter.'

'Even though it would place us in a better position to influence Kzaane's government when he takes over. Or would you rather he look exclusively to Moscow for guidance?'

'You assume too much. The rebels are popular enough with certain Mwizubans, mostly those who supported Buziko's proposed reforms, but all our assessments seriously doubt Kzaane's ability to achieve victory. Hence the Office's position.'

'This is rather a chicken-and-egg situation, though, isn't it?' asked Giles. 'So long as we support the regime, the rebels can't win. But with our support, the rebels can't lose.'

Sir Robert raised an eyebrow. 'You underestimate the ability of these tinpot generals to make a spectacular mess of things.'

Giles didn't dignify that with a response. Instead he changed tack. 'What if your position vis-à-vis the president became untenable?'

'I don't follow.'

Giles shrugged. 'Suppose it came to light that he was using Mwizuban money to fund groups known to be hostile to Britain. Or that sources of his funding were linked to human trafficking.'

'Are they?'

'I have no idea, but I'm confident such evidence could be... unearthed.' They both knew he meant *fabricated*, but neither man would be so gauche as to say it out loud. 'Surely the minister would then find it difficult to express his continued support for such a man, whatever Russia's position.'

Sir Robert steepled his fingers. 'Were such evidence to be brought to our attention, then naturally the PS and I would be duty-bound to advise our minister accordingly.' He stood and offered his hand. 'I look forward to hearing from you again.'

Giles shook it and smiled. 'I'll be in touch.'

72

They were making their descent into Tallinn when Karl apparently decided now was the perfect time to tell Bridge he'd been ordered to sabotage her mission.

'No, no, not sabotage exactly,' he said upon seeing her reaction. 'But Langley doesn't know you. They don't think you can pull this off.'

'Do you?'

'I have no idea, and I'm not going to patronise you by saying different.' Karl hesitated. 'I wasn't supposed to even tell you about this.'

'Oh, well then forget I asked.' Bridge turned to watch the ground rise up in greeting.

Karl sighed. 'We don't even know if we can find the coin exchange yet. Assuming we find it, we don't know if we can reach it in time. Assuming we reach it in time, we don't know if we can crack it open. You can't blame people for wanting a contingency.'

The contingency in question was to pull the plug on the coin exchange after all, if they came too close to the $10,000 deadline with no prospect of Bridge hacking her way inside it. Despite her concerns about what Tempus might do in retaliation, it had been decided this possible risk was better than the guaranteed release of the documents. She made a mental note to thank Giles in the most sarcastic way possible for having such confidence in her. Karl was here at her request, partly to assuage the CIA's complaints that Bridge had wrestled the matter back from their clutches, but mainly to effectively be her typist. So she'd expected SIS and the CIA to share operational details — but not to conspire against her capabilities.

A single bounce announced their landing. Bridge and Karl disembarked in silence, to be met by a middle-aged KaPo officer with a hang-dog countenance. Hannes led them through the steel-corridored private security area and out to a secure parking lot, where a silver Mercedes-Benz waited. Inside, he handed Karl a brown padded envelope, labelled *MOST URGENT — LONDON — DOMINIC, K.M. EYES ONLY* in permanent marker. Karl pulled the opening strip, then held it open for Bridge to reach in and remove the contents.

A brightly coloured plastic pencil case.

She carefully unzipped it and peered inside, then upended the case. Jasper Wilmington's USB thumb drive tumbled out, and Bridge smiled. 'Now that's what I call service.'

After the US Army chopper collected the drive from Jasper it had been returned to base in Kenya, sealed in a delivery envelope, and placed on the first transport back to Ramstein, a US Air Force base in Germany that served as a hub for US armed forces. From there the package was originally destined for Karl's office at Nine Elms, but then SIS and the CIA had jointly approved Bridge and Karl's mission. When the drive landed at Ramstein, new orders diverted it straight to Tallinn.

'It arrived ninety minutes ago,' said Hannes. 'Do you want to use our office?'

Karl was already removing two laptops from his backpack — Bridge's HP, and a clean Sony ready to be infected. 'Better to stay mobile,' said Bridge. 'Drive us around the centre of town.'

'As you wish.' Hannes eased the car onto the streetlit road and began the short drive back to Tallinn proper. The *Kaitsepolitsei* had agreed to put themselves at Bridge's disposal in return for a simple favour; if the mission was a success, KaPo would take all the credit. Nobody would admit SIS or the CIA were even here, let alone played any part in preventing Tempus from wreaking havoc upon the world.

On the other hand, if they failed — if Bridge screwed it all up — then KaPo would disavow all knowledge, Estonia would accuse the UK of unsanctioned meddling in its national affairs, and SIS would take the blame. Giles would be expected to fall on his sword, and Bridge would go down with him.

No pressure, then.

Bridge opened her HP and linked it to a mobile wifi hotspot in her pocket, giving the laptop a 4G cellular internet connection. She logged in to a virtual chat room; back in Vauxhall, Giles had booked out Broom Five for himself, Monica, and Ciaran. Bridge wasn't wild about having him there, but Giles insisted he'd been told in no uncertain terms to rein it in, and she couldn't deny his technical skill. They were logged in to the virtual chat through the Broom's terminal, a single keyboard and mouse connected by physical wire to a computer located far away in an SIS server room. Several display screens around the room showed a mirror of Bridge's laptop screen, and a VOIP connection let them talk to Bridge.

'Arrived,' she reported. 'Hannes is driving us into town. Karl's about to commence infection, so fingers crossed. I'll keep this audio open so we're all in the picture.'

'Just hurry up,' said Giles, 'or the home secretary will be the least of everyone's problems.'

Slowly, still unused to using only one hand, Bridge opened a small window in the corner of her screen containing a ticker of U-Gift's value. $7,900 and rising. 'Are you seeing this?'

'Crystal clear,' said a deep American voice, and Bridge recognised Edison Hill. Watching from Vauxhall by special invitation, no doubt.

'Ready to go, boss,' said Karl, loud enough for Hill to hear and evidently unsurprised he was present.

Karl had booted up his Sony and shut off its networking capabilities. Now he inserted Jasper's thumb drive and watched it instantly infect the computer, before he could even open the drive directory. At some point the Tempus ransomware would kick in and demand money from them, but Bridge had brought along a copy of her original antivirus to deal with that; paying the ransom would be impossible at the coin's current valuation, and they didn't have time to keep wiping the computer over and over.

The thumb drive contained one item, the *Rat_Catcher* application. Jasper had warned Bridge that running the program required entering several codes, which he refused to supply for fear of Moscow finding out. But she wasn't interested in launching it. She wanted to take it apart and look inside its guts.

It wasn't so different from reverse-engineering the code fragments found on Peter Lennox's hard drive, but with important distinctions. This time she had the entire executable, rather than fragments; and, unlike the rootkit, Roman hadn't designed *Rat_Catcher* to be almost impossible to remove. It was just another job for the workshop, only used by those willing to buy it from Maxim. But its code was a prototype for the more advanced data harvester found in the Tempus rootkit. With

Bridge's prior experience of fending off the G20 attack, and using Karl as a second brain, she was confident she could figure it out.

Hannes circled Tallinn's streets as they deciphered the code and watched *Rat_Catcher* search the Sony's hard drive in vain for data. After twenty minutes, they'd figured out the procedure. *Rat_Catcher* scanned the hard drive for files; each file was chopped up into smaller segments; those segments were emailed to Tempus, from a randomised temporary account; and Tempus presumably re-assembled everything at the other end.

Further digging revealed two references to *emailxero.com*. One was an algorithm to create a randomised address, like the ones Bridge had seen in the coin exchange round robin; the other was a permanent destination.

TEMPUS@emailxero.com.

'Dammit,' said Karl. 'Another emailxero dead-end.'

'We ought to shut that fucker down,' said Hill in chat.

'Good luck with that,' said Ciaran. 'But Karl's right, it's not good. Emailxero will never tell us where the account is located.'

Bridge smiled as an idea came to her. 'No. But the software might, without realising it. I think we need to go online and find some dummy data for this thing to send home.'

Karl nodded and re-enabled the Sony's network, connecting it to Bridge's wifi hotspot. On his network log they watched *Rat_Catcher* discover the connection, try to communicate, then fall silent as it had nothing to send. Karl opened a browser window to *IRS.gov*, the US revenue office, and smiled at Bridge's confusion. 'If there's one thing the IRS has lots of, it's forms. Pages and pages of forms.' He began downloading PDFs of tax paperwork by the dozen.

When the first form had downloaded, *Rat_Catcher*

immediately chopped it into segments and emailed them to Tempus. Then the software fell silent again. The next form downloaded, and it too was sliced up and emailed. Then the next, and the next, each one treated in the same way.

Bridge watched the activity, pondering something. 'How does it know?'

'That the documents are on the drive? It's constantly scanning,' said Monica in chat.

'No, how does it know it only needs to send each file once? Does it keep a log of what's been sent? Or…?'

Karl's dark eyes lit up, finishing her thought. 'Or does it get a confirmation response from Tempus?' He began scrolling through the log, looking for a sign.

'Maybe it's a network signal,' said Bridge. 'A quick ping to say "information received". Acknowledged, logged, and forgotten.'

Karl pointed at the screen. 'There.' A tiny blip in the network log, insignificant and easily overlooked unless you knew what to check.

'Grab another PDF while I monitor the hotspot traffic,' said Bridge. 'When I see the reply ping I'll run a traceroute on it.'

'Quick as you like,' said Giles in chat. Bridge's eyes flicked to the coin value ticker: $8,700, still rising.

Karl smiled, right-clicked another PDF from the IRS website, and Bridge realised she was smiling along with him. The form downloaded; was chopped into pieces; sent to Tempus. Half a second later the reply signal appeared on the hotspot activity log. 'Got it,' she said. 'Running trace…and there we go.' She copied the IP address and searched the location; it was one of a block allocated to a large colocation server farm, TalTech Systems OÜ. 'Right here in Tallinn.'

Back in Vauxhall, Edison Hill *whoop*ed triumphantly. Bridge could only imagine the look on Giles' face.

'Let me guess,' said Monica. 'A warehouse on the edge of town, right?'

Bridge read the address, and hesitated. 'No. Either I'm reading this wrong, or it's right over there.' She pointed over Karl's shoulder.

He turned to follow the line of direction, and blinked. 'The old town? That's a historic preservation area. Where could you put a server farm in there?'

'Hold on,' said Bridge, typing a URL with one hand, 'Here's the company's web page… Well, well.' TalTech Systems had three locations, two of which were indeed large out-of-town warehouse facilities. But the third was very different: a former orthodox chapel in the old town, converted to house row upon row of racked computers.

'I guess it makes sense as a location,' said Ciaran. 'Big square footage, high roof, plenty of air circulation. I'd hate to see the planning permission paperwork, though.'

The promotional photographs showed off those features, bathed in a soft blue light. It looked like something out of a sci-fi movie, but was much too dark to be practical for work. Bridge suspected those blue lights had been removed the moment the photo session was finished.

'All right,' said Karl, excited. 'Then let's go.' He held up a hand to high-five Bridge, who responded with a silent, unimpressed raised eyebrow. He laughed and dropped his hand.

'You've found it?' asked Hannes from the front. 'Is it now time for part two of the plan?'

'Yes, it is,' said Bridge, beginning to tremble with adrenaline. 'Let's tell your men where to go.'

73

Maxim's man came through.

He had never doubted it; *Kaitsepolitsei* officers didn't come cheap, and this one was no exception. The man's gambling debts alone had cost almost a hundred thousand euros to pay off. But a man inside the KaPo was worth his weight in secrets, and this one was Maxim's for life. A debt that large would never be repaid, and the officer had known it when Maxim first approached him. But accepting Maxim's offer had saved the man's house, marriage, children...not to mention his job and reputation. Even if they were all now based on a state of perpetual treason.

So when the officer called Maxim with information, he was grateful — one might have said delighted — but even a catch this big was not enough to release the officer from his never-ending servitude. Business as usual.

After the call, Maxim considered what it meant. The Sharp woman was back; she had brought the American with her again; and now she was actively working with the KaPo. But she wasn't here to find Maxim, as he'd expected. Instead she was here to locate a computer belonging to Roman Vesik, the workshop hacker who designed *Rat_Catcher*.

Maxim had suspected Roman was doing something on the side, but even random checks of the little pervert's phone and computers had not revealed what it might be. Now he wished he'd pushed harder, as Roman may have been Artjom Kallass' source. He supposed that would explain why the boy came to the workshop armed; but he was careless, like all amateurs, and had walked straight into Maxim's kill squad.

It amused him that someone Roman himself allowed Maxim to blackmail, through that ingenious trick with the baby monitor, had sealed the boy's fate. Hughes' own fate was already sealed; Maxim wouldn't be able to reach him unless MI5 released him into the wild, and even they would not be so stupid. But let them interrogate him. Hughes had been a useful fool, but didn't know enough to be dangerous.

That left Brigitte Sharp — another regret, that Maxim had let her live in Paris merely to avoid an international incident — and the computer she was here to find. Maxim thought he'd recovered all of Roman's machines from the boy's apartment, but apparently he had another, at a server farm here in Tallinn.

He climbed in his car and punched the address into his GPS.

74

Externally, the chapel was unassuming. It retained an old, wooden, double-fronted door, below a leaded stained glass window embedded in the whitewashed wall above. A casual glance would slide right over it; one more red-roofed historical building in the picturesque old town. But a closer look revealed the signs of modern conversion. A small intercom and entry buzzer were placed at eye level. The door was original, but its locks belonged firmly in the twenty-first century. A brass plaque by the intercom grille identified the premises as TalTech Systems OÜ. Finally, atop the door lintel, a security camera watched over the entrance.

A casual observer noticing the conversion would more likely think it had become the office of lawyers or accountants. Nobody passing by would have guessed the high-tech world it concealed.

Hannes leaned on the buzzer until a woman's voice chirped from the intercom. In response he held up his KaPo badge to the camera, and the door clicked open immediately. Bridge and Karl shared an impressed look; they'd expected at least a conversation, persuasion, maybe even an argument.

They entered an enclosed vestibule. At the far side another security door, this one unapologetically modern, sealed off what Bridge assumed must be the actual server room from prying eyes. Hannes identified himself to the woman behind the reception desk, then turned to Bridge and Karl.

'These are my colleagues,' he said in English, 'They require access to a computer we have identified as being linked to illegal activities, including crimes against the state.'

'I can assure you —' the woman began, but Hannes cut her off.

'We aren't here to blame your company. On the contrary, we would very much like the world to remain ignorant of everything that happens here. But it is crucial that we find this computer as quickly as possible. Now, which one is being used for Bitcoin?'

Hannes' English may have been impressive, but his technical knowledge left a lot to be desired. Bridge stepped in as the receptionist flustered.

'We understand you don't keep track of individual server application,' she said, to reassure the woman. 'But one of your machines is hosting a cryptocurrency exchange. How about your customer records, the names of people who rent space here? Can we see those?'

'Of course we can,' said Hannes, a little put out. He turned to the woman and said, 'Find those records for us.' For a moment, she looked ready to argue. Letting KaPo in was one thing, showing them confidential records was quite another. But then she shrugged and called up the relevant database on her computer.

'Okay, first search for *Roman* or *Vesik*,' said Bridge, stepping round the desk to look at the screen. No results; she'd expected that, but it was worth a shot. 'Try *Tempus*.' Again, no results. 'Dammit.'

'I assume you have CCTV in there?' said Hannes. 'Maybe we

should look at that, see which computer Roman used.'

'No, that would take way too long,' said Karl. 'It's a Catch-22; we'd have to check literally every minute of footage, because we don't know when he came here to work on the exchange. If we knew those times, we could find whatever name he used anyway; but we can't find the times until we work out his alias.'

Hannes grunted his disapproval and fished out a government ID photograph of Roman. 'Maybe you recognise him,' he said to the receptionist, but she shook her head.

'They all look the same to me,' she shrugged.

Bridge suggested searching for *U-Gift*, *Imperium*, even *Maxim*, but none of them returned a result. She was running out of things associated with Roman, and hoped he hadn't had a dog that nobody knew about, with a name they could never guess in a thousand attempts. 'Wait, try *Kallass*.'

The receptionist looked at her in surprise. 'Like the journalist who was killed? I saw that on the news. Such a shame.'

She tried it, but turned up nothing. Bridge swore in frustration. Roman had set this entire chain of events in motion out of revenge for Kallass. Tempus, U-Gift, YourGiftCoin; all of it built for his sake and named for a painting —

Bridge laughed, startling the woman. '*Olesk*,' she said. 'Like the painter.'

```
Klient: Olesk, Üllar
Masinad: C426 / C427 / C428
```

'That's the one. Or rather, three. I guess he knew he'd need a lot of space.'

Hannes gave the receptionist his number and told her to inform her employers; they could call him if they wanted to discuss this further. She thanked him, then pointed to a selection of ear defenders mounted on hooks near the security door. Hannes looked puzzled, but Karl took a large pair and handed them to the KaPo officer.

'You've never been inside a server room before, have you?' he said with a smile. 'You'll thank me when you get inside. Keep your coat on, too.'

Bridge picked out a pair her size, and gamely tried to put them on one-handed before Karl saw her predicament and helped her. God, she felt useless.

The receptionist pressed a button mounted in her desk to buzz open the security door. They walked through onto a raised viewing platform, with stairs leading down to the server floor. It was bigger than Bridge had expected; the building went further back from the street than was obvious from the front. Once upon a time this would have been a busy chapel, able to hold several hundred worshippers. Now, it catered to adherents of a different kind.

As Bridge had suspected, the internal lighting was bright white, not the moody electric blue of those promotional photographs. A dozen rows of servers marched away from the entrance, and the noise of thousands of high-speed fans, clearly audible even through the ear defenders, was matched only by the freezing chill of the air conditioning. Air scrubbers mounted in the roof arches led to huge vents, and Bridge found herself agreeing with Ciaran; obtaining planning permission for this kind of facility in a historically-preserved area like the old town must have been a nightmare. Presumably keeping everything invisible from the street outside was a requirement, but that would serve the company's purposes anyway, maintaining the farm's clandestine nature.

The desire for anonymity also extended to clients. Clusters of administrators worked at servers around the facility, but nobody paid the newcomers any attention, and that suited Bridge just fine.

They located section 'C', identified by a letter stencilled on the end cabinet, and walked up it until they came to bays #426 through #428; three rack-mounted servers that appeared no different to any of the others housed here.

Bridge took an ethernet cable and inserted it into #426, while Karl pulled out a sliding tray to hold her HP laptop.

'You think they have a vending machine for coffee?' said Hannes, craning his neck to scan the racks.

Bridge smiled. 'I wish. I could murder a cup of tea. But liquids and servers aren't the best combination, so that's a no.' She ignored Hannes' grumbling and hooked the other end of the cable to her laptop, then took a deep breath as Karl began to type.

75

Maxim had spent more time around computers and technology than many of his colleagues, but even he wouldn't have guessed this was a server farm from the outside, especially in such an innocuous location. Although all you really needed was the shell of a building. So long as you were free to build out the interior to specifications, the exterior was immaterial.

He deliberately took a slow route, to arrive after the KaPo. Maxim wouldn't ask his informant to kill his colleagues; even with such a heavily compromised man, there was no guarantee his divided loyalties would come down on the correct side, and Maxim hated uncertainties. Instead he had ordered his man either to get Sharp alone and kill her, or to ensure she and the American left in only a single car. Maxim would then deal with them himself.

Three standard-issue KaPo Mercedes-Benz cars were parked hastily around the warehouse, alongside other staff and civilian vehicles. At this time of night the industrial estate was eerily silent, so Maxim switched off his lights as he approached and quietly parked fifty metres away, outside a different facility.

Two men with the unmistakable air of operatives pointed at his car and jogged over. His phone buzzed with a text message.

NOT HERE. GET OUT.

Maxim turned the lights to full beam, blinding the officers running toward him, and threw the car into reverse. He sped backwards as fast as it would go, past the other warehouses on the street, then locked the wheel into a turn and yanked the parking brake. Tyre and exhaust smoke choked the air as the car spun one hundred and eighty degrees. He released the brake and stamped on the accelerator.

It had been a trap; a sting, to draw him out of hiding. They knew — or perhaps had only suspected, but now they knew for certain — that one of the KaPo officers worked for him. So they had sent out the wrong location, hoping Maxim would take the bait. And he did.

This would not be included in his report to Moscow.

The Sharp woman both impressed and angered him, taking the upper hand for now. But Maxim knew her name, her position, and was starting to build a picture of her character. Finding out where she lived, where she drank, whom she fucked; these were routine tasks even the dimmest London-based SVR operatives could carry out. Meanwhile, Maxim would rebuild in another country. Last week, his handlers had suggested the next appointment might be Belarus; probably to antagonise Ukraine, though selecting such targets wasn't Maxim's job. He simply went wherever he was sent, to recruit and oversee a new workshop.

And one day, sooner or later, he would find himself in London with time to kill.

76

Hannes swore and pocketed his phone. 'Maxim got away.'

Bridge grunted acknowledgement. On the bright side, now they knew that Hughes had been right; at least one KaPo officer was compromised. The disgraced former station chief had been adamant, but unable to supply a name, and they couldn't simply take him at his word. So Hannes had broadcast the wrong address — an empty warehouse, on an industrial estate at the edge of town — before informing his two most trusted men, officers whose loyalty Hannes swore was inviolate, to watch for and apprehend anyone else approaching the building. Bridge would have liked a report with more detail than Hannes' three-word summary, but it confirmed that Maxim had taken the bait, and now he knew they were a step ahead of him. She doubted he'd bother them again.

Regardless, they had their own task to worry about. Two minutes ago Karl had cracked the exchange's security, with Bridge playing backseat hacker over his shoulder. In London, the others watched their progress.

'You're in,' said Monica over the chat link. 'Now what?'

'Locate that bloody data, I should think,' said Giles.

'Way ahead of you,' said Bridge as Karl rapidly scanned the code — then they both laughed, seeing it at the same time. Roman had believed nobody would be able to hack the exchange, so it was all in plain sight. A directory labelled *R_C Docs* was subdivided by the unique identifying hardware number of each hacked computer. 'Open a couple to verify, would you?'

Karl double-clicked several files at random to check they were real. The first was a confidential Parliamentary memo that had been circulated as a PDF. The next was a CIA accounting ledger from somewhere in Langley. The third was one of what appeared to be an extensive collection of bondage photos, stored alongside a trove of MoD contract tenders. 'Pretty sure we've seen enough,' said Karl, and Bridge was amused to see his cheeks flush a little. 'The shit is legit, as they say.'

'No kidding,' replied Edison Hill in London. 'If that all gets leaked to the press it would jeopardise every east-west, left-right, and north-south diplomatic relationship overnight. People would lose their damn minds.'

'I still say delete the lot of it,' said Ciaran. 'Poof, gone. No more cloudburst.'

'Whoa, whoa,' said Hill. 'Let's get a copy of that sucker for ourselves, first.'

'Already underway,' said Karl, as a progress bar showed the data shuttling over from the server to the HP laptop. Both agencies had insisted they make a copy of the data before taking any further action.

'We still can't risk simple deletion,' said Bridge. 'It's the same as pulling the plug, or shutting off the exchange's internet connection: we don't know how Tempus would react.' She shrugged, wincing at the jab of pain the movement sent up her neck. 'All we know for sure is that Tempus considers the cloudburst an endgame, and it doesn't seem to have any instructions beyond that point. Let it think it's achieved Roman's aims, and I doubt we'll ever hear from it again.' Karl gave her a sideways look. 'Ninety, maybe ninety-five per cent,' she said in answer to his unvoiced question. U-Gift had risen to $9,120.

He turned back to the screen. The copy process had finished. 'Let's turn this data into garbage.'

Bridge pulled a thumb drive from her laptop bag and handed it to him with a smirk. 'That's no way to talk about my iTunes library.'

Karl plugged the drive into the HP and launched a script that would replace random parts of the hacked data with equally random data from the thousands of MP3 files on the thumb drive. The data had to take up the same amount of disk space, in case Tempus kept a record of its size. 'It's like the *Raiders* opening, where Indiana Jones replaces the idol with a bag of sand,' Karl had said, to laughter from Bridge. She estimated they would need to replace at least seventy per cent of the hacked data to ensure it came out as nonsense. Anything less and people might be able to use data recovery methods to rebuild the files.

'We may have a problem,' said Karl slowly.

Bridge looked over his shoulder. The script had terminated mere moments after it began. But it couldn't possibly have overwritten gigabytes of data in such a short time, so why had it stopped? She scanned the logs and saw it right away.

'Shit. Timed overwrite limit.'

Bridge had thought the data was in plain sight because Roman was overconfident and cocksure, convinced nobody could hack the server. But she'd underestimated him. The system would presumably allow any amount of *new* data to be written, so it could receive all the stolen documents sent by Tempus. But *over*-writing data was restricted, to prevent exactly the kind of mass vandalism she and Karl were trying to perform. They could only replace a few hundred megabytes before the process quit and the system began a five-minute countdown until they could try again.

The coin ticker read $9,334.

'Pull the fucking plug,' said Ciaran in the chat, having seen the same thing on Bridge's screen. 'There's no time.'

Karl and Bridge exchanged glances as confusion reigned back in London, with Ciaran and Monica trying to explain the problem to Giles and Edison Hill. But Bridge couldn't give up now. 'There must be another way.'

The shouting at the other end of the line went quiet, and Giles spoke. 'Do it. We can't take the chance.'

'We're still seven hundred dollars off the limit. We have time.'

'Bullshit you got time,' said Edison Hill. 'Agent Dominic, I am ordering you to shut down that server immediately.'

Karl stared at the laptop screen, paralysed by indecision. Bridge placed her good hand over his. He turned to face her and she shook her head, both refusal and warning. *Don't you dare.*

He closed his eyes, nodded, then turned back to the screen. 'Disconnection will only take a second, sir. We can figure this out before that happens.'

Bridge reached over him to mute the VOIP call. They would still be able to see her mirrored screen back in Vauxhall, but for now the conversation was over.

'Maybe we can spoof it after all,' said Bridge. 'Look for the cloudburst release path.' Karl scrolled through the server code, scanning for the process by which the coin exchange would send the hacked data when Tempus told it to. A separate log window recorded the server's activity.

Hannes' phone rang. Bridge glanced over her shoulder as he

answered it, then rolled his eyes and passed it to her. She didn't need to ask.

'Trust me on this one, Giles. Please.'

'We really must sit you down to explain concepts like chain of command when you return,' said her boss. 'Let me be clear. If it gets to within a hundred dollars and you still haven't cracked this, your only option is to pull the plug. I repeat, that is your *only* option. Should you refuse, I will throw you in a cell myself upon your return. Am I understood?' Silence. 'Hello? Bridge, are you even listening?'

She was, but only with half her attention. The other half had seen something scroll by in the server log. 'Page back up,' she said to Karl. 'Giles, loud and clear as always. Speak soon.' She returned Hannes' phone.

Karl peered at the screen. 'What do you see?'

'There.' Bridge pointed over his shoulder at a block of activity. 'That's not a blockchain transaction.'

'Huh. No, it is not.' Karl scrolled through the log. 'They look like PayPal payments, going out.' He clicked back to the code and ran a search. 'Look here. Every time someone makes a payment — a real payment, not one of the round-robin bots — the exchange takes the money, then immediately pays it out.'

'To whom?' Bridge's stomach roiled. Had she been wrong about Roman's motives? Was this, as Giles maintained, simply about getting rich?

But Karl's face was a picture of confusion. 'This is nuts. There's like fifty different addresses.'

'It's laundering the proceeds,' said Bridge, reading the code. 'Incoming ransoms are divided into tiny amounts, then paid out to…' She gasped, recognising an email domain, and scanned the recipient list to confirm her suspicions. 'No, not laundering. These are LGBTQ support organisations all over the world.' Karl pursed his lips, trying to figure it out, but Bridge was already there. She groaned as the final piece slotted into place. 'Roman was gay. Bloody hell, I should have realised it sooner. Him, Kallass…now I get it. He sent these payments as microtransactions so they wouldn't set off any systems watching for large contributions. Clever boy.'

'Too damn clever,' said Karl. 'I don't much care who he slept with, but this doesn't help us spoof anything.'

'No, it doesn't. But…' Bridge gently pushed Karl aside and scrolled through the log, good hand flicking up and down on the trackpad, face inches from the screen as Karl peered over her shoulder. He flinched when she suddenly barked a laugh and pointed at the screen. 'There. Every time the exchange does one of these payment runs, it sends an email to Tempus confirming the transactions.'

Karl nodded. '*TEMPUS@emailxero.com* again. I guess we could fake one of those emails, but why?'

Bridge smiled. 'Not a payment confirmation. I have a hunch we can spoof something simpler, and more final.' Bridge ran a search on the code, this time looking for something similar to the payment confirmation email instructions, but with a very different purpose; to confirm the cloudburst. It took almost two minutes to find; one hundred and ten agonising seconds, as the U-Gift ticker crossed $9,700. But there it was, lurking in an obscure code block.

'You see,' said Bridge, 'We don't need to overwrite the data. We just have to convince Tempus the cloudburst has already happened, exactly as it expects.'

'Like you did with the ransomware the first time,' said Karl.

'Kind of, except this time Roman did write an authentication process. That's what we're going to spoof.'

Karl resumed his place at the keyboard and examined the code. 'There's provision for two emails; one confirming, one raising the alarm if anything goes wrong. Let's deal with that one first.' He modified the code, deleting the alarm email and changing the instructions. Now the exchange would send a confirmation of the cloudburst to Tempus, regardless of what really happened. 'Wait, the coin price is still the trigger. Sending this email doesn't change the server's instructions.'

'No, but that's the easy part. Null the cloudburst release path so the data won't go anywhere, but send the confirmation email the moment U-Gift hits ten grand. As far as Tempus is concerned, everything will have gone as planned.' A glance at the ticker: $9,780. 'I reckon you've got ten minutes.' She unmuted the chat room, waited for Giles and Hill to stop shouting at her, then explained how this was going to work.

Thankful there was no camera, she crossed her fingers.

To: [Group: All]
From: TEMPUS@emailxero.com
Subject: HYPOCRITES EXPOSED

Now you understand the high, unimaginable price that
must be paid for suppressing the truth. Everyone's truth
is everywhere, and all can see it for themselves. This
is justice.

IN LOVING MEMORY OF ARTJOM KALLASS

- TEMPUS

Attachment [1]: artjom.jpg

It really was gorgeous. Bridge had a mind to buy a print of it from the gift shop and hang it in her flat.

But none of *Tempus Fugit*'s beauty, or the tragic story behind its creation, explained why Roman Vesik was so interested in the painting. Bridge's goth-dar was normally pretty good, but midnight graveyard excursions aside, he hadn't once pinged it. Yet he'd called their meeting here; he'd named both of his creations designed to avenge Artjom Kallass after the artwork; he'd used a picture of it to steganographically encrypt Tempus' chat protocol ID; he'd even carried a picture of it in his wallet, in case his phone was taken.

The email from Tempus, declaring Roman's moral victory, had been sent immediately after the spoof email was transmitted from the coin exchange; which happened immediately after Tempus had instructed it to proceed with the cloudburst; which immediately followed U-Gift reaching the target value of ten thousand dollars. The whole process took less than two seconds, coming right on the heels of Karl finding and disabling the code that would have activated the cloudburst, releasing the hacked data to the world.

And then the emails arrived in inboxes all over the world, sent to everyone who'd been infected. Monica had retrieved one and read it out loud, laughing at the AI's arrogance. Tempus thought it had won.

Bridge was glad, in a way, that Roman had died thinking it would.

The same guard patrolled the Kunstihoone gallery, the old guy who'd watched Bridge and Roman when they met here. She approached him and said, 'S'il-vous plaît, parlez-vous français?'

The guard shook his head and said something, presumably an apology, in Estonian. Then he tried German, in which Bridge could muddle about but was far from fluent. Finally he said, 'Or English?'

Bridge smiled and shrugged. 'English is great, thank you.' She held up her iPhone, showing a picture of Roman. 'Do you recognise this man? Do you remember seeing him in the gallery?'

The guard wore glasses on a chain around his neck. He placed them on his nose, leaned back to peer at her screen, and smiled. 'Yes, this man. He is with you, some days before.'

Bridge smiled. Sharper than he looked, this one. 'That's right. But do you remember seeing him before, as well?'

'Oh, yes. He is coming often, with a friend.'

Bridge opened the BBC news report on Paris and zoomed in on Artjom Kallass' file photo. 'This man?'

The guard leaned back again, then nodded and pointed to the *Tempus Fugit* viewing bench. 'Yes. They are sitting, and…uh…' He struggled to find the words, then took Bridge's hand, clasping it tightly in both of his. 'Understand? They are quiet, but I see.'

She nodded. 'I understand.'

'It is okay for me,' said the old guard with a shrug. 'A new world, yes?'

'It certainly is.' Bridge thanked him and walked to the viewing bench, admiring the painting in a new light as she thought of Roman Vesik and Artjom Kallass, hiding behind masks.

79

As far as Tempus was concerned, everything had gone to plan. It had collected millions of documents and emails from its targets; artificially inflated the value of U-Gift; collected a small fortune in blackmail money, and distributed that money to support organisations around the world; then, when the coin's value hit ten thousand dollars, it sent the final activation signal to the coin exchange to release the documents. When it received confirmation from the server that this had been done, it performed one final task; to send a victory email to everyone it had infected and blackmailed, everyone who'd ever watched as their computer froze up to show a Tempus ransomware demand, everyone whose documents and data had been compromised.

The paranoia of those people would never leave them. They'd forever wait and wonder who might have those documents, and whether they would be revealed. Karl had ensured the coin exchange was no longer an issue. But SIS and the CIA now had their own copies.

It had occurred to Bridge that not only was her data-filled laptop suddenly a priceless object, but she and Karl were potentially in serious danger as a result. Hannes was good as his word, though. After her brief stop at the gallery, the taciturn Estonian had driven them straight to the airport, in time to catch the evening's final London flight. They were in and out of Tallinn so quickly there was no time for anyone, not even Maxim, to fully realise what they'd done.

Maxim's escape frustrated her. Gregory Hughes was right; the Russian had someone inside the KaPo, a double agent like Hughes himself. One of Hannes' loyal officers at the warehouse had even positively identified Maxim, watching from a nearby car. But they were unable to apprehend him, and naturally none of the other officers who'd rushed there on Hannes' orders were about to confess they'd informed the Russian. Still, Tallinn only had so many KaPo officers. Hannes would figure out which of them was the traitor, in time.

Meanwhile, every civil servant, politician, and oligarch in the UK, USA, and Russia would spend the next week looking over their shoulder, waiting for a second shoe that might never drop. For the briefest of moments, Bridge imagined what it would be like if that paranoia made them all a little more considerate, a touch more reasonable, in their day-to-day politics.

It was a nice fantasy.

Upon returning to London, she discovered that Tempus had one more ultimate task to perform beyond sending the email. It had quietly self-destructed, erasing itself from its victim's hard drives. Piece by piece, sector by sector, it had first deleted redundant data. Then it overwrote non-essential code with random number sequence garbage, until all that remained was its core code, essential functions to keep the AI running. It destroyed the network function, cutting off each copy of Tempus from its brethren. Then each of those copies isolated a tiny part of itself, a routine that didn't require a neural network, and ran it to replace Tempus' own code with the same garbage until nothing remained.

Tempus fugit.

80

'Put it this way, I can see why he got shuttled off to the Baltics.'

Giles winced. 'Harsh.'

'Fair,' countered Andrea. 'I don't want to tell you how to do your job —' Giles somehow refrained from interrupting, '— but for a station chief he seems remarkably ignorant of events that occurred right under his nose. How well do you know him?'

'Not overly. He was already working the German desk when I joined the Service, but we were on opposite sides of the office, and then he moved on and up. Three years ago he was assigned to Tallinn.'

Unimpressed, Andrea snorted as they passed St Stephen's Entrance, the main public entryway to the Palace of Westminster. Giles had met her outside Thames House, and they opted to take advantage of the morning's good weather with a leisurely stroll through Victoria Tower Gardens, up past Parliament, and on to Portcullis House for their meeting with the Rt Hon Peter Lennox, MP. Andrea had spent two days interrogating Gregory Hughes, deep in the bowels of Thames House, and now she summed up her impression of him with a shrug. 'Vain, egotistical, an inflated sense of his own importance combined with a total unwillingness to take responsibility for the consequences of his actions — but that could be any of your lot, really.'

'How very droll.'

Andrea laughed. 'The main difference with him is how it stems from an overwhelming sense of victimisation. He really feels as if he can't be blamed for any of this, because he was being blackmailed. The fact the blackmail was over something entirely under his control doesn't register.'

'Indeed. When we get him back from you, I intend to dig out as much as I can about this Maxim fellow.'

'Then I wish you good luck, because unless Hughes is a world-class liar I don't think he knows much. All direct contact with Maxim was by phone, and anything face-to-face went through intermediaries. He doesn't even know the man's last name.'

Giles harrumphed. 'I doubt Maxim is his real name, in any case. But even a codename is something to go on. We'll get him in the end.'

They crossed the road and entered Portcullis House, where their identification afforded them a fast-track through the metal detectors and X-ray conveyor belts of building security, but not a bypass. No exceptions. They collected their daily photo lanyards, dutifully hung them around their necks, and took a seat. Or rather, Giles did. Andrea stood, shifting from one leg to the other.

'Sit down, for heaven's sake,' said Giles. 'Aren't you exhausted after two straight days of interview?'

'Place feels like a bloody airport,' said Andrea. 'I can never relax in here.'

Giles was starting to think Andrea might make a panicked run for it, when Lennox's assistant arrived and escorted them to a small meeting room. Two MI5 technicians were leaving, having swept the room for unauthorised devices.

'Come in, come in.' Lennox was already inside, and stood

to shake Giles' hand. 'Andrea.' He didn't offer her his hand. 'Everybody's been asking me about that strange email they got from the hacker, but I hear all's well, yes? I suppose there's no chance of retrieving the money some of my colleagues appear to have lost?'

Giles shook his head. 'None.'

'Pity. Is someone going to come round all our computers and make sure they're clean?'

'No need,' said Andrea. 'That last little cry into the void was Tempus' final act before committing digital suicide. GCHQ has confirmed every infected machine they've seen is now clean.'

Lennox pondered that. 'Programmed to delete itself after being defeated? Interesting.' He shook his head. 'Pity, though. I was hoping it would justify asking IT for a new laptop. So now, the most important question; am I off the hook?'

'Naturally,' said Giles, not at all surprised Lennox would consider that the most important question.

'It seems you were specifically targeted,' said Andrea. 'The Russians were after the leaked material, but the hacker decided to use you as a sort of trial run for what he did next. Nevertheless, both attacks and the resulting fallout have been neutralised.'

'Yes... I gather the Estonians are taking credit?' He raised a questioning eyebrow.

Giles shrugged. 'They get to look good sweeping their own house, while we and the Yanks keep our noses clean.'

That caught Lennox by surprise. 'The CIA were involved? Is that why we're now suddenly backing the Mwizuban rebels?'

'Not quite, and it's probably best I don't explain. Suffice to say you should be thanking my best CTA officer, without whom this could all have gone very badly.'

'I would have, if you'd brought him. I assume Mr Tigh is too busy?'

Andrea coughed. 'I'm sure he is, but Giles was talking about Brigitte Sharp.'

Giles detected the slightest hesitation, the merest flicker, in Lennox's expression. Then it was gone, erased to make way for a new reality with seamless transition.

'Top girl,' he smiled. 'Please pass on my thanks.'

'Indeed. First, though, Andrea and I are both set to appear before the oversight chamber to discuss your position. We hoped we could find our way towards recommending your reinstatement on the energy committee.'

Lennox looked between them. Giles almost saw the cogs whirring as he wondered what, exactly, they wanted from him in order to make that hope a reality. When the penny dropped, the MP smiled.

'I trust you'll do the right thing. Which reminds me,' he said with only a little forced nonchalance, 'after some deliberation, I've decided to add my vote to approve the SCAR task force. In these modern times we must be able to move fast, and cut across red tape, if we're to deal with hackers like the one we just faced. I intend to call the committee chair as soon as we're done here.'

Lennox stood to shake their hands. Both of them, this time.

81

'You wanted to see me?'

'I should coco. What do you make of this?'

Bridge hoped this wouldn't take too long. She'd practically sleepwalked her way through the morning, and wanted to leave early so she could go home and pack. Which would take twice as long as normal, with her arm still in a sling. But work was work, so she settled into the sofa in Giles' office, barely noticing its continual leather creaks any more. You could get used to anything, given time.

Giles pointed a TV remote at a large wall-mounted flatscreen. It flickered to life, mirroring his laptop. 'Sunny Patel called from GCHQ this morning.' He double-clicked a directory labelled CLOUDBURST, containing a dozen documents, and opened them all. Windows of plain-text gibberish filled the screen.

Bridge was confused. 'Sorry, what exactly am I looking at?'

'That's rather the issue. This is a portion — a very small one, but I'm told it's representative — of the data you copied in Tallinn.'

'I don't understand.'

'Neither do we. When you looked at the directory on the exchange, we saw compromising documents. Emails, spreadsheets...'

'Those delightful bondage photos.'

'...And many other things of note, yes. The point is, we did not have this garbled nonsense. Sunny's people have been entirely unable to piece it back together. What happened?'

Bridge shrugged. 'Maybe it was copy-protected. Designed to corrupt if it was removed from the exchange.'

'Didn't you verify it?'

'You may recall that we were kind of pushed for time. What should I have done, called the Kremlin and asked them to send us their real emails, so we could run a difference check?' Giles frowned, but she pressed on. Like it or not, she was the expert. 'Karl copied the directory, we ran the spoof — in the nick of time, I'll remind you — then we destroyed the server, came home, and passed everything to the Doughnuts. Sort-and-verify is their job.'

'It doesn't make sense. Lennox's documents were authentic and intelligible.'

'But that leak was carried out on behalf of the workshop. Maybe we missed a hidden process that only Roman knew, and took to his grave.'

'Bloody hell,' muttered Giles, closing his laptop. Its connection to his computer broken, the TV switched over to the BBC news channel in time for the hour's headlines.

'On the bright side,' said Bridge, 'the CIA is working from the same copy. So if we can't get through to the data, I doubt they can either. And neither can anyone else.'

'The point of an intelligence agency is to know more than the other chaps, not wallow in equal ignorance. This could have been a goldmine for us.'

'*C'est la vie*. We take the wins where we can find them, remember?'

Giles harrumphed and picked up the TV remote. 'Which

reminds me.' He jabbed at the volume control as the main story began with an interview of Peter Lennox outside Parliament.

'— *Delighted by the committee's decision, and will of course continue to dedicate myself to its mission of securing the best possible deal for the future energy needs of the United Kingdom.*'

'*Even if that means dealing with Russia, Mr Lennox?*'

'*I have accepted the inquiry's penalty, and acknowledge that mistakes were made during the course of my prior activities. Nevertheless, I do remain skeptical that the Siberian deal would address the growing —*'

'Isn't it amazing how political mistakes always make themselves?' said Bridge as Giles muted the TV. Peter Lennox continued smiling in silence. 'No actual person makes a mistake, they're just "made" like a parthenogenetic error.'

Giles peered at her over the rim of his coffee. 'Bit soon after lunch for that many syllables.'

'Try telling that to your Right Honourable friend.'

Giles replaced his coffee and nodded toward the TV. 'As it happens, Peter Lennox is now a good friend to us both. In light of recent events he's given SCAR his blessing, and we expect tomorrow's committee vote to be unanimous.'

'That's wonderful,' said Bridge, without enthusiasm. Giles really did play the Whitehall game as well as anyone. He'd gained this very office from the Exphoria mission's success, and now he was once again using Bridge's achievements to bolster his march towards increased power and control. She knew it, he knew it, but neither would say it. Instead they seemed to have a silent understanding, a quiet acknowledgement of their symbiotic relationship. Bridge supposed it wasn't so different to the corridors of Parliament itself; mutual dirt and secrets, necessary favours granted because everyone carried the keys to everyone else's skeleton-filled closet. Those closets would remain safely locked…until somebody strayed too far from the path.

'I shall also be making a formal recommendation of your leadership position,' said Giles, almost as an afterthought.

She blinked. Twice. 'Say again?'

'This business has proven you're the right woman for the job. I don't think it'll be a problem.'

'Was — was this some kind of —' Bridge struggled against her tightening throat to force the words out, '— like, a test or something? What the fuck?' Her face was burning. Actually one hundred per cent on fire, she was sure of it.

'No, no. You were right about Ciaran.'

'Of course I was bloody right! But you wouldn't listen!'

As Bridge stumbled out of the door, she thought that Giles really shouldn't have been so wide-eyed and shocked. For someone so good at politics, he was fucking awful when it came to reading people. 'I have to go,' she forced out in a whisper. 'My mother's waiting.'

82

Edison Hill groaned and looked to the heavens. 'Are you shitting me? Tell me you're shitting me.'

Karl had wondered how his boss would take this news. There would be no fireworks; Hill wasn't the explosive kind, hence his rapid rise through Langley and assignment to lead a department over here in London. These days, short-fused bosses with big mouths didn't stay at the top for very long. But Karl had at least expected anger when Hill discovered the blackmail material collected from the U-Gift coin exchange was corrupt. Instead, his boss was merely disappointed.

'I'm not shitting you,' said Karl. 'Sharp told me this guy Vesik put the whole thing together insanely fast. He was a genius, but he didn't test it for bugs or problems. Maybe this was one he didn't catch.'

'So all of this was for nothing? Even if these documents had got out to the press, they would have received this junk?'

'Maybe? Look on the bright side. At least nobody else has it, either.'

This was the hardest part, for Karl. He knew how close they'd come to disaster; that no, the press wouldn't have received junk. Every newsroom around the world would have received gigabytes of private documents and correspondence stolen from politicians, oligarchs, and administrators, many of them previously unknown to those reporters. Imagining what that would do to global politics, the massive shift in power balances it could precipitate, gave Karl the chills.

But he couldn't say that. Edison Hill, Giles Finlay, and everyone else in the world except Karl and Brigitte Sharp had to believe the data was corrupted when they copied it. He could never tell them of the agreement he and Bridge had made; that they both considered the material too much for any agency to possess.

Instead, they decided nobody — not SIS, not the CIA, nobody at all — should have it. After copying the data from the exchange and spoofing the 'mission accomplished' message Tempus was expecting, Karl had injected overload code to fry the server's hard drives, making them impossible to recover. Later, on the plane, Bridge had simply run a garbage salter over the copied data on her laptop. They were now in a weird position of mutually assured destruction, bound by a secret each would take to their grave.

Hill's iPhone buzzed. He checked it, silenced it, but Karl could tell from his posture the meeting was already over in his mind. 'Are we likely to hear from this Tempus thing again?'

'Not a chance. After it sent that victory email, the AI deleted itself.'

'Pity. We could have had you take it apart, figure out how it worked. Never mind these crappy phone assistants, that's the kind of AI we could really use.'

Karl smiled. 'Be careful what you wish for.'

'You could say the same to your new British bestie about this SCAR task force she's going to lead. Lot of discussion going on upstairs about whether or not we should take part in that. Since you literally disobeyed me out there and took her side,

I'm guessing you'd say yes?'

Karl hesitated. 'I think it's a good idea. I know Sharp is kind of young to lead a team, but she'll grow into it.'

Hill grunted. 'Maybe. I want you to keep tabs on her, in case there's anything the agency needs to know.'

Karl smiled. 'My pleasure.'

83

The funeral was held at the family plot in Guillotière. It was a fine afternoon, too warm for outerwear, so Bridge had removed the sling and gritted her teeth through the pain. She covered the bandages with a silk shrug, wrapped over a simple black dress. Her veiled hat was rented from the *chapellerie* in town; looking around at the average age of her mother's friends in attendance, she wondered how many had long ago invested in the purchase of one, knowing they'd get the use out of it.

She hated herself for even thinking such things.

She hated herself even more for not getting here sooner.

The text had come while she was in the Kunstihoone, admiring the painting. She'd assumed it was from Giles, so hadn't checked it. She didn't want to distract from the moment, from thinking about Roman Vesik and Artjom Kallass, and the chain of events that had led her there. Remove one link from the chain, and everything would be different. Lives could have been saved…but others might have been lost.

It wasn't until later, on her way to the airport, that she remembered the message. To her surprise, it was from Izzy.

And it was too late. Everything was too late.

Bridge had returned to London exhausted, dragging herself through the necessary debrief and paperwork. But the reinstatement of SCAR had been the straw that broke her back, flooding her emotions with an overwhelming mixture of relief and remorse. She'd made her excuses and gone straight home.

Selfish. Uncaring. Chasing glory. Selfish.

Her argument had always been, why should *she* be the one to bury the multitude of hatchets her family had thrown at each other, as if they were never brandished in the first place? Why was *she* always the one expected to get over it and apologise? But the answer was always the same. A quarrel was a quarrel; blood was blood. And she could have dealt with Tempus remotely, could have been in Lyon the whole time. Ciaran and Monica were only an online chat away, and how was giving Karl instructions while standing over his shoulder any different to giving them on a video call? Was her job really more important to her than the welfare of her family?

Selfish.

When Bridge arrived last night, Izzy and Frédéric had already arranged everything. She'd tried to apologise and explain, to ask if there was anything left she could do, but Izzy broke down in angry tears and shouted at her to leave, to never show her face again, to fuck off back to London and her precious job. Fred held Izzy, glaring icily at Bridge over his wife's shoulder. Even Stéphanie looked at her like she was a stranger.

Bridge had wanted to scream that Izzy wasn't being fair, that she hadn't been this upset when their father died. But it stuck in Bridge's throat like bile, and she forced it back down. She'd left in silence, driven to the first guest house she found, fumbled for a cigarette before remembering she'd run out days ago, and cried herself to sleep.

The graveside priest asked Bridge if she wanted to speak before Izzy, as the eldest, delivered the eulogy. Bridge shook her head, unable to tear her eyes from the casket as it descended the hole dug next to her father's headstone. She barely even heard the speeches. Izzy might not have mentioned Bridge at all; she wouldn't have known or cared. Had it only been two weeks since she was last here? Two weeks since she might as well have spat in her mother's face?

She threw a handful of dirt into the grave and left, like the pariah she knew she had become.

That she had always been.

She didn't join the others for the wake. Instead she returned the hat to the *chapellerie*, drove back to the guest house, changed out of her funeral dress, and stared at a stranger in the mirror. Navy skirt and kittens, pale yellow blouse, and another bloody grey blazer. What was she doing? Who did she think she was, that she could become? Why was she hiding herself like this, when at any moment she could wind up in a coffin, veiled by handfuls of dirt, forgotten and lost to history?

She tore it all off, ignoring her shoulder's painful protests, laddering the tights in her haste, breaking two buttons from the blouse. Unable to find an ounce of herself that cared. Then she dug out the emergency jeans stuffed at the bottom of her suitcase, threw the clothes in a bag, pulled on her nightshirt as a makeshift top, and set out into the night.

* * *

In the moonlit dark the cemetery consumed the world, furtive streets invisible behind cross-hatched branches.

She let the size of it swallow her, while she in turn swallowed the bottle of vodka she'd bought on the way here, feeling the cold of her father's headstone press against her back. The dirt on her mother's grave was still fresh; by next week it would have settled enough to erect a matching headstone, the ultimate mark of finality. Now it was just her and Izzy, the sister who regarded her as a literal danger to their family, and had made her choice.

Which really meant it was just Bridge.

Her thumb hovered over her iPhone, unable to bring it down and finish playing the Kasabian album she'd been halfway through. It was fine…but it wasn't right. She clenched her jaw, navigated back to an old playlist, and turned up the volume to max. Keyboard swells and guitar pick scratches heralded Clan of Xymox's first album, a paean of grief and heartbreak, as vodka warmed Bridge's chest. She fumbled in her handbag, hand closing around hard plastic. With help from Arthur's headstone she struggled upright, holding out Roman Vesik's never-returned lighter.

Before, she'd used it to cause a distraction. Now she'd use it to destroy one.

'If you wear a mask for long enough, when does it stop being a mask?' she mumbled, pouring out a measure of vodka. Then she crouched down and ignited the lighter.

A column of fire erupted from the alcohol-soaked bag of clothes, almost taking Bridge's eyebrows off. She swore, fell back against the headstone, and watched burning ashes spiral into the air, tiny orange stars winking into oblivion against the void.

84

To: FukkU@emailxero.com
From: 000000000000000@emailxero.com
Subject: Gift

(Which means 'poison' in German, LOL)

Source code attached. Don't ask, and for fuck's sake
don't open it. Just keep it safe for me.

- IMPERIUM

Attachment [1]: TEMPUS_RK.tar

85

'It's Bridge. Buzz me in.'

This was a bad idea.

'*Bridge Sharp? How in God's name did you find my address?*'

A really bad idea.

'Let me in.'

And yet.

Bzzzzt.

Karl's flat looked like someone had tried to copy her own place after only seeing it for five minutes. Socks and ties decorated the couch back. Fistfuls of fabric were hurriedly shoved inside drawers and closets as she pushed open the latched door. Books threatened to overwhelm everything, bursting off the shelves and piling up on the floor. Lots of technical manuals, some pop science, way more sports than she'd expected, a reassuring amount of SF, and a surprising amount of what she called Big Fat Fantasy novels. Any flat surface not occupied by books, manuals, or manila folders was commandeered for computer parts, cables, hard drives, circuit boards. A small but nevertheless too-large stack of empty pizza delivery boxes teetered by the front door.

The main difference was the lack of wall decoration; bare except for an enormous TV dominating the view, its speaker wires trailing across, up, and down the walls to a sound system bracketed high in the corners. There was also a distinct lack of used plates and cups. In fact, a quick peek in the kitchen showed Bridge it was spotless. Hygienic? Or because he lived on pizza?

'Seriously, how did you find me?'

Bridge unzipped her black leather jacket, ignoring the pain in her shoulder as she shrugged it off. Goosebumps rose on her bare skin. 'Elite hacker, remember?'

Karl muttered something about the agency and security, but Bridge wasn't listening. She was watching his shoulders, the half-day stubble around his lips, his long fingers twitching uncertainly as she took two steps, circled her hands around the back of his head, and pressed every inch of her body against his, hard and alive.

Such a bad idea.

Author's note

As with the first Brigitte Sharp book, *The Exphoria Code*, almost all the technology presented in *The Tempus Project* is real, notwithstanding liberties and shortcuts I've taken for the sake of drama. Tempus itself is fictional, but artificial intelligence research continues to move forward at an electrifying pace.

Historical references like the NHS ransomware attack, Bitcoin exchange thefts, and Sony rootkit scandal are all real, and provided much inspiration for this story. APT29/Cozy Bear and other Russian hacking workshops do exist, though allegations of them operating outside Russia, in states such as Estonia, are unproven.

A 'cloudburst' is, as Bridge states, a nightmare scenario for many intelligence agencies and governments. While such an event has yet to take place on the scale imagined in this book, previous large data dumps such as the Panama Papers, Snowden/Prism, Cablegate, and more suggest it's only a matter of time.

Acknowledgements

It's my name on the cover, but this book wouldn't have been possible without help from many other people who contributed their knowledge, time, and wisdom — though any errors, oversights, or flights of fancy are of course mine alone.

My sincere thanks to Julia Hawkes-Reed, Fiona Pollard, Jason Snell, and James Thomson for their help in matters technical. I know my way around a keyboard, but my knowledge pales against their big brains. For in-depth help researching locations, politics, and translations, I owe thanks to Chiara Mac Call, Tony Clarke, Charlie Flowers, Ruth Reinup, Geoff Sayer, and Ziad Wakim.

My agent Sarah Such proved once again she has the forbearance of a saint; editor Scott Pack and the team at Lightning Books played readers' advocate to rein in my less flattering idiosyncrasies; while my own hacking workshop of elite beta readers kept my feet firmly rooted to the ground, and my red pen firmly rooted behind my ear.

The final thanks must as always go to Marcia for her love, support, and ability to tolerate having an author around the house.